INTO
WHAT
FAR
HARBOR?

Also by Allen Drury

The Advise and Consent Series
Advise and Consent
A Shade of Difference
Capable of Honor
Preserve and Protect
Come Nineveh, Come Tyre
The Promise of Joy

Other Washington Novels
Anna Hastings
Mark Coffin, U.S.S.
The Hill of Summer
The Roads of Earth
Decision
Pentagon

Novels of Ancient Egypt
A God Against the Gods
Return to Thebes

The University Novels
Toward What Bright Glory?

Other Novels
That Summer: A California Novel
The Throne of Saturn: A Novel of Space and Politics

Nonfiction
A Senate Journal
Three Kids in a Cart
"A Very Strange Society"
Courage and Hesitation (with Fred Maroon)
Egypt: The Eternal Smile (with Alex Gotfryd)

INTO WHAT FAR HARBOR?

A NOVEL

ALLEN DRURY

William Morrow and Company, Inc.
New York

It is the policy of William Morrow and Company, Inc., and its imprints and affiliates, recognizing the importance of preserving what has been written, to print the books we publish on acid-free paper, and we exert our best efforts to that end.

Library of Congress Cataloging-in-Publication Data

Drury, Allen.
    Into what far harbor? : a novel / by Allen Drury.
        p.   cm.
    Sequel to: Toward what bright glory?
    ISBN 0-688-07714-5
    I. Title.
    PS3554.R8I5   1992
    813'.54—dc20   92-24129
                                    CIP

Printed in the United States of America

First Edition

1 2 3 4 5 6 7 8 9 10

BOOK DESIGN BY LYNN DONOFRIO

Dedicated to the Independent-Minded

*For, yea, verily, they shall
not be permitted to enter into
the kingdom of Heaven, neither
shall they inherit the Earth.
Like unto the frantic bleatings
of sheep rise the cries of their
critics in the land.*

Note to the Reader

The characters of this novel were introduced in the novel *Toward What Bright Glory?*, which covers their senior year, 1939, as fraternity brothers on the eve of the outbreak of World War II. There you will find them just as they are beginning to mature into manhood, about to be called from relatively sheltered peacetime lives to play their parts, willing or reluctant, brave or foolish, in the greatest conflict in the history of humanity. Therein will be found many of the themes and quirks of character that find their further development in this present novel, *Into What Far Harbor?*

About *Toward What Bright Glory?* a sampling of readers from a broad spectrum of interests and backgrounds had nice things to say.

The Harvard history professor, retired after forty years' teaching:

> *Above all, you have triumphed as a novelist in your sensitive development of the young men who I presume will carry your narrative through subsequent volumes. They are living, complex human beings, especially in coming to grips with their sexuality. Your insights make this the most illuminating novel I've read about college youth.*

The sophomore at the University of California, Berkeley:

> *It is certainly comforting to read a novel that carries such familiarities with it as to lend understanding to the most trying, and at the same time, most exciting and pleasurable period in one's life. . . . We push ever onward to learn and*

8 NOTE TO THE READER

grow and I must say that your novel has helped to make that realization much easier to accept. Thanks again!

The sergeant-major (ret.), U.S. Army:

You managed to integrate most of the major issues of that particular period in our history. The Nazi threat, concurrent with Hitler's "Jewish solution," was covered especially well. Your handling of the situation with By Johnson, a black, and the prescience of the future implied is exceptionally well done . . . From my first exposure to your writing thirty years ago when I read Advise and Consent, *your use of dialogue has always impressed me. Again, Mr. Drury, please accept my sincere appreciation for a truly wonderful reading experience.*

The barrister, London, England:

I am writing you a "fan letter" to thank you for a marvelous book . . . a splendid book. Thank you.

The Catholic priest:

Toward What Bright Glory? *seems to be a tour de force of issues-before-their-time (race, anti-Semitism, homosexuality) and of characterizations—thorough, consistent and believable throughout. . . . Excellent work!*

The realtor:

After the first few pages I thought, "This is just another ho-hum book about college life." Suddenly the characters emerged as real people. I was hooked! By the time I reached the end of the book, I didn't want the story to stop; and I am looking forward to its sequel. It has been a long time since I've read a book which "reached me" to that extent.

The stockbroker:

It's a splendid job and you have caught the atmosphere of that past time exceedingly well. . . . My congratulations and

I look forward to reading further about Willie and his friends and classmates.

The housewife:

Thank you for touching my heart.

Now, in *Into What Far Harbor?*, the fraternity brothers who began their fictional life together in *Toward What Bright Glory?* find themselves in another world—a world dominated by the special mind-set of the Western intellectual community:

"With an increasingly grim determination since the war, the establishment has refused to admit, greeted with scathing sarcasm or deliberately looked the other way when evidence has surfaced of Communist suppressions and brutalities in the Soviet Union, Communist suppressions and brutalities in Eastern Europe, naked Communist imperialist aggression in the Baltic States and elsewhere, unceasing Communist attempts to subvert peace and stability everywhere in the world.

"With similar ruthlessness the establishment has glossed over, where it has not blatantly refused to report, the facts about Communist-incited dictatorships in newly freed Africa and many Third World nations. . . .

"The broad, complacent forgiveness extended to the Soviets is granted to any tin-pot dictator or piece of human scum who overthrows an established order, providing he is smart enough to give himself the correct political label. All that is necessary to win favorable standing with the opinion-makers of the West, as the shrewd realize—and some of them, like Fidel Castro, are very shrewd—is to work on the guilty conscience that seems to pervade the Western intellectual community. If you are a murderous thug who can successfully con the West into considering you "progressive," it doesn't matter how many horrors you perpetrate. You have the establishment's official seal of approval, and are home free.

"As the years draw away from the harsh realities of the wartime struggle for survival, the integrity and courage needed for an honest view of the world have become too much for the establishment. Hardly anyone in it has the guts to face up to the facts, or to the implications of doing something about them if one does face up. Consequently it has become the fashionable, the right, the only acceptable thing, to pretend that they are not there. Consequently, much more often than not, both perspective and reportage have become sadly skewed—sometimes unconsciously, more often deliberately, suppressive of the truth.

"The inevitable result has been that readers and viewers, having nowhere else to turn for their knowledge of events, have become as skewed in their perceptions of the world as the creators and purveyors of the news themselves. Told incessantly that the Communists are just earnest, idealistic, misunderstood nice guys, occasionally a little cruel, perhaps, but essentially salt of the earth, many innocent millions in the West have begun to believe it.

"Told incessantly in many direct and indirect ways that their own country is no damned good, many millions of innocent Americans have begun to feel uneasily that this may be so. . . ."

This is the mind-set that challenges the characters in *Into What Far Harbor?*—some directly, some not so directly, but all conditioned and affected by it, as the whole world is conditioned and affected by it, to this day and far into the future.

It is against this background that the characters herein move on through the fat fifties into the unglued sixties and begin to worry about *their* kids as they face an ever more chaotic and ominous future in a world slipping ever more rapidly into free-fall.

Allen Drury

Members of the House,
1945–1964

TIMOTHY MERRILL BATES, *The Washington Inquirer*, Washington, D.C.

DR. GILBERT GULBRANSEN, La Jolla, California; m.
KAREN ANN WATERHOUSE, s. Grant, d. Gracia

EDWARD PAUL HAGGERTY, Rome, Italy; m.

1) FRANCINE MAGRUDER;

2) FLAVIA LAMPADINI; s. Paolo, d. Sophia

DR. NORTH McALLISTER, Salt Lake City; m.

BETTY JUNE LETTERMAN, s. Jason, d. Eileen

FRANCIS ALLEN MILLER, Sullivan Buick, Medford, Oregon; m.

MARY KATHERINE SULLIVAN; s. Francis, Jr., d. Rose

THEODORE KRASNIK MUSAVICH, the University; m.

DIANA SORENSON, s. Michael Roger, d. Mary Diana, s. Martin Theodore

DR. CLYDE GAIUS UNRUH, Honolulu; m.

MARGUERITE JOHNSON, s. Wilson, s. Peter, d. Elizabeth, d. Abby

HON. RICHARD EMMETT WILSON, United States Senate, Washington, D.C.; m.

DONNAMARIA VAN DYKE, s. Latt, s. Amos, d. Clayne

11

ANTONIO ANDRADE, Collina Bella Winery, Rutherford, California; m.

> LOUISE GIANFALCO, s. Antonio, Jr., d. Aurora Louise, s. Loren, d. Theresa

DR. GALEN BRYCE, "Overlook," Mulholland Drive, Hollywood, California

SMITH CARRIGER, Carrigcorp, Philadelphia, Pennsylvania; m.

> ANNELLE CHABOT, s. Chabot, d. Evangeline, s. Smith, Jr.

LOREN DAVIS, Davis Oil Company, Long Beach, California; m.

> ANGELINA D'ALESSANDRO, s. Anthony, d. Helen, s. Henry

JOHN THOMAS HERBERT, the University

DR. ALAN FREDERICK OFFENBERG, the University; m.

> RACHEL SHAHNA EPSTEIN, s. Alan, Jr., d. Ruth

DR. RENÉ SURATT, the University and Hillsborough, California

JEFFERSON DAVIS BARNETT, Barnett Plantations, Charleston, South Carolina; m.

> MARY DELL BRYANT, s. Bryant, s. Jefferson Davis, Jr., d. Mary Helen

BISHOP RANDOLPH RAMIREZ CARRERO, Archdiocese of New Mexico, Albuquerque, N.M.

DR. ROGER LEIGHTON, International Atomic Energy Agency, Vienna, Austria; m.

> JULIETTE CAMBRON, s. Roger Theodore, d. Yvette, s. Robert, s. Philip

MARCUS ANDREW TAYLOR, Taylorite Corporation, Pittsburgh, Pennsylvania

WILLIAM HENRY WILSON, Wilson Ranch, Terra Bella, California; m.

> ELIZABETH JANE MONTGOMERY, d. Leslie, s. Thomas

RUDOLPH JOHN KROHL, Krohl, Inc., Ridgewood, New Jersey; m.

HELGA BERGER, s. Rudolph, Jr., s. Hans Friedrich, d. Lotte, s. Herman

BAYARD WHITTINGTON JOHNSON, Washington, D.C.; m.

MARYETTA BRADFORD, d. Tianna, s. Melrick

YOSOHIRO NAGATANI, Nagatani Farms, Fresno, California; m.

IBU ISUNO, s. Hiro, d. April, d. Mary Ibu

ARAM KATANIAN, Katanian Rolph Mercer Katanian, Fresno, California; m.

HELEN SMITH, s. Aram, Jr., d. Margaret

1

From all the corners of the earth the mad magician bade them come and from all the corners of the earth they came to offer themselves up as sacrifices on his monstrous bloody altar.

He unleashed horror.

He unleashed agony.

He unleashed death.

He said he did it to create the Thousand-Year Reich.

Fifty million dead and a world uprooted, later, they would scoff at this.

It took them a while to realize that he had accomplished something far more fundamental.

As only a tiny handful in all of history, virtually single-handed he had changed the course of humankind—

Forever.

It was only much later, as the second half of the twentieth century with all its heavy burdens of global chaos raced on, that they realized fully that something great and truly terrible had come their way; and that although he lay dead by his own hand in a bunker in Berlin, he was not really dead at all but had risen like the anti-Christ to cast his shadow over all the days of humanity to come.

Fifty years later, bright young "revisionist" historians, born long after his war, possessed of no experience of it, little concept of its human realities, no real sympathy for the untold agonies it had inflicted upon so many, many millions, would tell Richard Emmett Wilson and his contemporaries what it was all about.

They would tell Willie and his generation what they had felt—what they had done—what it all meant—why it all happened.

Quite frequently also they would tell them how basically shabby their government's motivations had been, how pointless their own efforts, how empty and futile their sacrifices.

Speaking from the smug security of the world their parents had saved for them, rocked in the cradle of their parents' ancient, terrible victory, these commentators would teach and write and pontificate about it with a serene intellectual arrogance that knew it all.

For Willie and his generation and for all the many millions who lived through it, the war was not quite that simple.

When you existed in a world where you literally did not know from day to day what was going to happen—

When the whole globe was a roiling turmoil with all rules broken, all certainties destroyed—

When the awful, erratic, death-dealing chances of actual ongoing worldwide conflict were with you every minute of every day for seemingly endless periods of time—

When you literally did not know when you went to bed whether you would find the enemy triumphant on the morrow and your nation, and with it all your hopes and dreams, destroyed—

When the heavy burden of the war rested upon heart, mind, body, soul and every human activity, a relentless, ominous, ever-menacing, actual, palpable *thing*—"the war"—an awful, grinding never-ending weight upon the whole world—

It was not so simple then.

Then it was not a neat, trim, all-questions-answered, all-edges-smoothed, all-problems-solved researchers' delight, its terrible uncertainties safely answered in the pages of a book or the magisterial pomposities of a classroom—

It was all real then.

Observe a survivor of its terrible agonies as he stands on the steps of Carlton House Terrace overlooking the Mall in the besieged and battered city of London, in the ancient, hard-pressed land of Britain.

His name is Richard Emmett Wilson—"Willie"—sometime lover, ofttime philosopher, not so long ago, in the half-affectionate, half-ironic words of his college fraternity, P.B.P. (Perfect Boy Politician) and S.M.O.C. (Superman on Campus).

It is "V-J Day," August 14, 1945, the final ending, with Japan's surrender, of the war in Asia, three months after "V-E Day," its formal conclusion in Europe.

V-J Day has come about as the direct and immediate result of the dropping of atomic bombs on Hiroshima and Nagasaki. The hysteria of war's ending is enormous but a great uneasiness underlies it in the minds of many.

Willie feels this as much as anyone. But, like almost everyone, his relief at the conclusion of hostilities is so great that it successfully, for a while, pushes back the ominous thoughts brought forth by the apocalyptic fireballs over the main Japanese island of Honshū.

Across the heads of the wildly celebrating crowd moving slowly along the Mall toward the Palace he can see the once and future beauty of St. James's Park, disfigured, as it has been for almost six years, by the trenches and antiaircraft emplacements of an exhausted but indomitable people.

Those few who happen to glance his way see a tall, lanky, pleasant-faced but not inordinately handsome American, toughened, sobered and noticeably matured by his experiences in the war.

He has traveled very far indeed from the day, soon after war's beginning, when he left the peaceful campus where he was educated and said a goodbye, destined to be longer than he knew, to the hot, brown, endlessly fertile San Joaquin Valley of California where he grew up.

He is twenty-seven years old, six of them passed in war or the shadow of war. Sixteen million of his American generation, mostly men, a few women, are in the same situation. They have fought in Europe. They have fought in the Aleutians and in the islands of the Pacific. They have fought in the jungles of Southeast Asia. They have fought wherever their cause was challenged, everywhere on earth. They have seen horrors, suffered horrors, given horrors back. They have achieved fantastic triumphs, made colossal blunders and, ultimately, won out.

More than 400,000 of them have not come back, 200,000 fewer than died in the American Civil War but a terrible figure in its own right which includes many youths, decent, bright and able, who now will never contribute what they might have to their parents, their families, their friends and their times.

Nothing will ever quite assuage the grief of those they have left behind, or quite bring into balance a reckoning so grim, so implacable, so essentially and irretrievably unfair.

Thoughts like these come often to Willie on this final day of Allied jubilation. They will continue to haunt him from time to time down the long corridor of the years, coming upon him unexpectedly for the rest of his life in the silent marches of the night or the treacherous little interstices of the day into which doubt and uncertainty, submerged but always present, creep.

"Somebody had to do it"—the adage of the pragmatic, which Willie himself often uses. But need it have been done like that? Was it necessary to have such infinite waste of life and treasure? Was there in it somewhere, aside from the obvious bravery and endurance of so many millions, that glory whose name he invoked, in desperation and irony, on the day it all began?

"What will they do to us, in their pride and their anger? Where will they send us drifting, on the darkening flood of the years? Toward what bright glory? Into what far harbor? . . ."

He will never know for sure. The debate will always remain open.

The mad magician in Berlin and his savage allies in the East had to be stopped if any decency at all was to be preserved in the world. But the destruction, the death, the death, the universal death—could not some of it have been avoided by more forethought, better planning, the prudent husbanding of effort and of lives instead of the gigantic wastefulness of a giant hand?

For himself and for the moment, he thinks he can honestly say, as he pauses a second longer before plunging into the crowd to try to make his own way to the ancient tribal ritual at the Palace: sufficient unto the day is the triumph thereof. He will not admit doubts now. The joy is too great all around him. Willie the analytical, he tells himself, had better stop analyzing and give himself up to it.

With a sudden flash of insight he realizes that in all likelihood he and the rest of humanity will never see the like of this day again. Never again in his lifetime—or perhaps ever—will so much of the world be so genuinely united, in heart and feeling, as it is this day of final victory in World War II.

Willie's war, like that of everyone else, has been fought on many levels. Thanks to its random chances and to some urge to hang on to old friendships as anchor in a whirling, suddenly anchorless universe, he has been able to keep in touch with most of his friends as they have survived, or fallen victim to, the roaring, tumbling, all-devouring juggernaut.

The three with whom he first came to England, for instance, within days of the outbreak of war in Europe on September 3, 1939. Amiable "Buff" Richardson, Arthur John III from Montclair, New Jersey, friendliest and most generous of youths . . . Guy Unruh, Clyde Gaius from Honolulu, Hawaii, bosom friend since the day they first met as freshmen roommates at the University in the fall of 1935 . . . Aram Katanian from Fresno, California, "Ari," the "next-door roommate" and permanent friend against whom Willie was to run three years later, successfully, in the election for student-body president.

And their girls, or, rather, his and Guy's—his wife, Donnamaria "Donn" Van Dyke from West Park, New York, her bright and ever-cheerful personality worn down a little now by the war but basically still as resilient, good-natured and determinedly optimistic as it had been when she was his vice-president of the student body at the University; and plump little Marguerite "Maggie" Johnson, whose gentle persistence had finally brought free-swinging ladies' man Guy to a domesticity he still sometimes honors more in the breach than the observance, but whose sympathetic support and calmly enfolding love provide him haven that he deeply values and for which he never ceases to be grateful.

Ari and Buff, bachelors when the war began, are finishing it as bachelors still—or Ari is finishing it.

The thought of Buff can still bring tears to Willie's eyes, though it has been almost a year now since his last letter to Buff in the Pacific was returned by Buff's commanding officer with a sympathetic little note.

Buff, "one of our bravest and most popular officers, a great aviator who was, I think I can say, universally loved by all ranks," had finally succumbed to the Japanese off Rabaul after successfully surviving without a scratch four long years of war against the Germans.

"It was a mission on which no one asked Lt. Col. Richardson to go," the general wrote. "It was to some extent a suicide one. But he said that some of his friends were going and he wanted to be with them. It is a good thought to which to cling. He was doing what he wanted to do, in the company of officers and men with whom he wanted to do it. He knew the chances, took them gallantly and, I am sure, happily, for as you know, that was his nature. We here all sympathize with you and his other friends from college days, of whom I am sure he had very many."

And so he did, Willie thought, so he did. Lovable, easygoing Buff, whom everybody liked; big, good-natured puppy dog, never hurting anybody in his whole life. Willie feels again the blind, bitter protest he has felt for so many friends in the course of the war, and asks himself again the question always asked and never answered: why him? Why not me? Why do some survive and others go? Why does the luck of the draw play such havoc with the young, the decent, the worthy, and leave some others noticeably less worthy to wax and flourish and live mediocre lives?

Willie does not, of course, put himself in the latter category but he knows plenty who fit and they are doing just fine as the war ends. Poor, gentle, easygoing Buff, who could have contributed so much, lies picked clean by the sharks on the bottom of the Pacific while some sour bastard like Renny Suratt lives and flourishes. It never makes sense. . . .

Willie is being pushed, shoved and carried along toward the Palace in the crush of happy celebrants who, seeing the familiar uniform, shout, "Good on you, Yank!" But he cannot escape his thoughts of the too-early dead.

He often reads and hears the determinedly comforting cliché: They are "forever young, forever perfect, nevermore to be troubled by the savage storms of life."

Well, that's very kind of you, he thinks bitterly, but I'd rather have them alive, thank you very much.

His mind goes to the second of his fellow seniors who has not lived to enjoy this day. Again the sadness grips him. Less outgoing than Buff, far too serious to be the ever-ready party boy, steadier, graver, quieter, more solid yet with a saving grace of wry good humor and good natured tolerance, Ray Baker will never find the ideal Miss Right with whom he had planned to make a happy home and raise a happy family in his quiet little town of Arvin, sixty miles south of Willie's Terra Bella in the southern end of the San Joaquin Valley.

Ray had planned to be a lawyer. He would have been a very good one, Willie thinks now. He almost feels like shouting, *"He would have been a very good one!"* But there is no point in that. Probably half or more of his companions in the Mall have lost a family member or members, close friends or pleasant acquaintances. If they haven't suffered that kind of loss, they've lost an empire. They have a right to shout in anger, too. But nobody's shouting, except in happiness. It would ill behoove him.

Ray, unflappable, quietly efficient, no-nonsense "backbone of the company" as he had once been the "backbone of the house": first lieutenant in the Army, lost in the Battle of the Bulge in the war's closing months in Germany. Another good man gone, another empty space in the fabric of humankind, infinitesimal in the scheme of things, much larger in the hearts of family and friends. And again, why? And again the bitter, never-to-be-answered questions, recurring monotonously as they always do.

And quiet little Hank Moore, sophomore when Willie first knew him in his own senior year, earnest and steady and unobtrusive like Ray, who had stayed on in school for two and half years until the Monday morning after Pearl Harbor, when he left the house at 8:00 A.M. to hurry down to the hastily erected recruiting station in the Quad to enlist in the Army. A nice, quiet, decent little guy, never flashy or particularly notable: just "a good citizen," Willie thinks as he finds himself barely inching forward along the broad graveled expanse of the Mall, its lovely old buildings unnecessarily grimy and worn from wartime neglect.

Just "a good citizen."

But needed.

The world is vastly different now from what it was on September 3, 1939, or even December 7, 1941. The challenges of war, by now routine and all too familiar, have finally, and it seems almost abruptly, yielded to the mysterious, unknown challenges of a peace for which very few governments and peoples are prepared. (Only one, the monolith in Moscow, seems to know exactly where it wants to go and is burrowing, burrowing, burrowing busily toward that end.) "Good citizens" are needed everywhere to help restore stability and decency in the return to civilian life.

A great many will not be there, including Hank Moore, who died in Italy at Monte Cassino, that futile campaign inspired by the headline-hunting competitions of generals who, with some rare and honorable exceptions, have not died with quite the frequency of enlisted ranks such as Corporal Henry Ellis Moore.

And finally, last of the four lost from the house, Bob Godwin from St. Louis, Missouri.

Godwin—"God," as his brethren sometimes nicknamed him behind his back with a frustrated combination of liking and exasperation—had succeeded Willie as student body president after running desperately for the office from the day he first hit campus as a freshman.

The ups and downs of his sometimes embarrassingly naked ambition formed the butt of many jokes at his expense. Some he noticed in his headlong drive for campus prominence. Some he was too humorless and self-centered to realize.

The vast gel of human bodies, Willie in its midst, oozes slowly past Marlborough House. Distantly, being six feet three, he can glimpse over the heads of the crowd the back of Victoria's statue, and just beyond the gray-brown, dingy-dull facade of the Palace. "God," he thinks as he is propelled along virtually without conscious effort on his part, was a good citizen, too, if a terribly earnest one.

Bob had enlisted in the Marines on the day he graduated in June of 1940 because the Marines, he wrote Willie—and Willie could imagine his earnest expression as he considered all the political advantages to be gained later from such an association—were very likely to win a lot of glory in the war that was daily coming closer to America.

And so, with all the implacable inexorability of random fate, he had joined the Marines—shared in and, being a brave youth, contributed his fair share to the glory—and had died, in the last weeks of the Pacific war, on the slopes of Mount Surabachi on Iwo Jima.

For him, too, Willie feels a deep regret. He knows Bob was quite humorless, more than a little ambition-driven, but he was a good-hearted, good-spirited youth who made many civic contributions along the way to becoming president of the student body. He had once confided to Willie, in one of those late-night college bull sessions in which vast dreams and great imaginings are exchanged, that his political ambitions went far beyond the University.

"Our Congressman is getting pretty old—probably about fifty," he said, "and I've been giving it a lot of study. I think he's vulnerable. If I come back a war hero and he's just been sitting around Congress on his duff doing nothing, which is what he usually does, then I think I can take him. And then, after that, both our Senators are getting along, one's got a famous name but he's a famous drunk, and the other is an innocuous little guy named Truman who has no background or qualifications at all. I think I could do it, Willie."

"And then?" Willie had asked, trying not to sound too dry and discouraging.

"Then," Bob had said, eyes alight. "*Then* we'll see."

But now he never would, poor "God" who tried so hard. Now all that drive and ambition and eager willingness to take on any public task as long as it carried a modest—he didn't ask too much—bit of publicity for him are gone, completely gone, bones bleaching somewhere on the gutted slope of Surabachi. And the world and his America, which might very well—and who, now, could say not?—have one day seen him rise to the ultimate eminence he obviously so deeply desired, even at twenty-one—will never know him now.

Waste, waste, waste! Willie thinks bleakly as the crowd pushes him along past the back of St. James's Palace and begins to flow into the broad river of humanity already crowding every inch between Victoria's monument and the gates of Buckingham Palace.

Waste compounded by the millions.

The mind cannot conceive, as yet, the extent of it.

Perhaps it can never be accurately assessed.

It is in a somber mood that he finds himself immobilized at last by the mass of bodies all around him.

A hush falls over the vast crowd. Only the distant bleat of a taxi, far on the outskirts, momentarily breaks the silence. Then the hush resumes, deepens, intensifies almost beyond endurance.

Suddenly a great excitement grips the world.

Tiny figures appear upon a balcony.

Thoughts, regrets, concerns, forebodings about the terrible new atomic force abroad in the world, all vanish in a great happy roar of tribal exultation.

On the balcony that during the twentieth century has become the sacred high altar of the tribe, linking its members to a glorious past winding back into the mists of ancient time, the little icons smile and smile and wave and wave.

Far from Willie, shouting now in mindless, exultant release like all the rest in front of Buckingham Palace, the other members of the house who once were so close to one another at the University greet this hour from posts, battle stations, homes, jobs, wherever the inexorable demands of the world convulsion have taken them.

Those who have gone to war are scattered from one end of the globe to the other.

Those few, like Tim Bates and Marc Taylor, who have been deferred because of physical or mental handicap, are closer to home, but also swept up in the day's euphoria.

All, underneath the universal rejoicing, have one basic, recurring thought.

Whether they were in the war or out of it, a great unspoken relief sings in all their hearts. They would be ashamed to admit it, but it is there.

Warrior or non-warrior, armed participant or civilian, they all feel the same secret, triumphant joy.

The war is over.

And they have survived.

*   *   *

For Tim Bates, watching the news of worldwide rejoicing coming
in over the ticker in the National Press Club offices of United Press
in Washington, D.C., the hour is one of mixed joy and uneasy foreboding.

Unlike most, Tim thinks ahead.

He has always thought ahead.

Therein lies his lifelong advantage and his lifelong burden.

He reflects now that he had seen the war coming when he was
editor of the campus *Daily* in 1938. In a time when it was not popular
to point out what lay ahead, he had warned his contemporaries re-
peatedly in editorials, columns, news reports. "Timmy's at it again,"
was the general reaction to his hortatory efforts. But damn it, he had
been right. Hitler *had* plunged the world into war. Japan *had* struck
in the Pacific, just as he had been fearful that it would, even though
Bill (Yusohiro) Nagatani, his associate editor then and subsequent
successor as editor, had pooh-poohed the idea. Bill's tone had been
such that it had persuaded Tim that Nagatani, "nisei" second-
generation Japanese from Fresno, might know more than Tim did
about what was going to happen.

Which in retrospect, Tim has to admit honestly, appears now to
have been nonsense. Bill had been interned briefly at Manzanar
when the Japanese were swept from the West Coast; had helped to
edit the camp newspaper for a short time; then had enlisted in the
442nd Regimental Combat Team, "the Nisei Battalion," and had
served with great bravery and distinction in Europe.

So much for suspecting Nagatani.

But he had been right on all the rest, Tim thinks now as he watches
the news come in with his fellow newsmen—and women, for the
business has rapidly opened up in the wartime absence of many male
staffers.

Even now in the midst of universal rejoicing his ever-present instinct, comprised partly of native intuition and partly of an innate
pessimism surprising in one so young, tells him that there is much to
be concerned about in this newfound, euphoric peace.

Greatest of all is the awesome new force unleashed at Hiroshima
and Nagasaki.

Tim's war has been on the whole an exciting one, though not as
dramatic as he had hoped. His first job in Washington had been as a

humbled beginner in the Washington bureau of the New York *Daily News*. He had hoped, as so many young newsmen did in those days, that he would be assigned immediately to Europe to help cover the war he had long seen coming. Somehow his superiors did not seem as impressed with his scrapbook of editorials and columns as he was. He was assigned to cover the Commerce and Agriculture departments, a dull beat at best and doubly so when one had his dreams of journalistic glory. He tried to enlist but was rejected because of eyesight, a factor that had not interfered in his student pilot training at the University but seemed increasingly important to officialdom as war came closer.

After Pearl Harbor, restless and frustrated, he had secretly gone job-hunting and had landed in the ramshackle, run-down offices of perennially threatened, perennially penurious United Press. There he had at least been given a few assignments at the State Department and now and again, on a fill-in basis, in the Senate. A year later, in 1944, he had been assigned full time to the Senate and had settled in, comfortable and at last on reasonable terms with his ambitions, to pass the remainder of the war covering that always unique and frequently astounding body.

There he had known the great ones of the war years, Bob Taft of Ohio, Walter George and Richard Russell of Georgia, Alben Barkely of Kentucky, Arthur Vandenberg of Michigan, Tom Connally of Texas, Claude Pepper of Florida, Hiram Johnson of California, and all of their colleagues—that colorful pantheon, then holding office, that had given the Senate an intellectual stature and human fascination it was not to know again in his lifetime. There he had seen them conduct the wartime business of the nation with the sometimes petty self-interest and sometimes soaring patriotism of which free men are capable.

There he had seen Vandenberg, his thinning hair carefully combed to hide his growing bald spot, looking like a portly, pompous pouter pigeon, change the Republican party and the course of American history with his thundering endorsement of the United Nations, setting the United States on a course of world cooperation from which it will not deviate.

There he had seen the ill and terribly aging President who had dominated the years of his youth address the Congress for the last time, apologizing for his seated posture because "it makes it a lot easier for me in not having to carry about ten pounds of steel on the bottom of my legs. . . ." Six weeks later he was dead, succeeded by

Bob Godwin's "innocuous little guy named Truman who has no background or qualifications at all"—who has proved to be anything but innocuous and has already overcome whatever lack of qualifications there might have been.

There in the Senate Tim has watched the postwar world being formed: not very astutely, not in any organized or profoundly thoughtful fashion, but rather in the blundering, forward stumble typical of America as it has moved, good-hearted and uncertain, toward goals inchoate and dreams not often clearly seen.

Through it all he has kept firmly in mind his ultimate ambition, which is to become, first, a foreign correspondent, and then, in due course, a nationally syndicated columnist with the potential, as he puts it privately to himself, to "do something" to help guide his native land in what he regards as its largely feckless plunge into the future. It never occurs to him, as this constantly recurring thought again goes through his mind in the midst of the war's-end jubilation in the UP office, that this could be regarded as a somewhat pompous and youthful idea. He has never doubted his ability to advise his country on what it ought to do. Having been proved right about the war, he feels more competent than ever.

This, as Willie has written lately from London, is the first requisite of being a good columnist—"the basic conviction that you are absolutely right."

"You demonstrated this amply on the *Daily*," Willie wrote with that dryness characteristic of him. "Now, watch out, world! Here comes Timmy!"

Well, he thinks now, Willie can kid him about it if he wants to, but he's going to do his damnedest to make it come true. United Press is only a temporary stop along the way. He'll use it for what he can get out of it—and give it good service, too, he tells himself—as long as he stays. But it certainly isn't going to be the last stop on the line for him.

Someone lets out a happy whoop—"Live ones!"—and all the men crowd to the windows that look across Fourteenth Street to the Willard Hotel. The two pairs of office binoculars are passed from hand to hand, focused on the view that has helped to while away so many wartime hours.

On this day of universal rejoicing no one, at three in the afternoon, has paid much attention to the angle of the blinds.

In a room one floor down, a male and female are enjoying each other to the utmost.

In the room directly below them, a sailor and a Marine, both still wearing their uniform caps at a jaunty angle in some last, sardonic defiance of service authority, are doing the same.

Tim reflects, as he takes his turn at the binoculars, that one could learn a great deal about human nature in wartime from the side of the National Press Building that overlooks the Willard.

In fact, one could learn a great deal about the basic nature of war itself, which always unleashes a great tidal wave of desperate sex that nine times out of ten has the automatic result of replenishing the race when it gets into one of its periodic spasms of self-decimation.

The two entertainments end, almost simultaneously, in obvious satisfaction.

Their terminations prompt raucous disappointment in the UP office. Then everyone turns back to the news, coming steadily in over the wire, of a world gone happily mad.

For Guy Unruh from Hawaii and for Gilbert Gulbransen from Minneapolis, Minnesota, the war is ending in much the same fashion as it is in the Willard.

Guy, like Willie, is in England, stationed at an American air base in the Midlands. At the moment he is in a bed-sitter in Chelsea, half aware of sounds of jubilation but some distance from the wilder scenes of celebration in central London.

Gil Gulbransen is in a small hut somewhere in the Philippine jungle near Subic Bay, celebrating both the end of the war and his first chance to relax in almost seventy-two hours of seemingly endless medical duty.

For these two valiant warriors, who, as their fraternity brother Franky Miller once remarked, "unsheathed their swords in high school and haven't sheathed them since," the war has been one long round of backbreaking, mind-wrenching, emotion-dulling medical service interspersed with infrequent but happily riotous explorations of the female species in all its interesting national varieties.

Guy has now been married to Maggie for six years. She and the two children, a boy and a girl, are with her parents in New Jersey.

His present activity with a robustly cooperative young female Royal Air Force lieutenant whom he picked up half an hour ago in the King's Road is simply one more of the matter-of-fact relaxations he has routinely sought whenever he could get away from duty.

This has not been very often, actually, and has usually been in the company of Willie, in much the same fashion in which they used to go up to San Francisco from the University on the occasional Saturday night.

In London Willie, in the final year of the war, has shared a flat in South Audley Street with two young fellow officers attached like himself to the Supreme Commander's headquarters in Grosvenor Square, a five-minute walk away. The assignment has not made him privy to the thoughts of the Supreme Commander—he has not, as in some fictional recreations of the era, helped great men conduct the war from a junior officer's position—but it has permitted him a relatively safe billet in the capital after five years of very tough combat that he has somehow miraculously survived. There Guy has found safe haven on his infrequent visits to town.

His own survival, Guy thinks now as happy noises from Cheyne Walk distract him somewhat from the pleasant business in progress, has often been as miraculous as Willie's. The youthful idealism with which they came to England to enlist in the Royal Air Force in late September 1939 had soon given way to a more mature but dogged conviction that what they were doing was right. Very soon they came to regard the war as their hosts the British did: a nasty job that must be completed as fast as possible so that everyone could go home.

In its early months—"the phony war," in which all was relatively static and nothing much seemed to be happening anywhere—this mood was a little hard to sustain. Very soon this changed. Starting in February 1940, there came in fast succession the terrifying collapse of nations, the pathetic roll call that issued seemingly almost every night from the radio:

"Norway fell today. . . . Denmark fell today. . . . Holland fell to-day. . . . Belgium fell today. . . ."

And finally:

"France fell today."

And the heroic retreat from Dunkirk, and the Battle of Britain begun in earnest. And on December 7, 1941, the cruel American awakening at Pearl Harbor, and a hesitant homeland in the war at last.

"Pearl Harbor solved a problem for Franklin," Eleanor Roosevelt remarked later; and so it did.

For him and for his country.

In those early hectic days of "the real war" in Europe, both Willie and Guy underwent their baptisms, flying with the R.A.F. on the desperate heroic missions that met the challenge and ultimately turned it back. When America entered the war, they transferred to the U.S. Army Air Corps, as it was then. Willie continued to fly, 143 combat missions before his assignment to Grovesnor Square. Guy's aerial assignments diminished rapidly as his pre-medical training at the University was soon transformed into the terrible realities of war as a medical officer. The services, notorious for their misuse and misassignments of talent, creators of kitchen help out of scientists and ditch-diggers out of mathematicians, did have sense enough to use medically trained men for medical purposes. As casualties shot up, the need became too desperate to permit of wasted competence in this particular area.

And he has been competent, Guy reflects as the period of lull in which he has had time for reverie gives signs of turning into something more delightful and more demanding of attention. He has learned things, helping to care for returning flight crews, that he would never have learned in three years of medical school, and he has learned them with the headlong fury of war. There has been no time for niceties, no time for anything but what was wryly referred to as "on-the-job training."

He is still planning to complete med school when he returns home, but it will be as a much older, wiser and more seasoned man. They may be able to teach him the niceties, but the realities he has already learned in the grimmest school there is.

Far away in the Philippine countryside Gil Gulbransen is thinking the same as the firm little brown body under his writhes and twists and emits ecstatic sounds. He has been her American daddy for six weeks now, ever since the successful drive on Manila that began with the landings at Linguyen Bay. She was hastily recruited as a nurse's assistant, had appeared at his elbow in the operating room; desire was virtually instant, and they have retreated whenever possible since into her village near the great naval base. The little hut has seemed then to encompass the world—the only world he has known in recent months, aside from the other world of wounded who seem to come at him, in dreams as in reality, in one long, charging, incessant, bloody stream.

Perversely, even as things reach their pleasant climax in the hut, the wounded are charging him now. For a few brief seconds he can banish them as he lies exhausted on her breast; but only for a few. In moments they are back again, faceless, nameless, sometimes limbless and almost headless, too, demanding all his attention, consuming his emotions, obliterating his mind.

Gulbransen in college had never been the most introspective of youths. Gulbransen the mature veteran of three and a half years of war in the Pacific is different now. Since he did not join the idealists in their volunteer early entry into the war, he has had time for a couple of years of formal medical training before entering service. But as with Guy, most of what he knows he has learned in the savage cauldron of battle. He is a much better doctor now than he would have been: older, wiser and sadder, too.

He has always had a certain fatherly streak, surprising under the sensational blond good looks that have guaranteed him mastery over the female population. His attempts to befriend shy, unhappy Marc Taylor in the fraternity house, his good-natured bantering relationship with Karen Ann Waterhouse, whom he still intends to marry now that peace has finally come, his many other good-hearted and likable qualities, have been put to good use in the war. His bedside manner is a highly effective one, eliciting from the wounded the sort of willing-to-oblige response that is often the extra ingredient needed for recovery. Many more times than he can now remember, his sympathetic air and kindly approach have proved to be the turning points for sailors who have come to him dreadfully wounded and in the last depths of despair. To his own delight he has become not only a good physical doctor but a good psychological one as well.

He is beginning to get a glimpse of a practice in Karen Ann's hometown of La Jolla near San Diego that may be more than the fashionable time-serving, money-making treatment of rich widows he has sometimes cynically imagined for himself.

Now, as the sound of firecrackers and jubilation outside in the little village tell him that war's end has been officially announced, he smiles down at his companion and says regretfully, "I've got to go."

"Will you come back next week?" she asks with the slow, accepting smile that had first endeared her to him.

"I will indeed," he says crisply; but when he reaches Manila, he finds the orders sending him home immediately. And though he tries desperately to get word to her, he is unable to do so. He has an address, of sorts, and assures himself that he will try to contact her someday; but being a realist, doubts, regretfully, that he will.

He thinks wryly that this will not be a reprise of Madam Butterfly. She is also a realist. That, too, has endeared her to him.

For Guy in Chelsea, no such thoughts, even mildly sentimental, occur. He and his R.A.F. friend understand each other; this is strictly a war's-over celebration, and like the war, it is over too the minute the bed is abandoned, the clothes are back on and a final warm hug has been exchanged. It has all been very practiced and practical, highly good-natured and delightfully companionable. But now it is time to try to get across town to rejoin Willie and then return to the base to prepare for the homeward journey that now cannot be long delayed.

At home wait Maggie and Donna and peace.

The reality of it suddenly hits Guy in Chelsea as it is suddenly hitting Willie in front of the Palace, Gil in the Philippines and indeed all of them, everywhere.

Peace.

And then what?

It is a question that is hitting no one harder than it is the small, wiry figure in Marine uniform, crouching beside the pilot of a fighter plane, flying over the ruins of Hiroshima. He is staring down in frightened awe at the devastation below.

Roger Leighton, straight-A student in physics, determined heretofore to return and complete his courses at the University just as soon as war ends, is looking down upon the ultimate consequences of his chosen trade.

He has been through almost all of the Pacific war and has seen, and been involved in, many terrible things. But none he has ever seen, done, or imagined, has been as dreadfully, awfully, soul-devastatingly terrible as this.

As far as the eye can see—obliteration. As far as the mind can stretch—desolation. As far as the imagination can reach—the silent indifference of the universe, the casual shrug of God, the ending of the world.

Oh, Christ, he keeps saying to himself. Oh, Christ, oh, Christ, oh, Christ. Look at *that*.

"Pretty bad, Major," the pilot observes in a matter-of-fact tone, and Rodge thinks: what an imaginative bastard you are. He nods without turning his head, unable to be reasonably civil or even speak as he contemplates the final result of what man can do to man.

He knows the reasons, understands the rationale; he can even, in some other area of his brain, admire the technical skill and the scientific achievement. But having been a youth with compassion he finds himself in these few minutes transformed into a man with a mission. It mustn't happen again, he thinks over and over. *It mustn't happen again.*

He stays in the cockpit for a few more minutes while the plane swings slowly over the gray annihilation and then turns east and north toward its base on board an aircraft carrier anchored in Tokyo Bay. Three years as a Marine have hardened Rodge to many things; but his mind for a while cannot encompass this.

When it does, somewhere on the flight back, it appears to make a mockery of everything he has done in the war. He has been a dedicated Marine, a fine officer, a recipient of two battlefield promotions as a result of heroic action under fire. He will emerge, though he does not know it now, as the most decorated member of the fraternity; presently he will be awarded the Congressional Medal of Honor. This will be given him for the rescue of seven enlisted men trapped in a cave on Iwo not far from the spot where Bob Godwin, unknown to Roger, fell on the same day to the savage bayonet of a dying Japanese.

The fact that one of the enlisted men was his old buddy Theodore Krasnick Musavich from the house will not be noted in the citation, but Rodge knows with a wry little smile that Moose's presence explained the heroism that day. He had to save Moose. Nobody could abandon Moose.

But this—this *thing* that destroyed Hiroshima and three days later Nagasaki: what good was heroism in its presence? It abolished everything. In a second one hundred thousand worlds were not only shattered, they were gone. In the terror of that revelation, he suspects for a few optimistic moments that never again will there be a place for war. He will prove to be entirely wrong about this in his savage century of unceasing little wars, but the thing that will become known simply as "the Bomb" will underlie his own thinking and that of his generation for the rest of their days.

It will not, unfortunately, inhibit the leaders of successor generations when they become used to, and casually dismissive of, its fearsome potential. The little foxes, undeterred, will continue to spoil the grapes; and as a result of their headlong irresponsible drive toward conquest and ethnic domination, their own appointments with the Bomb will sooner or later become inevitable.

There will be much need for heroism then.

Right now, however, neither Rodge nor anyone else can foresee this. The plane on which he had been first an eager, now an appalled, passenger reaches its carrier, touches down. He returns to his temporary quarters below.

"How was it?" a fellow officer asks.

"Awful," he says tersely, and finds no other adequate words. "Just awful. You have to see it to believe it."

And even then, he thinks, you don't really believe it. The mind doesn't possess the capacity to *really* believe it.

Nor to really comprehend or accept what he murmurs to himself as he strips down and steps into a shower:

"Let's don't have any more children."

"What?" demands a startled friend in the next stall. But Rodge only shakes his head and does not reply.

He knows in his heart that he is absolutely right. He also knows that neither he nor anyone else in the ever-hopeful world is really capable of believing, or following, so bleak a proposal. For better or worse the human race will keep on instinctively perpetuating itself as its leaders impel it ever more blindly and ever more irretrievably toward the ultimate abyss.

Fighting his temporary but overwhelming sense of doom, he tells himself sternly that surely humankind cannot be so self-destructive. Surely its collective common sense will rise up and say: enough! An end to insanity! An end to mindless struggle! Welcome, new dawn and new day! And the earth will resound with peace, and infinite will be the blessings thereof.

Rodge is not quite that much of an idealist, of course: war has taken care of any really wide-eyed dreams he may have had. Yet it is possible to think, in this moment when he comes to grips with the Bomb and tries to fashion from its horrors some glimpse of a better future, that out of it may just possibly come a unity of thought and purpose that will strengthen men and women of goodwill everywhere and help them to prevail over the darker forces of their collective nature.

Such, at any rate, is the thought that comes to him; and it is one, he realizes as he washes up and prepares for evening mess, to which he must cling despite the intimations that he also has, of a colder wind already blowing.

He wonders as he joins his fellow officers and compares notes with the few who have also been privileged to fly over one or the other of the two last great targets of the war, how many of them are striving as desperately as he to hold on to hope. Not too many, he realizes sadly; at least not hope in his sense of it.

"We can wipe those bastards in Moscow off the face of the earth with this," a cherubic Air Force colonel about his own age says with great satisfaction, and the sentiment is echoed fervently all around.

Only two or three catch his expression of dismay and exchange sympathetic glances with him. The rest are obviously all for it. He decides he won't even argue. But to himself he says: we have to do better. Mankind has *got* to do better.

As often happened at the University and has often happened in the past three years during which he has managed to arrange for their service to run roughly parallel, he wonders what one of the most good-hearted oafs he has ever known is up to now. Is he, too, filled with philosophic forebodings? Not, he thinks, if he knows Moose.

But in this, even though he knows him so well by this time, he is making the mistake many do when judging Moose. On this day of universal celebration, even Moose has become philosophical.

He would be a little resentful, even of his friend Rodge, if he were to know that Rodge doesn't consider him capable of really deep thinking about things.

He often, Moose tells himself now, thinks about things. Just because he doesn't make a big show of it like some people do, it doesn't mean he doesn't think.

He is lying in bed at the naval medical facility on Treasure Island in the center of San Francisco Bay between Oakland and San Francisco. Through the window of the room he shares with a fellow Marine savagely wounded on Okinawa, he can see across the wind-whipped, whitecapped waters the gleaming white city as it wanders casually over its hills. It is, at this time, a human-sized city composed of low-lying houses and a few taller commercial buildings. It is a modest, beautiful and amiable city, a pleasant place made for pleasant, comfortable living. It is a city still in proportion.

Moose knows it well from his days at the University, some thirty miles down the Peninsula. Like most who make its acquaintance under those conditions, he has fallen permanently in love with it. He finds it difficult to conceive of a life in which San Francisco does not, sooner or later, play some part.

In his case, he knows it will. His professional future, which in his senior year seemed to him highly uncertain, is happily decided now. His campus football career, dogged, erratic, yet finally triumphant in what Franky Miller always referred to as "his fucking asshole touchdowns," had brought him, at the last possible moment just before graduation, an offer from Coach and the University to join the coaching staff. This had been his secret dream, never revealed to anyone but Rodge, ever since he started college. When Coach called him to break the news, he had dissolved in tears, so great had been his tension and so hopeless had he considered the dream.

In a great rush of gratitude he had pitched in and worked like a dog, he thinks now, an absolute fucking dog, all through the next year and a half. When the '41 season ended in late November, he had received a promotion to third assistant coach and the implied promise of a permanent position with the athletic department if he so wished. He so wished, fervently. Ten days later came Pearl Harbor. A week after that he was in the Marines with Rodge. But not before he had received personal assurances from both Coach and Dr. Chalmers, president of the University, that his job would be waiting for him when he came back.

If he came back, he thinks wryly now. That had been a close one; and again, as with a lot of other things, he has Rodge and his loyal friendship to thank.

If it weren't for Rodge, he wouldn't be here right now; and even though he certainly isn't enjoying the best health in the world at the moment, it beats what could have happened on Iwo. He has a severe head wound, which will always leave a scar extending from his right temple down to almost his right eye, and he will always have a gimpy right leg and a right arm that will always be an inch or two shorter than the left; but at least he's alive and in relatively good shape. The fucking Japs had almost gotten him and six of his buddies, but thanks to Rodge, they hadn't. Only about sixty feet had separated Rodge and the seven of them in the cave, but it was sixty feet of continuous raving hell, mortar fire and slippery scraps of bodies all over the place, slithering treacherously underfoot, slapping you blindly in the face as they dripped from blasted branches. But Rodge had made it, covered their escapes and, one by one, taken them back to safety.

Moose had seen a lot of brave things in his years in the Pacific, but nothing quite as brave as Rodge's seven round-trips under fire; and because he realizes that his being there was probably what gave Rodge the extra strength to carry it off, he is humbly grateful once again for the friendships forged in the house.

The house! How distant that all seems now, those kids back there who didn't really dream, when they debated Hitler and F.D.R. and whether war would come, what the years immediately following would bring them—such comradeship, such bravery, such mind-bending horror for many of them, until on this day of universal rejoicing those who have been through the fire are emerging so hardened and changed that he wonders if they can possibly fit back smoothly into civilian life.

A lot of islands and a lot of savage seas have been hosts to his own dreams on that score. The University and particularly the deep green oval inside the stadium have danced tantalizingly in his head on many a lonely night in the barracks, aboard troop transports and on beaches and jungles under fire.

But now he wonders, as he groans and shifts position to ease the constant pain and discomfort, if those visions will really be as wonderful and soothing when he returns to them as they have been so many times when his life was in the balance.

"Hurtin'?" his roommate inquires, voice drowsy with medication and also difficult to understand because of his injuries—more a squawk than a voice, Moose thinks.

"Like hell," Moose says. "You?"

"Oh"—the guy grins, or at least his tone sounds as if he is grinning, although with so many bandages and most of the left side of his face blown off, nobody can really tell—"oh, yeah. But I'll survive."

"Good for you, buddy," Moose says. "Won't we all?"

"I hope so," the guy says, less cheery now. "I've got to go home and—and face my wife—like this."

And quite suddenly he utters a great convulsive sob and starts to cry.

"That's O.K., buddy," Moose says. "Let it all out. And don't worry. They do miracles with reconstruction these days." He utters a wry chuckle. "They've had to learn. Fast. They'll have you patched up as good as new before you know it. If she loves you, she'll stand by."

"Maybe," the guy says through his tears. "But I so wanted to be more to her than just a—just a—patch." And his tears increase.

Moose sighs heavily and repeats, "Let it out. It'll do you good."

There isn't much he can do, this time any more than the hundreds of other times in the last three years when he has tried, awkwardly and helplessly, to comfort guys with wounds as bad as this and sometimes much worse than this.

War is so damned *awful*, he thinks as he rolls over and looks again at the gleaming white city, fresh and pristine in the cool morning winds. So fucking *awful*. You're lucky, city. Most of you will never, ever, really have to know.

He is a good-natured man, Moose—man, now, not college kid—but he can't help feeling some of the universal bitterness within the services toward the bastards who have stayed home. Some of them, he knows, have had no choice; some of them, like Marc Taylor and Johnny Herbert from the house, wanted to go but haven't been able to because of disabilities of one kind or another. But there are others, he thinks darkly, like Renny Suratt and that Hitler-lover Rudy Krohl, who have pulled all the strings and worked all the angles to stay out of it.

He doesn't know this for sure, of course, the war has disrupted so many communications, but the last word from the house, a mimeographed list entitled "Who's Where" that Johnny Herbert had somehow managed to put together and send out a couple of years ago, had shown six of them as civilians.

He knows Timmy Bates has bad eyes—and Johnny Herbert has permanent lung problems—and he isn't surprised that Marc's attempted suicide in college was picked up by the medical examiners—and Franky Miller is subject to migraine headaches—and Randy Carrero has a permanent back injury from the auto accident in which Bill Lattimer was killed—so all those deferments have been legitimate enough. But Suratt and Krohl—suddenly they symbolize all the reasons why he and the poor fucker across the room are where they are and others aren't.

He sighs again: probably there's no point worrying about that now. It's all over and everybody's back to square one—except that those who have been exempt from service have of course had a chance to get a head start on all the rest of them who will soon come flooding home in their millions to try to get jobs, enter into or renew marriages, begin to think of families and homes, try to pick up their interrupted lives and start all over again.

He knows he has his coaching position to come back to, but now it doesn't seem quite so wonderful and satisfying as it did before the war. And the world, seen for three and a half years through the prisms of war and war's excitement, has suddenly become duller and less interesting.

For all its horrors and awfulness, he thinks, war, let's face it, is more often than not a unique and fascinating experience. And peace, let's face it, is drab in comparison when all it can offer, for most, is everyday routine.

He suspects that these sad truisms, unfashionable to articulate, are the ultimate explanations for war.

It is horrible, but if men are honest they will admit that they do enjoy it—more afterward than during, at times, but nonetheless they do enjoy it.

It appeals to the child that is always in them.

It is the greatest excitement many of them will ever know—the last great dangerous game, which tests their capacities to the utmost and frees them of all cares—except for themselves and their fellows—and all responsibilities—except to themselves and their fellows and to the common goal.

Which is why, he suspects as he shifts position once again and suddenly sees his future as pretty dull and unexciting, some poor fucking bastard will be fighting some other poor fucking bastard, into eternity.

No such philosophic overtones complicate the emotions of Moose's two most unfavorite people in all the world as they make the transition from war to peace on V-J Day.

Rudolph John Krohl, breaking out champagne for employees in Warehouse No. 3 of the greatly expanded family business in New Jersey, can see only an end to the easy wartime profits that have taken a small manufacturer of heavy moving equipment from somewhat less than $500,000 a year to a clear net this quarter of $5,650,000.

René Surratt, lying in the sun beside the pool in Hillsborough, California, while the radio blares forth the news of the world's jubilation, is thinking moodily that his rather unique position as a conscientious objector—unique in Hillsborough, anyway—must now come to an end and he must get back to the potentially dull business of making a living.

Both he and Rudy have had a pleasant war. Rudy's father, civic leader, member of the draft board, respected community figure despite his earlier—now greatly muted—sympathies for his German homeland, has been instrumental in arranging Rudy's war.

Renny's father, similarly placed in Hillsborough, has been equally effective on behalf of his son.

It has been true, of course, that both the senior Krohl and the senior Surratt immediately and with considerable public fanfare disassociated themselves from the respective draft boards' judgments of their offspring. But it is an open secret in both communities that, as it was put in New Jersey, "Them Germans stick together," and in Hillsborough, "Nobody's going to give Leon Surratt's son a hard time. After all, they've been here since the Gold Rush, or just about."

So, as happened in many communities across America where special situations overrode patriotic duty, Rudy, claiming to suffer from recurring bouts of asthma—not noted by his former fraternity brothers during his brief sojourn in the house but supported by a compliant affidavit from the family doctor—was promptly classified 4-F. And Renny, who made no secret of his disparaging views of what he called his country's "blind following of the Anglo-Judaic–Wall Street–Bank of England line," was promptly granted the conscientious-objector status he wanted and so was able to spend three healthy years in a camp in the Sierras, clearing underbrush, helping to thin out dead trees and enjoying frequent leaves back home in Hillsborough.

For Rudy, who had never approved of his government's increasingly open opposition to what was still called in the privacy of the Krohl household "the Fatherland," his deferment gave him the chance to join his father, somewhat earlier than they had planned, in the family business. One minor but satisfying bonus was that he was able to satisfy those racial feelings that had caused him to be labeled "Hitler-lover" by some of his enemies in the house: no one of Jewish background was employed by Krohl & Son during the war. The sentiments that had led Rudy into the disastrous campaign against Duke Offenberg in the fraternity that had resulted in his own expulsion could be freely exercised now. This gave him a lot of satisfaction, a satisfaction compounded by financial success as the business grew and Rudy began to reach an economic level he was convinced would enable him both to win the envious admiration of his former fraternity brothers and permit him to exercise considerable influence on his alma mater after the war, if he wanted to.

He does want to. He has something of a permanent grudge against the University as a result of the stern dressing-down administered to him by Dr. Chalmers, the president, after he, Helga Berger and the German exchange student Wolfgang Hubner had disrupted an anti-Hitler rally on campus. The rally had been organized by that pompous half-ass Willie Wilson, that other pompous half-ass Tim Bates and their willing stooge Aram Katanian. The memory of it even now, six years later, makes Rudy boil. Even as five hundred robust Aryan employees cheer and mill about excitedly under the persuasions of the champagne he and his father are pouring for them, he can still be angered by the gross injustice of the house in expelling him for his perfectly justifiable dislike for Duke Offenberg, and the subsequent cold verbal chastisement by Dr. Chalmers.

Helga Berger, who of course is now Mrs. Rudy Krohl—"Such good stock!" his mother murmurs complacently, with two towheaded little

Aryans already toddling about the house—enters the happy hall and is cheered by the employees. Rudy greets her with a rather patriarchal kiss (he is already beginning to feel that way as his father, though only sixty, increasingly gives him command of the company) and smiles and waves as the employees cheer again. Inwardly he is already busy calculating how the company can go on making profits, and increase them, when its War Department contract expires, as he knows it soon will now that the Fatherland is in collapse, humiliation and defeat.

Already he sees a glimmer. Underneath the florid exterior, increasingly pompous and proprietarial far beyond his years, underneath the quick temper and the racial prejudices, Rudy is beginning to be a very shrewd businessman.

The Fatherland may be down and out now but he has a lot of faith in its ability to recoup.

"Never discount the Germans!" his father keeps saying, in a time when Germany's utter collapse makes it easy to do so; and even though a lot of this may be hope and tribal superstition, Rudy never does.

Somebody is going to be on the inside of Germany's comeback early, he thinks now; and in this moment of the world's complacent jubilation at the defeat of the old country, there comes to him in a sudden revelation: *I'm going to be the one.*

In that thought, which some instinct—or hope—or faith—or message from Wotan—or whatever—tells him is absolutely correct, the world suddenly becomes bright and exciting again.

Not for Rudy Krohl the moody wonderings about the future that are plaguing some of his former fraternity brothers in this noisy moment. He knows what he's going to do.

The future looks just fine to him.

For Renny Suratt, lying on his back on his pad by the pool stark naked—the folks have gone into the city today, the maid is off, the cook doesn't come in until late afternoon—the thoughts are moody. But in his case, also, final clarification comes before he rolls over the concrete lip and lets himself flop lazily into the cool, refreshing water.

His war has been a moderately strenuous but very healthy one, and one of its dividends has been the opportunity to do a lot of thinking.

It has also given him a lot of time to read and study and prepare himself for the vocation to which he has finally decided to devote himself.

Renny Suratt the skeptic, always sarcastic about everything, always unsettling to the assumptions and self-confidence of those around him, curiously hostile to a world that has never treated him badly, has decided to teach.

He's going to show the coming college generations what this overbearing and hypocritical America is all about. He is going to get at least a few of them grounded in reality instead of in the flag-waving hogwash that so many of his generation seem to have swallowed hook, line and sinker. With a little luck he will send at least some of the kids forth to fight the system and help to bring about the changes he considers necessary.

He knows it will be an uphill battle in the wake of victory in the war dictated by America's money, greed and desire to rule the world, but in his own small way, he reflects wryly as he contemplates his sinuous dark-haired body floating on the surface of the pool, he will do what he can.

Nearby, firecrackers go off. Neighbor kids, probably, or maybe even their parents. Typical, he thinks, typical. The silly bastards, celebrating something whose implications they will never understand as he does. Typical of America, the half-baked giant. How like its citizens, to think one lucky triumph has settled the dreadful scores of the world, and that they can turn their backs, celebrate and forget all about it with happy times, happy days.

Renny is an interesting study, now as he was at the University. There various fraternity brothers like Guy Unruh the future doctor and Gaylen Bryce the know-it-all psychology major had spent quite a few idle moments trying to "figure out Suratt." He had eluded them all. He is not a "radical" in the glib sense of the word: he despises the so-called "Communist ideology" as much as he does the complacent-Dumbo mind-set of his countrymen. He doesn't follow anybody or fall into any easy categories. Obvious, though never very strong adolescent rebellion against the easy wealth of his parents doesn't explain it. After a while, most of his contemporaries have given up. "Just a sour, sarcastic, antisocial, uncomfortable son of a bitch," Franky Miller finally put it. "Fuck him. Forget him."

But nobody forgets Renny Surrat, he thinks with satisfaction as his body begins to react to the sunlight and the gentle currents of wind and water and a pleasant tumescence overtakes it. And they won't be able to forget him in the future. He intends to become one of the great social critics of his time.

He has done a lot of reading in history, sociology, political science, during his comfortable years as a conscientious objector. War's demands have not distracted him. He has not come to grips with reality as Bob Godwin dying on Surabachi, Willie bombing Germany, Rodge Leighton at this moment flying over Hiroshima, have had to come to grips with it. By his own deliberate choice and the amiable compliance of the local draft board, that kind of reality has not come his way. But as a potential academic gadfly, a theoretician sarcastically scornful of society's structure and beliefs, the sort of perpetual "aginner" who can always shock and delight adolescent minds, he is already well equipped.

After the graduate studies he intends to take at the University in the next couple of years in pursuit of a master's degree and ultimately a Ph.D., he will be ready to take on all comers, and to challenge and absolutely thrill many of the young minds who will take his courses.

Because of its steadily growing national prestige and influence, he wants to come back to the University to teach. In this, he reflects sardonically, he is not alone: Many will be wanting to return to that warm womb. He hasn't heard from anyone in the house—neither he nor they have had any particular desire to keep in touch after graduation—so he doesn't know if they are still alive, although by the law of averages a good many must be. If they've survived, he is sure that dumb slob Moose will be coming back to the coaching staff. Duke Offenberg, that insufferable overbearing ego, will be trying to return as a teacher in the School of Education; Renny will undoubtedly run into him. And he has already run into Johnny Herbert, one day when he was on campus in pursuit of some young sophomore gal he had met at L'Omelette this spring. Johnny, foreclosed from service by his frail lungs, is already entrenched as an assistant in the history department.

Renny notes the tumescence has increased, though it hasn't been on the surface of his mind. Maybe, he thinks wryly, he should call his young sophomore gal, whom he is still pursuing in a desultory fashion, and see if they can't do something about it tonight. Abruptly his thoughts shy away from the prospect and the tumescence promptly dies.

He likes the young ones, always has, but they don't often seem to like him. He tries not to be too sarcastic, at least until he has achieved his objective, but a lot of them seem to sense something hurtful and threatening to their egos and their necessary concepts of themselves. His fraternity brothers could always sluff off his destructive tongue with a few crudities: women don't seem to have that kind of uncaring defense. Most of his "romances" are over before they've begun.

It is the one defect he has been able to find in the character of Renny Suratt, and it disturbs him. But what the hell, he thinks as he pulls himself out of the pool, towels off and lies down again in the sun, there are other satisfactions. He will be an awfully big guy in the eyes of many worshipful students. He has seen it happen with a lot of teachers and he is sure it will with him. The girls will come with it. He is sure of that, too.

He closes his eyes and drifts off to sleep. More firecrackers don't disturb him. The war is ending nicely for Renny Suratt, and he has his future comfortably defined.

For the other four house members deferred from service, V-J Day has come as a welcome sign that the long years of uncomfortable status are over. None has deliberately sought deferment, all have wanted desperately to go. It has been no satisfaction to stay restlessly at home while fraternity brothers and friends have been suffering the dangers, the excitements and recurring boredoms of war.

It isn't my idea, Johnny Herbert thinks defensively whenever he receives the scathing glance of some serviceman or civilian girl. *Fuck you, buddy,* Randy Carerro flares silently when he receives the same treatment. *I want to go,* Marc Taylor insists in the same inward way when his eye catches theirs. *Screw you, too,* Franky Miller tells them in the same furious private dialogue, having learned on one sad and violent occasion that you didn't say this aloud, particularly to several servicemen in a group. You could get away with it with one or two sometimes, and he has, but he learned the hard way that it's best to keep one's resentment to oneself. Two black eyes, a sprained ankle and excruciatingly sore ribs have taught him that.

V-J Day finds the four of them widely separated. Marc Taylor is at his parents' home on the outskirts of Pittsburgh, Pennsylvania. Johnny Herbert is at the University preparing for the opening of fall quarter. Randy Carerro is in Albuquerque, New Mexico, arguing with a young Catholic priest. Franky is just about to close the doors of his father-in-law's used-car business in Medford, Oregon, and go

home to his father-in-law's house to join the impromptu neighborhood celebration hastily organized by his mother-in-law.

He is still smarting, mentally and physically, from his run-in with
the servicemen, which took place just a couple of weeks ago. Thank
God everybody will soon be back in civilian clothes and the war will
begin to sink into reverie and reminiscence in which tolerance will
gradually reestablish itself. Enforced civilians like himself will be able
once more to walk down the street without being scorned, and once
more be able to say freely what they think. Having always had a
carefree and irreverent tongue, he is especially pleased about this.

He reflects now, as he locks the doors, limps out and climbs into
the thirdhand 1935 Ford his father-in-law has given him, that those
who think civilians, particularly young civilian males, have had it easy
during the war have another think coming. It hasn't been easy in the
auto business, where production has been stopped for the duration
and gas rationing has drastically curtailed driving. Handling used
cars, about the only kind available, Mr. Sullivan has done well and
Franky has prospered with him. He and Katie have also had the gift
of a good many extra gas coupons Mr. Sullivan has mysteriously been
able to get, although they have had to be discreet about it and not do
much pleasure driving. But, even so, it has been a long, dragging
haul.

And now, he wonders as he drives carefully through the small-town
streets in which other celebrants mill along the sidewalks and occasionally spill over, what will he do with himself? Here he is at twenty-
eight, older, plumper (always has been fat, though denying it with
injured dignity when his fraternity brothers rudely pointed it out),
pleasant dark looks beginning to flesh out through neck and jowls,
beginning to look more and more like a prosperous businessman. But
is that what he really wants? That's what Buck Sullivan wants, he
knows that, and maybe Katie, too. But does he want it?

He frowns, his usual cheerful expression shadowed as he avoids a
couple of drunks and narrowly misses their happy wives.

When he reaches the big old house on the tree-shaded street he
finds a lot of the neighbors already there. Everything is very bright
and noisy and self-congratulatory. They've all won the war. Presently
Buck Sullivan, fortified by a couple of martinis, says to him, "Well,
Franky, so it's all over, over there!"

"Guess so," Franky agrees, fortified himself. " 'Bout time!"

" 'Bout time for you to decide what you want to do, too, boy," his
father-in-law says with heavy good humor. "You going to stay with me

and make a million or move out and be a—what was it you took in college?—sociologist or something? Whatever the hell that is."

"If I want to do that," Franky says carefully as Katie comes alongside to take his arm protectively, pert little face trying not to show her concern at her father's loud tone, "I'll have to go back to school and become a teacher, I guess."

"Who wants to do that?" Buck inquires scornfully. "Never make a dime that way. Never support my gal in the state to which she's accustomed *that* way. Right, doll?"

"Daddy," Kate says firmly, "I don't believe this is the time to discuss that."

"Well," Buck says, unabashed. "I was just going to offer you a partnership, Franky. In fact, I *am* offering you a partnership. How's that for a war's-over present?"

"It's great," Franky says, realizing with a lot of self-disgust that he's grinning idiotically, which Buck will probably take as acceptance, which it isn't at all. "It's great, really, Buck. But—"

"All settled, then!" Buck cries triumphantly. "Hey, folks—"

But Franky interrupts with a sudden harshness—"No, it's not all settled!"—and turns, Katie still clinging to his arm, and pushes his way through the startled neighbors who obviously think he's gone crazy not to accept at once. "I'm sorry, but it's not all settled."

And even though they stay up there in the room they've occupied all through the war, arguing and debating and discussing, until Katie's mother comes up and snaps, "Good for you, Franky, you've really got everybody talking now"—and virtually drags him back down by main force—even though his obvious hesitation and worry create the scandal of the day—he doesn't really know what he wants to do, just then. Except that he knows he's got to have some time to think about it.

And finally persuades Katie to come up with him and leaves the party and hops in the old Ford, lets her drive, and they rattle off to a favorite spot on Bear Creek and sit there talking and talking and talking until finally V-J Day fades into afternoon and evening and so at last, daylight exhausted and they exhausted, into night.

No such uncertainties trouble Marc Taylor, who has known since childhood that his destiny is to enter the family business, which is adding machines and office equipment. Like Rudy Krohl's family business, Marc's has flourished during the war. Steel and other materials have sometimes been hard to get, but the great need for better office equipment to help run the war effort has resulted in lucrative government contracts and rapidly growing business. Taylorite ("Tay-

lored to Your Needs") is emerging in excellent shape on this happy
day, and with excellent prospects for future expansion as peace returns. Marc's future, like Rudy's, seems certain and secure.

But what of Marc himself, he thinks gloomily as he and his parents
prepare to go downtown to have dinner and "join the crowds for an
hour or so," as his mother puts it, "so we can just say we were part of
this very historic moment." *Very historic moment* she says, and of
course he knows it is. It is for him, too.

He will now—at least officially—be relieved of the obvious public
stigma of not wearing a uniform. In his heart he knows he will never
be fully relieved of it. It will be a long time, if ever, before he can find
the suitable locution to help handle the inevitable "What did you do
in the war?" And it will probably take him longer—maybe a lifetime—to adjust to what he is afraid will be the permanent shame of
the real reason why he did not serve.

The ghost of the terrible mental depression he had felt in the
fraternity house in his sophomore year—the depression he couldn't
understand, change, conquer, the depression that had finally impelled him to his aborted suicide attempt—will always haunt him.

The terrible mystery of it is with him now, even in this very moment when everyone around him is rejoicing—the terrible thing he
will never be able to escape: "When I was sick . . . That time I was
feeling bad . . . When I wasn't well"—the lame phrases he uses with
his parents and his fraternity brothers, who know it all, his more
recent friends who don't.

It was mysterious to him then, it will always be mysterious to him.
But it has fundamentally and permanently affected his life.

When he recovered and returned to school after the spring and
summer quarters he spent at home, it was with him, even though the
house was almost unanimously supportive. With the exceptions of
that superior jerk Galen Bryce, who fancied his psych major gave him
inside knowledge of everybody, and unpleasant Renny Suratt, who
could always be counted upon to take advantage of any weakness with
his savage, unforgiving tongue, everyone had been compassionate
and helpful. Even when Gil Gulbransen and Guy Unruh used their
future-doctors' privilege to probe a bit, it was always with an encouraging and helpful gentleness that protected him.

Nonetheless, there it was; and there, he thinks bleakly now, it is
going to stay.

When Pearl Harbor came and he went down to the Quad with

Hank Moore and Moose and Rodge to volunteer, it was there waiting. The doctors, no doubt tipped off by the University—which really had no choice, it was part of him, how could it be hidden?—had consulted earnestly for a few minutes, with the result he had feared.

"We'd like to take you, Marc," they had said, not unkindly, "but you can understand why we just can't. Military life isn't easy . . . and the possibility of combat, with all its tensions . . ." Their voices had trailed away and he had said humbly, "Yes, of course I understand."

But in some last, final recess of his being, he didn't.

So he was classified 4-F, finished his studies and in due course, following graduation, returned home.

There his father had been at elaborate and obvious pains to give him duties and responsibilities so demanding that he wouldn't have time to brood about it.

"The best thing to do now," his father had said in the only direct reference he ever made to it, "is to do the very best you can. We have a big job here helping the war effort and it's very important that you contribute everything you can. I can't do it all, I need help. I'm counting on you."

And so, like Rudy but without the same slick evasion of duty or the relish in having "put one over on Uncle Sam" (as Rudy has often remarked happily to his friends in the now-underground German-American Bund), Marc has pitched in earnestly to help his father and the company. Purpose and profits have blended into a manufacturing achievement that has indeed been of value to the war effort as well as to the company.

Now, as he and his parents mingle sedately with the celebrating crowds in Pittsburgh's dingy downtown, he knows what his professional future will be: He will go on as vice-president, and in time as president, and the company, with reasonable enterprise and luck, will continue to grow and flourish and quite likely diversify eventually into areas of manufacture at present only dimly glimpsed in the writings of science's more far-out prophets. All of this, he feels, will be more or less inevitable in the postwar boom that will almost certainly follow when America's fantastic and unsurpassed industrial machine shifts gears into peacetime channels.

And what of Marc Taylor the man, now twenty-five, who lives inside? Can he handle all this? Will the future bring him the personal security he perhaps has never had, and certainly has not had since his attempted suicide? Will he—something he hardly dares hope at all,

so little does he feel he has to offer—find a wife who will help him and
keep him safe and share the burden and achievements with him
someday?

His expression changes, for a fleeting moment becomes set and
quietly desperate. His parents, normally attentive to his every mood,
do not notice as the happy excitement grows in the streets. In the
midst of the increasingly raucous crowds he is dressed neatly in suit
and tie, at his mother's behest. "We have a position to maintain," she
often says, and though they love one another dearly, he sighs in
protest as he obeys. But it is a silent protest and one that does not
trouble the accustomed placidity of their relationship.

He moves through the crowds as he has already learned to move
through life, small, neat, quiet, reserved; an object of admiration to
many; of a certain silent pity to some sensitive, perceptive few.

Thus, also, Johnny Herbert—John Thomas Herbert from Philadelphia, Pennsylvania, at this moment the only member of the house
still on campus. He is sitting quietly in Memorial Church, drawn
there by the excitement of V-J Day and the thought that here, perhaps, in this beautiful place that has given comfort to so many over
the years, there may be found some strength and reassurance for the
new day being born.

The chapel is silent save for the muted strains of the organ, played
by someone with obvious skill and a gentle, mood-answering, mood-
building touch. A handful of others are scattered among the pews, a
few women students and staff members, a few men like himself not in
uniform, a small group of soldiers, sailors and Marines, apparently
visiting campus as tourists while on leave, drawn to the chapel, like
himself, by some lingering childhood pull in this hour of triumph and
new beginnings.

Johnny, too, carries the burden of the world's respect and the
world's pity and, like Marc, he carries it with dignity—and with a
certain grace, for he has had longer in which to do it. His burden goes
back to freshman year and the innocent Big Game Night prank that
got out of hand when he was strapped to a bed and, with careless lack
of thought on the part of the youthful pranksters, left out in the first
chill rain of November. His lungs have never recovered from the
onslaught of that night. His generally erratic health has kept him out
of the service, out of the war and, as he recognizes once again with a
small, resigned, unhappy sigh, out of life.

At least out of the normal life that most of his college contemporaries have enjoyed. Not for him the athletics, horseplay, walks, hikes, physical adventures, rough-and-tumble known to so many others. Not for him the freedom to pick up and go, heedless of the weather . . . not for him, even, the normal round of girls and dating that have enlivened school life for so many.

He has always had to be cautious, careful, full of hesitations, reservations, advance planning. Life since freshman year has not been spontaneous for Johnny Herbert and he is sure that it never again will be. He is already settling into the habit—and more important, the frame of mind—of the permanently half-well, made more poignant in his case by the fact that the condition is not complete. He is not frail enough to be a real invalid, just frail enough to have half a life instead of a whole one.

But this, he thinks as the organist moves gently into familiar hymns, is self-pity verging on the maudlin, and he must not give in to it. It is hard enough to sense the pity of his friends and colleagues in the history department without succumbing to his own. He realizes he can't afford to let himself go all the way from: I shouldn't do that, to: I can't do that. The difference, he realizes, is small but vital. If he yields altogether, he really will be a sad case.

And he isn't. He thinks he can tell himself that with perfect justification. He doesn't whine, pout, malinger, excuse. He is always cheerful, always steady, always there. He tells himself that just because quite often there's a little hell inside, it doesn't mean Johnny Herbert is quitting. Far from it.

It has been a great disappointment to him that he has had to sit out the war. He would much have preferred to have gone and done his part, whatever it might have been, in the national effort. He had known at the start that it was impossible, but still he tried to enlist when the others did. He and Marc had consoled each other with assurances that they'd find something to do that would help. No doubt Marc, with his family business to work at, had done so. Johnny wasn't so satisfied with his own efforts, even though everyone at the University from Dr. Chalmers to the head of the history department was always reassuring him that he had been invaluable.

"We're on a reduced crew here, as you know," the president had said, "with half the faculty gone to war. And when people do as good a job as you do, Johnny, it makes us extra grateful."

He had just this morning received a letter from his closest pal in the house, Tony Andrade, sent from "somewhere in Germany" under an Army frank, and this reminds him anew of how much of his generation's life he has had to miss. For a while there during their undergraduate years he and Tony had made up a casual and happy foursome with "the cousins," Angie D'Alessandro and Louise Gianfalco. They had dated in the carefree no-strings, no-promises mood that Tony in particular seemed to want, and it had been a happy time for Johnny—perhaps the happiest, he thinks now, that he had known in adolescence. Their dates had been spontaneous then, but always with a certain unspoken consideration for his health that he much appreciated. He had the feeling then that they were looking out for him, surrounding him with a warmth he did not often receive, and for a while he had permitted himself to hope that something permanent might come from it with Louise. Then Tony had taken a shine to their fellow sophomore Loren Davis with his sensational blond good looks and amiable personality, and little by little Lor had been introduced into the foursome, which became increasingly an awkward fivesome. After a while Johnny had decided to bow out of it while he could still do so with dignity.

At first his decision was received with disbelief and a determined effort to keep him in the group. But before long his repeated refusals and excuses, which he was always careful to state in a perfectly friendly way, were accepted—with disappointment, as they earnestly assured him, but with an inevitable adjustment to what he apparently seemed to think was best for himself. He had still been included from time to time, but not with the old casual acceptance that had always meant so much to him. It was, he decided, just part of the lot in life that his often-uncertain health made inevitable.

Tony had remained close, as Tony seemed to have a knack for doing with a lot of people even though Lor seemed to have become his special pal—"his asshole buddy," Renny Suratt had once remarked with jealous sourness, though there was nothing to warrant that except a friendly closeness that Renny himself could never achieve with anyone. Johnny, in common he suspected with many, received occasional notes from Tony all through the war, welcome examples of his talent for friendship—the standard serviceman's "V-mail," short and censored, which arrived at first from training camps in the continental United States, then from North Africa, then from Italy, France and finally Germany.

The latest had come shortly after the Battle of the Bulge, "a real tough go. I'll tell you about it someday"—and Johnny had heard nothing since. Neither had Lor. Just a couple weeks ago Johnny had received a note from him, written under Army frank, from "Some-where in the Pacific," To which Lor, in a tiny scribble that the censor had somehow missed, had added, "or about to be."

"Since you're the guy who's sort of keeping tabs on everybody," Lor wrote, "I thought maybe you've heard from our buddy Tony. I haven't had a word from the bastard in the last three months, which isn't like him, and I'm kind of worried. Let me know if you hear anything, O.K.? I hope everything is O.K. with you back there on campus. Lucky guy! Keep the home fires burning. We'll all have a big reunion when we get home. If you hear from Tony, let me know."

But he hadn't heard from Tony. Nor has he heard from a number of others, although he had written a blanket note early in the war and offered his services, as a permanent civilian and "a sort of resident clearing house," as he put it, to keep track of everyone. Some, like Tony, had responded fairly regularly, some he has not heard from since Pearl Harbor. War's silence has swallowed them and he can only hope they are all right.

Now as he emerges from Memorial Church into the somnolent heat of summer in the Santa Clara Valley, he hears firecrackers going off somewhere up the Row. The University's sparse summer-quarter population is celebrating along with the rest. He determines that he will now make a real effort to track everyone down. A letter begins to form in his head that he will send from his permanent place here at the University to the home addresses of all his fraternity brothers:

"Dear———: Hello again! I'm trying to find all you guys and let everybody know what's happened to all of us in the war. If you'll send me a brief account of your experiences I'll put it all together and send out some sort of newsletter. Maybe it's not too soon to begin thinking about a reunion, too. We've got a whole new world opening up and it would be great to compare notes and find out what everybody's plans are. Let me hear from you. . . ."

Maybe, he thinks, this is too sentimental an effort; maybe the time has already passed for that kind of collegial closeness. War may well have speeded up the gradual lapse of friendships that often came with graduation and the beginning of new lives. Now their generation, like their parents', was separated from adolescence by the great gulf of war. What had meant a lot on the far side of it perhaps would not—perhaps could not, given war's profound experience—mean so much now.

But, he tells himself, you have to hang on to a few things in a world as chaotic as that of the twentieth century. He is already beginning to realize, as an historian, that perhaps no century in all history has seen so many profound and far-reaching changes—and it's not even half-over, yet. What will it bring, before it comes at last to an end with the start of a new millennium he and most of his contemporaries probably won't even live to see?

Enough, he has no doubt.

Quite enough.

He shivers, in the soft, embracing day, as he walks slowly back to the bicycle rack to which he has chained his transportation back up the Row to the faculty residential area beyond, where he rents a modest room and bath in the home of one of the history department's younger professors.

He has the sudden, almost desperate feeling that he ought to gather around him all the people who have meant something to him up to now and they'll all huddle together against the cold winds of a savage century. But of course that isn't how it works: you each have your own little segment of it and you just keep slogging along a step at a time, a day at a time, and hope your friends will make it, too, and won't get hurt too much along the way.

For Randy Carrero, engaged at the moment in earnest argument, quite oblivious to the V-J Day celebrations going on all around him in a small dusty park in Albuquerque, thoughts of the future are not quite so gloomy—although he, too, has realized with maturity that whatever is to come has to be faced alone and with as much strength as one can muster.

His companion, dark, earnest, intent and humorless, is trying to convince him that he will find the greatest strength of all in the Catholic Church. Randy, pragmatic, realistic, skeptical and impatient as always, is not so sure.

"You're telling me," he exclaims indignantly, "that I'll find peace of mind in being celibate all my life? Are you crazy?"

But the earnest young priest who faces him across the stained wooden table where they are consuming a couple of hamburgers and milkshakes is his cousin who has known him all their lives. He isn't giving ground.

"Has the alternative made you happy?" he asks doggedly, and Randy, having made the mistake of telling him about Fluff Stevens and his college agonies, suddenly grins his charming, candid grin.

"I suppose I could jack off when the pressure gets too great," he says. His cousin can't help but smile, but he shakes his head almost angrily.

"Be serious, will you?" he demands. "I'm talking about a lifelong commitment here."

"So am I," Randy says, "I don't intend to abandon sex anytime soon."

"That isn't the *point!*" his cousin says indignantly. "You won't face up to things, that's your problem."

"Hell I won't," Randy says, face suddenly grim. "I've faced up to more things than you'll face up to, buster, in your snug little protected church world. And you want me to join *that* and give up everything I want out of life? I repeat, are you crazy?"

"Just listen to me," his cousin says. "Just listen to me and you'll see what I mean."

"But why me?" Randy asks in a bewilderment quite genuine. "What makes you think I'm suited for the Church, even if I wanted to? Which I don't."

"I've just got an instinct," his cousin says. "I just think you'd have a lot to give people, that's all. A lot to contribute."

"I can do it without wearing a chastity belt," Randy says, irreverent again. "And be a lot happier, too."

"Not in your mind," the young priest says. "Not in your heart. That's what I'm talking about."

"You're being medieval," Randy says. "I always thought you were a little weird, Juan. Now I know it."

"O.K.," Juan says. "Go ahead and laugh. But I'm not going to stop talking to you."

"I may stop listening," Randy suggests. Juan shakes his head, serene in faith and convictions.

"The Lord won't let you," he says, crossing himself. "He'll pursue you."

"I know," Randy says. "Down the nights and down the days. But I'll outrun him."

"A year from now you'll be preparing to take orders," Juan says in a tone of serene certainty.

"No, I won't," Randy says. "No, I *won't.*"

And dismisses it indignantly from his mind as several carloads of teenagers, shouting wildly about the end of a war they have just barely been old enough to experience, careen down the street alongside the park. Somewhere a mariachi band is playing, somewhere church bells are ringing. Albuquerque has joined the world for a long, celebratory night.

Into it Randy presently passes with his priestly cousin. He will stick with him for a while, then they will separate as they have on many occasions before when Randy has come up from the ranch, and Juan from the seminary, to reunion. Juan will say goodbye with a smile more wistful than he realizes, because he is sure that Randy is off to some bar, or an even more reliable establishment, to find a woman.

When he does, Randy knows, the result will be the same. It is always the same. Momentary, agonizing, routine—flat. A brief, boring release in which he finds neither satisfaction nor the oblivion he might be willing to accept as a substitute. He goes in with the burden of his attractive but difficult and uneasy personality and comes out with the same burden. Nothing much of lasting interest, no matter how willing or inventive his partner, seems to happen in between.

"Fluff Stevens and Bill Lattimer," he remembers saying once, bitterly, aloud, when he stepped into the hot desert night after such an episode. "Fluff and Latt."

He told himself then that he was oversimplifying, being as phony a psychologist as Galen Bryce in the fraternity house. But maybe, he thinks now as he emerges once more into the hot desert night, on this occasion still raucous with V-J Day celebrations, he is closer to it than he likes to think.

Once again, as he has done a million times, probably, since that awful winter night in 1939, his mind races over the old insoluble conundrum. His passionate, bitter, unrequited involvement with Fluff, her personality as lightweight as her nickname, her brain completely inferior to his straight-A, Phi Beta Kappa mentality, everything about her inferior to himself—and her physical being such that he had been unable to keep himself from being obsessed with it . . . their last bitter quarrel . . . his return to the house with his mind in such turmoil that he could barely function . . . Latt's unfailing kindness, the miracle of his always-caring personality, his refusal to let Randy drive alone into town to satisfy his totally senseless and in this case totally fatal urge for a late-night snack . . . the fog, the slick pavement, Randy driving too fast up Palm Drive . . . the car swerving out of control, the tree, the crash, oblivion . . . the slow awakening, heavily bandaged and sedated, to find his fraternity brothers standing white-faced around the bed . . . their refusal to answer when he demanded drowsily, "How's Latt?" . . . the terrible realization, prompted by their silence, that Latt's grave, gentle, unfailingly kind and considerate personality would be with them no longer . . . that he was gone forever . . . and that *I did it . . . I killed Latt. . . .*

He had never seen or communicated with Fluff again. Even when he recovered from his injuries—the unspecified "internal injuries," the broken back and fractured pelvis, whose residual effects would keep him out of the war and thus change his life forever—he did not see her. Occasionally he would glimpse her in the distance on campus as he completed his sophomore, junior, senior years, but they never spoke. He deliberately made elaborate detours to avoid even coming near her. Twice he had actually changed a class when he found she was in it. She always looked frightened of him and he used to think grimly that, by God, she had better. Because he was in no mood to forgive her—ever. And in no mood to forgive himself for Latt's death, which had come so directly out of the mental and emotional turmoil she had caused him on that awful, unforgiving night.

All this he had told, gradually and haltingly, to Juan, who had been his best friend in high school and continued to be as the years went on and Randy found he needed a support his fraternity brothers and his family, as supportive as they all were, could not seem to give him. Juan had decided very early that he wanted to be a priest and, once committed, had become a fine and thoroughly devoted one. It was only normal that he would suggest that Randy, obviously at times still in such deep anguish, should seek the same path of peace. And since it had been obvious from a very early age that he was a very bright youth and a natural leader, Juan was convinced that he would find a great reward, not only in peace of mind but in the service he could render.

"If you ever do become a priest," he had told Randy not too long ago, "you'll be heard from."

"Pope, maybe?" Randy asked with his quick-flashing grin. "I used to think I'd like to be President someday. If you get me in the Church, will you make me Pope?"

"Can't guarantee that," Juan had replied with his own earnest smile. "But something, I'm sure of that. Something."

"Too much of a prison," Randy said. "Sorry about that, but just too much of a prison."

"On the contrary," Juan insisted. "You'll see."

But he doesn't think he will, Randy tells himself now as he walks soberly through the still-celebrating crowds, back to the hotel room he is sharing with Juan in the center of town. He finds him there, of course. Praying. As usual.

"Praying!" he exclaims, half-mocking, half-affectionate. "Don't you ever stop?"

"Why don't you try it?" Juan inquires. "The war's over. Isn't that something to pray about? Better celebrate it that way than—than—"

"What?" Randy demands sharply, but Juan doesn't back down.

"What you've been doing."

"I haven't been doing anything," Randy says defiantly, but the aura is on him and Juan knows. He just stares and after a moment Randy's eyes drop and he gives him a shamefaced grin—and yet, why be shamefaced? It's perfectly natural.

"So's praying, to me," Juan says. "Why don't you join me?"

It takes Randy a few minutes but he finally drops to his knees beside him in the old accustomed, childhood way. And they pray together.

What a thing to be doing, on the night of V-J Day! Randy thinks wryly. But he's doing it, just the same.

Six thousand miles away and about a quarter of a mile from the Soviet camp with which they are sharing watch on a bridge in defeated Germany, Tony Andrade is lying in his bunk reflecting on a wild, exciting night and a tense, disturbing day.

His paramount thought is: the war is over and I won't be sent to the Pacific after all.

His secondary one, which threatens from time to time to become paramount, so disturbing is it to his quick, intuitive intelligence, is: Those bastards are God damned tough and they have plans we Americans don't even dream about.

He has been dealing, as a first lieutenant on the liaison team, with their Soviet counterparts, who have consistently shown the crafty intransigence he is coming to recognize as characteristic.

For a few hours the excitement and relief of V-J Day, freeing the Americans from the demoralizing prospect of still more war in the Pacific after two and a half years in Europe, have overwhelmed him. Discipline has been temporarily abandoned. Americans and Soviets have roamed the streets of the ancient town together, linking arms, hugging and kissing (the Soviets are very good at that, Tony thinks dryly, but watch the other hand behind your back, it's probably holding a knife), laughing, shouting, exchanging drinks, gloriously happy and gloriously drunk.

Somewhere during the course of the night he had wound up in an old half-blasted house with a lot of others, some American, some Soviet, a few local girls, frightened yet eagerly compliant. In some instinctual, overwhelming urge, sex had demanded an outlet and found it. It didn't much matter whom you had it with, you just had it:

five times, Tony recalls in amused wonderment now, in about six hours. That beats *my* record, he thinks wryly: if you're only young once, I'm elderly now. I won't achieve those heights again, that's for sure.

Now he lies in his bunk, trying to get at least a little sleep before the dawning of the first day of peace but too keyed-up to find it yet. Inexorably and with increasingly ominous insistence, there comes the memory of the events of the last day of war. He wonders gloomily just how much has been accomplished by the global conflict, after all.

It was not, he remembers, as though there was anything very vital at stake: just how the Soviet and American troops were to be placed while they "guarded" the bridge. There was no real need for "guarding"; the war had already been over three months in Germany and was about to end in the Pacific. But the daily routine of "guarding" was still being maintained, basically because neither side wanted to be the first to withdraw from it. And so the daily jockeying about which troops would be closest to the bridge, which a little farther away; solved for three months by alternating the duty, but suddenly turned into symbolism on the last day of world war, by a small battle of wills at a minor bridge in Germany.

Which the Soviets, he recalls, won.

He wonders if maybe the foreboding isn't too dramatic and too extreme, given the really very minor circumstance involved; but then he shakes his head, in the murmurous, snore-filled darkness around him, and tells himself with a sigh: no, I don't think so.

How had the Soviets won? Simply by looking grim, huffing and puffing and insisting—insisting—insisting. And how had the Americans lost? Simply by being good-natured, disbelieving of the importance of tenacity, unwilling to make a fuss, and yielding—yielding—yielding.

So the Soviets had taken their place at the bridge, out of regular order, on the last day of world war. And after two or three hours of further futile arguing, Tony's superior, a colonel who talked all the time about how anxious he was to "chuck this whole fucking thing and get back to living my life again," had finally said, "Shit, let's go," and had withdrawn them altogether back to the barracks. There he had dismissed them, to loud cries of approval, to "go on into town and raise whatever hell you want to. The fucking war is *over*! Everywhere!"

But is it? Tony wonders uneasily now. Is it? And what did it all mean if it isn't?

He wonders whose attitude will dominate America in the days to come—his own, of misgiving and uneasiness and caution toward their erstwhile ally—or that of the colonel, "chucking the whole fucking thing" in the happy conviction that "the fucking war is over" and that from now on it will be happiness and light and "raising whatever hell you want to" in peace, glorious peace, forever after?

He decides presently that these are heavy thoughts for a man of twenty-five in his condition, exhausted from too much liquor, sex and celebrating. He can't shake them entirely—they will condition much of his thinking in the years ahead—but for the time being the euphoria of war's end reasserts itself. For him it has been a good war, all things considered, and there isn't much about it he would have changed.

Above all, he knows he has been a good soldier, in combat duty and in the more boring administrative side to which he has from time to time been assigned. Not many have been in it so long, seen so much action, or received so many commendations and medals. He knows with his customary pragmatism that these are soon going to lose all but their sentimental value when he returns to civilian life, but at least they are proof that he has performed well in the tasks he was given to do. Which is not such a poor satisfaction to carry away from war, or such a bad recommendation for what will come after.

He has had his fill, and more, of blood and agony. He has seen so many fine youths die, so much appalling waste of men, materiel and idealistic purpose, that he sometimes thinks it a wonder that he is still sane. But the human animal adapts, as one of his professors at the University used to say: the human animal adapts. It doesn't take long, even in the midst of horror: twenty-four hours under fire, and you've seen and done it all. The rest is repetition, awful and terrible but basically just more of the same. Some go under in the face of it, some ride the wave. Tony Andrade, short, wiry, tough, resourceful, has stayed the course.

This has been so even though he has had more than the usual recruit's burden to carry. Life long ago laid its special challenge upon him: he was tough before he went to war because he had to be. Thinking back, as he often does, over his college years, he realizes that various episodes in it, one in particular, helped to give him strength to answer war's demands. Again, some facing similar pressures have gone under. He has not only survived but been strengthened.

In the war, careful and cautious as he has always been—with the one exception at the University—he has gone through the challenges of battle and boredom with his outwardly pleasant and self-contained personality intact. He has killed men when he had to and narrowly escaped being killed in return. Miraculously he has suffered no major wounds. He has managed to maintain his private life even in the midst of the most public atmosphere known to men, the atmosphere of barracks and bivouacs. He has found a few good friends to help him along the way, has "kept the faith," as he puts it to himself, and has emerged with stability, good humor and reliable personality firmly in hand.

And now, he thinks as he lies in the darkness that is beginning to give way to the first faint grayness of day—now comes peace. And what of that?

He rather suspects that he is going to do three things in the weeks directly ahead: tell his father that he definitely won't be coming home to help run the butcher shop in Brooklyn, which his father suspects already and has in effect already accepted; resume his friendship with Lor Davis, which has remained unbroken via the mails all during the war; and marry Louise Gianfalco and with her return to Napa Valley and join her father in the opening stages of the reviving wine industry that both he and Mario Gianfalco are convinced will before long become a major factor in California's postwar agriculture.

He remembers that when they were all at the University, it was generally assumed among them that if anybody were to marry anybody, it would be Lor and Louise and perhaps her cousin Angie D'Alessandro and Johnny Herbert. But Johnny's health had gradually taken him out of the main activities of their tight-knit little group, and by the time of Pearl Harbor, when Tony and Lor had been called up in the draft, Lor had seemed to be gravitating toward Angie with her sunny temperament and even disposition, away from Louise with her dark good looks, bluntly practical mind and shrewd perceptions of human nature. These were qualities Tony liked, having them himself; and now at war's end he has become so accustomed to thinking in terms of marrying Louise that he can't really conceive of things turning out any other way.

For some reason, partly boredom, partly genuine desire to keep in touch, he has become quite a correspondent during the war, sending his V-mail messages to a surprisingly long list of friends. His brief notes to Louise and her equally brief responses have become increasingly full of shared attitudes and an implicit understanding that they will at least give marriage very careful thought after the war. He had finally indicated as much to Lor, and Lor, ever faithful and obliging, wrote, "O.K., then I'll go after Angie. Is that all right?"

"Of course, stupid," Tony had written back. "Do you think you have to have my permission?"

But Lor did seem to think so, just as he had in college about virtually everything. This was flattering and Tony didn't mind at all. He liked the feeling that he was in command of Lor's life; providing he wasn't mishandling it, and he was very confident he wasn't.

Now he wonders where old Lor is at the moment. Tony has been rather bad about his correspondence in these winding-down months of the war in Europe; part of the universal war-weariness among the services has begun to affect his usual precise routines. But he is sure he would have heard something if anything had happened to Lor: Lor and Louise are going to be the first phone calls he makes when he returns to the States.

Finally, just as dawn brightens and reveille sounds, he starts to fall off to sleep. There won't be much doing on this day of the new world dawning. He may just write them one last note from "Your boy in the Army," as he always signs himself. They'll both be pleased to know that war is really over, for him—and that peace, in some inner way, is really beginning for them.

At this moment Lor is three thousand miles west of Hawaii on a troop transport wallowing through the Pacific on its way to more war—or at least that is what they had all been gloomily anticipating until the news came over ship's radio that the Japanese had finally, indubitably and irrevocably, surrendered. Wild yells and sounds of jubilation had broken out, the captain had ordered whiskey for everyone, discipline had been abandoned for a while. The dreary voyage had suddenly been transformed into a triumphal passage over seas that now belonged, beyond all challenge and beyond all question, to them.

The exuberance had lasted maybe an hour. Now it is beginning to simmer down and boredom is setting in. The apprehension about further combat, wiped out by the news of the capitulation, has been rapidly succeeded by a great impatience to go home. The prospect of another week at sea, followed no doubt by the usual interminable delays and red tape before everybody can get out of Japan and get back to the States, is a hell of a boring prospect. Not least for Loren

Davis, who wants to get on home to Long Beach, the family business, Angie and Tony.

The business, like that of Rudy Krohl and Marc Taylor, has prospered during the war. The modest five oil wells with which his father had gone into business now number twenty-three; the small refinery at nearby Seal Beach is about to be expanded again. The logo of DAVIS OIL—a fan of three oil wells supporting a sun, is beginning to appear at many gasoline stations in the West. There are plans to expand distribution to the East Coast, plans to buy into Texas. Lor is coming home with a handsome inheritance. In his amiable, easygoing way he is looking forward to it. He probably won't have to work too hard, which is just as well. His major talent is for friendship, and he suspects there will be plenty of use for that in the oil business.

At the University, where he had studied the minimum amount necessary to reconcile his rather modest mental abilities with his desire for an engineering degree, his studies, like the rest of his life, had been largely dominated by Tony Andrade. They had met on Registration Day, freshman year, and the instant liking established then has only seemed to grow stronger over the years. It will, Lor is sure, continue to be a major part of his life "as long as they both are around"—which is what he had said to Tony when they said goodbye at graduation and prepared to go off to war.

The draft had taken them into the Army but from there their paths had diverged, Tony's into the campaigns of North Africa and southern Europe and so into Germany in time for the Battle of the Bulge and the final fall of the Reich. Lor first to England, then France on D-Day, then the long, slogging push into Germany and finally, two weeks before the surrender, the sudden order to the Pacific that had brought him to his present unwilling sea passage. At one point in Germany, though they didn't know it, they had been within two miles of each other. But it was a long two miles, filled with hell and horror and death and destruction, and they had passed and gone their separate ways unknowing. They had corresponded quite faithfully all during the war, frustrated sometimes by the long delays of censorship and the hazards of wartime communication but managing to keeping in touch every two or three months, which was a pretty good record, Lor felt. They had been able to arrange leave together twice, once in London, where they had run into Willie quite by accident in Piccadilly one night, the second time in liberated Paris just about six months ago. Both had been great occasions, filled with endless talk, as much good food as could be found in the war-strapped capitals (not much), a lot of bars and cabarets and a certain number of girls who, although at times creating a certain awkwardness they tried to hide from one another, were what was expected of them in such circumstances. They both managed, quite valiantly and quite well, and anyway, it didn't matter much: the rest of the time they had each other's company and, with so much to get caught up on, that seemed quite sufficient.

Lor wonders wearily how in the God damned hell he is going to get through the inevitable boredom of the next few weeks before he can get home. And he wonders where Tony is on this triumphant day, and whether he, too, is anxious to get back in touch. The bastard hasn't written in the past four months, but some instinct tells Lor not to worry too much, he's O.K. He knows that the first thing he is going to do when he gets back to the States is call Tony's home in Brooklyn. They will probably have heard something.

And he will call Angie, whose faithful letters, written at least once a week, have followed him persistently, if somewhat sporadically, all through the war. They have been like her—cheerful, optimistic, filled with the small details of civilian life.

"We can't complain," she has often written, and then, with a typical gentle humor, has added, "After all, 'Don't you know there's a war on?' "

The standard civilian phrase—which, along with the services' use of the universal four-letter word and its variants has pretty well dominated American conversation during the war—has summed up her attitude, and that of most of their countrymen: wry, protesting but basically good-humored and good-natured; in there for the duration; not enjoying it, but committed for the long haul.

And now the long haul is over, and ahead lies a new world. Contemplating it, as he runs for the fifteenth time around the deck, Lor wonders: should he marry Angie? Tony seems to think so. And will Tony marry Louise? His recent letters seem to indicate it. And when Lor takes Angie from her close-knit family in San Francisco's North Beach down to the oil wells of Signal Hill and Seal Beach, and Tony joins Louise on her father's vineyards in Napa Valley in northern California, will he and Tony be able to see each other then?

They'll find a way, Lor thinks confidently, tossing the blond locks that always fall perfectly around the classic young-Roman-emperor head. They'll find a way.

He can't conceive of a life that doesn't include Tony in it somewhere.

*   *   *

At this moment—his reaction if he knew it would be an astounded, "For Christ's sake, why?"—Lor is undergoing analysis, in absentia, by that brilliant psychiatrist and infallible student of human nature Galen Bryce from Burlingame, California.

Gale is accompanying two of his senior medical officers on their rounds of the psychiatric wards of Bethesda Naval Hospital just north of Washington, D.C. He has been stationed there for the entire length of the war, having early managed, with his winning combination of genuine if annoyingly smug intelligence and his smooth adaptability to the moods and egos of his superiors, to ingratiate himself beyond dislodgment. The bright young man whom many of his fraternity brothers at the University remember as "one of the supreme ass-kissers of all time" has metamorphosed in the war into what his commanding officer calls "one of the *very best* of our 'young indispensables.' "

It has guaranteed him an easy berth.

Now, prompted by the case of a young Marine officer still racked by almost uncontrollable sobs four months after losing his best buddy on Okinawa, Gale is thinking that the closest thing he has seen to that kind of fixation so far has been Lor Davis and Tony Andrade in the house. Only he and Renny Suratt seemed to have been aware of it then, but both considered it pretty obvious and pretty disgusting the way Lor, the subservient one, had seemed to be engulfed in the friendship of the dominant Tony. Neither he nor Renny, Gale remembers now, could seem to convince anybody else that there was anything obsessive there. Franky Miller, in fact, had exclaimed scathingly, "Why in hell can't you filthy bastards keep your filthy minds off a good friendship? Because you haven't got any?"

Gale had started to give him an equally scathing retort but then had shrugged and given up: it wouldn't have been becoming. *Be aware that you are always invulnerable to personal attacks inspired by envy and spite,* his professors had taught him, and he always was. It didn't apply directly in this case, but the general thesis was sound; the psychiatrist is always superior to the rest of the world *because he is the only one who knows why people do what they do.* It was a comforting, and usually impregnable, armor.

He wonders now, as he considers the case of "the two lovebirds," as Renny had taken to calling them behind their backs, what has become of them in the war. He does not often think of his fraternity brothers, except as their critical attitudes toward him have implanted them in his mind, but on this day in which war's-end jubilation has penetrated even Bethesda's antiseptic corridors, he can't help but speculate idly on their fates and whereabouts.

At first he had responded to Johnny Herbert's occasional appeals for news, until it occurred to him that to keep reporting that he was "still in Bethesda" might lead some jealous souls to assume that there was something wrong with him that barred him from sea duty. This would be such a canard, given his eager and often expressed desire to "get out there and see some action" that he realized he didn't want to lay himself open to it. It wasn't true and he didn't want to encourage it. He did often say that he wanted to "get out there and see some action." If he was careful to say this only in the presence of his juniors, not his seniors, well, that was his business. He suspected his superiors knew he was as ready as any other healthy, red-blooded American youth to get into battle. Just because he had made himself "indispensable" to them didn't mean that he wasn't as brave a warrior as anyone could desire. Somehow, though, he never did get moved out to more dangerous duty. Others came and went. Lt. Galen Bryce stayed where he was and became Capt. Galen Bryce at age twenty-six. His future, everyone said, was brilliant.

It doesn't at the moment include wife and family, but he has them on his list and one of these days he knows he will get to it. Everything generally fits into its proper place in his life, and he is sure that will, too. There have been many opportunities in a wartime Washington awash with females in government and service, and he has made use of some of them with the clinical, observant approach that he considers suited to his profession. If this has antagonized some and even embittered a few, he considers that a small price to pay for all the things he has learned about feminine nature that he will apply in his practice later. And in due course, he will find some younger woman suitably subservient—and at the same time beautiful, intelligent and adept at motherhood and household management—who will be the Perfect Psychiatrist Galen Bryce type.

Secure in this knowledge, he makes his way now through the halls filled with excited nurses and grinning patients to the orderly room that has been transformed with balloons and streamers into an impromptu V-J Day party. He will kiss the nurses, shake hands with the patients, congratulate his commanding officers on their stalwart service during the war.

He is pleased with his own, and why not? He has listened to many sad tales, heard many difficult stories, told many shattered minds what they must do to better face the challenges of their lives when peacetime comes. He has always known that he knows more than most people. In the war he has acquired an absolute sense of superiority that has increased, if possible, his already monumental intellectual arrogance. He knows this will make him virtually invincible when he ministers to the distraught souls who will be the foundations for a distinguished, and no doubt very lucrative, practice in his native California.

Unable—being a much more perceptive and therefore much more uncertain man than they—to meet the future with the calm arrogance of a Gale Bryce, a Rudy Krohl or a Renny Suratt, Edward Paul Haggerty from Springfield, Illinois, is sitting out front at a small bar in Piazza Navona in Rome, moodily drinking a Campari and soda and wondering what the hell happens now.

Hack Haggerty, whose great musical talent made him one of the most popular students on campus in college days, has gone through the war with his talent satisfactorily employed. His original assignment, as the records clerk of an Army infantry unit, had plunged him into deep despair at the whole fucking assininity of the Army system—"the right way, the wrong way and the Army way," as everybody said, with varying degrees of woeful truth. Very fortunately, this had lasted only a month at Fort Ord, California, where he had been assigned following completion of basic training.

A camp show had been scheduled—he had been sitting at a piano in the rec room idly, and bitterly, rambling over the keys—his company commander had come in and overheard him—"My man, you must join us in our show!" as Hack recited with ironic exaggeration, later—"All very Hollywood, all very Mickey Rooney–Judy Garland. 'Give that kid a break, he's got Real Talent'—and by God there I was. It was onward and upward from there."

And so it had been, much to his relief and the enjoyment of many thousands of servicemen in the three years following. In all likelihood he would have made it anyway, having already sent through channels his application for Special Services, the "entertainment wing" of the Army where they dumped all the square pegs they couldn't find round holes for, "but my discovery made it all so simple for higher authority. They didn't have to think about me anymore. 'Thank God, that takes care of Haggerty!' They don't want to think, anyway, and I'm sure it was a great relief to them to have me out of the way. Out of sight, out of mind."

Which was typical wry, self-putting-down Haggerty, because of course he wasn't out of sight or of mind at all, but instead was a well-known and very popular figure wherever he was assigned. He had been passed along with highest recommendations from command to command, had finally, when sent overseas, a year and a half into his service, been authorized to pick his own sidemen and organize his own combo. "The Sad Sack Ramblers" became widely known throughout the European theater. "Colonels and even generals vie for our services," Hank wrote to Fran. "The mad scramble to acquire us results in toppled chairs and flying fists. We are *popular*. Gad, are we popular!"

Looking back now as he absentmindedly sips his Campari and surveys the always-fascinating passing parade in Piazza Navona, he reflects that writing to Fran had been his principal occupation in the war every time he has had a free moment away from planning and playing in Army shows. The uneasy peace the United States enjoyed from the start of war in Europe on September 3, 1939, to Pearl Harbor on December 7, 1941, had given them two years of marriage and some reasonable time in which to get to know each other and embark on the difficult task of reconciling their divergent ambitions. Their running argument at the University over his desire to follow a musical career and her devotion to the law had taken on a more serious dimension once they formally committed to each other. "We haven't got the luxury of arguing about it forever," Fran had said in her most practical tone on the day they came home from their honeymoon. "Now we've got to make some decisions."

But they hadn't made any, really; and then came the war and a year and a half of transferring from camp to camp before he was sent. Fran, gracious and unflappable as always, had abandoned arguments for a while to become "the perfect little housewifey camp follower," as she put it. And now he is sitting alone and uncertain in Piazza Navona, the busy life of eternal, indomitable Rome beginning the surge again in the giddy days of war's conclusion.

Two drunken Italian soldiers stagger toward him across the ancient rectangle where the Emperor Domitian once staged horse races and mock naval battles to entertain the populace. They look about fourteen, dark-skinned, dark-haired, dark-eyed. Impossibly rosy-cheeked. Impossibly young.

"*Signor?*" one manages to articulate and he gestures them to take the empty chairs at his table. They collapse into them gratefully and gracefully, a couple of classic statutes come to life. But not much life, at the moment, he can see that.

"Have you had a good war?" he inquires in English.

"*Signor?*" says the articulate one. Hack repeats it in the creaky Italian he has picked up in the past four months. They break into rosy, beaming smiles.

"*Bene!*" says the one.

"*Bene!*" says the other.

"Want a drink?" he inquires.

"*Signor!*" says the one.

"*Molto bene!*" says the other.

A while later, feeling more fatherly by the moment and having established that they both come from small hill towns north of Rome, he asks what they plan to do now.

Go home, they say, as soon as they are demobilized, and get married.

"Tell me about your girlfriends," he suggests, and they look at him blankly and then start laughing.

"Oh, we haven't met them yet," the articulate one confides. "But as long as they————" specifying one requirement.

"And————" suggests his friend, specifying another. And concludes, "*Then* we will marry them!" Happy laughter again erupts.

Presently they depart, unsteadier than they came, and once more he is alone in the midst of Piazza Navona while the children and the prostitutes parade and the ordinary Italians wander through the Piazza giving each other the eye, and the jugglers juggle and the musicians play and loud family parties fill the tables all around to eat and relax in the long, humid twilight of August. If there's any place in the world where you can truly say, "Life goes on," he thinks with an amused admiration he will always feel for the boisterous race, it is Rome.

And how about Hack Haggerty, twenty-seven, musician, composer, entertainer, shrewdly intelligent mind, greatly talented individual, celebrating V-J Day in his typical lone-wolf fashion four thousand miles from his native shore and seven thousand miles from his wife, now waiting for him in the little apartment she has found on Nob Hill in the cool white city by the bay?

He is tempted to make use of the feminine companionship being offered him every time he glances up from the table and doesn't remember to make his gaze impersonal as he looks around the old imperial rectangle of the loveliest piazza in Italy. Some of its professional patrollers are quite lovely, too; and there are also a lot of giggling nonprofessionals out for what they can find on this final night of the war.

Somehow he doesn't feel like any of them—or any of the others who wander by, most of them drunk and in uniform, Italian, American, British, Aussie, the Allies on parade for the last time in a most individual way.

Hack gives them all a friendly but completely unresponsive glance that stops them right there. The professionals, the casuals and the Allies get the message, nod or smile with varying degrees of wistfulness, and pass on. He wants Fran: he always wants Fran. And he is probably one of the very few on this exciting night in Rome who isn't willing to accept the first attractive substitute that comes along.

So he stays at his table for a while longer. Presently he orders ravioli, a salad, half a bottle of red wine; consumes gelato and a huge cappuccino; and presently pays his bill, gets up, joins the parade for a while and then concludes his week of leave with a last walk through one of his favorite cities of all the world, to which he knows he will return as often as he can over the years.

His walk through happy, noisy crowds of celebrants takes him to the Pantheon, overwhelming and massive against the clear night sky, still alive after almost two thousand years with the spirit of great Hadrian; then slowly and determinedly, because he has all night, to Fontana di Trevi, its waters silent in wartime but its figures of Neptune and his horses plunging out of the sea powerful and commanding as always; and so presently to the Forum, closed but its ruined temples and arches visible over the modern walls; and above it the Palatine, the ruins of its imperial residences still alive with the ghosts of an ancient, bloody time; and finally the Colosseum, bloodiest and most moving of all, place of awful deeds, impossibly gallant men, tyrants cruel beyond dreams of cruelty . . . and then, having been lucky enough to catch one of the few decrepit taxis still working at that late hour, back along the Tiber to Castel Sant' Angelo, (again the ghost of great Hadrian and his wedding-cake tomb) and at last the vast expanse of the piazza of St. Peter's, filled now with thousands moving restlessly yet silently, rustling through the night in whispering groups, unable to go home, unable to sleep. Ah, Fran, he thinks.

I want to come home and be with you and have kids and be a good husband and make a good home for my family and be with you always. . . .

And gently, insistently, inescapably, quite unbidden yet overpoweringly demanding as always, there come to him the first tentative chords of some new melody whose final outline and ultimate shape he cannot now discern.

But he knows he must answer it.

And so, at 5:00 A.M. on the morning of the first full day of peace, Staff Sgt. Edward P. Haggerty, Special Services, U.S. Army, is still sitting in yet another small *ristorante*, just off Piazza di San Pietro, patiently writing down bars and chords and musical notes on sheets of butcher paper furnished by the sleepy but still cheerfully obliging proprietor, who is quite excited to have the obviously talented young American *signor* gracing his establishment while the tides of genius move him.

The sun is just beginning to gild the dome of the great basilica. All around it the city is beginning to come alight with its characteristic soft umber glow in the clear, cool hush of eternal Roman dawn.

Far from basilicas, music, Piazza di San Pietro and the lovely Roman dawn, Smith Carriger on V-J Day is somewhere deep in the jungles of the southern tip of Mindanao in the Philippines.

Neither he nor his prey is aware the war is over. He will not be certain until he reaches the small city of Davao days later. His prey will not survive to know it at all.

Smitty Carriger, scion of a wealthy Main Line family in Pennsylvania, big man on campus in his days at the University, inveterate worker in a hundred good causes, chairman of this, co-chairman of that, "incessant do-gooder," as Franky Miller used to call him, has spent his war in pursuits very far indeed from the opulent world in which he was brought up. His small, compact, determined-looking figure, always bustling about campus on some errand of goodwill or other, has been seen—or more often, not seen—in many strange and dangerous places since he left the University. His shrewd, pragmatic mind with its unceasing devotion to detail has had to come to grips with many realities far from his busy life on campus and far from the ideals with which he had enlisted in the Navy on the morning after Pearl Harbor.

Sometimes he has wondered whether what he is doing in the war has had any relation at all to those ideals. Then he has chided himself that of course it has, given the ultimate objective of preserving freedom in the world. Smitty has been a small but very active element in this endeavor. When he tells his fraternity brothers about it later at some reunion, he knows they will greet his circumspectly sketchy accounts with a certain air of polite astonishment, bordering on disbelief, that will sometimes upset him a little. But after all, he reflects, he has been places and done things they couldn't conceive of unless they had been there themselves, and he is the only one in the house who has. It is exotic and unbelievable, but there it is. As it recedes into memory there will be times when even he will wonder if it ever really happened.

Now, while far away Hack is wandering through Rome, in London Willie and Guy are pushing their way through wall-to-wall Piccadilly, and nearby, outside Manila, Gil Gulbransen is engaging in pleasant war's-end activity with his little lady, Smitty is lying concealed in a tree on a small knoll overlooking a Japanese outpost, in the dense forest traversed only by a narrow, hidden footpath linking village to village.

He is getting ready to kill a man, or maybe, if he is lucky, two or three. For the past five days he has been scientifically picking them off one by one. Now he is getting ready to close in on his five remaining nervous targets. With a little luck he will have them all wiped out in another twenty-four hours. The last Japanese command post for southern Mindanao will be gone, his mission will have been accomplished and he can go on to the next.

Smitty has been an early enlistee in what is known as the Office of Strategic Services, and it is quite a long way from the report-reading, evidence-analyzing, patient, devious, bureaucratic Central Intelligence Agency it will become. Right now, it is a brood of killers.

Smitty Carriger, to his recurring surprise when he stops to think about it, but fortunately he has the kind of mind that doesn't very often, is one of the best of them.

When he had volunteered for the Navy after Pearl Harbor, he brushed aside his father's suggestion that he "talk to my friends on the draft board and see if we can't get a deferment." Smitty regarded this as very un-Carriger-like, and now and for the rest of his life, his otherwise deeply respected father will always carry a certain unhappy taint in his mind.

"That's never occurred to me," he said tartly. His father, taken aback by his tone, hastily apologized. Smitty's stern reaction sent him off to the naval recruiting office that same afternoon. He was welcomed with open arms, sent to training, given a swift commission as lieutenant. From the very first he was intrigued by naval intelligence, which he thought would suit his careful, dedicated personality and his very intelligent interest in the world. When the O.S.S. came recruiting from the services, Lt. Carriger was highly recommended. Three months later, trained to infiltrate, trained to observe, trained, if necessary, to kill, he was off to the Pacific.

There life became a long series of infiltrations, observations and killings. His life has been at risk so many times he can't recall the number. Because he is small in stature like the Filipino people, his face and body have lent themselves well to disguise and camouflage. Increasingly fluent in Tagalog and several of the major dialects, he has become very adept at passing as a native.

Sometimes the risks have been relatively minor, sometimes so great that it is a miracle that he has escaped death. Twice he has been captured, facing certain execution if his disguise had been penetrated; but having an incisive personality capable of instant decision and able to take advantage of every possible lucky break, he has escaped both times when guards have grown careless with the labor force in which he was placed. Each time he has faded instantly into the jungle and lived to kill again.

Now he is engaged on what he is sure will be his last mission. Even in his lonely one-man war he has native contacts; he could not have survived this long without them. Jungle telegraph has brought the news of some awful unknown devastation falling from the skies upon Japan. He is confident this means the end and his return to civilian life.

He wonders now, as he lies supine in a tangle of vines on a limb and waits patiently for one or more of the enemy to pass beneath along the narrow jungle trail, how he will readjust to civilian life after so much killing. There was never a more civilized, well-mannered, responsible, decent youth than Smith Carriger, he remembers wryly: he can see him in his mind's eye bustling about campus on unceasing errands of goodwill. How long ago and far away that other world is, off there on the other side of war! How far he has traveled since.

Killer into responsible civilian again? He thinks he can make the jump—two generations of wealth, privilege and earnestly discharged social responsibility by the Carrigers will assist him. But he really isn't sure. Peace is going to mean a great transition. He wonders if he can meet its demands. For the first time in his life, staid, steady, stable Smith Carriger is not sure he can handle life on the terms his wartime service has imposed upon him.

He hears the slightest rustle of branches, the softest sound of footsteps, the approach of the enemy. They are being very quiet and very careful now, since his in-and-out tactics have taken four of them in the last five days.

There are two of them this time.

He tenses on his branch above, and waits.

Hushed and waiting, too, is Jefferson Davis Barnett of Charleston, South Carolina, deep in a canyon of the Atlantic off the coast of Iceland, preparing with his fellow submariners to participate in one of the very last engagements of the war. Like Smitty Carriger's death-dealing sortie in the Philippines, the conclusion of the mission of Jeff and his mates will come slightly after war's formal ending. There are quite a lot of such loose tag ends all over the globe—"little final scores that have to be settled," as Jeff's captain wryly puts it.

How a German sub is still prowling the Atlantic three months after the surrender is one of those mysteries no one will ever solve.

But it is there.

And it is up to Jeff and his mates to ignore it, capture it or send it down.

There is little doubt in anyone's mind what they are going to do. It is probably illegal under "international law," but "international law" never stopped men in their pursuit of conquest or revenge. It gives a certain sporting fillip, in fact, to their concluding days of service.

Word has been received of the Japanese surrender. They have enjoyed a brief period of celebration, interrupted now by the German presence. Only the most earnest and conscientious crew members have doubts about seizing the opportunity for one last kill.

It does not occur to them that they might be killed. They are the victors, and suddenly after three years of warfare they feel invincible.

"Ah thank it's goin' to take us 'bout five minutes to sink that silly suckah," Jeff observes to his fellow lieutenant at the torpedo bay, his accent seeming to become broader as the tension grows. "He's got one hell of a nerve comin' 'round heah at this late date."

"Maybe he can't find his way back home," his friend suggests. Jeff snorts.

"Then he'd bettah cry 'uncle' raht now," he says, "or he's goin' to be on the bottom so fast he can't say Adolf Hitluh."

It appears, however, that the German is not going to cooperate. Though challenged, he is not responding. He appears, in fact, to have decided to make a run for it. Just before he turns, as the ugly craft hang suspended like two sea cows facing off, he fires two torpedoes, whether ill aimed or intentionally off the mark, no one can say. In any event, they miss by a wide margin. But their presence says defiance. Then he swings rapidly about. A thrill runs through the Americans as they begin the chase. Apparently they are in for a real hunt-and-kill. For the last time they are back fully in the war, its desperate dangers and visceral excitements surging through them.

"Jes' lahk ole times!" Jeff exclaims happily.

"You like it," his colleague remarks dryly. "*I* want to go home."

"Me, too," Jeff says with his quick grin, the puppy-dog amiability of college days a lot older but still very appealing. "But I want to get this suckuh first."

This is what you become, he thinks wryly, when you go to war awhile. You get just a wee bit bloodthirsty. You become a hunter. You enjoy the kill. You get a thrill from closing in on some poor bastard as anxious to go home as you are. And you wonder, just like Smitty Carriger, whether some basic decency essential to civilized behavior has not been eroded, and whether you can recapture enough of it to make you fit to live with again.

Not that he has anybody to live with at the moment, of course. He hadn't found anyone before Pearl Harbor and the war hasn't given him much opportunity since. He has been home a few times on leave, attended several cotillions, noted how many hasty marriages that had been rushed into were rapidly falling apart under wartime pressures, tensions and separations. He has decided that he will wait awhile. Lots of pretty little girls have indicated unmistakably that they would like to become Mrs. Jefferson Davis Barnett of the big house, the great bloodlines and the substantial family fortune, but he isn't looking for that type. He wants someone he can really respect and cherish and that's why he's waited. Or so he tells himself. In that conviction he has remained throughout the war a charming but elusive figure among the companions of his youth.

Elsewhere has been another story. Not that he has been "a real wild man," as he puts it to himself on occasion, but he has not hesitated to take advantage of whatever wartime opportunities have come his way.

Late in the war in London, on leave from his base far in the north of Scotland, he, like Tony and Lor, had quite unexpectedly run into Willie in Grosvenor Square, where Jeff had gone to see the headquarters of the Supreme Commander. This had resulted in an immediate invitation to stay with Willie and his roommates for the remaining five days of his leave. Guy Unruh had been there, too, and they had enjoyed a great reunion, talking about old times in the house, their experiences in the war, their plans for the future—and women. Old Guy, as always, was full of a lot of b.s.; Willie, always more reticent, had apparently had some flings, too; and Jeff, not to be outdone, confessed to a fairly sizable number of conquests among the nubile females of the British Isles. Guy and Willie, though, were both married and had something stable to come home to when the war ended. Jeff was still out there in the "wahd opin spaces," as he put it wryly. "I can get *them*," he said with confidence, "but I haven't found the one I want to have get *me*."

They had assured him he would when the time was ripe.

"How about when I'm ripe?" he inquired. "I've been ripe for years."

They had laughed and ruffled his hair affectionately as they used to in the house; and presently the talk turned to other, more serious matters in their mutual past. Jeff began it, since there was still a certain slight tension between him and Willie, and they both knew what it was.

"Whatever became of your boy By Johnson?" Jeff inquired casually. Willie gave him a long look.

"I don't know," he said. "We don't write."

"I thought maybe you'd kept up with him," Jeff said, "after puttin' on that big battle in the house"—which Jeff won when Willie tried to persuade the house to admit By, the only black student on campus in those days. Jeff had rounded up the votes to blackball him because, as he told the house in their tense formal meeting on the matter, "I grew up with boys like him. Some of 'em's goin' to be my best friends all my life. But I don't have to live with 'em. I don't have to have them in my house."

"He should keep up with you," Jeff suggested, "after all you did for him."

"Doesn't always work out that way," Willie said dryly. "I think he blamed me more than he did you. I tried and failed. You were conditioned by the Old South. He thought I was Superman. He knew you were a bastard."

"Oh, come on," Jeff said, laugh a little uncertain. "I just did what I felt I had to do."

"So did I," Willie said.

"Have you learned anything in the war?" Guy inquired.

"On that subject?" Jeff said. "No, sir. Not a thing."

"Better," Guy said. "It's coming. Goin' to git you, little Suthun boy."

"Maybe," Jeff said tightly. "We'll see."

Then they realized that they were all becoming too serious about it again, and shifted the conversation rapidly back to women. It had been a really great reunion, as he told them gratefully when he left. It was wonderful to see them again, and the brief renewal of their differences over By had been only a minor part of it.

Nonetheless, Jeff thinks stubbornly now as the submarine shudders in its increasingly rapid pursuit of the fleeing German, he was right and he still knows he was right.

He hasn't seen a great many of 'em in the war, the Navy hasn't anywhere near as many as the Army, and the ones he has seen have been pretty much on a menial level—or at least, as he supposed Willie and Guy would maintain, have been kept on a menial level. There are two of them on board, as a matter of fact, working in the mess: nice boys, pleasant to converse with, pleasant to be around, always doing their duty with big grins and a willing air. It was perfectly natural to him to see them in these positions but he had been quite surprised to learn that the older one was a chemistry graduate of Howard University, the younger a not-quite-finished English major who intended to go back to the University of Chicago after the war and get his degree.

"How come you're doin' duty like this?" he had inquired, his tone so naively surprised that they couldn't help laughing, though they kept it kindly and he couldn't take offense.

"Well, Lieutenant, sir," the older said, "you'll have to ask Uncle Sam about that. We just do what we're told."

"With a smile," the younger said, suiting expression to words so broadly that Jeff couldn't quite decide whether he was being kidded a bit or not. A lot of 'em did have a sly sense of humor when it came to dealing with white folks, he had seen that many times at home.

"Well, you keep smilin'," he said with his own easygoing grin, "and we'll all get out of this in one piece."

"Yes, *sir*," the younger said, and suddenly they went off into a roar of laughter together that did annoy Jeff a little. But he decided to let it pass; after all, they were all in this together. And no matter how uppity some of 'em like By Johnson might be, they weren't going to get anywhere with it, leastwise not while Jeff and his friends still ran the South. And they had no intention of lettin' anybody else do it, particularly anybody of color.

Still and all, he reflects now as they begin to pick up even more speed and the German, flagging, looms larger ahead, he won't be surprised if there's some unrest when they all get home from the war. They've been out and around the world, now, just like the white boys. And a lot of those who haven't been in service have been drawn by war industries up North, to the East, the Midwest, and on west to California and the Seattle area. Because he's interested in the problem, he's noticed these changes in "demographics," as it is coming to be called: the science of where somebody's movin' to threaten somebody else's job, he describes it ironically to himself. He is glad quite a number of 'em have left South Carolina. It will make it easier for everybody, in the postwar years.

He can't help wondering, at this moment when he and his fellow submariners are beginning to grow tense with the excitement of the coming clash, what has become of old By in the war. He wouldn't be surprised if they all heard from By again, he'd been so embittered by the house's rejection. If he was still runnin' with that little white gal who'd glommed onto him at school, Jeff knew she wouldn't let him rest. By might be a quiet boy but Maryetta was hell on wheels, with all her radical ideas and her hatred for things as they rightly ought to be. She'd make sure By was out there whoopin' and hollerin' and carryin' on, Jeff was sure of that.

His thoughts become concentrated on the German, now just ahead. Jeff's captain is beginning to request him, calmly but firmly, to heave to and surrender. The German is apparently paying no attention. More torpedoes may come at any moment. Jeff stands by to direct the firing of his own.

Surrender or die, you sucker, he thinks exultantly. We don't want to kill you but we're sure as hell goin' to if you don't behave. Then I'll be off this garbage can and home to Charleston, the beautiful mansion on Broad Street and the dear old state of South Carolina where Barnetts have always had a big part to play, and I will, too.

The captain shouts, they scarcely have time to brace, evasive action yanks them suddenly off balance. The German has fired another torpedo. It misses by perhaps twenty feet: this time he means business. They swing wide and begin to circle in on him. Jeff is ready to fire. A happy excitement fills his heart. He tells himself he shouldn't feel so good about the imminent death of fellow human beings even if they are German. But after almost four years of war, he can't help it.

Sweating heavily, like his fellows on Jeff's sub though not for the same dramatic reason, Bayard Johnson is standing sentry duty at the main gate of beautiful, historic Fort Leslie J. McNair on the banks of the Potomac in the District of Columbia.

At this moment he couldn't care less of a damn about its beauty or its history. V-J Day is like any other August day in Washington, hot, humid, suffocating, insufferable. Air-conditioning is primitive and in-efficient, mostly bedraggled old water-stained window-box units, many broken-down or near to it. They are restricted to officers of the upper echelons, anyway. There is none in the sentry box.

Nobody, as one of his friends remarked the other day, "worries 'bout us niggers. They think we *made* of sweat."

By surely is at this moment. It oozes out of him, runs down him, inundates his lithe basketball player's body in all its parts, makes of him a miserable, unhappy, uncomfortable mess.

His physical discomfort is aggravated by all his bitter memories of his service in the war, now, thank God, apparently coming to an end.

By has not had a pleasant war, and it has only confirmed him in the conviction he brought home to Richmond from the University: no-body really gives a damn about helping the Negro. If he wants to achieve something better, he's got to help himself.

He is not entirely sure what his definition of "something better" would be. But he acquired at the University a pretty good under-standing of what it will take for the Negro to "help himself." Aided by Maryetta's constant prodding and his own unhappy experiences, he is coming out of the war filled with a militant determination far indeed from the gentle protest of the mild-mannered youth who arrived on campus as a sophomore transfer, became a basketball star and then went into an emotional tailspin when Willie's attempt to get him into the fraternity house was blocked by a triumphant Jeff Barnett.

For a moment the curious relationship he has had with these two overwhelms him, as it often does, with its paralyzing contradictions. He still admires and, yes, deeply likes Willie, even if he does still resent the way Willie failed him by building his hopes of acceptance so high and then being unable to deliver. And for Jeff he feels that

deep, frustrating, ever-shifting but ever-constant emotional dichot-
omy of so many southern blacks for so many southern whites.

"Stuck together like Siamese twins," he had told Maryetta bitterly
not long after their hasty marriage in January of '42 just before he was
drafted into the white man's army. "We can never get rid of each
other. Never."

"Well!" she had said tartly, sharp-featured little face grim and humorless as it so often was beneath its tightly drawn bun of hair.
"Maybe that's why I'm here. They're no Siamese twins to me."

And indeed they aren't, he thinks wryly now as he salutes the car
of an incoming general and reads the unspoken comment in the general's eyes: there's a right smart colored boy. We've made some
pretty good soldiers out of some of them, anyway.

No matter how many thousands of times he has been patronized in
the past three years, By feels the sting just as sharply as though it
were the first time.

He used to tell himself: you're touchy, boy. You're imagining
things. You're oversensitive. Not every white man feels that way. But
now, after what happened at the University, and after three years of
Army life, he finds it very hard to cling to even that shred of tolerant
attitude.

In fact, he realizes now, as from somewhere in the nearby slums of
southeast Washington he hears sounds of V-J Day rejoicing, he is no
longer tolerant at all. The emotional process begun when the house
rejected him has reached final culmination in the Army. Now he is as
ready as his wife to make war against them.

This frightens him in a way but he welcomes it, too. Maryetta is
always telling him he has a mission to help his people. He has finally,
after much uncertainty and fretful cogitation, come to agree.

Like millions of his fellow blacks, By has been sidelined to menial
employments during the war. He has had constant proof in front of
his eyes that many, many white boys also have had their abilities
misassigned, misdirected and misused by the impersonal machinery
of the services. How in hell they ever won the war, he thinks, he
doesn't know. It's a miracle. But even so, he thinks stubbornly, they
have treated us worse. They really have treated us worse.

When he was drafted he had assumed naively that his mechanical-
engineering training would be put to some worthwhile use. Instead,
he had immediately been assigned to a supply unit at Fort Bragg in
North Carolina. There he spent endless boring days passing out clothing to nervous, wide-eyed recruits. Six months of that and he was

suddenly transferred to another supply corps unit at a camp in Georgia. Six more months and he was abruptly sent overseas in a kitchen
unit with an infantry battalion in Britain. A year of washing dishes,
scrubbing pans and mopping floors followed. Next he found himself,
a month after the D-Day invasion of Europe, assigned to a medical-
supply unit at a base hospital in France. Shortly after V-E Day he
found himself at Fort McNair, for no logical reason discernible to
him, assigned to the guard unit on base. Now on V-J Day he is still
there. The War Department has already announced the imminent
demobilization of some two million troops. Nobody has said anything
yet about his demobilization but he is sure it won't be long. He thinks
grimly: it had better not be.

It has been his general misfortune—and, Maryetta tells him with
satisfaction, America's as well, "They'll see!"—to serve under non-
coms and officers whose attitude toward their Negro troops has been
one of conspicuous boredom and resentment alternating with insufferable patronizing patience. Twice he has had to suffer the most
unpleasant type of Southerner, rednecks whose racial intolerance has
not been mitigated by the slightest trace of human sympathy. Twice,
also, he is honest enough to admit to himself and to Maryetta, who
sniffed skeptically and refused to believe it, he has been fortunate
enough to serve under the Jeff Barnett type, genuine gentlemen
genuinely decent within their lights and limits to "their" colored
boys. But in most cases he has drawn the bad types all the way, not
only in command positions but in barracks where all the normal petty
harassments springing from the forced conglomeration of men have
been exaggerated by too close proximity, boredom and too much
opportunity to do cruel little things to one another in the name of
racial superiority.

It has been, he thinks bleakly now as he waves out a busload of
happily singing white soldiers, off to downtown Washington to take
part in the happy chaos in the streets, a hell of an experience and it
has left him with the conviction that he will never allow himself—or
his people, if he can help it—to be patronized, harassed or demeaned
again. How he is going to achieve this aim in postwar America he
doesn't know at the moment, but he does know one thing: Maryetta
is right. He has got to take a really active part in what he has already
come to think of as "the struggle." He can't do it sitting on the
sidelines.

For some reason, Maryetta has always been convinced that he is a
"born leader." He has told her on many occasions that she wants to

put too big a burden on him, a burden he doesn't really want and doesn't think he is really equipped to carry. A sort of missionary zeal has come over her face and into her voice when faced with his honest attempts at humility.

"You've got the brains, the looks and the personality," she says in the dismissive tone she applies to all his hesitations. "All you need to do is learn how to speak to a crowd and you'll be all set."

He tries to explain patiently that he has to find a job to support her and the children that he, at least, desires. He says the practicalities of everyday living will prevent the sort of crusade she apparently sees him leading. He says that leading such a crusade could be a highly dangerous business in many parts of the South.

"You're not a coward!" she says scornfully, and he sighs.

"No, I'm not a coward, but you have to be practical about these things, Maryetta. You have to see the realities. You can't just challenge a whole society."

"Why not?" she demands. "It's the only way to get anywhere. You won't accomplish anything sitting around wishing. You've got to *do* things."

Now at war's end he has finally concluded that she is right. He doesn't know exactly where to begin, isn't sure how to take hold of it, but he knows he is going to get involved somehow. There are organizations, the National Association for the Advancement of Colored People is one, and others newer and more radical about which he has heard vaguely during the war.

"Start your own!" Maryetta says flatly.

Maybe he will, he thinks as he turns over sentry duty to another colored boy and prepares to go downtown to join her in the V-J Day celebration that she scorns with ostentatious contempt. Maybe he just will. Wouldn't that be something, for quiet, soft-spoken, well-behaved By Johnson.

Also quiet, soft-spoken and well behaved—and likely to remain so, for no such inner angers could possibly drive him as drive By Johnson—is Billy Wilson, Willie's sibling, the "little brother" or "baby brother" of easygoing fraternity reference.

On V-J Day Billy is still a quiet and amiable soul, but in subtle and inescapable ways he is "little" and "baby" no longer.

Like most who have survived the war, he is older, wiser, more mature; more reserved; less naive and trusting; not quite so automatically open and welcoming to the world.

Baby brother has grown up.

He is twenty-five, and shows it.

On this day of worldwide Allied relief and rejoicing, Billy is winding down his war at a base on the tiny island of Adak, far out near the tip of the Aleutian Islands in the vast, forbidding Bering Sea. As befits a warmblooded native Californian, he doesn't care if he never again sees glaciers, moose, bears, musk oxen, walrus, salmon, Eskimos, Aleuts, Arctic seabirds or even, with a few exceptions, the fellow Americans with whom he has shared almost two years of frigid discomfort.

Officially they have been there to guard against an attempt by the Japanese to repeat their thwarted invasion of the islands in the opening months of the Pacific war. In actuality, due to the invaders' preoccupations elsewhere, it has been one long siege of frozen boredom with practically nothing to report but false alarms and not much to see but one another.

This had not been enough, he has often written Janie, to keep them healthily occupied. There have been fights among themselves and with the natives, at least one unsolved murder, several suicides. The eternal cold, the endless storms and savage winds, have frayed even Billy's gentle nature. All he can think of now, as they stand about toasting one another in the steamy atmosphere of the Quonset hut that passes for officers' club is: thank God it's over. And, how soon can I go home?

These virtually universal sentiments, shared by everyone from his brother and Guy Unruh in Piccadilly to Jeff Barnett in his sub off Iceland and Smitty Carringer lying along a limb three thousand miles to the south on Mindanao, would have struck Billy as disloyal and somehow demeaning had they come to him earlier in the war. Then he had been one of the idealists, not waiting for the draft, enlisting right after Pearl Harbor, going off to war with an enthusiasm and dedication that had quite upset Janie.

She said she had never seen him like this. He responded that he had never been like this because there hadn't been a war to inspire it. She said with a rare bitterness that he seemed to like war better than he liked her. He had stopped that with a kiss and told her he would be back in no time to marry her and start the family they both wanted. A year later he had come home on leave from Elmendorf Field outside Anchorage, where he was then stationed, and done both. Now she and their daughter Leslie are with her parents in Portland, Oregon. Tonight he plans to write his last letter datelined "From God's Icebox." Within a month, he hopes, they will be reunited.

Billy's war has been largely one of cold and boredom. Why an education and dramatic-arts major in college should have been assigned to Jap-watching duty in Alaska, he will never know but decided early to stop fretting about. Billy's nature is not combative. Unlike many of his fellow G.I.'s who constantly go around exclaiming, "Now why in the *hell*—" do they do this, that or the other, Billy's response usually is to shrug and let it go. He has never been in any particular danger, except from freezing to death, which has always been a very real and present danger and not to be scoffed at. Ten minutes unprotected exposure to Alaska in the dead of winter, and you were a goner. One of his best friends had gotten it that way when his truck broke down one January night between Elmendorf and Anchorage. You gained great respect for nature, very fast, in Alaska. It suffered you as long as you were circumspect. The minute you slipped, you froze to death, or were eaten by a polar bear, as had happened to another of his pals, or you went stark raving mad in the seemingly endless glacial wastes and the pitiless desolation of seemingly endless winter.

Billy has come to love Alaska, as so many do, but unlike quite a few of his friends who say they want to come back after the war and be part of its last-frontier life, he has no desire to remain. A hot, brown, fertile valley in California is calling him home. He finds, to his surprise, that he can't wait to see it again.

The desire is so strong, in fact, that it is forcing him to confront a question he had thought was completely settled when he left the ranch to go to the University.

Does he really want to tackle the world of theater and movies, as he has believed for a decade, or does he want to return home and run the ranch, as his parents want him to do?

If he does, he knows that it will greatly please Willie, because it will relieve him of his own uneasy feelings of obligation. Should Billy please his older brother, whom he has worshiped for as long as he can remember, or should he think solely of what he wants for himself? And might they not be, as he suspects, the same?

"The ranch" has dominated his life for so long, virtually from the time he became old enough to realize what it was, that he has somehow not realized, until now, what a really striking independence he and Willie have shown in thinking they could break away from it. Some five hundred acres sloping up the foothills of the Sierras, two hundred planted to oranges, the rest fenced for the running of beef cattle, it had grown under their father's careful management into one of the major properties in the Valley. Now his father is dickering with their neighbors on the east to buy their two hundred acres of oranges, lemons and grapefruit; he is also beginning to think about violating his own rule of "always buy contiguous property" and is considering purchase of another three-hundred-acre cattle ranch near Springville, fifteen miles farther up in the mountains.

All of this requires, and will continue to require, skillful and increasingly demanding management. Their father will be able to continue that for perhaps another ten years—he is now sixty—but the time will inevitably come when he will need help. With the new properties, he will probably need it right now.

They have had a terrific manager, Jose, for the past twenty years; he has raised the Wilson boys along with his own, teaching them everything they know about the outdoors, how to ride, how to care for, rope and manage cattle, how to harvest oranges, how to husband the fields and nurture the crops—all the challenging, treacherous, frustrating, exciting, unpredictable, rewarding and wonderful world of the land. But it takes more than Jose's instinct for the land to run the ranch. It takes a mastery of facts, figures, finance, managerial skills, that he might have had if he had been privileged to have an education suited to his abilities. But unfortunately, in those days, he did not.

So it comes back to Willie and me, Billy thinks now as he lets himself be talked into a poker game in one corner of the Quonset hut. The colonel has promised them "something special" for dinner tonight to celebrate V-J Day, which they suppose means more of the half-thawed turkey that forms the customary "treat" on special occasions. The poker, which this particular group of Billy's friends plays more for fun than money, will serve to pass the time until then. There isn't much else to do, on Adak.

Insistently in Billy's mind and heart the ranch keeps returning in these hours of "celebration," if one can call them that, on Adak. Willie has made it clear that he isn't coming back to run it. Billy hasn't thought for a long time that he wanted to. But now it looms suddenly as something not so bad, not so unattractive, not so burdensome. He still wants to write plays, act, direct. His parents have never objected, though clinging wistfully to the hope that he will change his mind. He might just do that, and fool them, he thinks now: he just might.

First, though, he has a date in Portland, Oregon, with "the two women in my life."

The thought of Janie and Leslie fills him suddenly with a warmth so great he thinks he may explode. Billy, with his open, amiable face, his ready smile, his short, somewhat roly-poly figure such a contrast to his brother's lean six feet three, has always seemed to think and act in conventional, if not downright clichéd, terms. "Impossibly dull," Renny Suratt once dismissed him. "Your basic American Legion material," Galen Bryce concurred with a superior smile.

But somebody has to be nice and average and gentle-natured and happy. And now, contemplating Janie and Leslie and how soon he will be with them again, Billy is all of these.

He would have been surprised—or perhaps he would not, for sometimes Billy reveals a sympathy and understanding unknown and unsuspected by all but his brother—to know that on this day of war's ending his fetching air of happiness and goodwill, so pronounced and to some rather unsettling in college days, is still vivid and alive in the mind of an older fraternity brother, many thousands of miles away at the U.S. naval base in Guantánamo Bay, Cuba.

North McAllister, husband, father, increasingly skillful internist and soon-to-be full-fledged doctor, is stationed in the hospital there. He is a brilliant and respected officer, a sound, steady and stable man—and almost as eaten by devils as he was in college.

No matter how often he has appeased them during the war—and there have been fairly constant opportunities in his first assignment in San Diego, then in Greenland where he was stationed for a year, then in Buenos Aires for another year and finally in easygoing, complacent, anything-goes Cuba—they are with him still. He is not as desperate about them as he was at the University—he is relatively safe behind a barrier of matrimony and fatherhood now, and has learned to fit them in without jeopardizing the stability he values and has to have in his profession. But he knows he will have them to contend with all his life.

Mostly his sacrifices at their altar have been anonymous, fleeting, almost momentary. No involvement, no commitment, sometimes not even faces. Just mutual help, freely and quickly given—what he thinks of as "the casual generosity of the open road." Often dangerous, rarely denied. The chances of war on a different level.

But, as always, still vivid and insistent in his mind, the laughing face of Billy Wilson and the love that had threatened to tear him apart in senior year—until Billy, threatened with an unhappiness almost as great as his, had turned to Willie for help and between them they had persuaded North to do what almost everyone, all unknowing, confidently expected—marry Betty June Letterman.

Convinced finally that there could be nothing with Billy, and no really lasting happiness in the open road alone, he had done so, making "the brightest girl in the University" so happy that he could never turn back from the path that he had set himself with the encouragement and help of the Wilson brothers. B.J., who had alternated with poor Latt in receiving the top grades in school each quarter, is an ideal wife, loving, devoted, absorbed in her growing family and her circle of friends and activities in Salt Lake City. And, fortunately, not remotely intuitive or perceptive of the darker underpinnings of what seems to her to be their ideally happy situation.

He often thinks, in the moments of still-gnawing despair that sometimes overtake him after some casual encounter with civilian or fellow serviceman, that what she doesn't know won't hurt her. And after a while, although he knows this is an entirely selfish and self-comforting way to look at it, the despair lightens, the balance returns, and he is, as he tells himself with a wryness so delicately balanced between bitterness and anticipation that he can't make the dividing line, ready for the next one.

But now the war with all its easy sex of all kinds is over and he will soon be going home to Salt Lake to complete his specialization in internal medicine and take up the practice that is already being arranged for him by influential friends of his father-in-law. Mr. Letterman is not a Mormon and so does not have the full influence he might have in the church-dominated community; but he is highly respected and has a great deal. Several of his gentile friends, equally respected, are doctors. Two are aging and need young blood in the office. North has already in effect been promised a partnership when he completes the formal training interrupted by the war. Like Guy Unruh and Gil Gulbransen, he has learned many things in combat that would have taken years to learn in civilian practice; the degree will be only necessary gloss on an already highly competent and experienced medical skill. The future lies before him filled with good medicine, good

deeds and a worthy and lucrative practice that will give him and his
family, assuming no unforeseen derailments, a comfortable and happy
life.

He thinks of them now as the sounds of V-J Day excitement ani-
mate Guantánamo and the nearby villages—B.J., her quick trusting
smile, her absolute honesty, her susceptibility to being hurt, which,
he has found, he can so easily damage; Jason, five, as earnest and
honest as she, always plunging headlong into life's challenges, often
bruised but always bouncing back; and Eileen, three, shy and beautiful and no doubt destined to grow up and marry some unworthy
fellow who may break her heart.

What if he is like me? North thinks, and the thought paralyzes him
as he stands waiting for the bus that will take him into the nearby
town. For a moment he can hardly breathe. What if he lives two lives
like I do? And how would I handle that, if she came to me for counsel
and help? Or if he did?

For a few moments the exhilaration and relief of the day are overshadowed by a wave of a melancholy so dark it almost physically
cripples him. He has to be nudged from behind by other eager bus-
boarders to snap out of it; and even then, it is some while after he
arrives in town and is swept up in the melee of excitement before he
can shake it off. It is only when he catches an eye in the crowd, drifts
imperceptibly but steadily closer and finally exchanges a casual hello
that he forgets it momentarily; afterward it comes back even stronger.

The big war is ending for North MacAllister, but the personal war
goes on. He looks forward with happiness and with dread to the
reunion with his family. His future, for all the world knows, is bright,
certain and secure. But like Willie in London, Moose on Treasure
Island, Marc Taylor lonely in the midst of noisy Pittsburgh and most
of their other brethren from the fraternity house, it does not look at
all certain or secure, to him.

Nor does it look secure to the tall, dark, earnest, sometimes
haunted-looking member who is concluding his service with a brief
stint in the Allied occupation forces in southern Bavaria.

Duke Offenberg—Alan Frederick, education major from Cleve-
land, Ohio—is assigned to a unit stationed in Berchtesgaden, charged
with responsibility for guarding the headquarters high on the moun-

tain above, and the fantastic aerie, still higher above that, from which the mad magician from time to time performed his awful tricks.

Duke often goes up there, walking through the devastated rooms where so much of the world's agony—and above all the agony of what he now considers, in the universal embracement forced by the mad magician, as "my people," was conceived. From there he goes on higher to the mountaintop retreat, the "Eagle's Nest" with its breathtaking view over Bavaria and east to the magician's native Austria—mountain upon mountain, valley upon valley, lush and green and peaceful in the sleepy summer sun. . . . It is unbelievable that this spectacular spot, with the bucolic countryside stretching away far below, should be the place from which so much horror flowed. This, and the bunker in Berlin.

The bunker is gone, and there are rumors in the occupation force that the headquarters buildings also will soon be destroyed, a deliberate act to prevent their use as a sentimental focus for the feared postwar revival of Nazism. "The stake in the heart," Duke writes his wife, the former Shahna Epstein. "But whether it will really kill him, who knows?"

Now as he stares upward toward those haunted heights from the peaceful little village below, he is increasingly and ominously uncertain. Officially, all anti-Semitism is now suppressed; officially, everyone, including the hearty Germans who now love their conquerors so, and whom he does not trust for one second, are the Jews' great friends. With the heightened sensitivity Hitler has imposed upon the world, Duke is still frightened. Hitler opened the doors to ancient hatreds, inflamed them, directed them, used them to consume a people insofar as he could manage. As a member of that ethnic entity Duke has the unhappy conviction that he and his generation, and their children and their children's children unto the last generation, will never really, truly, rest easy again.

Officially, of course, this is banned thinking. The war has been won, the magician destroyed, his monstrous toys and tricks forever put away. All is peace and happy tolerance in the world . . . and within steps of the street corner where he is standing now there are alley walls new-scrawled with obscenities against his people . . . and in a jolly rotund face that comes bouncing and oom-pah-pah-ing toward him now he can catch in a sudden quickly shifted glance the embodiment of self-conferred superiority, and contempt.

Before coming here, he had been a member of the Allied inspection group going into Belsen. The experience had almost killed him. His superiors, who had assigned Maj. Offenberg there with the typical unthinking callousness that so often accompanies assignments in the military, finally became alarmed: the camp of horrors was so obviously ravaging him and other Jewish members of the detail. As if in awkward compensation, someone had conceived the brilliant idea of sending him to Bavaria—"It's so beautiful down there."

And so it was, but not, perhaps, for a Jew in Berchtesgaden.

However, he does have to concede its beauty; and the contrast between the physical setting and the monstrous schemes hatched there is so great to his highly intelligent and sensitive mind, that it has forced him, almost unrelated to any conscious ratiocination, into a renewed dedication to his chosen profession.

If this was what men could do in such a setting (or indeed, any setting, but the contrast here was especially overwhelming), then education became more important and imperative than ever. He had decided when he first entered the University that he wanted to be an educator, preferably at the college level. Now he knows with even greater urgency that education is the only answer—a slow answer, he knows, taking years, decades, generations, to leave its civilizing mark. But it *is* the only answer in the long run, though it may be weak and feeble and lacking the quick-fix patness beloved of his countrymen.

Years ago in one of those late-night college bull sessions that settle the affairs of the world, he had confided to Willie that his ultimate ambition was to return to the University as its president. He has come to realize that the ambition then was more an ego satisfaction than a really profound dedication to education. Now he is emerging from the war with a purpose much deeper and an ambition much less selfish. Now he wants to become a university president so that he can direct, guide, teach—educate. He tells himself with inner irony but profound conviction that it is a relatively ponderous method of saving the world; but whatever it takes to implant some enthusiasm and constructive response in youthful minds, he will give.

He feels a sudden sense of exhilaration and euphoria. All doubts are momentarily swept away as he wanders along the little village street, carefully avoiding the eyes that carefully avoid his. The war is over—he will return to the University to complete his master's degree and Ph.D. in education—he will teach, direct, guide—educate.

His euphoria lasts perhaps two minutes. Then he meets a heavyset, red-faced, broad-beamed country woman whose eyes do not leave his, and as they pass, he hears tossed over her shoulder the hissed word, *"Juden!"* And the day is shadowed again for Alan Frederick Offenberg.

Night has fallen on the jubilant Allied world and on the members of the house. V-J Day is over. Only Hack Haggerty, writing, scratching out, rewriting again, is still scribbling away in perfect happiness and absorption in the cool, hushed dawn of Piazza di San Pietro.

Tony Andrade, yielding at last to too much liquor, sex and excitement, has finally fallen asleep near his bridge in Germany. He will be some time waking. When he does, it will be to find his orders home waiting for him.

Smitty Carriger, having with neatness and dispatch killed two Japanese without so much as a single human cry or rustle of branch beneath falling body, is in his customary thin-sleep mode in the hollowed-out bore of a tree on Mindanao. He will come instantly awake if there is the slightest variation in the animal-insect chorus of the night jungle around him. If necessary, he will kill again.

Rodge Leighton, after staying awake for a long time in his temporary quarters on the ship in Tokyo Bay, has finally drifted off to horrendous dreams of a great light and a great destruction falling on some vaguely discernible land that he fears, helplessly, may be his own. He comes bolt upright, sweating, in his narrow bunk.

Nearby but completely unknown to one another, Gil Gulbransen, on another ship in the bay, is fighting his constantly recurring dream of faceless, headless, limbless men, ripped and bloody, staggering toward him out of some endless cavern whose outlines he can only dimly see. He, too, comes suddenly, joltingly awake and tries, without success, to stay awake for a while. It doesn't work, he is too tired. The terrible procession resumes.

On Treasure Island in San Francisco Bay, Moose, sleeping the sleep of the exhausted and the just, is jolted awake by a horrible strangling sound from his roommate, who is hemorrhaging frightfully all over his pillow. Moose heaves himself out of bed, bellows for the medics, tries to help the poor guy, but it is hopeless. He is gone when they get there.

Rudy Krohl in New Jersey, celebration over, congratulations received, war contributions suitably praised and profits happily remembered, is snoring gently alongside bountiful Helga, having planted another seed of the master race, U.S. division, before drifting off.

Marc Taylor in Pittsburgh, after tossing and turning for several hours, has finally said to himself, "Well, I tried!"—and then has promptly started sobbing and has not been able to stop for quite a long while. But, finally, mercifully, he has tired himself out and gone at last to sleep.

On the transport still plowing slowly and inexorably toward Japan, Lor Davis has been having confusing dreams in which Tony and Angie D'Alessandro seem to be all mixed up with him in some way he can't understand. He finds it pleasant, though, and there is a pleased little half-smile on his lips as he, too, snores gently through the night.

Randy Carrero in Albuquerque, having been "prayed out and sexed out," as he told his cousin (who, to Randy's amusement, flinched openly), has dropped into a heavy, dreamless sleep. Across the room in the other bed Juan is still awake, earnestly praying for Randy's soul and asking God to send him to the Catholic Church. Juan doesn't think he has made much progress with Randy tonight, and Randy, before dropping off, told him bluntly that he is correct. But Juan knows that there is considerable unhappiness underlying his strong-willed cousin's outward certainties. On that foundation, much can be built.

In Washington, D.C., in the little room he rents in a shabby war-time rooming house on Sixteenth Street, N.W., overlooking Rock Creek Park, Tim Bates has finally gone to sleep after listening to a few last radio reports from around the world. He is more anxious than ever to get overseas and find out what is going on over there, but for the moment he doesn't see quite how this is going to happen anytime soon. He decides, however, that he will go into the office tomorrow and lay all his cards on the table with the bureau chief. At least then they'll know that he wants to be something more than just one of the agency's good old reliables who stay there forever and never budge out of Washington.

In Medford, Oregon, after an agonizing argument with Katie, Franky Miller has decided to accept his father-in-law's offer and stay with the auto business. He has never considered himself a tradesman or businessman of any kind. His plans have always been amiable but inchoate. He has had vague, good-hearted ideas that he might do some kind of social work, but there's Katie to think about, and while they have no children yet, he has to consider that, too. He isn't equipped to teach, he doesn't have much to offer society but his good heart—it isn't enough, he and Katie have agreed after a long, long talk about it. But they are going to move out and get their own home, now the war is over. He has persuaded her to agree to that. With that assurance, he has finally been able to go to sleep.

Unfettered by family ties and sure of coming home to a set and accepted place in society, Jeff Barnett is sleeping soundly in his narrow bunk aboard the submarine off Iceland. They have killed the German, after a brief discussion about what to do with him in this unexpected coda to the war. The decision has come down to a simple proposition: it would be too much bother to take him captive and shepherd him to Reykjavík, the nearest Allied port. With only a few exceptions, Jeff not among them, the consensus has been to get rid of him. He has been given no quarter, and in minutes, tumbling helplessly, he has disappeared from sight into the cavern below, coffin for some sixty or seventy Germans who never had a chance. But, as Jeff said crisply to an uneasy shipmate, "The bastard wouldn't have given *us* any quawtuh, so why should we worry 'bout *him?*" He has felt a pang of remorse, thinking, You've got a ways to go to get back to bein' nice little Jeff Barnett, boy, a ways to go—but hasn't worried about it for more than five seconds before sinking into a dreamless sleep. He'll make it with no difficulty, he's sure of that.

Galen Bryce in Bethesda, Maryland, is also sleeping in perfect confidence with no dreams. Tomorrow his superiors, with flattering reluctance and many compliments on his work, will begin the process of disengaging him from the service. After that, he will be off to California to complete his training and take up his work as counselor and guide to a troubled humanity.

No uncertainties disturb Gale's dreams. They wouldn't dare.

At the University, home to him now for six years and destined, he knows, to be home to him for probably another forty more, Johnny Herbert, having had a very quiet V-J Day all by himself, is sleeping soundly in his room on the now quiet and deserted campus. His dreams, if any, revolve around the start of the new fall quarter in September. Like Gil Gulbransen in Manila Bay, he, too, sees a procession, but it is a procession of fresh young faces and fresh young hopes as college life resumes and the long unfolding saga of the University begins to move back to peacetime normalcy again.

In Berchtesgaden the University is remembered, too, as Duke Offenberg finally shakes off the heavy hopelessness he has been fighting all day and deliberately tries to make himself think of pleasant things.

First and foremost, he has Shahna to come back to, her shy but fiercely protective love for him even stronger now that she is eight months pregnant with their first child; and second he has the University, whose peaceful image has fortified him many times during the war. The promise it embodies excites him now as it has excited him ever since that night, bull-sessioning with Willie in the house, when he first articulated his ambition to someday be president. Whether he will achieve this goal he has no way of knowing, but to it he expects to devote his professional life. There in that soothing climate, where he is sure the defeat of Hitler has removed the last traces of racial tension—or is he sure? It's as though he has hit a brick wall. The hopelessness comes back. All happy things vanish. Sleep scurries away once more and Duke Offenberg lies a while longer, uneasy and unhappy, in the warm, comfortable—if you're the right race—German night.

Billy Wilson, also with wife and child to come home to, happily by accident of birth free of Duke's terrors, sleeps peacefully on Adak.

Renny Suratt, confident as Galen Bryce and, if possible, more superior in his relations with the world, is equally dreamless in Hillsborough.

Bayard Johnson, returned to Fort McNair after a long afternoon spent listening to his wife jeer at their country while most around them celebrated its victory over Japan, is as usual so mixed up by race and Maryetta that his normally sound sleep is punctuated by incessant tossings and turnings.

Equally restless, though for far different reasons, is North McAllister in Guantánamo. Conflicting desires—or is it one great universal desire? he has often wondered helplessly—do not always permit of easy sleep for one as sensitive as he.

Guy Unruh, returned to his base in the Midlands after a long day spent in Chelsea with his buxom British lady friend and then roaming jubilating London with Willie, is dreaming now of Maggie, the kids and home. He is, as Willie has so often remarked, a rover by habit but a homebody at heart.

And Willie himself? Again one must observe him, as one must observe his generation, poised on the edge of peace. At this moment Willie, much as he prides himself on being different, is probably as close to the norm as anyone.

Not the mindless norm, concentrating only on one obsessive thought: *when in the hell am I going to get out of this fucking place and go home?*

But the thoughtful norm, that wonders now, in the late-night hours as when the day began: what did it all add up to? And what purpose have I served in giving up the best years of my life to it?

Not that many have had a choice, of course. Willie and a fair number of others have gone of their own free will but the great majority of their comrades have been drafted. Their lives have been removed from their control for six years, or four, or whatever it has been before death or disability, or now peace, have terminated their involvement. Once committed, their experiences have basically been the same. Their governments have flung them far across the world for purposes they have only dimly glimpsed. Blindly they have gone, and in many cases, blindly and bravely died. Those who remain are left with the conundrum that will return to haunt them many times: what did it all mean, the abyss that opened at their feet and broke their lives in two?

Sometimes Willie feels that he is standing on a cliff on one side of that abyss looking back across its roiling depths to a pleasant green land of order and serenity never to be found again.

Over there lie youth and happy days, lack of care, lack of worry, freedom to hope, plan, live.

Over here all is uncertainty, no matter how confident one may try to be in facing it. Here, too, one can only hope and plan—and now, thankfully, with war's ending, live—but here all is shifting, confusing, unclear—serenity only a dream, if attainable at all.

So must his parents have felt. He realizes that now as the noise in South Audley Street finally diminishes and V-J Day begins to end in London. He has never quite appreciated it before. No wonder their nostalgia for those final years of the nineteenth century, the first seventeen of the twentieth. They, too, had come to an abyss, by some fluke of fate or good fortune crossed over, and stood here looking back. The future that to him seemed so established and secure in 1939 had been fully as unknown and forbidding to them twenty years before.

Only twenty years! He wonders how long his generation will have before the future lies shattered again, for them or their children. On his last visit to the ranch before leaving for England in September 1939, he had come across a faded newspaper clipping, saved in a drawer, that said: ARMISTICE ENDS WAR TO END WARS.

"Oh," he had said with deliberate irony, "so *that's* what it was."

His mother's face crumpled and she began to cry.

"Well," she said, "that's what *we* thought it was."

His father had looked very sad.

He remembers now and thinks to himself: what a shit.

But he couldn't know—none of his generation could know.

Then.

They do now.

Now they are veterans of the greatest war in the history of the world.

Now they, and with them their county, have been yanked from their homes and their lives to be projected full speed into that world, never to be able to retreat into their happy isolation again. Now farm boys who knew only Iowa and city boys who knew only Manhattan are at home around the globe, walking with a new knowledge, walking with a new swagger: "We're the Americans, world!" They feel it big, their country feels it big, together they cannot help but show it in the way they think, live, act, conduct themselves and their affairs.

It will give them great power to influence, control, dominate, lead, in the years ahead; it will give them overpowering position in the world. It will also, he suspects, make them many enemies, great and small. Like Andrade, he, too, in his recent months in Allied head-quarters, has seen a little of the greatest of them. He shares with millions of his fellow servicemen who have fought in Europe a gut instinct that a grimmer reality underlies the fine, hopeful statements of pompous men. On the ground, the troops have caught a glimpse of what underlies the ringing pledges of cooperation on high.

Two scorpions in a bottle do not live together peaceably for long. Like Tony and many of his comrades in arms, he fears the conflict is not off there in the future somewhere: *"These bastards are God damned tough and they have plans we Americans don't even dream about."*

If he is right in this, he wonders, where does little Willie Wilson fit in? What can he do, as one individual, one heart, one mind, one citizen, to influence the course of events, help to keep the country strong and if possible help to avert what could be the final disaster of the world? What luggage will he carry into the future, when he turns away from the abyss and starts inland?

He has a good brain, this he knows—quick, intuitive, generous, kind, compassionate, nonjudgmental . . . broad, he likes to think. Also, self-satisfied, a trifle arrogant and a bit superior. These latter characteristics have all been much, and for the better, modified by the war, but still they are a part of him. Now and then he still reacts like the president of the student body, as Unruh told him the other week, "when really you're a half-assed major who's just a scab on the butt of humanity. Just a scab—on the butt—"

"All right, God damn it," he had replied with the laughter Guy had intended to arouse. "Maybe I'm not perfect—"

"Hunh!" Unruh exclaimed. "That's all I can say. Hunh!"

"Well, I'm not," he said. "But at least that's better than half the paper-pushers over there in Ike's office."

"How come you haven't told him how to run the war, then?" Guy inquired.

"He knows I'm here if he needs me," Willie said with a grin. "Just because he's been able to manage on his own doesn't mean that I haven't given him a needed feeling of security."

"If I didn't know you so well I'd think you might almost mean that," Guy said, throwing a pillow at him. He returned it, Guy shot it back, he responded and for a few moments they were back in college, romping without a care in the world. But they would never be in college again and in two minutes' time they were veterans of the war again, older, more settled, more—slowed down; he guessed he would put it that way if he had to use a term. He didn't like to think of them as slowed down, but they had been through a tough war and they were twenty-seven, and well aware that time, particularly wartime, did something to you even if you were still relatively young.

So the war is over, and he is going home in another two or three weeks at the most. He will take with him many terrible memories of hope and horror and emptiness and loss; a good mind, a decent heart, basic good health, basic optimism, basic goodwill toward the world in spite of what he has been through. He will, in short, take home the same luggage as the majority of his fellow servicemen. He hopes it will be sufficient. But like most of them in this moment of leaving war's awful but familiar cocoon for peacetime's unknowables, he feels an inner trepidation far from the confident exterior he manages to maintain.

It is almost 3:00 A.M. and fully quiet now in South Audley Street. In the Palace the little sacred icons are sleeping soundly, in Piccadilly Circus the last few drunken remnants of their people snore at the foot of Mercury's statue. For the most part, London, in common with most humankind, has gone to rest.

Into his mind comes home. The ranch. His parents and Billy. Donna with her parents in upstate New York. The need to decide whether he will complete his Rhodes Scholarship, formally complete the readings in the law he has managed to pursue for six years in spite of war's interruptions. The resumption of full-time marriage after wartime's fleeting, chopped-up, home-leave contacts. The necessity of coming fully to grips with his commitment to his wife and hers to him. The question of children, deferred but soon, he knows, to be inescapable given Donna's anxious desire to have a family "before I'm too old" . . . and the burden of time, lost and irrecoverable, and what its passage has done, and will continue to do, to them.

Career, marriage, family—all the things deferred for so many years for so many millions.

He considers them somberly for a moment as he looks down upon the deserted street, its tall red-and-white facades marching away in stately Victorian procession on either side.

Then his mood lightens, as it manages to do, at some moment or other in the aftermath of this final, triumphant day, for all of them.

Warrior or nonwarrior, armed participants or civilians, they feel the same secret, overriding triumph:

The mad magician's work is done, and horrible it has been.

But the war is over.

And *they* have survived.

What they will do with this gift of life each will have to determine in his own way. The deep, almost superstitious awe of it will remain with the more sensitive for many years to come.

2

H e was thirty-four when he ran for Congress.
　　　 Lawyer.

Rancher.

Father of three.

Observer of life (with a capital L, irreverent friends suggested) and participant therein to the best of his abilities, which, if he did say so himself, seemed to be developing quite satisfactorily.

And already target of the media, well aware that the probabilities were great that throughout his public life he would have to contend with the smug assassins of column, editorial and news story, the snidely arrogant, pompous, self-righteous destroyers of reputation, character and accomplishments who launched their relentless unremitting attacks upon all who raised head above water and ventured to stray in the slightest degree from rigid ideological orthodoxy.

At the moment, he and they were not the constantly sparring antagonists he sensed they would become. But the certainty was there, implicit in his own independent character and quizzical, free-ranging mind. They could not abide anyone who concluded that their ideological emperor had no clothes. He had early realized the fact and said so. Being dutiful followers of the emperor, some of them already could not abide him. The antagonism could only grow.

"It's going to be a rough ride," he predicted to Billy.

Billy's serenely sunny conviction that everything his brother attempted would come right in the end did not fail him.

"You'll beat it," he said.

"I'm not so sure," he replied moodily. "But"—egotism and self-confidence, as always, coming to the rescue—"I'm going to give it a damned good try."

Willie Wilson was growing up.

He was also becoming a stickler for detail. The "Willie" was an example.

Somewhere in Europe during the war there had come to him the thought that "Willie" was perhaps a little too informal for the life he was increasingly sure he would pursue. The nickname had sufficed through four successful years at the University, through academic and political triumphs, through his presidency of the fraternity and, in senior year, the presidency of the student body. It had sufficed through six years of warfare, the 143 flying missions over Germany and German-held Europe, the seemingly interminable months of desk duty that had intermingled with and finally, after his wounding over Frankfurt, taken their place.

It had even sufficed on the rare occasions—two, in fact—when as Major Wilson he had been privileged to be asked for advice by the Supreme Commander.

"Well, Willie," that roseate, legendary figure had said, giving him the full treatment of the big, all-embracing grin, "what do *you* think?"

The question had been phrased exactly the same on both occasions and on both occasions the Supreme Commander, supreme politician that he was, had remembered exactly Willie's name, rank, service record and nickname.

What shall I put on my tombstone, he had asked himself with the wry inward humor he often felt: *Ike called me Willie?*

Probably not—but now, about to embark simultaneously with that ultimate paradigm of the American democratic system on a political campaign, he only hoped he could somehow link his effort with Ike's and perhaps elicit another, public "Willie" to impress the electorate with their fond, comradely, wartime closeness.

Basically, though, he told himself as he prepared on this hot, suffocating July 4 to start his first motorcade through the southern end of the San Joaquin Valley, he was on his own. And on his own he had wrestled for some time with the name he should use for the long haul:

Richard Emmett Wilson, a dignified appellation for an aspiring statesman?

R. E. Wilson, which left out some really rather imposing syllables?

R. Emmett Wilson, which sounded too elderly and somehow not right? ("Emm" as a nickname? Hardly.)

"Dick" or "Rich" or "Rick" Wilson, which were perhaps a little too informal even in the all-engulfing informality that was beginning to erode the gentler graces of American society and put everyone on an unctuously lowest-denominator level of instantaneous first-name familiarity?

It had to be one of the six unless he invented something else. He had invented "Willie" and it had served him well. Maybe it could still serve him. The full signature, "Richard Emmett Wilson" for official correspondence, official biographies, official reference; "Willie" for friends, media. Perhaps in the *Congressional Directory*, "Richard Emmett (Willie) Wilson, —th District, California," etc.

Which was a hell of a presumption to make, he thought, suddenly sobered as his "motorcade"—only two cars, as a matter of fact, himself, Donna and his parents in the Studebaker, Billy and Janie and Willie's own three kids in the Ford—pulled out of the ranch gates in Terra Bella to the desultory snappings of one (1) photographer from the local weekly and headed northwest the short distance into Porterville. A hell of a presumption, to get a mind's-eye glimpse of your listing in the official roster of Congress when you were, at the moment, only a brash and hopeful candidate possessing little money, only a handful of dedicated supporters and with only—as one of the larger papers in the district had put it kindly just yesterday—"the chance of a flea on a St. Bernard" of beating the district's shrewd, longtime, good-ole-boy incumbent.

Well, he thought grimly, this will start the ball rolling, anyway. I may lose this time but I'll be in position. People will know me. The name will be much bigger. And next time I'll show old Spit-on-His-Hands, Slap-My-Back-and-Call-Me-Howdy, vest-pocket buddy of all the big landowners in the district.

And then what, run their errands for them the way he does, so that I can stay in the House sufficient time to prepare for the next jump up the ladder? Is that what Richard Emmett Wilson—R. E. Wilson— R. Emmett Wilson—Dick Wilson—Rick—Willie—really wants to do? And had to admit honestly to himself:

Yes, that's what I want to do. What's the use of getting into the game in the first place if you don't intend to go as far as you can? Sure, I want to go further if I can, maybe governor, maybe even—

I'm as good as the next man.

Why not?

But this conviction, necessary if one is to undertake all the endless destructive rigors of the American political game, was, he knew, only as good as the last election. If he didn't win this one, there probably wouldn't be any more. Some managed to rise out of defeat to forge later victories but it wasn't easy. More often than not the chance, once missed, did not come around again.

"My goodness!" Donna exclaimed beside him in her cheery way. "You're in a mood this morning! Make Willie laugh, somebody! He's got to meet his constituents in fifteen minutes. We can't have him looking as grim as this!"

"I'm not grim," he protested mildly. "Just thinking."

"They might not understand that in this district," his mother said.

"It sounds pretty radical to me," his father agreed.

"Oh, stop it," he said amicably. "I can't have you encouraging me to look down on the voters. That would be fatal."

But he realized as they entered Porterville, were greeted vociferously by eight or ten enthusiastic friends and took their place toward the end of the parade that was forming up behind the library, that he really was in no danger of this. Even though the parade's organizers had placed the Wilson cars toward the back and the incumbent's up front one car behind the parade marshal, he was surprised and gratified to note in himself a certain unruffled serenity despite this deliberate or inadvertent snub. He didn't know which it was but found he didn't care.

Bless your hearts, he told them silently, I think you're wonderful with your small-town Fourth of July parade, and I love you all. Just vote for me, damn it, and I'll be yours forever. And whatever happens, I won't look down on you or patronize you. As a vote-seeker I can't afford to, and as a fellow being I suddenly seem to be in the grip of a sentimental tolerance toward you in spite of your nasty little hurtful tricks. I forgive you all.

Which is very noble of you, Willie, he told himself. You're a great kid.

So off they went, driving very slowly and importantly along Main Street with the rest of the procession to the good-natured applause of the crowd, most of whom had known him and Billy since high school days.

The incumbent got a big hand but so did he, not as big, maybe, but generous and respectful. They didn't seem to think he was as crazy to be the challenger as he had feared they might. He realized his candidacy was moving into the realm of the possible. Suddenly it had become respectable. He could sense that the incumbent, who gave him a big grin and a patronizing wave when their cars passed the turnaround and started back along the route, was not quite as confident as before. Apparently he was feeling some erosion of his own position, some strengthening of Willie's.

When he and Donna said goodbye afterward to his parents and Billy and Janie and prepared to head out across the valley floor in the suffocating 105-degree heat toward their first overnight stay, with friends in Tulare, his mother gave him a thoughtful kiss.

"For the first time," she said, "I'm beginning to think you may have a chance."

"Me too," he said with a grin increasingly confident. "Wish us luck."

"Isn't it exciting?" Donna demanded as they drove off, kids bouncing in the backseat in some convoluted game organized as usual by the oldest, six-year-old Latt.

"What would I do without your endless enthusiasm?" he asked, and instantly regretted it though it had been entirely in jest. As often happened, he had underestimated the way his casual sallies could sound like sarcasm. As often happened, she had misinterpreted. She shook her head with a sudden involuntary grimace; a little pain was there for just a second.

"I mean it," he said soberly. "You're a great strengthening to me, Donn."

"Well!" she said, smiling but not sounding entirely sure. "I hope so."

"Absolutely," he said, and just then Latt and No. 2, four-year-old Amos, began hitting each other and she had to turn to the backseat and restore order.

The two-lane macadam shimmered before them in the suffocating heat. He sighed and concentrated on his driving.

Two hundred thousand potential voters suddenly seemed like an awful lot of people. How could he possibly contact them all?

He couldn't afford to worry about Donna or the kids or anybody if he was to succeed in this political career he was choosing for himself. Somehow he would have to keep a balance, though, or his family life would really go to hell.

But first he had to win this election.

Fortunately the kids kept Donna preoccupied—or she pretended they did—all the way to Tulare and there was no opportunity for further discussion. He didn't want to talk, anyway. No doubt he was inside what she referred to as "Willie's Castle." He didn't mean it to hurt but he knew it did. He couldn't help it. Sometimes he was just *in* there.

He drove toward his destiny in silence, essentially alone as he always was.

"Seven years have passed," wrote the would-be political columnist of Anna Hastings's *Washington Inquirer* as he began a special piece on the state of the world, "and the euphoria of war's end is long gone. Already it is becoming apparent to many thoughtful citizens that far from being the harbinger of a new world, the peace following the great conflict of 1939–1945 has become only the breeder of unending crises, the spawner of more wars.

"In such a situation it seems likely that a powerful, deep-seated yearning for a return to a peaceful, untroubled America is going to propel Dwight D. Eisenhower into the presidency. After all the long agony of the Second World War—the death of F.D.R.—the seemingly endless, cantankerous Truman years with all their hectic domestic or foreign problems culminating in the Korean War, America appears to want—and need—a 'return to normalcy.'

"Not in the Warren G. Harding sense of trying to roll back the clock after the First World War, but in a more modern, more caring way worthy of the enormous sacrifices of World War II.

"If the victor of World War II can triumph over Senator Robert A. Taft of Ohio in the upcoming G.O.P. convention and then go on to beat former Gov. Adlai Stevenson of Illinois in November, he will have before him a crazy horrifying awful terrible God-awful gee-whiz blah, blah, blah."

"And *blah*." Tim scoffed at himself as inspiration temporarily floundered and his hands fell still on the typewriter. I'm getting entangled in my own rich, purple prose. Best back away and take another crack at that third graph. And how am I going to work Willie into the Whole Big Picture? He wants me to, and anything to help a dear old fraternity brother, but the stretch from F.D.R. to Harry to Ike to Willie may be more than even a freshly minted pundit can manage. Though of course I'll try.

Anything to help Willie.

"Personally, I think you're crazy," he had written when he received a cheerful note from California announcing, "I'm going to try it, so rally 'round." But of course his misgivings hadn't stopped Willie. "You've thought I was crazy before," he wrote back, "and it's worked all right, so get busy and get me into that column of yours, I need all the help I can get. Congratulations on that, incidentally. It's a great boost for you and I couldn't be more pleased."

Neither could he, Tim thought now as his mind temporarily abandoned the victor of World War II and the would-be Congressman from California and wandered off into the past seven years of hard work that were finally, in his estimation, about to be rewarded. He had come a long way from the UP offices in the National Press Building, and although he was back in Washington and again at the National Press Building—on a nonview side—it was only after three employers and some five years of assignments abroad that he had achieved the column he had always wanted. This was not bad for thirty-four years old in the highly competitive world of Washington journalism, but he had learned a lot about patience in the interval.

He had also learned a lot about the world, having been stationed first in London for two years, then in Paris for two years, in Rome for a year and finally in Bonn in the increasingly vigorous Federal Republic of Germany. Upon his recent return from Bonn, where he had been employed by the *Inquirer* to cover most of Middle Europe, he had been assigned once more to his first and lasting love, the U.S. Senate. Some of the players had changed since he had last worked in the press gallery but the game of power, personality and politics went on as vigorously, and with as much fascination for participants and observers, as before.

He began a quiet but determined campaign to give his coverage as much analysis and commentary as the copy desk would allow. This was quite a lot, since he wrote well and with an increasing maturity; the free-swinging approach of the campus editor was still there when he let himself become really aroused about something, but mostly he was settling into an older, more sober and less vehement mode.

Quite soon it paid off.

He hadn't been back more than two months when Anna Hastings, with whom he had become pals when they were reporters together in early Senate days, called him in and asked if he would like to do a series of political features.

"If you do them well, there's a possibility of a full-time column when"—she named the *Inquirer's* veteran commentator, now pushing seventy—"retires. Would you like that?"

"Would I!" he exclaimed, for once openly overjoyed. Anna smiled and sent him on his way with an encouraging "Good luck!"

Timmy, he reminded himself more soberly later, you haven't got it yet. You'd really better give it hell, boy. The whole world's watching.

Which of course it wasn't: only his parents in Baltimore; colleagues of his own age in the press gallery, some openly envious of his opportunity; some members of the Senate with whom he had established genuine personal friendships. But if he proved to be good enough, he might acquire in time a solid body of readers who would look for, and place some value upon, his opinions. He felt a sudden surge of feeling for them, the sort of fatherly, proprietary emotion that had sometimes come over him as editor of the *Daily* at school when he made some point that he knew, simply *knew*, was in their best interests and for their benefit.

"If anybody pays any attention," Franky Miller had once dryly remarked when Tim confided this sentimental emotion. "That's the question."

Well, the main point he had made for them then, in that year just before the war began in Europe, had been entirely correct whether they paid attention or not: Hitler menaces the world, the war is coming, we've got to get into it and help shape a new world of peace and justice in which war can never happen again.

And where did that world stand now? he wondered with some bitterness as he contemplated the chaotic scene that confronted humanity seven years after the great conflict ended. Just seven years, and already irrevocably bent out of shape. Irrevocably . . .

His fingers returned almost without conscious volition to the keyboard. The words began to flow again:

"The peace that looked so exciting and so promising on V-J Day has dwindled and withered and tumbled us into many unhappy things since then. For a few brief months there was an illusory calm in the wake of the final exhaustions of battle. Then it all began to come apart again.

"It was only six months after the Japanese surrender on August 14, 1945, that Winston Churchill spoke at Fulton, Missouri, on March 5, 1946, and warned that 'From Stettin in the Baltic to Trieste in the Adriatic, an iron curtain has descended across the Continent.' Six months only, and in the seven years since, only a steadily rising tension, the steady death of hopes, the development of danger after danger that could, at any point, at any moment, bring the whole flimsy structure of international relationships down.

"In the easy jargon of the day, a third world war is 'unthinkable.' "

"But the threat of a third world war is ever-present and in many places increasing every day.

"America no longer holds her atomic monopoly. The Soviet Union, aided by Klaus Fuchs, the Rosenbergs and perhaps others as yet undiscovered, is in the club now. So are Britain and France. China and West Germany, possibly Japan, are working on it. Other potential players, some of them among the so-called 'undeveloped nations,' cannot be far behind. Now the thing is loose in the world, there is no telling where it will pop up next. Obviously its spread cannot be stopped. Nobody has the ability—or the will.

"The United Nations has been established but its principal activity so far has been talk with little action and with little indication that it will ever be more than a windy forum for airing of national interests and national prejudices. India has been released by Britain and split into Hindu India and Moslem Pakistan, with enormous consequent slaughter and the potential of continuing wars between them. China has fallen to the Communists under Mao Tse-tung, Chiang Kai-shek has fled to Taiwan with his Nationalist government. The Soviet attempt to choke off Berlin, met by the United States with 277,264 flights of the Berlin airlift, has ended in an expensive 'victory' for America but with Soviet intransigence unabashed.

"Israel has been created, a tiny sliver of country afloat on a sea of Arab hostility, a client state that America is tied to by the need for a strategic toehold in the Middle East and the importance to would-be Presidents of a potential toehold in New York and Hollywood. Who knows when, or with what, we may be called upon to defend this difficult infant among nations?

"The French have withdrawn from Vietnam, a new state has been created under the Communist Ho Chi Minh; the United States has joined France, Vietnam, Cambodia, Laos, in a military assistance pact. But there are signs that the government is already beginning to crumble, that the South may break away; civil war looms on the horizon. It is, at best, an awkward situation for the United States, and likely to become more so.

"Africa, its disparate and often warring peoples finally freed by their colonial rulers, is rapidly reverting to tribal dictatorships, tyrannies and wars. South America lies supine under various forms of military dictatorship from Argentina to Cuba. Eastern Europe, its peoples consigned to the tender mercies of Soviet Russia by the agreements made at Yalta by the dying Roosevelt, truly does reside behind an 'iron curtain' of dictatorship, duplicity and distrust.

"Only the Marshall Plan, that amazing and unprecedented act of international generosity, stands to the credit of America and the Truman administration in foreign affairs, West Germany its prime example of success. In the Orient, we have freed the Philippines and, under MacArthur's proconsulship, have restored Japan to a reasonable national health with a reasonably democratic form of government. Both West Germany and Japan give promise of becoming worthy junior partners of the United States in a reviving world economy; but given the devastations of war, it seems safe to predict that they will probably be able to play no more than a minor role for many decades to come."

He paused. A slight doubt intruded. His mind flashed back to an unexpected and unpleasant little encounter a couple of weeks before he left Bonn. Perhaps he was being too positive?

He had just left a session of the Bundestag. Ahead in the corridor he suddenly became aware of a figure he had never expected to see again, its tall blond bulk moving forward with a slow, sure and arrogant stride—very similar, he noted dryly, to the slow, sure and arrogant strides of many now coming to power in this reviving country.

Instinctively he slowed his pace; reunion with Rudy Krohl was not his idea of the fun occasion of the year. But maybe Rudy wouldn't even see him or speak to him: he had been so furiously embittered by Tim's editorials in the *Daily* attacking Rudy, Helga and the German exchange student, Wolfgang Hubner, for their open pro-Nazism on campus before the war.

But, of course, no such luck. Rudy turned a corner, became aware someone was close behind, swung about. For a second his expression froze. Then it went from hostility to disdain to an open, sarcastic and unsettling amusement.

"Well!" he said. "You meet the damndest people in Bonn. What are you doing here?"

"I'm a correspondent," Tim said. "What are you?"

"A friend of Germany," Rudy said with a certain smugness, and Tim could see that he was well fed, prosperous and now very sure of himself.

"Doing well at it," Tim suggested.

"Yes," Rudy said crisply. "And we're going to do better. The days are coming when Germany is going to lick the pants off you economically and I'm going to be part of it."

"Well, good for you," Tim said with some sarcasm. "I don't see many signs of that yet."

"It's coming," Rudy said. "You wait and see. You're riding high now but you'll be scrambling to catch up before long. You wait."

"What are you selling them?" Tim asked dryly. "Munitions?"

"Heavy moving equipment. We're making a mint on it at home and we're going to make a mint on it here. Plus, we'll be helping Germany regain her rightful place among the nations."

"Are you still actually saying pompous things like that?" Tim inquired in a tone deliberately offensive. Rudy gave him a sudden glare.

"Write me up, correspondent. I can tell you about the future over here."

"As a matter of fact," Tim said. "I'm going home in a couple of weeks to work in Washington again and I may just do that. You're a bridge. It would make a good story. Are there many like you?"

"Enough to help," Rudy said. "You'll find out. Here—" He took out a card with exaggerated deliberation. "I'm here at least once a month, the rest of the time at the plant in New Jersey. Look me up. Maybe I can give you a story."

"I'm sure you can. You're an interesting study."

"Always have been," Rudy said with a sudden open bitterness. "But you bastards at the University never had enough sense to see it." And he turned on his heel and left, leaving Tim to think: well, well. Next he'll be claiming Adolf wasn't in that bunker.

Nonetheless, he still had it in mind to do a piece about Rudy one of these days. He *was* a bridge, and as such a possibly significant figure in judging the future of Germany, and of the America Rudy had always seemed to resent being a part of.

Even so, Tim could not believe Germany, or Japan, could recover sufficiently fast from overwhelming defeat to be major factors in the world economy "for many decades to come." He decided to let the last sentence stand and moved on toward his conclusion: "And finally in Korea, partitioned at the 38th parallel at the end of the war, the attack of Communist North Korea upon U.S.–sponsored South Korea still drags on as casualties mount toward 50,000. Truman's firing of MacArthur has increased the already bitter divisions over the war. A major headache awaits the new President, whoever he may be. How do we stop it? How do we get out? And once out, how do we stay out and remain true to MacArthur's own sound principle: 'No more land wars in Asia'?

"At home, the major advantage of a new administration must surely be the inauguration of a new 'era of good feeling,' a new period of domestic tranquillity to succeed the bitterly squabbling Truman years—the battle over the Taft-Hartley Act imposing moderate restrictions on the power of the labor unions, passed by Congress over the President's veto . . . the President's squeak-in victory over Thomas E. Dewey after a bitter campaign featuring the President's attacks on the 'do-nothing, good-for-nothing' Congress . . . the trial of Alger Hiss, the rise of Senator Joseph McCarthy and his attacks on alleged Communists in the State Department . . . the President's attempts to preempt the issue and his veto, also overridden, of the MacCarran Act providing severe restrictions on Communist activity . . . the President's denunciation of the coal miners' strike, the administration's securing an injunction to stop the threatened rail strike . . . the constant tensions over almost everything, the seemingly endless noisy controversies.

"Looking back, it seems now as though Americans, led by their President, have spent seven long years shouting at each other in bitter, strident tones. We're worn out, exhausted. It's time for quieter tones, softer voices: time for raucous little Harry to quiet down and go home. America, it seems likely, would just like to stop shouting for a while.

"The hope must be that a new administration will have something of this effect, domestically. In foreign affairs the prospects are not so bright for even the most sanguine of Presidents. Possibly Ike can cast the glow of his grin upon the turbulent scene; perhaps Senator Taft, as volatile in his way as President Truman in his, can sternly order the waves to subside; or maybe Adlai Stevenson, witty of word and stylish of gesture, can lead us skipping gracefully over the surface of events. But the prospects do not encourage."

In fact, Tim thought as he prepared to wind up with some suitable burst of words to bedazzle and impress, he was reminded, and not for the first time, of something a friend of his father's had said before the war. It was still a time when men did not often indulge in vulgarities in the presence of women, but the friend was so full of some frustration in love or business that he said it right out in the midst of the startled company:

"Life is a sea of shit. You just have to swim through it, if you want to get to the other side."

Sure that for the rest of his professional life he would probably be commenting publicly upon current events, Tim was almost tempted to conclude his piece by narrowing the sentiment down to the specifics that faced the world:

The twentieth century is a sea of shit. We just have to swim through it, if we want to get to the other side.

But of course one didn't write that way in a family newspaper.

Particularly if one was a would-be pundit. And if one felt an obligation to offer at least a modicum of optimism to readers as troubled as oneself.

He hadn't been able to include Willie, either, he realized. Well, maybe next time: "Typical of the earnest young veterans who are beginning to seek a well-earned place in American public life is the would-be Congressman from California Richard Emmett Wilson, who—etcetera, etcetera, etcetera, etcetera," he typed ironically, "creeps in this weary pace from day to day—"

He tore the sheet of copy paper out of the machine, inserted another. He had millions of words ahead of him as a commentator on world affairs. He knew subjects would never fail him. The sea would always be there for him and his generation, swimming to stay afloat in their sick, chaotic century.

Far from Tim and far from such gloomy thoughts—which would not have surprised him, because he knew Timmy—the assistant coach of the University football team was also contemplating life at thirty-four. He wasn't gloomy, because that wasn't his nature, but he had to admit he was feeling a little moody as he stared down from his seat high in the deserted stadium upon the team, on campus early for its first run-through of the season.

August's heat lay on the Peninsula. As always, heat was stirring his wounds from the South Pacific. The jagged scar that ran down from his right temple to just above his right eye was throbbing, his gimpy right arm and right leg were kicking up. His limp, always present, was noticeably worse today. For the time being he was unable to raise his right arm high enough to comb his hair. The awkward left-handed result this morning had left his head looking a little lopsided.

But what the hell, he told himself as he often did, he was alive. And deeply thankful for that. Deeply thankful, as always, to Rodge Leighton, from whom he had just that morning received the usual every-other-month-or-so letter with its mixture of upbeat optimism and overriding worry about what he always capitalized as "the Bomb."

"Dear Moose," Rodge wrote, "I suppose you're busy already on fall practice out there. I envy you the simple life. [Huh, Moose thought. You don't have to deal with adolescent kids and meddling alumni and pressure from the administration and carping by the *Daily*—but, anyway.] Over here in Vienna at the International Atomic Energy

Conference we're having the usual go-around about trying to control the Bomb, and as usual getting nowhere. As I wrote you the last time, the Association of Concerned Atomic Scientists has asked me to go along as a member of the American delegation, which I suppose is an honor and certainly a responsibility. But it's all trailing away in talk again, as it always does.

"The nations just can't seem to come to grips with it—can't or won't. The chief stumbling block, I feel, is our own country. We've never understood power, have always been afraid of it, duck its responsibility every time we're called upon to do something. We had the monopoly: we could have laid down the law then, when we offered to put all atomic energy under international control.

"True, the Soviets balked, but at that time we had the power and we could have insisted. Sure, it would have been tough. Sure, it would have carried great risks of a political explosion from the Soviets. So we waffled and let ourselves be afraid and now the Soviets could really put on an explosion if they wanted to.

"Now all the duplicities of big-power politics are in play when it comes to controlling lesser powers in atomic areas or indeed in all other kinds of weapons. We have our clients, they have theirs. Theoretically, neither of us want any of them to develop it, but the British are in it, too, and of course dear old France, which can always be counted on to be the international spoiler. We and the British might possibly be able to persuade the Soviets even now to help stop the spread of the damned thing; France will always find a way to sell parts and material and encourage anyone who will oppose us, just so we can be opposed. So humanity, betrayed by its leaders as always, sits by helpless and the cancer grows and grows—

"Well. Enough of that. How is practice going? How is the University? Do you ever walk up to the dear old house? How are Diana and the kids? My four are doing well and Juliette is fine. That's one good thing about these trips to Vienna, frustrating though they are otherwise: I did find her over here, and that's been a blessing. She's with me this time and we're going to swing through Provence and visit the relatives before coming home.

"Write when you can. We'll be in D.C. in two weeks. Know you can't travel during the season, but maybe next year? We'd love to see you both, as always.

"Give 'em hell, Mooser. You always were my favorite football hero.

"Take care.

"Rodge"

Just like him, Moose thought as he automatically noted that Jones, right end, and Murphy, quarterback, needed to get the summer lead out and get moving if they were to shape up for the stiff competition in the fall. Just like good-hearted, earnest, intense little Rodge, who had become a great advocate of atomic-arms control but at the same time couldn't help enjoying domesticity even when he concluded, as he often did, that the world is doomed.

He enjoyed domesticity, too, Moose reflected. Diana was the daughter of Professor Sorenson of the geology department and he met her soon after his return to campus after being discharged from Treasure Island in the spring of '46. He had been an interested wallflower at a campus dance, looking, to those few who still remembered him, like plain old Moose but carrying with him for others the romantic aura of the crutches he still depended upon and the medal he still wore pinned to his sweater. Diana had been an official hostess, which gave her, shy though she was, sufficient courage to approach him and start talking. When she relaxed, which he soon persuaded her to do, she was lively, bright, cute. Something of the hectic imperatives of wartime still lingered. By evening's end Moose had decided this was it. He asked her on their second date, she accepted immediately. The family felt he was a bit big and bulky for their little daughter, but soon realized the good heart and decent personality that went along with it.

They were married in Memorial Church like so many thousands before and since, and so far had lived happily ever after. He saw no reason why they should ever change: he was absolutely faithful (college insatiability long forgotten, or at least buried beneath present responsibilities), absolutely devoted and absolutely pleased with the whole thing. ("Who would want a dumbbell like me?" he had inquired with a wondering shake of the head when he somehow found himself proposing. "I do!" she said fiercely. He had been so humbled and overwhelmed that he still hadn't entirely gotten over it.) In rapid succession had come Michael Roger Musavich, now five; Mary Diana Musavich (Diana liked alliteration), now four; and Martin Theodore Musavich, pushing three. Diana had indicated that this was probably enough and he agreed, although he was still very active and accidents did happen.

They occupied, on one of the tree-shaded streets of the nearby town, a modest but pleasant little house, which, like millions of other veterans, he was purchasing with a thirty-year, low-interest loan under the "G.I. Bill of Rights." The bill, one of the greatest achievements of Congressional foresight, had also financed completion of his master's degree in physical education four years ago. Life on the whole was well ordered, generally happy and snug. He told himself that this was what it was really all about, when you came right down to it: a nice house, a good wife, having kids, making a good home for them, hoping they'd grow up to do better than you had.

That was the basic American dream.

Hell, that was the basic human dream.

He had lately noticed an increasing tendency in academic and other circles to scoff at this. That jerk Renny Suratt, for instance, whom Moose had never been able to abide in the house and whom he fortunately only saw infrequently when their paths crossed accidentally on campus, had recently been quoted in the *Daily* as telling his sociology class that this was a "banal and bucolically insipid concept of life." What would Suratt know, that nympho bachelor whose pursuit of young female students was already notorious in faculty circles? That "banal and insipid concept" of home and family required a self-confidence, a mental ability and emotional security that Suratt and his fellow critics would never know. But their criticism and the attitude it represented was growing.

It worried Moose in some instinctive way. He felt it was beginning to work on the foundations of America society, and he didn't like it.

Fortunately for his own peace of mind, he didn't often think about it. He lived in a nice, tight little family world and his present happiness and future dreams were so bound up in it that he didn't have much time left over for Suratt and his kind.

The only thing that meant as much to him as his family, he reflected now as the sun slanted low across the stadium as it had on so many well-remembered occasions of adolescent gore and glory, was football. To that he owed an allegiance that had been instantaneous and permanent from the first moment he had run on the field as a member of the freshman team. Others found fulfillment in a great bridge, a great painting, a symphony, a book. Moose found it in helping to field the best possible team, and this, he felt, was just as valid as anything else. It was what *he* had been put here to do, and if he did it well, then that was dignity and justification enough for him.

This gave him an inner assurance and integrity that could not be shaken. Today he knew what he was and where he stood. Adolescent uncertainties had rolled away in the crucible of the South Pacific. His goals were not as high as many men's, he recognized, but they were suited to him. He knew he pursued them well, and that was bedrock enough for a good and worthwhile life.

There was talk now that Coach might be resigning after twenty long years of battling administration, alumni and press and fielding a generally successful series of teams. An alumni search committee would be appointed soon, he told Moose, and Moose would be his own most highly recommended choice. The thought made Moose shiver, though heat still lay heavy even at 5:00 P.M.

He didn't dare think about it too much. If it happened, he felt he was ready. If it didn't, well, he'd keep his nose clean and keep on doing his damndest. Sooner or later, he'd make it. God wouldn't let him down, he felt, when he worked so hard and so earnestly to be good and do right.

Elsewhere on campus as the year turned toward autumn the three other house members who had returned to school to take up academic careers were also, according to their lights, leading productive and worthwhile lives.

If Renny Surratt's was devoted to mocking, and he hoped undermining, a society he saw as stupid, complacent and corrupt, then that might upset Moose, whom he despised anyway, but it suited him just fine.

Johnny Herbert, snugly entrenched in the history department and moving steadily toward the full professorship he had set his heart on, was fitting more and more permanently into the sort of neat bachelor-scholar's life that appealed to his mature and orderly mind. It filled the void that he believed his shaky health made it impossible for him to fill with wife and family.

And in the education department Duke Offenberg, supported loyally, as always, by faithful Shahna, was also well on his way to becoming one of the leading younger members of the faculty. He had never confided to anyone except Shahna and Willie his secret ambition to become president of the University someday. But he felt that so far he hadn't put a foot wrong; and while Dr. Chalmers at fifty-two seemed in perfect health and good for another fifteen or twenty, Duke had learned long ago the value of a fixed intention and the unwavering pursuit of it.

"Look at this country!" Suratt would exclaim, and over his class there would come the intensely quiet listening that he knew, to his delight, signaled their absolute, enslaved awe of him.

"Look at it! Seven years out of the war, and what is the major goal of a majority of our countrymen? Why"—his tone beginning to drip with the sarcasm for which he was already famous on campus—"to get married, buy a house, raise a family, be a little cog in the wheel, just like all the other little cogs in the wheel. Materialism, materialism, materialism! That's the goal for America now. We fought a war, presumably to make the world safe for democracy because we didn't make it safe in 1914–1918 and had to go back and do it over again"— this always got an obliging titter—"but it isn't democracy we're interested in, it's money. It's getting a bigger house than the other guy, a flashier car, a bigger salary, belonging to fancier clubs, sending your kids to fancier schools, not only keeping up with the Joneses but passing them on the turn. Millions of Americans haven't made it yet, but they're all scrambling in that direction.

"And as a result, what's happening to art and music and culture and all the things that should make this country worthwhile—including democracy itself? What *is* happening to our democracy, by the way? It isn't doing too well. We still have too many people who aren't working, too many who are illiterate, too many who live in squalid conditions, too many who can't get adequate educations, or medical care. And what about the Negroes, our main national disgrace? Harry Truman ordered the services desegregated but do you think that's made any difference *in people's hearts?* That's where it has to be decided, this racial-equality issue. It's how you think of the other guy, not how you treat him because the laws force you to. They don't, yet. They may someday, but it will be a long time coming. And when it does, there will still be ingrained attitudes and long-standing prejudices that won't give way to legal or societal pressures in our lifetimes, because whatever the legal pressures say, the societal pressures will still be all the other way.

"And you. What about *you?* When I got out of this place thirteen years ago, we all faced a war but a lot of us thought that somehow out of it would come a better world. [He carefully always refrained from saying what he had done in that war, or what his own scathingly skeptical predictions of its results had been.] Imagine our surprise when it turned out to be the mess it is. Imagine our surprise when we realized that you, the generation that is going to have to come along next and mop up the horrible mess we have made of things, are facing such poor prospects as you are. Oh, I know, some of you are optimistic, some of you are dreaming, some of you think everything will be all right.

"That's permissible: there's always room for a few fools in each generation. [This always brought titters, too, though increasingly uncomfortable.] Good luck to you, I say! Keep on dreaming! Listen to the glowing words they'll give you on graduation and then go forth and try to make them come true! You'll find it isn't so easy, my young friends! Not so easy. You have to be realistic. It's a hell of a world, and you're going to have to set it straight *if you can.* So good luck and good dreams to you, I say! You're going to need them!"

And later, as he passed groups of them in the Quad arguing furiously over his words, he would feel the secret inner satisfaction he always felt. He'd knock their complacency into a cocked hat before he was through with them. He'd stir them up. They wouldn't forget Professor Suratt!

Nor did they, of course; and, as always with faculty members whose chief stock in trade is attacks upon the status quo of their own country and their own society, his fame increased and his classes grew until today, five years after joining the faculty, Assistant Professor Suratt was one of the most known and most popular members of a body that included a good many increasingly notable people. He was also writing his first book, *America: The Myth That Couldn't.* When it was published (already under contract to a major publishing house, national tour and extensive exposure on radio, and the rapidly emerging television that was beginning to dominate American thought, already scheduled), he knew that "Professor Suratt," an entity already almost separate from himself, would be recognized far beyond the University.

He would receive that instantaneous benediction and loudly applauding canonization that came automatically to all who declared loudly enough, and persistently enough, and obnoxiously enough, that their own country was no damned good.

Duke Offenberg, passing along the sandstone colonnades one day, had overheard the positive, sarcastic voice, familiar from so many house bull sessions, rising from a nearby classroom. He agreed with some of it, but the overall tone and import—Jesus, it was all so much crap. He had paused, listened for a moment in amused disbelief, then slipped in quietly and seated himself at the back. His presence was instantly perceived by the lecturer, who hailed him with an ironic, "Ladies and gentlemen, we seem to be privileged to have with us one of my oldest and should I say—or no, I shan't say 'dearest'—friends and fraternity brothers . . . anyway, welcome and stay as long as you like. Assistant Professor Offenberg from the School of Education."

And then he had proceeded to be even more histrionic, outrageous and extreme than usual, to the point of crying sarcastically, "Oh, wait!" when after five minutes Duke, fed up, shook his head with deliberate amusement, rose and tried to slip quietly out again.

"Can't take it anymore," he said. "Too brilliant for me, Renny. Much too brilliant."

"Come back anytime!" Renny called, while the class tittered in dutiful appreciation. "Anytime!"

But he didn't think he would, Duke reflected as he concluded one of his own factual but, he hoped, interesting lectures on education a couple of days later. Never had liked Renny—never would. Some of what Renny said Duke could agree with—he still didn't feel, in postwar America, that his own minority was doing much better, in a societal sense, than the Negro—he still didn't see that inflaming the situation with deliberately provocative statements, as Renny obviously was trying to do, could make it much better. He could understand the motivation, of course. Professors who were deliberately provocative were always the stars of the faculty, fawned on by the students who flocked to their classes in droves, fabled in song and story along the Row and in the dormitories, always good for a shocker or two when approached for comment by the *Daily,* soon so famed and entrenched that the administration was rarely able to dislodge them even if their personal conduct began to achieve a notoriety as great as their lectures.

There was always that type on every campus, usually blessed with considerable intelligence and always blessed with a shrewd sense of how to manipulate publicity for their carefully nurtured me-against-the-system reputations. Renny, Duke conceded, was probably set for life, with a tenure in notoriety far more permanent and unshakable than any he might earn for longevity in the system. Even Dr. Chalmers, Duke suspected, would have a hard time dislodging Renny, no matter how much scandal he created with girls who were already approaching the half-his-age category.

Such, he reflected, were not for him. For one thing, he considered it too dangerous, and for another, he had no interest. He was a handsome soul if he did think so himself, six feet three and possessed of the aquiline features, deep-set dark eyes, curly dark hair and classical bone structure of his heritage. Lots of his students, lots of faculty wives and lots of the quieter mousy types who found their niches in the administration made it abundantly clear that they were strongly aware of his presence as he was of theirs. But his heritage also had a tradition of loyal and long-lived domesticity, and he considered himself content to adhere to it. The other was just too much bother. And, as he often told himself, not worth the risks.

Plus the fact, of course, that it would be a betrayal of Shahna, and betraying Shahna was the last thing he wanted to do. No one could ever be more loyal and loving to him, or give him more complete and absolute support. Not very exciting, perhaps—that had passed very quickly in their wartime marriage, and now, ten years later, much was routine; but the fact that she was always there, always steadfast, always supportive, partner in, and encourager of, all his dreams and hopes and plans—what more could one ask? He was damned lucky to have her, as Willie and the others in the house had often told him before the war, and he firmly intended to remain completely and entirely faithful for the rest of his life.

Particularly was this true because, when he returned from Europe to join the faculty and she rejoined him from her enormous family home in Hollywood, they had agreed that the anti-Semitism that had worried them so during the rise of Hitler was still unhappily present in American society.

Her father, now one of the movie industry's major producers after seven patriotic films that had won him three Oscars and contributed greatly to the war effort, had offered Duke a vice-presidency and, in effect, the moon. Duke had said no, thanks, he preferred to stay in education. Her family and his thought he was crazy but secretly admired his integrity.

"Maybe," his father-in-law said wistfully, "you can do better with them than I can with all my movies and wartime contributions."

He had not defined "them"—didn't need to. He and Duke had discussed it before, and what "doing better with them" meant. It meant being accepted totally without that secret little edge that both of them felt was always there and that always made them slightly uncomfortable even in the midst of the most apparently cordial surroundings. Money was Hollywood's only language and in that his father-in-law spoke as loudly as any Goldwyn or Mayer; but while money was power, it was not true acceptance. And that, Duke sometimes despairingly felt, they might never achieve.

And yet, as he had concluded at Berchtesgaden in the war's-end days that now seemed so long ago, in education there might be a key—the only key, perhaps, slow, difficult and sometimes thankless as it might seem. It was not thankless, he often told himself stubbornly. It did produce results. Tolerance did flow from the educated mind. He had to believe that: he had dedicated his life to it. And he did not intend to fail.

So he went about his lecturing and his counseling and his teaching with an earnest, concentrated and often humorless air that caused some of his colleagues to regard him as "stuck up" and some of his students to regard him with an awe bordering on genuine fear. He did not slash them down, as Renny loved to do with his razor tongue, relishing their supplicant status, but his withdrawn disapproval could be monumental for the faint of heart. They did not realize how much of it came of shyness, compounding his basic seriousness; the combination, unfortunately, made him inaccessible to many even when they admired him. Shahna often worked on this but did not succeed in persuading him to relax much.

"Life is real, life is earnest," she sometimes remarked with her gentle little smile.

"Well, it is," he said, and couldn't understand the tenderness with which she sometimes put her hand against his cheek and responded, "Oh, come on, now. Relax."

But he couldn't, that's all, he couldn't. Even when he was at rest in their home in the hills behind campus and was playing with Alan, Jr., seven, and Ruth, four, he couldn't really let go. And of course they sensed this too, and withdrew a little, and he was made unhappy by that. And so he sometimes wondered, carrying the weight of the world on his shoulders as he did, whether he could ever find real peace and contentment.

He intended, however, to become president of the University. To that intention he did not admit impediments.

Johnny Herbert, who had seen Duke only yesterday on the Quad when both were on their way to meet waiting classes, was not one privy to this ambition. But he was aware, as always, of a driving preoccupation in his classmate and fraternity brother. It made Duke one of the easier subjects to write about for the annual newsletter Johnny was putting together to send to the scattered members of the house.

"Hey, Duke!" he hailed the tall figure striding on purposefully ahead. "Slow down for a sec. Where are you going?"

"Oh, hi, Johnny," Duke said, breaking his stride and turning back. "Meeting a class. Haven't seen you in a long time. How've you been?"

"Oh," Johnny said, and in spite of himself a certain underlying wistfulness was present in his voice. "I'm fine. Always fine. Nothing new, really. Just fine."

"Well, good," Duke said, taken out of himself for a moment by Johnny's tone and looking a little puzzled by its insistence. "I hope so. I thought you said you were going to come see us one of these days? Shahna'd love to cook us a meal."

"I will," Johnny said. "I promise."

"Call me on Monday," Duke said firmly. "Don't let it trail away, O.K.?"

"O.K.," Johnny said. "Oh, by the way, do you have anything you want to put in the newsletter this year? I'm getting ready to send it out, probably in September so people will know where everybody is in case anybody wants to send Christmas cards or anything."

"You're very faithful about that," Duke said. "That's good of you. Most people wouldn't care."

"Well, maybe not very many of us do after all these years," Johnny said. "But I do sort of like to know where everybody is, and I'm assuming others would, too."

"Oh, I love to get it," Duke said hastily. "I don't mean that. And it was a special time, and a special bond. Life just gets in the way of that, though. Too many things going on, as you get older. But by all means, don't stop it. I'll bet you'd get a lot of complaints if you did."

"Some of the guys don't even bother to write me anymore," Johnny said, and again the wistful note came in to his voice. "But I enjoy doing it."

"Keep after 'em," Duke advised. "And mention it in the letter, if they don't respond. Nail 'em. They'll get to it eventually. You know where Moose and I are, anyway. And Renny."

"Renny!" Johnny said with a snort. "That insufferable jerk! Have you heard what he's telling the kids these days?"

"Yeah, I stopped in one day a while ago. Quite a lecture, from the little I heard of it."

Johnny gave his head an annoyed shake.

"I did the same, once. Once. That was enough."

"He's building himself a reputation, though," Duke remarked thoughtfully. "He'll be heard from nationally, which is what he's aiming for, obviously."

"You and I don't know the opportunities we're missing," Johnny said with a rare sarcasm. "Have a good class."

"You, too," said Duke, peeling away. "Call us."

But whether he would or not, Johnny wasn't sure as he walked on across the Quad to History Corner and the class he was teaching on "America and World Peace: Intervention and Isolation." He wanted to—but felt shy about it, even though he knew Duke was perfectly sincere, and he had always liked Shahna and knew she would love to cook for him. They were good people, and he a sad soul if he didn't take them up on it, and renew and strengthen a friendship that, like so many, seemed to have trailed away when college's close intimacy gave way to adult concerns.

Maybe he was a sad soul, really. Maybe that was all there was to Johnny Herbert, a sad soul who would never be anything much more than an adequate teacher, a modestly accomplished historian and scholar—and a human being, crippled by perennial poor health, who would never know half of human living as he mused his way through endless years of quiet teaching on a college campus.

He told himself sternly as he entered the classroom to see the faces of his waiting students—friendly, anyway, not hostile or challenging, they liked him, everybody liked Johnny Herbert—that this was the sort of thinking that could only end in a blind alley. It was self-pitying, self-weakening, ultimately self-defeating if he let it run on. He reminded himself, as he so often had since the night of his fateful abandonment fifteen years ago, that he was just as sick and sorry as he let himself be, just as sad and pathetic as he let himself be. Look at his students: they obviously didn't regard him that way. In their eyes he was Professor Herbert, fount of knowledge.

O.K., fount, he told himself with the returning humor that always came to his rescue, get with it and perform.

And so he did, as he always managed to, perhaps not as sensationally and notoriously as Renny, perhaps not with the earnest erudition he knew was coming to be associated with Duke's name, but with the solid scholarship and touches of humor he hoped were coming to be associated with his. He had decided to become a history teacher at the suggestion of Bill Lattimer, who had been his chief mentor in the department until the terrible accident that resulted in Latt's death in the car driven by Randy Carrero. At the time Latt had been the student with the highest grade average in school. Most of the house had been devastated by his death and Johnny and some others had found the courses of their own lives directly affected. Randy, conscience-stricken, had apparently been impelled into the priesthood—Johnny had just heard from him the other day while preparing the newsletter—and Johnny for his part had decided to make a permanent commitment to the teaching of history. Latt had predicted, in his gravely quiet way, that this would be needed by the country after the war in a way it perhaps had never been before.

The concept of doing something "for the country" that was outside and separate from the military service most of them were then facing had seemed somewhat pompous and pretentious to some; but to Johnny, who could not serve, and for Latt, who never would, it had seemed real enough. Some people did live by conscious adherence to what they thought was the common good—not many, Johnny conceded dryly, but some. Now after the war he was impressed by Latt's prescience in perceiving that helping Americans to understand how their country had been created, the storms through which it had passed and what it was all about, was a major and imperatively necessary contribution.

Many Americans did not realize it now, but without a clear understanding of the history of their own land they would be adrift in a chaotic world without anchor, with no points of reference or contact to guide them; and while he realized that an increasing number of teachers, such as Renny, encouraged scorn of the past because its absence furnished fertile ground for implanting their own misshapen views of the present and the future, Johnny was not one of them. History, as clear and accurate as he could transmit it, was becoming something of a Grail for him.

He told himself that this *was* pompous and pretentious. But it made sense to him.

"Americans don't believe in history," Renny had told him one day before the war. "Why should you bother to teach it to them?"

"Because I don't want you to rewrite it for them," he had retorted with unusual vigor.

Renny had only smiled in his superior and sardonic way and now, of course, he was, as Duke said, well on the way to establishing a solid national reputation based principally upon his misuses of history. How many students, Johnny wondered bleakly, would be sent wandering into the world without guideposts, because Renny had destroyed them all when the students were at their most impressionable?

He shook his head in annoyance with himself when he reached this point in his thinking. He told himself that he devoted too much time worrying about Renny, when Renny wasn't all that important. Except that Renny, and the growing school of anti-history and anti-responsibility that he symbolized, were very important indeed.

For the purpose of the house newsletter, however, no more important than anyone else, Johnny told himself firmly, and he had best get on with it or it wouldn't be ready to send out in the fall. So far he had heard from seventeen of the members who had survived World War II. Some of the major ones were still missing, no doubt too busy with their own preoccupations to write; the rest had reported in.

Two of the three doctors, Gil Gulbransen and Guy Unruh (North McAllister had yet to respond) were doing fine. Gil was in La Jolla, had finally married Karen Ann Waterhouse, and they had two kids, Grant, six, and Gracia, four. Guy was back in his native Hawaii, his pre-war marriage to Maggie Johnson apparently in good shape; they had four kids, Wilson, seven; Peter, five; Elizabeth, four; Ann, three. Gil's general practice was apparently going very well; Guy, now one of the leading oncologists in the country, was dividing his time between practice and research. A certain smugness crept into both their letters.

"Everything's going great here," Gil wrote, "I can't complain."

"Good wife, good kids, good practice, good patients, good research opportunities and the chance to live in my Hawaii, still pretty much unspoiled," Guy wrote. "What more could a guy ask? Come see us, you-all."

Equally as smug sounded Galen Bryce in Hollywood, where he had decided to set up practice on discharge from the Navy. "There appears to be a real need for good psychiatrists here," he wrote. "And they're prepared to pay for it, too. I have never seen so many mixed-up egos in my life pushing each other in the door. It is a golden field. I'm attempting to do my best, and must say I seem to be achieving some success." So far, though, he noted, "no Mrs. Bryce on the horizon, but I keep hoping."

The note from Tim, recounting present prospects and future hope, contained news of Willie's campaign, which Johnny had already received in a telephone call from Willie soon after his announcement. Tim also mentioned Rudy Krohl: "Sounds as if he plans to take over the New Germany. From what I've seen, they may deserve each other. Not a major item," Tim concluded almost apologetically, "but in case anyone is interested. It was surprising to see him over there."

Marc Taylor also sounded apologetic but as usual about himself. "Things are just going along here," he wrote. "The company is doing well and I'm trying to be useful to my Dad. Keeping busy: nothing much to report." He enclosed his card, however, listing him as "Vice-President, Administration," which seemed to indicate a fairly important hand in things; and when an innate researcher's curiosity took

Johnny to the pages of *The Wall Street Journal,* he found Taylorite listed on the New York Stock Exchange and a report indicating second-quarter profits of more than $10 million. Marc was determinedly modest, Johnny reflected, but something was obviously going right. He wondered, not for the first time, whether they hadn't underestimated Marc—or if Marc hadn't underestimated himself. "Like me," he had added honestly. It wasn't good for either of them. He thought he was getting over it, and hoped Marc would, too. No Mrs. Taylor there, either.

Billy Wilson, abubble as usual with his big brother's activities, wrote from the San Joaquin Valley that he was "doing my damndest to help my Dad keep the ranch running, and at the same time doing what I can to help Willie. He's got a tough opponent in the incumbent but he's definitely making headway. In fact there was an interview story the other day that quoted a lot of Valley people, and the ratio was almost 50–50. So, we're all pitching in to give it an extra punch as we head into the fall. The house may have a 'Congressman Wilson' in November. Wouldn't that be an interesting kettle of fish." His own dreams of a stage and theatrical career, he added with a wistfulness that came through clearly, "are sort of on the back burner now. I try to keep writing some, but farming is a hell of a demanding life if you do it right. Dad needs me here, and Willie depends on me a lot, and between the two I don't have too much time to think about anything else. I still want to, though, and maybe someday—anyway, Janie and the kids join in sending their best to everybody. VOTE FOR WILSON!"

Tony Andrade wrote, with a certain calm assumption of proprietorship, for both himself and Lor Davis. "Louise and I," he noted, "are now into our fifth year here in Napa Valley, and we're beginning to feel really at home in the vineyards. We've built our house on a knoll near her father's, and it's a beauty if I do say it myself. We hope you'll all stop by—this is really a beautiful part of the world. We have room for us, the kids (now four) and a couple of guest houses, so don't hesitate. Everything is going well with the grapes—obviously! My father-in-law, Mario, now owns 500 acres and doesn't seem to want to stop there; he's even talking about our own winery, which would be nice if we can. Speaking of dropping by, Lor and Angie and their three kids were recently here for a week from Long Beach, where the family oil wells apparently continue to gush forth goodies. You've probably used their products in your cars; he says they're planning a big expansion overseas if things continue to go well; Kuwait and Saudi

Arabia, he thinks, are the most likely places. He and Angie seem fine, the kids are flourishing and all seems to be well. We talk on the phone at least once a month. He said to say hi to you all when I write so hi to you from both of us."

(They had stayed up, talking a lot and drinking mildly, until after midnight, until after Angie and Louise and all of the kids were safely long abed. Then they put out the lights in the study, stood for a long moment listening: all was still.

They left the study, slipped silently out, went down the long line of vines to the abandoned old caretaker's hut at the far end of the home property.

There they stood another long moment, staring at one another through the soft interior gray of the fading moonlight.

"Well, Mr. Davis," Tony whispered. "Let's do it."

The golden head tossed, the Roman emperor curls fell into the carefree disarray that had captured his heart so long ago when they first met as sophomores in the house. Lor grinned, still and forever boyish at thirty-three.

"O.K. Mr. Andrade," he whispered back. "Let's.")

"Well, here I am," Smith Carriger wrote from Carriger Corporation in Philadelphia, "carrying on the old Carriger traditions. Married six years now, to delightful Annelle, father of three, vice-president, etc., of the boring old company. Things haven't changed much since the last newsletter [which in spite of Johnny's best intentions, had appeared for two years running, then tailed away to a sporadic maybe-every-other-three or four]. The oil business, as Lor Davis can probably testify out there in Long Beach, is good; other ventures moving well. We're expanding a bit, adding a couple of other interests; maybe more to come. Other than that, life drifts along in typical Main Line fashion. Lots of socializing, lots of parties. Very important to the girls, not so important to me. Active in a lot of charities, as usual. You know me! If anybody ever gets to Philadelphia—who *ever* gets to Philadelphia—look us up. We'd love to see you. I may be on the West Coast on business soon. I'll try to drop by school, anyway, and see Johnny, Duke and Moose. Keep in touch, everybody."

This, Smitty congratulated himself as he prepared with two other colleagues to go back for their third trip into the jungles and rice paddies of North Korea, sounded suitably innocuous—suitably Main Line. He had written it months ago, sent it to Annelle with directions to readdress it and send it on to Johnny. She had been terrified of his going back into what was now the C.I.A., but the agency had known how to appeal to him: the Communists were on the move, America was threatened, we have to hold them—he agreed with all that, and he knew few had been as skilled as he was in what he did during the war. He was good at infiltration, good at killing. Smith Carriger, who moved so gracefully through charity balls and social entertaining in Philadelphia, was still a whole other being when he applied himself in the service of his country.

This was the third time he had been asked to return and he had promised Annelle it would be the last. But now that he was back in the fearsome and fascinating game, he had to be honest: he might be back again, if he survived this time. If he did, he would come home to San Francisco, visit the campus and see the guys—except for Renny, of course, whom he couldn't stand—and put on a good show. He'd have been in Indonesia, say, checking out oil prospects—or Hong Kong, seeking business contracts—or maybe Taiwan, where the newly established fugitive Nationalist government of Chiang Kai-shek was already showing signs of commercial growth and enterprise.

He was enjoying himself thoroughly in Korea. Dangerous as hell—deadly as could be—but for him the most fascinating and challenging thing he had ever undertaken. Typical of Smitty Carriger—what had the *Daily* said once? "Small, compact, dynamic, pragmatic, ever-efficient Smith Carriger"—he was doing it extremely well.

Franky Miller's was the most recent communication Johnny had received, just yesterday; he hoped the remaining members would report in soon, although the thought had occurred to him, reading Billy's, that it would make sense to hold the newsletter until after the election in November. Then he could report an exciting triumph—providing Willie had one. If not, a note of condolence, support and better-luck-next-time would have to be expressed. But he was confident it would turn out the way Willie wanted. Like most of them, he still had a lot of faith in Willie. He only wished he could get down to the Valley to watch the campaign for a day or two. It would be fun.

Although rarely an impulsive man, he was stopped abruptly by the thought. Why not? He didn't have a class on Fridays or Mondays; the modest little Ford coupe he had bought after the war when cars began to come back onto the roads for civilian use was still in good shape; he could be down there in eight or nine hours barring flat tires, poor roads and other hazards of the highway.

Two minutes later he was on the phone asking the operator to put through a long-distance call to Terra Bella. A minute after that Billy, sounding delighted, was urging him to come on down. Two days later he was on his way. Inevitably, he could see, this issue of the news-letter would be dominated by Willie. But then, hadn't their years as fraternity brothers always been?

Candidate for Congress was a role he had secretly thought of for himself ever since his election as student-body president fourteen years ago. There had been times during the war, particularly when the flak was coming up to surround his plane in Germany, when he was not sure he would live to see the day; but if he did, he often told himself then, Congress would be his objective. Politics had early fascinated him, the game of power and people, the mechanics through which some modest good might be achieved for the country—the means through which, if one was lucky, some small imprint of one's own dreams and character might be left upon the times. At the University his schoolmates had seen a tall, handsome, dashing figure whom many romanticized with a glow of youth and glamour. What his potential constituents saw now was a solid-looking citizen, handsome, dignified, distinguished, already showing a touch of weight, already turning a little gray at the temples, projecting an air of respectability, responsibility—and a subtle aura of being just a cut above his ostentatiously homespun, down-to-earth, country-boy opponent.

This could work either way, Johnny thought.

"Either they're going to decide he's the above-average type they want to have represent them," he told Billy after the Saturday of campaigning with Willie through the district, "or they're going to feel he's a stuck-up s.o.b. who is patronizing their favorite boy and in the process patronizing them."

"It's a danger," Billy admitted. "He's aware of it. He tries to get down on the same level with Jerk Head but sometimes he can't. At that point, I'll say for him, he says the hell with it and gets back to being himself, lump it or like it. They ought to recognize there's integrity in that."

"They should," Johnny agreed. "I'm sure a lot of them do—I do. But then, I'm not a Valley boy. How does it look right now, seriously?"

"Close," Billy said. "We're behind, but we've still got a couple of months. We'll make it."

"It would be great if you did," Johnny said, thinking that it *would* be great to see old Willie get on the national stage and justify the trust and admiration most of them had built up for him over the years. There were a few like Suratt who disliked him and who wouldn't feel this way; for most of them there would be real satisfaction. It would, in a small way, be an endorsement of themselves and of the happy, golden days that now already seemed so long ago and far away.

"How's Donna liking it?" he asked, and just then she came out onto the shady porch from which they were looking across the orange groves and the bare brown hills stretching away down the valley in the late afternoon sun.

"Donna," she said firmly, "likes it just fine." She uttered her merry, undaunted laugh and sat down beside Johnny in the big porch swing. "I haven't had so much fun since Willie was running for student-body president and I was running for vice-president. We made it then and we'll make it now." She chuckled. "I'm already decorating his House office for him. How about that?"

"I think it's great," Johnny said. "And I hope you're right. I understand it's not such an easy life."

"Very challenging," she said. "Willie's ready for that . . . aren't you?" she added as Willie, barefoot, clad in frayed canvas shorts and tattered khaki shirt, came through the door still vigorously toweling his shower-damp hair and sat down in one of the old wicker rockers facing them.

"You bet," he said, dropping the towel on the porch railing. "How about a drink, anybody?"

"I'll get them," she offered and rose quickly before Billy, similarly responsive, could move. "Johnny?"

"Gin and tonic, please. Light."

"Same," Billy said.

"The usual," Willie requested. "I do like a good martini at the end of the day, and Donn mixes a mean one."

"I'm glad I'm good for something," she said, but with a cheerful laugh that appeared to rob it of any sting; although not entirely, Johnny thought, and apparently Willie didn't, either, because just for a second a sad little expression crossed his face—almost instantly gone, but, Johnny thought, he'd make a note of it and see what developed later.

Nothing did, of course, at least on the surface. One or two little remarks that could have been interpreted one way but were summarily dismissed, with laughter, another; one or two sudden changes of expression that were quickly hidden.

They ate dinner on a wooden table under a giant live oak on the lawn. Mrs. Wilson had prepared it, refusing all offers of help and describing it as "one of my campaign contributions to the Congressman." The kids were well behaved, the adults mellow. Jollity and good nature reigned supreme. Johnny reflected that all appeared well with the Wilson family as an obviously rising optimism encouraged them to relax and enjoy their comfortable old ranch house in the groves.

The kids were put to bed after what they considered necessary protests; Mrs. Wilson and Donna disappeared into the kitchen to clean up; Billy, Johnny, Mr. Wilson and Willie returned to the porch. The warm velvet of twilight lingered for a while as distant sounds became muted and fireflies came out to dance above the lawn.

"What do you see as your purpose," Johnny inquired presently, "if you do get elected? As we're all sure you will," he added quickly, in case Willie might think he heard uncertainties. Willie chuckled, face shadowy in the dusk.

"Are you?" he inquired. "You don't sound so positive, Brother John. I'm not, myself, actually. But it's getting better by the day. I'm really getting a response now. I think there's a feeling that the old boy has been there an awfully long time and maybe it's time for younger blood—and, maybe someone who served in the war has a right to have his chance. He served, too, of course, but it was the last war, not our war. So, there's that feeling.

"And then there's a feeling, I think, that it's time for new ideas all around. He hasn't had a new one in thirty years, so I tell them. But of course"—his voice turned wry for a moment in the darkness—"his are big things like farm subsidies and opposition to 'civil rights,' as they are calling them, and stuff like that, that go over very well here. I have to buck the fact that it's really a very conservative constituency, dominated by big ranchers, oil, cotton, citrus, cattle. Agriculture is a formidable power."

"I thought you and Donn always intended to live in San Francisco," Johnny said. "Don't I recall you saying something like that at school?"

"I did," Willie said, voice again a little wry. "But we have the ranch—and there are certain pressures—"

"Oh, now," Mr. Wilson interrupted vigorously. "That isn't fair, Willie, and you know it. Your mother and I never insisted on a thing. We gave you boys your heads entirely. Isn't that right?"

"Right," Willie conceded. "I'm sorry. You and Mom have been fair, all along. But there's Billy—and the ranch as such—and you folks just *being* here—I didn't feel I should dump it all on him, even though I know you told me to, Billy.

"But those were obstacles. And when I got my law degree after the war—well, the logical place to start seemed to be right here. Maybe it's something like Antaeus—I like to touch my own earth, you know? When it came right down to it, I found that it meant more to me than I had anticipated. And Donn agreed—and nothing could be healthier for the kids than growing up on a ranch—and so we're here. Although soon," he added with a chuckle, "to depart for more glamorous climes, I hope. So what do I see as my purpose?

"I think"—his tone became musing—"it is basically to bring a middle view to things. I'm not an extremist, on either side. I'm liberal on some things, perhaps more conservative on others—somewhere down the middle, I like to think—which is not popular in America right now, particularly if you express it as 'a plague on both your houses' and 'the emperor has no clothes.' There are emperors on both sides, and God, they get furious if you say they have no clothes! They can't stand it, either one; although I'm afraid the liberals who dominate the press are the most vindictive emperors of all. They can dish it out but they just can't take it. And they're already zeroing in on me, thanks to Timmy, who inadvertently alerted the pack in his column. He wanted to do me a favor, bless his heart, by running a special piece on the gallant young would-be Congressman from California who's challenging all the odds. All it did was attract their attention."

"Have they been out here?" Johnny asked in surprise. Billy snorted.

"Four or five major dailies, the wire services, some radio people. And more to come."

"And they're not favorable?"

"Don't sound so disbelieving," Willie instructed with something of his old tartness. "It's flattering but unrealistic. My opponent, or Jerk Head, as Billy calls him, and I squared off on the issue of civil rights the other day and we also got onto Communism and the U.S. versus the Soviet Union, and I made the mistake of trying to be fair to both sides. He was rabidly against and so I wound up in the middle, you see. I didn't satisfy some of the constituency who agree with him entirely, and I also made the error of not satisfying some major people in the press who insist you've got to be all-out on the pro side or they'll attack you. I held to what seemed to me a balance, but there are plenty of people in this world who don't want a balance because it upsets their comfortable pre-conceived, one-sided notions. Some of the most powerful are in the press."

"You're damned if you do and damned if you don't," Mr. Wilson remarked and Willie agreed with a hint of glumness, "Yes, it's damned difficult. Anyway, Johnny, they're categorizing me already. 'Disappointingly conservative for one so young,' one of them put it. 'Obviously unaware of the dangers of his rabid-right attitudes,' said another. I'm no more conservative or rabid right than the man in the moon and certainly way to the left of my opponent, but they're already organizing themselves to portray me as that. If I do get in, I'll be neatly sealed, packaged, labeled and filed before I ever arrive in Washington. Every reference to me thereafter will come with a ready-made 'conservative' label. It's vicious and unfair but who gives a damn about that? I can see it coming . . . But," he said, and his voice, though bleak, was determined. "I'm damned if I'm going to let that stop me from trying to articulate a middle way on things." His tone turned wry. "If I get there at all, that is, which is unknown at the present."

They were silent for a moment. Far off on the country road somewhere a car changed gears and honked at some night thing in the deepening dusk.

"It isn't as easy as student-body president, is it, Willie?" Johnny inquired with a wryness of his own. Willie grunted.

"It isn't easy at all. That was child's play, of course, looking back now."

"Important at the time, though," Johnny said. "It meant a lot to all us then. You shouldn't scoff at it now."

"Oh, I don't," Willie said. "I really don't. It was good training, for one thing. I tried to do good, and I want to do good here. But it's a rougher road, by far."

"But you're going to make it," Billy said stoutly.

"Maybe," Willie said. "I'm sure as hell trying hard."

And he was, he reflected on Monday afternoon after they had all stood on the porch and waved Johnny off on his journey back to the University. The visit had been good for him, it was heartening to find that some of the old respect and adulation still clung, and that not only his family still made the connection between youthful promise and mature fulfillment. The campaign was getting to him more than he wanted anyone to know, and if Johnny and Billy and Timmy still saw it as a romantic challenge in which he appeared somewhat larger than life, a Young-Lochinvar-Come-Out-of-the-West to ride out and conquer the dream city by the Potomac, well, that was good for his ego and a needed shot in the arm for a campaign that sometimes seemed to him to have no formal ending, just an eternal slog from one small dusty town to another until he thought his endurance must finally break under the relentless pressures of it all.

This, for instance, had been a rare time at home, a few precious hours snatched from the maw of politics. In the past week he had once again traveled the entire district; spoken at fifteen at-homes arranged by members of the Women for Wilson Committee; addressed Rotary and Lions lunches; appeared at five small campaign rallies; been on three radio and television programs; given four newspaper interviews and issued through his campaign headquarters two "position papers" on major issues. He felt uneasily that these last could seem a little pompous and pretentious, and Donna had questioned their wisdom, but he had decided stubbornly that if his views were worth anything, they were worth putting on the record and articulating well.

As a result of all this, one small weekly paper in the far southern end of the district had switched endorsement from his opponent to him, and three members of his campaign committee had called to report a "very favorable response" to his appearances. If that meant votes, who could tell? It was all so amorphous, so uncertain, so— wearing.

But you went on, because that was the way it was done in America. No neat, short campaigns dictated by custom and by law, no swift, inexpensive decisions. It just went on, in a chaotic, costly fashion, until it ended, somewhere off there in some future that was really only a few weeks away but often seemed forever.

Physically, he seemed to be holding up well. If there was a tendency, which had alarmed him a little lately, to acquire a slight bulge around the middle, meals on the run helped to keep it under control. If he found himself thinking too much when he finally got to bed, sheer exhaustion drove him to sleep.

If tiredness drove him to being impatient with, and in some ways slighting, his family, well—that was a problem.

Thirteen years of marriage, three children, a companionship that until recently had always provided him with bright, sunny, determinedly optimistic support—it was hard to realize that now there seemed to be threatening things. He told himself it was not his fault, not Donna's fault. But they were threatened, all the same.

How this had come about he wasn't exactly sure, except that he was certain it could be attributed principally to the damned campaign—or could it? Thinking back now as the unusually quiet Monday afternoon unfolded, he was beginning to see that its roots went deeper, to a growing boredom he did not like to acknowledge because it was unfair to Donn. She certainly never failed him in any way he could honestly single out and say: this is it. The physical side of their marriage had never been ecstatic after the first few months, but he assumed, since it was such a universal cliché, that this was no different from nine tenths of the population. Aside from some regret that he decided was an inevitable part of maturing, he had not concerned himself with it overmuch. It would be nice to have moonlight and roses forever after, but who did? Not Guy Unruh, probably his all-time best friend, with whom he discussed it several times. Not Billy, who admitted that even what everybody considered "the perfect marriage" to Janie had become comfortably routine over the years. People settled: comfort and routine were what they settled for. Why should he expect his life to be any different?

For a little while after the war when the excitement of marriage was briefly revived by his return, as it had been for so many, he had hoped this would not be the case. Then, like so many, it had "returned to normal," as he supposed it could be stated. Again like so many, he had entertained brief ideas of supplementing it with more exciting adventures. He supposed old campaigners like Unruh and Gulbransen probably did this all the time, though Gulbransen certainly indicated that it was rather empty for him. The two or three brief occasions when Willie had tried it had been empty for him. It was also time-consuming, worrisome and demanded a concentration and craftiness that he found not worth the game. He had too many other important things to think about. And, when all was said and done, there was Donna—too good to be true, as people had been saying about her all her life, and certainly too good to ever give him cause for worry. Being unfair to her was being unfair to himself, he decided. So he stopped it.

That, however, did not alleviate the increasing boredom he felt with her, with their family and with his life. There again, there was no tangible justification. The kids were developing well, though Latt, darkly handsome, extremely intelligent, aware of his own charm at age eight and already showing signs of a fierce and domineering independence, was now at the point at which parents suddenly think:

This kid could be a real handful. This kid could be a challenge. This kid could be an enemy someday, unless we play our cards right. And where are the rules that tell us how to do that?

Amos at six was a complete contrast, gentle, outgoing, trusting, instinctively kind—his mother replicated. Clayne at two was still a roly-poly little doll, her blond beauty and shy, pleased little smile melting all adult hearts; still unformed in many ways but giving signs of fitting temperamentally somewhere between her brothers, determined but with enough of Amos' gentle goodwill to permit her to negotiate smoothly around life's harsher corners. "Wonderful kids," people said, "a beautiful family."

"But of course," Tony Andrade had remarked just a few weeks ago when he and Louise stopped by to see the ranch on their way up from a weekend with Lor and Angie in Palos Verdes, "nobody would expect you and Donna to have anything else, Willie. The Lord wouldn't dare." Which like many of Andrade's remarks, did not have the sting of Renny Suratt's sarcasm but had a characteristic little bite in it somewhere, under the amiable and instant grin.

Well—Tony. He and Andrade had shared knowledge between them, but all now seemed to be well in that sector. Tony's life was moving along smoothly, his kids were bubbly little Italian extroverts all, Louise with her shrewd intelligence seemed content. What more could you ask of Tony? He had paid his dues, whatever might have gone before.

But even if Willie's own family appeared "wonderful" and "beautiful" and even if Donn was still the relentless fountain of love, support and goodwill—that wasn't fair, either, that word "relentless"; but of course it fit—a certain restlessness had seemed to overtake him in recent years. In the average case, he supposed, this might well have pushed him toward renewed infidelities. In his case, life's sometimes startling timing seemed to have impelled him, somewhat sooner than he had intended, to try to transform his political dreams into action. One result of that seemed to be an even deeper impatience with his "perfect" domestic situation—which, in the eyes of many, he was required to have if he was to be the "perfect" candidate. So there he was.

Arrived at this ironic point in his musings, he has been interrupted by a series of telephone calls from campaign workers around the district and a visit from his secretary, an earnest, bespectacled high school classmate from the local Slavic colony, who was fast becoming the ideal old-maid secretary. She had the week's schedule of speeches and appearances pretty well worked out, and after they had gone over them in detail, accepted Donna's invitation to stay and have supper. The kids came in from the ranch, where Latt had been making his first tries at horseback riding under the tutelage of one of the younger Mexican hands while Amos and Clayne played quietly with the inevitable kittens that lived around the stable. His parents departed to visit friends at an adjoining ranch. The earth, exhausted from the day's 100-degree temperature, relaxed gently into the long, slow twilight. The great valley, and particularly his part of it, became quiet and at peace.

Supper ended. The kids were put to bed. Helena Ivancovitch, one of "the many itches and vitches" as his father put it, of the Slav colony whose members had settled in this part of the Valley years ago and now were quite successful growing cotton, fruit and vegetables out on the flat, said her shy good night and left. He and Donn were alone. An awkward little silence fell. He realized "awkward" was the word, didn't like it, but acknowledged that, increasingly, that's what it was. He didn't think it was fair, took it to be some sort of implicit criticism of himself, let it provoke him into impatience—knew he shouldn't— couldn't help it.

"You're awfully quiet tonight, for you," he said, more sharply than he intended, more sharply than he should. "Why is that?"

"Am I?" she said mildly across the ten feet or so that separated her wicker rocker from his. "I'm sorry, Willie. I should be more sparkly. That's always what's expected of me, isn't it? Good old Donna, full of beans. How could I fail the candidate when he needs me so much? Or does he?"

"No need to be sarcastic," he said, moderating his tone a bit. "I didn't mean to sound challenging—"

"Well, you did."

"I'm sorry."

"Don't be. It doesn't become you."

"Oh, listen—" he began, but quite uncharacteristically, she would have none of it.

"Don't. Just let it drop. All right?"

For a moment he was too taken aback to respond. Then he began again, tone much modified. He realized abruptly that this was apparently turning into something quite serious.

"I'm sorry if I sounded sharp," he said. "I get so tired and drawn so thin by this damned campaign that I forget sometimes that of course you must be, too. I don't mean to take it out on you."

"Well, you do," she said, and for once good old upbeat, bubbly, unfailingly bright and sunny Donna sounded like any other aggrieved wife confronted with the exclusionary demands of her husband's life. "And"—her voice trembled for just a moment—"I don't know why. I try to be supportive."

"Oh, you are," he said earnestly. "You are. Don't ever think you're not. I don't know what I'd do without you."

"So you say," she said, tone steadier and an unusual sarcasm creeping into it. "But I daresay you'd survive."

"What's the matter?" he demanded. "Do you want to go with me on the campaign? I thought you had your fill of that and wanted to stay home except for special occasions. But come if you'd like. You know the daily grind is no picnic. But you're welcome if you want to take another shot at it."

"It obviously means more to you than your family."

"Are you jealous?" he asked, suddenly feeling his bone-weariness a hundredfold. "In God's name, of what? Politics? Because if so, I thought you understood, 'way back in school, that politics is sometimes very consuming; particularly big politics, like this."

"Oh, I know all that," she said impatiently. "Of course it is. But I thought you would be able to balance it a little better with your family and—and with me. I thought if anybody could do it, Willie Wonderful could." Her voice sounded unsteady again. "I knew you were getting bored with us a long time ago. Bored with me. But now—now you have an excuse. You can stay away all the time and just—just *be* bored."

"I am *not*," he said desperately, although of course they both knew he was. "I am not. I have a great wife and a great family—"

"So everybody says."

"Well, damn it, it's true. I couldn't do a thing without you—"

"You've always been able to do without anybody. You've always been so—so—self-sufficient. I sometimes think it's a miracle that you've been able to fit us in at all."

"Oh, Donn—"

"Yes, 'Oh, Donn'! I've always been just an—an adjunct, not a part. And so are the kids."

"Well, if you think that," he said, "then what's the solution? Shall I give up the campaign? Do you want a divorce?"

"Oh, of course not! Of course not, don't be silly. You'll never give up your political plans and I don't want a divorce. The kids and I just want more—more attention, I guess. More attention and more— more love, if that isn't too corny for you. Is that too much to ask?"

He was silent for a moment as far off on the grove road they could hear a car begin the slow grind up the long shank of hill where the ranch house sat in its commanding position above the valley. Probably the folks, coming home from their visit. He hoped so. It would stop what he could only regard as a pointless conversation. Because nothing was going to change. They both knew that.

"Look," he said, trying to make his expression earnest and supplicating, though they were only shadowy outlines to one another in the full depth of Valley night. "I do love you. I do love the kids. I'm afraid it's part of politics, however, that inevitably people who go into it, at least on a major level, find that it is a very demanding thing and that it *is* hard to adjust family needs and obligations to the demands of public life. You know that, Donn. It's not exactly an original thought. It just happens to be our turn to find out that it's true. If I continue this—if I get elected now or next time or whenever—we're going to have to adjust to it. At least"—he tried hard to sound wry and self-deprecatory—"you know you're not competing with another woman. I can assure you of that. Where would I find the time, even if I wanted to, which I don't. All you're competing with is politics."

"All!" she echoed, equally wry. "Oh, Willie. You're incorrigible."

"But yours," he said as the folks' car lights flicked over them briefly and then swung away as they drove past the house to park in the broad graveled parking area in back.

"I'd like to think so," she said, coming over to give him a quick kiss as his parents came in the back door and went to their room upstairs. "But I've never really been sure." A certain dryness came into her voice. "You can count on me, though, you know that. You can always count on old Donn."

"In which I am very lucky," he said. "And don't you ever think I underestimate it."

But perhaps she did, he thought as she went on in to get ready for bed and he remained behind for a while to relax in the soft little wind that came to him gently from across the Valley. Perhaps she did. And perhaps rightly, for perhaps his attachment to domesticity had always been less than hers—less than most people's. Perhaps bigger goals had always instinctively been his.

Were there bigger goals?

He shivered a little in the gentle wind, which brought intimations of things he did not want to face right now. He told himself defensively that he had enough on his mind. He had to concentrate on winning. That was all that mattered, right now.

*   *   *

"Things are going O.K. up here," Franky Miller wrote from Medford, Oregon. "Katie is doing just fine. Franky Jr. is on the high school football team in his freshman year and little Rosie remains our sweet, gentle, lovable one. The doctors tell us she will never get much beyond age eight mentally but she'll always be happy and make everyone around her happy. So we have many blessings and can't complain. As for the old man, I'm still helping Katie's Dad in the auto business. Sales seem to get better every year. People can't seem to get enough new cars in the postwar boom and that's all to the good for us. Come see us. It's wet up here!"

Which, he thought as he finished his brief note to Johnny Herbert, would make everybody smile and say, "Good old Franky. Still playing it for laughs!"

He only wished he were.

He only wished he were.

None of them, so far as he knew, faced anything like a child with Down's syndrome. None of them, so far as he knew, faced a father-in-law like Buck Sullivan. None of them, he was sure, had seen, as devastatingly as he had, the bright hopes of college drizzle away into the looming threat of a dull and lifeless middle age, trapped in the wilds of Medford, Oregon.

That last, he thought, sounded like a shadow of the old, wry Franky—but just a shadow. He didn't think, at thirty-four, that there was much more than a shadow left. In fact, he was becoming sure of it.

A little earlier than most—but, he felt in a wave of the self-pity that seemed to be engulfing him more and more lately, with justification—he was falling victim to the here-I-am-almost-middle-aged-and-what-the-hell-have-I-accomplished-anyway? syndrome. Unlike Down's, which in one of nature's sadder jokes consigned you to seemingly perpetual good nature, the I'm-aging syndrome did not. It went through you, as they used to say in the house, like a dose of salts and every time you thought you had it licked, there it was again. Mocking and sneering. Giggling and gurgling. Knocking you down and each time letting you get back up just a little less tall than you were before. It was hell and he hated it. And he was beginning to feel, in a way whose dangers he recognized but sometimes seemed powerless to avoid, that it was getting a really serious hold on him.

Katie had noticed. Part of the trouble, in fact, was Katie, something he had never in all his college days, and for quite a while thereafter, dreamed he would ever think or feel. All through school their companionship had been recognized by everyone as coming as close to the ideal as envious housemates could imagine. "Miller and Sullivan are always doing some damned thing," everybody said. And enjoying it, too, always with jokes and laughs and a lightheartedness he looked back at now with a wistful and increasingly deep regret. If they could only just chuck it all and go to the beach or go to a dance or something. If only the old carefree days could come back. Those were the fun days, those were the golden times. Those were the years when all the world was right.

Maybe it had something to do with the war, whose universal burden had rested heavy even on those, like himself, who had not been physically engaged. Everyone who had been touched by it—and in one way or another it had touched everyone on the face of the globe—had been changed; some with an obvious, brutal impact, some more subtly but with equal consequence. He might have been one of its unknowing victims. Or maybe it had been destined to happen anyway, given Rosie's birth and Buck's overbearing dominance. And, as Katie—not his cute, ever-loving Katie!—had told him the other day in the midst of unbelievable, searing argument, "given what might be your own innate weakness."

Was he weak? Looking back in bewilderment after that argument, perhaps the worst of the steadily worsening series they seemed to be having, he could not find a weak Franky in the happy-go-lucky, wisecracking Franky who had been one of the bright spots of the house. He could make everybody laugh, he could always produce the wry or sly comment that would deflect anger and restore amiability when adolescent tensions and the forced nearness of living together had produced sudden flash points. Franky Miller weak? But everybody loved Franky, everybody laughed with Franky, Franky was just simply a great guy. Surely there had been some value in that. What had the years done to Katie, that she should have so easily forgotten?

Part of it, of course, was Rosie's condition, which had hit them both—and, he had to admit fairly, Buck and Edith as well—very hard, coming as it did after Franky Jr.'s easy birth and sturdy little mind and body. Nothing wrong with that kid, as Buck often said in his heavy-handed way, sounding judgmental even though he, like everyone else, soon came to love gentle little Rosie. And for a while Franky and Katie had gone through standard feelings of bitter guilt, regret, what-did-we-do and why-are-we-being-punished? Presently this had given way to why-is-*she*-being-punished? and on that more generous and worthy basis they had, he thought, managed to erect a loving and untroubled environment for her, and a deeper and more loving feeling for one another.

Which, he had to admit, still seemed to exist under his own increasing feelings of frustration and inadequacy. The foundation was still strong, he thought, but the superstructure was swaying in the wind a good bit right now. It did not make things easier.

Nor was he entirely sure that he could blame Buck Sullivan for it. Buck was a big, rough-hewn, basically limited man who rode roughshod over everybody and was sometimes quite brutal in his insensitivities. But Franky had to admit honestly that he didn't do so vindictively; he often said, with a puzzled defensiveness, "I'm not out to deliberately make anybody feel bad." He had a knack for it, though. "Your father's ability to cut people down to size may be God-given," Franky had remarked wryly to Katie not long ago, "but it sure as hell has developed into a major talent."

To this, of course, Franky's own relatively subservient position could only contribute. Having been deferred from service in the war, he knew that in his father-in-law's eyes he was something less than adequate, no matter how respectable the reasons and no matter how earnestly Buck really did try to accept the situation. And when Franky, not really wanting to teach sociology, as he had always claimed at the University, had taken the easy way out and accepted a job with the auto agency, that had done it. From then on, Franky sometimes told himself bitterly, he was relegated to "my son-in-law the secondhand auto dealer," no matter that those wartime days were over and the company's new-car sales were by far the major portion of its business.

The firm prospered and Franky prospered with it. He and Katie and the kids moved to their own house across town, began gently to dissolve some of the more obvious silken strands of Edith's compulsive oversight and supervision, creating "a life of their own, which is as it should be," as Edith, secretly upset but bowing to what she knew was inevitable and also right, publicly endorsed it. But the day-to-day contacts with Buck continued, and those, Franky felt, were wearing him down to a God damned frazzle.

"He's destroying me!" he had finally declared to Katie, who had snorted.

"Don't be so melodramatic," she ordered tartly. "He's providing you and us with a very good living and you with a perfectly respectable job. You'll probably inherit the business someday, since my brothers don't seem to be interested. So what is there to complain about?"

"But this isn't what I wanted to do," he could only retort weakly, at which she had snorted again.

"A little late to think about that. You could have gone back to school and gotten a degree and taught. The University might well have had a place for you. Duke Offenberg and Johnny Herbert and Renny Suratt and Moose are all back there now. You could have done it. Why didn't you?"

It was a little later in that same argument that she had struck out at "what might be your own innate weakness," provoking him to shout back at her, "I am not!" in a rare show of open anger and vehemence. The outburst was so foreign to his normally patient nature that the thought of it had actually made him cry later. He had apologized abjectly that night in bed. He noticed, however, that she didn't apologize to him; just, "Well, we all say things we don't mean sometimes," which was as close as she apparently intended to come to it.

It still stung like hell.

So here he was at thirty-five, writing his cheery little note for the newsletter and pretending to the fraternity that all was hunky-dory with him. A handicapped daughter, a domineering father-in-law, a meddling mother-in-law, a wife who was increasingly a long way from the "Katie Sullivan, always laughing, cute as a bug's ear" of campus days—a wife, he told himself morosely, who bites, which she hadn't used to. She understood and forgave me then. Now she doesn't seem to want to.

It was time, over at the high school, for Franky Jr.'s practice to get under way. He decided he would try to get over there and see part of it, as soon as he clinched the sale with the sniffy couple he was working on right now.

Franky Jr. was one who didn't fail him. Franky Jr. liked his dad, looked up to him, thought he was wonderful. Franky Sr. delighted in that. Franky Jr. made up for a hell of a lot. Franky Sr. could hardly wait to get away and go watch him trot sturdily up and down the field. He had lots of potential, did Franky Jr. Franky Sr. sometimes felt he could hardly wait to see what he would become.

*   *   *

Validation through one's offspring, that near-universal concomitant of parenthood, was something North McAllister also thought about a lot—virtually all the time, he reflected unhappily as he, too, scribbled off his response to Johnny Herbert. From his office window in Salt Lake City he could see the snow-topped Wasatch Mountains, clear and stark in the crisp October air. They looked pure—pure. He wasn't, he told himself, not by a long shot—not by a long shot. Two children and fourteen years of marriage had not changed his internal struggle. They didn't alleviate it any, even though in Jason he found a pledge to the future that he thought he might be able to keep. Jason gave promise of being the absolute, unthreatened male North had always felt he should have been. In Jason he placed many hopes and saw the promised redemption of many things.

Not that the handsome, dignified, seemingly steady and stable thirty-four-year-old whom his world knew as Dr. McAllister was ever regarded with anything other than respect by colleagues, patients and friends. His reputation as an internist and general practitioner was steadily rising; his standing as husband, father, increasingly active and increasingly respected civic figure was apparently unassailable. Only he, two other friends in Utah and the nameless casual contacts whom he met at medical conventions or in the anonymous bars when he went home, sometimes alone, to visit his parents in Los Angeles, knew anything to the contrary.

Certainly B.J., he was sure, had never suspected anything at all. Her honest, straightforward approach to life, as direct, innocent and uncomplicated as Donna Wilson's, held no place for even the remotest speculations. He had seen to it with the most careful circumspection that nothing would ever give her the slightest cause for doubt. He sometimes thought the strain of it would tear him apart but it never did because he knew with absolute certainty that it was worth it. Worth it for B.J. and the kids—and worth it for the other. Caught in the middle, he often told himself with a bitter defiance, and here, by God, I'm going to stay.

He would never leave his family, he knew that beyond the remotest question. And though he had tried very hard sometimes to leave the other, he had found it was not to be. It was too strong; different in some ways, ways he had finally decided were basically superficial, but as imperative, once recognized, as its competitor. He had come to perceive the two, in fact, as two sides of the same coin, "Sex," an older friend had once told him, "has no gender. It just wants out." It had taken him a while to accept that but it made things much easier when he finally did. Or as easy as he had decided they were ever going to be.

For Betty June Letterman, "the brightest girl in the University," which she indeed was, sharing with poor Bill Lattimer the highest grade-point average in school, he found as time went on that he had developed a deep and genuine love. He had never wanted to hurt her, which was why he had been so reluctant to commit himself to marriage. The Wilson brothers—Billy, whom he had fallen in love with, was still and always would be in love with, and Willie, dominant, persuasive and overriding—had told him that he must put aside his fears and hesitations. It was, they told him on the eve of graduation in 1939, the only way out.

He had been skeptical and afraid, but in those days that was the accepted wisdom. The tradition—and, though rarely admitted candidly, the hope—was that marriage would be the miraculous resolver of all things—from warts, as he had put it wryly to himself, to tapeworms, and back again. In the majority of cases that was the way it worked out. Many things were pushed back, drowned, submerged, when two people walked down the aisle. With luck they never resurfaced. It they did, divorces happened, though not so many, in his generation: divorce was not a casual matter then. You made your bargain and you tried to keep it; and although only he and the Wilsons knew how shaky his was, he had.

B.J., honest heart happy and honest nature unsuspecting, had plunged into marriage with the same enthusiasm as Donna. Willie's problems were not North's, North was sure, but he wasn't the easiest of characters to accommodate to. The two girls, who were famous on campus for being into everything, serving on committees, heading charity drives, organizing class functions, "chairing most things good and all things noble," as Franky Miller had put it, had approached their marriages in the same spirit. Believing in goodwill, good nature, good values, what their children would eventually call "good vibes," they went at it with a will. The results, three kids there, two here, respectable family lives, what the world saw as completely solid and unshakable marriages—what else, old classmates asked, was to be expected of B.J. Letterman and Donna Van Dyke? They had always been paragons on campus: it was assumed they would be paragons always. And although Donn was beginning to have some doubts, B.J. seemingly never wavered in her faith in the goodness of things. North was determined that she never would.

Which did not, of course, do much to ease the pressures. He was scrupulous about staying away from temptations, avoiding the slightest hint of the obvious. His two long-standing friends elsewhere in Utah, one older, one younger, both also married, joined him twice a year on fishing and hunting expeditions in the mountains. Otherwise, except on the rare occasions when one or the other happened to be in Salt Lake on business, at which times their meetings were hurried at best, their paths did not cross. All the wives were happy for them to have their joint chance "to just get away and relax," and, thus officially sanctioned, they managed. That, and "the casuals," as he thought of them, whom he met on his rare trips out of state.

So life was going along—or had been, until two months ago when he had "met someone," as he described it to himself. A young Mormon minister in his late twenties, also handsome, outgoing, likable, easy of manner, comfortable of nature—and what else? What was the magic? Hard to say: it just *was*. Who ever knew the reasons, in any sexual contact? It just happened, and there you were.

And so it had happened to him, and once again, as with Billy Wilson, he was plunged into heights of glory, depths of despair. There was no problem with Jack—what an ordinary name, for so extraordinary a person!—he didn't have Billy's reservations, the response had been instantaneous and, on the three occasions they had managed so far, wonderful. But now there kept nagging at North the unjustness of it—to others, not to them—and the impossibility "that anything could come of it," as he had said the last time.

"Why does anything have to 'come of it'?" Jack had asked, looking at him with the lazy smile that already had his heart forever in its grasp. "Why can't we just ride along and enjoy it? I don't expect to leave S.L. and you don't either. We don't intend to parade it in the streets or do it in front of the Tabernacle to the accompaniment of the Mormon choir. So why worry?"

"You wouldn't understand," North said. "You're not married."

"That's clear," Jack said. "But I'm not giving up. I expect it'll happen."

"And then what?" North demanded, alarm too obvious. Jack laughed.

"Will you stop worrying? I'm here. I'll always be here. I'm not the type that runs away. Once I've found somebody, I stay with him. Or I would have, if I'd ever found anybody. I never have. Now I have. So knock it off, O.K.?"

"Well," North said doubtfully. "All right."

"I should think so," Jack said comfortably. "I should think so!"

But of course it wasn't that easy for North, he thought as he completed his cheerful, innocuous little note to Johnny. All's well with old North, that's the gist of it, he told himself wryly. Old calm-and-confident over here in the desert is doing just O.K. with everything.

Hadn't his wife told him so, just this morning?

"When you write Johnny," she said as she prepared to dash off to some meeting of something somewhere, one of the ever-widening circle of activities that was already making her one of Salt Lake's busiest and most valued young civic-minded matrons, "you tell him that we have wonderful kids, a wonderful marriage and a wonderful life. O.K.?"

"Do we?" he asked with a smile that was slightly quizzical but genuinely loving and friendly.

"You bet!" she said firmly. "Don't we?"

"Sure we do," he said, responding to her kiss wholeheartedly, whatever his reservations. "We surely do. And I'll tell Johnny to tell the house that, too."

"You do that," she said, "and say I send my best to everybody. I wish we could see some of them. I'd like to see Donna and Willie."

"So would I," he said, sounding so heartfelt that for just a second she looked a little surprised. "Maybe we can one of these days," he added quickly. "The A.M.A. is going to meet in Washington in the spring. Maybe Willie will be in Congress by then and we can see them."

"Wouldn't that be great?" she said with a pleased smile. "I've got my fingers crossed for him."

"Me, too," he said. Maybe seeing Willie again would be a help, although in all probability Willie would just say: stay with it. Which is what he intended to do anyway, he told himself as he watched her busy little figure, beginning ever so slightly to go to fat, get into the car and prepare to pull out of the driveway.

Which is what he intended to do anyway.

Southeast in New Mexico the brightest—and, his bishop often thought with an exasperated but accepting little sigh, potentially the most difficult—young priest in the archdiocese of Albuquerque was contemplating the dreamed-of and planned-for future that was now, to his delight, apparently beginning to open up for him.

Randy Carrero—Father Carrero to you, bud, he had thought with fond amusement when he received Johnny's "Hey, Randy!" inquiry—was enjoying one of his favorite pastimes. Thinking—in the open—on a rock—with desert stretching away on all sides—with a rim of circling mountains on the far horizon in the hazy purple light of October afternoon—with only the furtive sounds of secret, busy desert animal life and a cool little wind rustling the sands and gnarled chaparral to break the antediluvian silence.

Time beyond time, he thought. Age beyond age. How small, man. And how important.

To himself.

And, he realized, almost hugging himself in his exhilaration, how important at times to others—others whom he had, with great determination and easy skill, cultivated in the five years since his graduation from seminary and his ordination as priest.

He had been what was known "in the business," as he put it ironically to himself, as a "late vocation" man, one who had come to the Church relatively late in life as the Church judged things. He had been turning twenty-five when the war ended and he had finally decided to "put Juan out of his misery" and take orders. His cousin Juan had been in the Church since age fifteen and had been the major influence constantly urging Randy to do the same. After many long struggles with his ambitions and his dreams of other things—and with what was officially described as "his carnal nature," although he had always realistically accepted it and never regarded it as all that bad—he had finally agreed to make the experiment.

"You can always leave," Juan said, "although I would certainly be greatly disappointed if you did. But it happens."

"If I go into it," Randy said, "I'll stay. I don't do things halfway."

"I know you don't," Juan said, half admiring, half wistfully mocking. "That's the only thing that worries me. You're so intense. If you go into it you'll probably wind up shooting your way onto the throne of Saint Peter. You're just the type."

"I won't go that far," Randy said; and added with a grin, "but, hell. Why should a guy settle for second best?"

It had taken him a while to get over the secret feeling that his entry into the priesthood was settling for second best, a while to fully accept his vocation. Many hours, many studies, many confessions later, he had finally made the crossover fully; or so he was able to convince himself. His "carnal nature" had demanded, still demanded, always would demand, he suspected, a little sterner handling. There had been times in the truncated two years of seminary that he had been required, as a college graduate, to take, when he had received various offers, had various opportunities: there was an underlayer of the Catholic establishment that everyone knew about, everyone pretended was not there. This he had rejected, since it had never been for him. The simple release of physical tensions, to which so many secretly resorted, he still used, knew he always would, dismissed it with his customary blunt, pragmatic, matter-of-fact realism. It was his business; so what? He doubted if the Lord would deny him entry into heaven for a "sin" so practical and universal. Like so many in the Church, he felt the whole concept of celibacy was the real crime against nature; but like so many under Rome's authority he kept his own counsel ("For once," Juan told him dryly) and prudently did not say so.

So at thirty-two he was, he felt, the same solid citizen he had always intended to be, if in a more specialized discipline than he had originally planned. The shock of Latt's death, for which he still blamed himself bitterly, his unhappiness over what he regarded as his self-betrayal in permitting himself to become so obsessed with Fluff Stevens, which had led directly to that last awful ride up Palm Drive with Latt—had probably combined, in some, powerful, subconscious way, to bring him to where he was now. He had promised Latt, when Latt was dead and he was lying in the hospital with his broken back and other injuries, that he would do something good with his life for Latt's sake. He had the chance now.

And so far, he told himself as the wind became a little cooler and stronger, the light a little less distinct, the ground darker, the mountains softer on the horizon, he had managed to accomplish a good deal.

He had served five years with the priest of a little church in one of the remoter towns in southern New Mexico, a town as primitive and ancient as though Spain still ruled and the twentieth century was yet undreamed of. To the Indian and Mexican parishioners he had been, as they told one another and eventually, discreetly, told him, "a fresh wind" compared to the elderly, kindly but almost hopelessly incompetent old man who was formally in charge.

Father Salvatore had served the Church for forty faithful years, and since he was a good but dull and unremarkable man, he had been carried on the rolls and passed from small parish to small parish all his life. Dull and unremarkable he might be, but not entirely a fool: he knew what was being done to him, but being too unenterprising and presently too old and too afraid to reenter the world and seek something else to support himself, he had found the solace so many did. Randy, like many another young priest, told himself bluntly that he had been sent to bolster up one of the Church's many charity cases— one of "the drunks or crazies you may be called upon to assist in some small parish," as the head of seminary had warned him. Father Salvatore was not crazy, just befuddled; but he certainly was drunk, most of the time. Randy knew his superiors in this assignment had counted on him to be kind, and since that was a basic part of his nature, he had been. Father Salvatore successfully survived his final five years on his way to pasture with his young aide's compassionate assistance.

From there, since Randy's conduct was carefully observed and much approved, and since he had also made it a point to get into Albuquerque as often as he could find excuse and become friendly with the archbishop, he found himself with satisfying suddenness ensconced at headquarters as one of the archbishop's junior secretaries. Basically, he reflected with some humor, it was much like campus politics or politics anywhere: it was whom you knew, how well you knew them, how skillfully you brought yourself to their attention and how astutely you convinced them that you were indispensable. And, of course, how diligently and well you made use of the opportunity once it had been given you.

So he had made himself "indispensable" to his superior to the best of his abilities, which were great. The Phi Beta Kappa intelligence, the shrewd, realistic mind, the physical attractiveness and smiling efficiency that made him so appealing to so many, brought their swift rewards. In two months' time, as one of his jealous fellows remarked, he was "the old man's darling." He heard this, ignored it at the time, later when the chance came, dropped a word that helped consign his detractor to a minor parish in the boondocks for a while, and made sure the word got around. "Don't fool with Carrero"—or, as one of his partisans put it delightedly, *"Non messum Carrerocum"*—quickly be came an article of local faith; blandly impervious, he did not have to make his point again. The archbishop heard, smiled, made note where note would have future value. Now at thirty-two Randy found himself in possession of the prize they all wanted.

He was on his way to Rome.

Rome. Rome! *Rome!* ROME!

He almost sang the name aloud in the growing sunset.

Assigned to the North American College. At the heart of the Catholic world. In the eye of the Vatican. Where the Pope, he told himself with a gurgle of laughter, might trip over him every morning.

"I'll make sure he does," he said aloud, to the surprise of a ground squirrel that gave a startled chirp and dived into its burrow. "Maybe I won't have to shoot my way onto the throne, after all."

But that was far off. Right now he had a great item for Johnny's newsletter. Right now he had enough for one ambitious young mind to handle.

"Latt," he said, more soberly, and started to cry. "Maybe I'll make you proud of me yet."

It was late, he just had time to make vespers and dinner.

He left his rock, walked up the worn little trail he had used so often, got into the diocese's rattly old Ford, drove off.

The sun died spectacularly in the west, the wind subsided, day sounds gave way to nocturnal.

Night claimed the desert.

Already in Rome, not entirely sure how he happened to be there, not exactly sure how he would explain it in his response to Johnny's note, Hack Haggerty looked out over the sprawling umber city to the dome of St. Peter's and listened to the growing cacophony from the streets below.

Noise.

Loud, brash, bustling, insistent.

Utterly unselfconscious.

Utterly self-absorbed.

Growing steadily louder by the minute.

Roman noise—life noise.

It was his first morning back in seven years and he loved it. Loved it and at the same time wanted to cry because here he was at last again in one of his most favorite cities in all the world—

Alone.

Fran, he thought. Oh, Fran. Where have you gone, beloved? Where have I gone? What am I doing here, so far from you? What are you doing there, so far from me? Where have the years gone, the brightness, the happiness, the love?

Except that he knew the love was not gone. Everything else might go but the love never would. That was what made it so terrible.

A wooden shutter clattered in one of the windows across the street. He realized that he was standing in his own stark naked with a full erection. A lot of good that will do me, he thought bitterly, but if it makes somebody else happy, let them look. He did, however, step back a foot or two. He wasn't quite that Roman yet.

He was still groggy from the flight over. He had intended to sleep late but Fran wouldn't let him. And the city, bright and crisp in late October light, called him. The jet lag would have to take care of itself. He was restless to get up, get out, get going. The grogginess would pass as he wandered the ancient streets. The real sleep would come later, when he had exhausted himself to his limit and could walk no more, think no more unhappy thoughts. When his daemon, unable to function in these past few hectic months of despair and dissolution, might come back again and reassure him, as it always eventually did, that he was a worthwhile human being with worthwhile achievements and aspirations, capable of doing further worthwhile things.

Dressed in T-shirt and jeans, eating breakfast on the roof terrace of Rome's most favored pensione, Scalatini di Espagna at the top of the Spanish Steps, he felt a little better. The city, which had known so infinitely much of human triumph, human despair, human degradation and human glory down the endless centuries, was settling into its characteristic universal hum, one of the great heartbeats of the world that would last until siesta and then be quiet for several hours before roaring back into life for the long Roman night. He finished quickly, descended into the street, walked slowly down the Steps, alive, as almost always in good weather, with the tongues and faces, mostly youthful, of everywhere. He planned a walk to his old favorites, first to the Forum and the Palatine, then back to Piazza Navona for lunch, then on to Castel Sant' Angelo, the Vatican and Trastevere. By then, if he lasted that long, he should be more than ready for sleep. And gnawing thoughts, if not banished, should be beaten down to the point where they could not, at least for a while, keep him from it.

As he progressed slowly, with the necessary automatic self-defensive nimbleness, through the incessant, heedless traffic that clogged the ancient labyrinthine ways, his mind kept coming back in helpless repetition to their last farewell—"last" for now, he told himself with a desperate defiance, even though she had seemed to indicate that for her it might be their last forever. He could not accept that. He was sure that in her heart of hearts she couldn't, either. He was Edward Paul Haggerty, after all; she was Francine Magruder.

They had been sanctified as one in Memorial Church in June of 1939. They *were* one. It was part of an ordered universe. How could she possibly feel otherwise?

He told himself, as one more snorting Vespa squeezed him against an ancient wall in its headlong passage, that he would not let her feel otherwise. He would not let her do this to them. He wouldn't let her do this to *him*. He *was* Edward Paul Haggerty, whose name was beginning to mean something. Things like this shouldn't happen to people whose names were beginning to mean something.

At which he had the grace to snort, which made a fat old lady carrying a basket of vegetables give him a keen look and a questioning "*Signor?*" as they edged past one another on the narrow sidewalk. "*Buon giorno,*" he said, managing a reasonably cheerful smile. He suspected he didn't fool her, though: Italians were on a special wavelength when it came to troubled hearts. And certainly his was troubled enough.

The last time he had been in this city he had spent the night of V-J Day sitting outside a trattoria just off St. Peter's Square, composing the first pages of what had turned out to be his *Roman Suite: The Caesars*, known generally now simply as *The Caesars*. Not exactly a threat to Respighi's *The Pines of Rome* but not all that bad, either. In fact, damned good, and, after seven years in which it had been played by five major orchestras across the United States, on its way to becoming something of a minor standard. Maybe he would come out of this visit with *Roman Suite II*. Or more likely, he told himself with another snort, "Kick Me, Baby, in the Head, I Can't Believe Our Love Is Dead."

He was not, in fact, a bad composer in either the classical discipline or the popular. He was getting better in both. And, as he had recognized at the University, his basic inspiration had been, was, and always would be, his wife.

Oh, Fran, he thought again. Why are you so—so—

He felt he really might cry, and that was no help, either. He shook his head and walked doggedly on, past the Trevi Fountain, toward the Forum. He thought he might stop when he reached the Palatine and sit there for a while surrounded by the ghosts of the terrible emperors, endlessly fascinating, eternally alive in their monstrous, exaggerated humanity. He could understand them: if everyone told you you were a god, how could you not believe it and do frightful things in the name of your own divinity? Maybe there, on the very ground where they had lusted, plotted, murdered, died, he would be able to forget for a little while the sad tangle his own life had lately become.

HOUSE OF LIVIA, a small sign said. Nearby a few fragmented pediments lay among the scrawny weeds and grasses under the whispering pines. He found the ruin of a moss-covered column and sat down.

He supposed it had really begun at the University, in those recurring arguments over future careers that he and Fran had indulged themselves in together. They shouldn't have, even then when it had seemed to be mostly in jest. His career versus her career, her concept of family versus his. Two strong personalities, always concluding with a laugh and a joke and the certainty that love would carry them through everything to a solid and steady resolution. Only it hadn't.

For a while after the war, perhaps yes, when she had joined one of San Francisco's major law firms and he had found a job teaching music and conducting the orchestra at one of the city's small community colleges. They had agreed that they would wait a while for children, then found that Fran, for all her professed desire for them in college, really didn't seem to want any.

"But I thought you wanted kids," he said with unconcealed dismay when he began to realize her reluctance. "What was all that talk about how it would be difficult to raise a family because I might be on the road with a band somewhere? I'm not on the road, I'm right here."

"I don't trust it," she said thoughtfully, a frown creasing her normally serene forehead, worry marring for a moment her gravely classical beauty. "I still expect you to take off sometime when I'm not looking. You have that band. You've already been down to L.A.—"

"Only that one weekend. And only because one of my students told his father about us and he paid our way down for the sister's wedding."

"It was a start," she said. "You won't be able to stop there, Hack Haggerty, I know you."

And of course he hadn't. He had formed the band from a handful of his best instrumentalists in the orchestra, which, like most student aggregations, was generally awful. But, as with many of them, a few with real ability stood out amid the off-key clarinets, uncertain trumpets and valiantly wobbling trombones. "Just for the hell of it," he had asked the best half-dozen to join him in playing contemporary music. Long before the practice became popular, he decided to choose the most incongruous name he could think of for the group.

CITY STRUGGLES TO MEET TRANSIT OBLIGATIONS a headline in the *Chronicle* said. "Transit Obligations" the band became.

As Transit Obligations they began to pick up engagements around the Bay, aided by invitations from several veterans who remembered Hack and the Sad Sack Ramblers from the European theater. Two were social chairmen for their clubs, one was on the organizing committee for a major charity ball in Oakland. Once rolling, the thing grew. It wasn't difficult if the group was good. Hack had been organizing and leading dance bands since junior year in high school. Under his practiced tutelage, as he often noted approvingly, Transit Obligations was damned good and steadily getting better.

Meanwhile his composing also progressed. He had never taken formal music courses, learned composition basically, as he said, "by listening and doing."

He was a quick study, an easy learner; and he did have, as everyone recognized, a genuine native talent that at times came close to genius. He read the scores of the great composers as others read books, played them over and over to himself on the piano, gradually discovered which techniques produced which results. His earliest compositions, such as *A Walk on the Quad* in his senior year at college, were derivative of Delius, Vaughan Williams and Debussy, but starting with *The Caesars* everything after the war had been distinctively his. He was now working on a *First Symphony*, a working title that struck him as mighty pompous but one had to start somewhere and the first, after all, was the first. If he had to pick some simulacrum for this one it would be Gershwin and *Rhapsody in Blue*. But its sinuous rhythms and startling climaxes were his own and, he hoped, exciting, and new. Certainly they were for him.

With *The Caesars* and several shorter compositions on contemporary themes, he was beginning to come to the attention of music critics. He found them to be as riven by fads, controlled by groupthink, besotted with favorites, demanding of worship and hostile to independence and originality as critics in any other form of artistic discipline.

Several of them had given *The Caesars* praise, then savaged his other efforts. Like Willie in a different context, he was beginning to suspect that he would spend a lot of his time swimming upstream against the conventional wisdom of the establishment. But like Willie, whose attitude would not have surprised him though they hadn't seen each other since school and hadn't compared notes, he basically didn't give a damn.

"Only one person in the world I really have to please," he told Fran in a rare moment of artistic arrogance, "and that's me."

And that, perhaps, was the heart of it, because her reaction had been a smile but a slightly edged, "And what about me?"

"I thought I did please you," he said. "I thought you always approved of my music. You certainly seemed to support me in school."

She frowned, her grave, dark beauty shadowed temporarily.

"You have a great deal of talent," she said, with an objective air, as though she were analyzing a case, which annoyed him. "In fact, I think you may be a genius—"

"I don't have long hair," he interrupted. "I don't cheat on my wife. I don't sleep with choirboys. How do you figure that?"

"Well," she said in the same objective way, "you don't fit a lot of the patterns, I'll admit, but anyway, you may be one. It's a difficult life, though. It isn't stable. It won't be settled."

"Is that the only problem?" he demanded, and answered himself. "Yes, I suppose maybe it is, the way *your* life is developing." He frowned, too, suddenly somber. "You're the one who seems to be getting swallowed up by the law. You're the one who's working overtime and not coming home nights—"

"No more than you."

"Well, as much. I'm only out a night or two on the weekends. You're at that damned office until nine and ten, three or four nights a week. Next they'll be wanting you to go to Sacramento and testify before the legislature. My wife the lobbyist—" He stopped at her expression. "Oh. When do they want you to go?"

"I didn't say they wanted me to go," she said, face flushed. He snorted.

"I know that look that says Fran Magruder is going to do exactly what she wants to do—"

"And I know that look that says that Hack Haggerty is going to do exactly what he wants to do! I'm going next week and I'll be gone for a week. They're trusting me with a lot of responsibility and I'm ready for it!"

"Well, so am I," he retorted, "and from now on I'll have no qualms about playing anywhere, and everywhere, and anytime anybody asks me. It's time to get a little proportion into things here. And I still want kids! And don't blame me for not wanting them! I'm not the one whose career would be disrupted by having them!"

"Exactly! Exactly! If that isn't a typical male attitude!"

"If I had a wife who had a typically female attitude," he snapped, "things might be better!"

"I'm going to the office," she said in a cold tone he had really never heard before.

"At this hour?"

"Nine-thirty. I can get a lot of work done, in peace and quiet. Don't wait up."

"I won't," he said, tone equally cold. "Be careful."

"I will," she said, yanking her coat out of the closet and flinging it on. "I'm not a child."

"Never that," he said as she slammed the door. "Never that."

And now here he was, a tortured year and a half later, sitting amid the scattered stones of Livia's house while the warm October morning lengthened and the sounds of Rome, still tumultuous but muted, rose gently to the haunted grove atop the haunted hill. Directly below in the Forum a few tourists wandered, an easy stone's throw away.

Livia, old girl, he thought, this isn't the only unhappy couple you've had at your house. Probably you would have known what to do with us. You could have poisoned one or the other, or maybe both, and that would have taken care of that. Things aren't so simple these days.

He became aware that someone was approaching behind him, treading softly on the graveled path. A woman, he judged perhaps thirty, came alongside, gave him a calm and perfectly self-possessed sideways glance and murmured, *"Buon giorno, signor."*

"Buon giorno," he said.

"Do you like Livia?" she asked in lightly accented English as he studied her more closely, thinking: standard Italian, big dark eyes, nice cheekbones, generous mouth, pleasant smile, good figure—tall, like Fran—quiet, like Fran—she reminded him of Fran—plus something soft and perhaps a little special coming through. Lunch, perhaps? Bed, perhaps? Any port in a storm, perhaps? How conventional, dearest Fran, how conventional! Where are you, dearest Fran, when I need you now?

"Livia was very bad," he said. "But fascinating."

"They all were," she said, sitting down, uninvited and without coyness, beside him on the stone. "So fascinating. And *so bad.*"

"They are alive here," he said. "Do you come here often?"

"Quite often. And you?"

"I haven't been here in seven years," he said. "Since the end of the war. I was in Rome then. I love Rome. But this is the first time I have been back."

"How sad for you," she said lightly. "You are American, I am sure, and you love Rome. You must come see us more often."

"I intend to," he said; and—abruptly, but what the hell—"I am going to walk to Piazza Navona for lunch. Would you care to join me?"

"How fortunate!" she said with a sudden laugh. "I have nothing to do until four o'clock when I must be at home to receive my two children when they are brought from school."

"Time for a Roman lunch," he said. "My name is"—he hesitated—"Hack."

"Hack," she repeated with a touch of irony. "How American! Mine is Flavia."

"Flavia!" he exclaimed. "How Roman. How really Roman!"

"My mother is a professor of classical studies," she said. "Very bright. My father is an agreeable businessman who doesn't object to anything. So—Flavia."

"You will forgive me if I fall asleep at the table," he said, standing up. "I just flew in from America this morning. I have had a terrible fight with my wife, we may get a divorce, I just more or less flew out just to—to get away somewhere—anywhere—for a few days. And I thought of Rome. It seemed natural."

"Rome is very natural," she said, standing also. "That is what Rome is all about. If you fall asleep I will put you safely in a taxi and tip the driver heavily to make sure that he takes you exactly where you want to go."

"But not before we have exchanged addresses and telephone numbers," he said, offering her his arm as they started down the steep little path into the Forum. "I hope. Flavia."

"Perhaps," she said, with another, perfectly comfortable, laugh. "We shall see. Hack."

Far from Rome, getting ready at last in Charleston, South Carolina, for the wedding family and friends considered long overdue, Jeff Barnett was thinking more of the South than of his own nuptials. He found he was paying more attention to aphorisms as he grew older: "Coming events cast their shadows before" was a recent favorite. There was a rising unease under the surface of things. He sensed it and it worried him. Unlike many of his contemporaries, who told each other nervously that there was nothing to it, he was convinced there was.

Characteristically, his instinct was to face up to it, sail right into it, and—what?

He had friends, driven by fear and inbred feelings of superiority and repulsion, who had joined the Klan. He had been approached and it had not been easy to refuse. But to himself he had expressed it stubbornly: "Ah'm too good to run with that kind of trash." And added, truthfully, "And Ah'm too decent to lower myself to that level. Anyway, that isn't the way to handle it."

But what was, he could not at the moment say.

By virtue of family and position as a Barnett, he was inevitably drawn into the unhappy tangle. He was one of those expected to lead. His father's generation, dead set against any form of racial compromise, had reared a generation not so completely sure of itself. They were sure "in a conditioned sort of way," as Jeff put it to his closest friends, and in his case the conditioning had been strong enough for him to take the lead in college in denying Bayard Johnson membership in the fraternity. Looking back now, thirteen years after that bitter episode, he found he was not so adamant and positive about things. He had defied Willie, who was so hell-bent on getting By, at that time the only Negro on campus, into the house. Jeff had rounded up sufficient votes to have By blackballed. But the serene conviction that prompted him to be so arbitrary then was undergoing changes now.

He marveled, in fact, at his own arrogant certainty then. Dr. Chalmers had asked him, in that last hurtful conversation on the subject that Jeff would never forget, if he wanted to look back on his campus career and think that one of his major accomplishments had been to embitter permanently a decent fellow student on no other grounds than race. He had been sure then. He wasn't so sure now.

Possibly he hadn't really been that sure then. But pride, stubbornness, the youthful insecurity that makes it difficult to admit mistakes, had combined with his social background to make flexibility impossible. Flexible, he was beginning to conclude, was what the South was going to have to be if they were all to come out of it in one piece.

The thought was revolutionary and repugnant to his father, who at fifty-four was accustomed to being lord of all he surveyed, which included cotton, tobacco, peanuts and cattle on three major plantations. He could not understand Jeff's increasing uneasiness at thirty-two.

"Why don't you just get married and raise us some grandchirren and forget all that Yankee crap?" his father inquired.

"I will," Jeff said with his characteristic quick, flashing, puppy-dog grin. "But"—more soberly—"I've got to give some thought to the kind of world I want your grandchildren to grow up in. Shouldn't you?"

"I don't see why," his father said complacently. "It's always been good enough for us."

And so it had, Jeff recognized, because the Barnetts had always been relatively—"enlightened," the Yankee word was—in their treatment of their farmhands.

"I've helped 'em get married," his father said, "given 'em good cabins to live in, seen to it they had decent clothes on their backs, sent some of their more capable kids to college, seen to it they were taken care of in their old age and given 'em a decent burial when they died. I couldn't have been better to 'em. Why are these Yankee bastards complainin' about that?"

"You have been good to them," Jeff conceded. "Nobody's treated 'em better than the Barnetts, I know that. The one thing you haven't given them is freedom."

"Freedom!" his father snorted. "Abe Lincoln took care of that. They're as free as you and I are. Who says they aren't free?"

"Not socially free," Jeff said. "Not economically free. Not treated like human beings. Not respected."

"I respect 'em!" his father cried indignantly. "I treat 'em like human beings. Point out to me one time when I haven't been decent and kind to 'em! You can't do it. And that's why I get so fed up with this equality crap. They're equal as can be and they know it. I can't stand all this stirrin' around. It goes against our whole way of life. And it doesn't gain them a damned thing."

"I think it will," Jeff said soberly. "Yes, sir, I think it will."

Which was a long way from Jeff Barnett at nineteen solemnly repeating to the house all the standard articles of Southern faith he had been brought up with. Or Jeff Barnett on V-J Day, still flying the Confederate flag.

Part of it, he supposed, was his fiancée, who like himself had left the South for her college education. He had gone west to the University, she north to Smith. He suspected sometimes that their parents might not really be as surprised as they professed to be by their children's changing opinions. Mary Dell Rundell was less outspoken than he but that didn't fool his father.

"I expect that little Mary Dell is goin' to raise a houseful of Yankees," he grumbled. "She's as radical as you are."

"I'm not radical," Jeff protested. "I just want to be realistic about things."

Mary Dell thought he was being realistic, and encouraged him in it.

And there was By.

By, quite unexpectedly—until Jeff stopped to figure out one day that that wild-eyed little Maryetta had probably put him up to it—was back in his life again. And that created further uncertainties, because he and By had always had a special sort of relationship, a very Southern sort of white-black relationship, even when he was fighting By's membership in the fraternity. They had understood one another then, he felt they understood one another now. And he could sense, not altogether comfortably, that in some subtle but inexorably changing way, their relationship was beginning to shift onto something of the same level.

Not quite "equal" yet.

But By was on the move.

You could have knocked Jeff over with a feather, he told Mary Dell later, one hot, sticky afternoon this summer when the heat lay oppressive over the jungly lowlands and a dull sky threatened the thunderstorm that presently came. He looked out his window in the plantation office, where he was helping with the books, to see a dusty blue Chevy coupe driving slowly up the rutted farm road. A minute later one of the hands knocked on the door and called out respectfully, "Mr. Jeff! There's a man to see you. Says his name is Mr. Johnson. Says you might better remember him as By."

He stood up, he told Mary Dell, not knowing what he was going to do. Certainly he would smile, because the past was long ago and because he smiled at everybody—"Mr. Jeff's smile," that abrupt, all-embracing benediction, was famous everywhere. But how informal should he be otherwise? Should he nod cordially—shake hands—offer By a chair? Remain standing, which would keep By on his feet too? Sit down and let By stand? Pretend he was busy and couldn't give him more than five minutes? Relax and talk as long as By wanted to?

Actually he was very curious, and as it turned out there was, surprisingly, no awkwardness at all. Jeff remembered By as quite a bit taller than himself, handsome, quite a commanding presence but very uncertain and very shy. A different By confronted him now, although he did begin hesitantly, "Hello, Jeff—Mr. Barnett—"

"Jeff," he said, smiled and instinctively (from college days, not his South Carolina upbringing) held out his hand. By took it gratefully and shook it with considerable vigor. "Sit down, By. [It all seemed to be falling into place very naturally, why had he been concerned?] This is a real surprise. What have you been up to since the war? And what brings you here?"

"I've been taking law," By said, sitting down rather gingerly in a chair across the desk. "I took advantage of the G.I. Bill and went to Hastings when I got out."

"Good for you," Jeff said, finding he was genuinely interested. "You're in practice now?"

By hesitated.

"In a sense. I'm working for an organization."

"What's that?"

"You may not approve," By said, and smiled suddenly with an assurance he had never shown in college. "The National Association for the Advancement of Colored People."

"That's all right," Jeff said, congratulating himself that he was perfectly matter-of-fact about it. "Good for you. Did you marry Maryetta?"

"Yes, I did," By said, smiling again. "She wouldn't let me get away."

"Very determined girl, as I remember," Jeff said. "*Very* determined."

"Still is," By said and laughed, quite naturally. "Keeps me hopping, I can tell you that. And into things? I tell you, Jeff, that little girl never slows down. If there's some cause Maryetta has missed, I want you to tell me. I can't keep track of 'em all."

"Must be quite an influence on you, I guess," Jeff observed and By laughed again.

"Tries to be. Thinks she is. And I guess she's right. She's the one thought I should ask to come down here."

"Oh? You goin' to be in Charleston?"

"And out and around. Like this."

"Well," Jeff said seriously, "let me tell you, By, I've changed some since—since we talked last. But a lot of folks haven't. There's a lot of feelin' still and some folks are very harsh about it—"

"I know," By said soberly. "I've been warned about that. I know it's dangerous."

"It can be," Jeff said, "unless you handle it right. I just want you to know that, before you get in too deep."

"Can I come to you for advice?" By asked, and for a second Jeff reverted to type and thought: unh-hunhh, you're clever, boy. But By looked, and obviously was, so innocent that he revised his impression immediately.

"I'll be happy to help you," he said quietly, "which I guess is why you're here"—By nodded—"but you have to understand, it can't always be too open. I can't move too fast. I'm part of my society here, and in some areas a fairly major part of it, and I'm sort of trapped, too. But if you go slow and are reasonable, then, yes, I'll help you. Providing"—he shot him a sudden sharp, appraising look—"providing you aren't out to turn the whole world upside down overnight. I'm sure that's what Maryetta wants to do."

"Pretty near," By admitted with a chuckle. "But," he added seriously, "I try to hold her down."

"Better," Jeff said. "Better. Otherwise there could be real trouble. Just remember, slow and easy does it."

"Maybe," By said gravely. "But maybe, for lots of us, 'slow and easy' and 'slow and reasonable' aren't enough anymore. The war changed so many things, you know, so many of us went north to Detroit and Chicago or out west to California and Washington State to work in the war plants. So many of us traveled all over the world to fight. So many of us found out that a guy bleeds and dies the same whatever his color. For so many of us, the world changed and it's never going back to what it was, ever again. That has to be taken into account."

"My father has friends," Jeff said slowly, "one of 'em a United States Senator who says"—he hesitated momentarily and then decided to let By have it—" 'Niggers don't vote in my state and niggers aren't going to vote in my state.' That's typical of what you're up against."

"We will," By said with a stubborn quietness. "We will. We'll vote and we'll run for office and we'll *be* United States Senators and Governors and Congressmen and mayors and school superintendents and police chiefs and *everything*, before we're through. You wait! *We will!*"

"Well," Jeff said, deciding it was time to lighten it up a bit, "I hope you'll leave room in Congress for Willie. Did you see where he's running out in California in his home district?"

"No!" By said. "I can't believe it! Or, yes"—he laughed, diverted—"I can believe it. That's Willie. Well, bless his heart. They think he'll make it?"

"Uncertain at the moment," Jeff said. "I saw a short AP piece on him last week that sounded doubtful. But you know our Willie. I believe in him. I think he will."

"I think," By said slowly with an air of political calculation that surprised Jeff, "that maybe that will be good for us. Willie's impulsive, sometimes, but he's fair. I'm going to keep in touch with that. I haven't really spoken to him since—since"—for just a second a little pain shadowed his eyes and Jeff recognized that it would always be there between them in some degree, even though cooperation that had once been impossible now seemed quite possible—"but I'm sure he'll be willing to listen to us if he wins." His tone became both shy and proud: for a moment the old By was back. "Willie was on my side, in that. It was always his idea."

"Well, forgive me," Jeff said. "It was thirteen years ago. People can change a lot in thirteen years. You have. You're much tougher now than you were then. You've changed."

"I hope it's me and not just Maryetta!" By said with a laugh that sounded quite relaxed. "And, realistically, there's not much to forgive. You hurt me like hell then, but that's just the way you were, you couldn't help it. I can see you're different now. There's some hope for sinners!"

Jeff grinned.

"A lot, I hope. But," he added soberly, standing up and holding out his hand, "do be careful. I can't yet invite you to my house, but I'm getting married in a week and there'll be some col—some Negroes—at the church and the reception, so you come to that."

"Me and the other family retainers?" By asked dryly as they shook hands. "I'll blend right in."

"Family friends," Jeff said firmly. "You come, now, and don't be hard on me."

"And Maryetta?" By asked in the same dry tone. "That will be a sensational couple, for South Carolina!"

"I've got to begin somewhere pretty soon," Jeff said, "and this is a good time to do it. Anyway, I want you both to meet Mary Dell. She thinks like I do. Our folks wonder if they found us under a kudzu vine."

"We'll see," By said. "I hope we can make it but I won't promise. Can I come back and talk once in a while? Is this a bad place to do it?"

"This is O.K.," Jeff said. "My father may be here, but he's got to adjust, too. He may bluster but he'll simmer down. It will be good for him. Here"—he wrote down two numbers on a memo pad, tore them off and handed them across—"the top number is my home, the other is the office here. I'd suggest here most days, but you do whatever you like, O.K.? In any event, the wedding is Saturday, so call me before and I'll give you the details. Hope to see you. And take care."

"You, too," By said seriously; and added with a shake of the head and a wondering grin, "isn't this fantastic after thirteen years? I can't believe it!"

"I can't either," Jeff said, "but it's got to begin somewhere."

But when By called his home on Friday morning before the wedding, it was to say that they were sorry but they just couldn't make it. He had appointments—there was business he had to attend to—he hoped to call soon . . . his voice trailed away.

"That's Maryetta," Jeff said bluntly.

"Yes," By admitted, sounding unhappy. "That's it."

"Damn it!" Jeff said angrily. "I'm trying! Let her try too!"

"I agree," By said with a caution that indicated she was standing at his elbow. "But there it is."

"O.K.," Jeff said shortly. "Call me when you can. And take care."

God damn it, he thought when he hung up, that's why By will never be the real bridge between the races he obviously hopes to be. That damned girl—woman—is going to fuck up his whole life and fuck up everything he tries to do. She's so "liberal" she won't accept a good chance at reconciliation when it's offered, so "liberal" everything has to be absolutely perfect before she'll condescend to touch it, so "liberal" everything has to be exactly on her terms and exactly the way she wants it or she won't play. Probably she wants By to be the best man and her to be maid of honor.

Fuck 'em all, he thought bitterly, fuck 'em all. Here I'm offering to take just as many chances as he is and because she has this phony, rigid, arbitrary, stupid "liberal" mentality, she'll barge in and mess everything up. Fuck 'em all.

But when he came to write his note to Johnny Herbert, he covered all that up with hopeful words and positive good cheer.

"You'll never believe who's turned up down here, or what's happened. I'm sure you all remember By Johnson—" and candidly and forthrightly he proceeded to write about their reunion, By's new maturity, his own changing attitudes, the hope he saw in their new relationship. No apologies, no hesitations: here you are, guys, marvel at the changes thirteen years have brought.

Not in Maryetta, though.

He refrained from all mention of Maryetta.

Fuck 'em all, wreckers of reconciliation, murderers of compromise. Their way or nothing!

He found he was beginning to despise that kind of crippled thinking so much that he couldn't ever begin to write about it or his words would burn up the page.

Billy had purchased a couple of spotlights, trained them on the house just in case. At 10:33 P.M., on a date, at a time, and in a place the family would never forget, he let out a yell and turned them on.

The ranch house stood illuminated on its hilltop. Looking down, they could see, coming from across the flat and snaking slowly through the orange groves along the narrow country roads, the headlights of cars approaching through the cool November night.

"In a stunning upset," the battered old Philco on the kitchen sideboard and the flickering new television set in the living room were reporting simultaneously, "challenger Richard Emmett Wilson has narrowly ousted veteran Representative Judah Baker from his congressional seat in the southern San Joaquin Valley.

"Mr. Wilson, thirty-four, defeated the twelve-term Congressman, sixty-seven, with a campaign based largely on what he calls 'new ideas' and 'constructive thinking.' These," the veteran network commentator noted dryly, "seem to be largely of what might be called a conservative nature. Their freshness has not always been apparent to national observers. But apparently they have appealed to Mr. Wilson's mainly rural constituency."

"Well, fuck you, you patronizing son of a bitch," Billy exploded, to the shocked laughter of Janie and his mother.

"Didn't know your little boy knew that word, did you?" he inquired with a grin. "But God damn *them*. Willie fought a hard campaign and a good campaign. His little finger is worth ten times that guy's whole body. And we're not the hayseeds he's implying. So fuck them!"

"All right, all right," Janie protested, amused but cautionary. "You don't have to repeat it. We get the idea."

"Thank goodness the children are asleep," his mother said with a chuckle. "They're still such innocents."

"On a ranch?" Billy said. "Come on, Mom. But I'll be good, since you insist. Have to get 'em up in a minute anyway, to meet the new Congressman."

" 'The Congressman,' " Janie said in a tone of awe. "So it's all come true. It's really come true. I can't believe it."

"I can't, either," their mother said, beginning to cry. "It's all so— so"—her voice sailed up in a shaky squeak—"so wonderful!"

It was so he found them when he and Donn and his father entered the room.

"So *wonderful!*" he mimicked in falsetto, coming over to give her a hug and a kiss. "Mom, you're great. But you'll have to be more dignified when the company comes."

"And they are coming," Donna said, going over to stand by the big picture window that looked down the hill. "It looks as though half the Valley is on its way."

"Have we got enough food?" Willie inquired. "I told you I thought probably about two hundred, with everybody I've asked and the extras."

"You know your mother," his father said. "Food for five hundred if there's food for one. Nobody ever goes away hungry from this house."

"I should hope not," she said, vigorously drying her eyes. "Don't worry. Food for five hundred won't be too much."

And by midnight, when things were going full blast, it was apparent that she was right. Excited friends and supporters filled the house, spilled on the patio and the parking area, sat on the lawn. The night was cool but they were bundled. In the exhilaration of the evening nobody really felt the temperature anyway.

Judah Baker conceded at 11:45, a statement somewhat grudging but, as Willie remarked, "after twenty-four years in office, not too bad."

"I have tried to serve you well," the Congressman concluded, "and I am sure my young opponent will try equally hard." ("Though he may not succeed," Donna murmured. Everybody laughed the easy laughter of triumph.) "Perhaps it is time to pass the torch to a new generation tempered by war and dedicated to a world at peace. I wish him well and I say to you, old friends, come see me anytime. You know 'Old Jude.' I'm always here for you. I will always be your friend."

"And I will run again in 1954," Billy said dryly, and again they all laughed. "But by then Willie will have done such a good job that you won't have the chance of a—but I'd better not say it or I'll shock my wife and mother again."

And again they all laughed, excited, happy, confident, congratulatory, brimming over with the day's delirious triumph.

Sometime during the long tumultuous night he received tele-
grams from Guy and Maggie in Honolulu, Gil and Karen Ann in
La Jolla, Tony and Louise in Napa Valley, Johnny and Duke and
Shahna at the University, Fran Haggerty (where was Hack?) in San
Francisco, Franky and Katie in Medford; and, surprisingly, from Bill
Nagatani, now a successful truck gardener and nurseryman in
Fresno.

Even more surprising was the phone call he received shortly after
1:30 A.M. his time, 4:30 A.M. theirs, from Charleston, South Carolina.

"Hey, Willie!" cried a voice he hadn't heard since wartime London. "How the hell are you, you ole Yankee Congressman, you!"

"Jeff!" he exclaimed, very pleased. "I don't believe it!"

"Believe it, boy, it's me, right enough [accent more pronounced, in
excitement]. Ah couldn't be happier for you, Willie, Ah really
couldn't. Now you goin' join all the othuh radicals up theah. Ah want
you to be good to us, Willie. Don't you be too hard on us now!"

"I won't," he said. "I'll try not to. How are you, anyway?"

"Just married," Jeff said. "Finally done it, Willie, and couldn't be
happier. Helpin' to run the family farms and keepin' busy. Hang on
there, somebody else wants to say hello to you."

"Hey!" Willie said. "You forgot to tell me her name—"

But the voice that came over was not feminine and for a moment he
was almost too astounded to respond.

"Willie?" it said, with the shy hesitation he had not forgotten. "You
probably don't remember me, but—"

"Well, I'll be damned," he said, in a voice so heartfelt that those
immediately around him in the beginning-to-fade but still exuberant
crowd abruptly quieted. "You'll never guess who this is," he whispered to Billy in a quick aside; and then, more loudly, "By! How are
you, By! I am very pleased indeed to hear from you, and that's no
lie."

"You never lied to me, Willie," By said, his voice suddenly shaky
with emotion and relief; Willie realized how difficult a step it must
have been for him to call after all these years. "And I won't lie to you.
I think this is just great but that isn't the only reason I'm calling. I
want you to help us, Willie. I want you to help my people. Will you
do that?"

"I'll do my best," Willie said solemnly. "I hope you know that."

"I hope you'll help us actively," By said. "I hope you won't sit back
and just give us lip service. Things are moving toward something,
Willie. I don't know what form it's going to take yet, but they're

moving—they're moving. We need you. Can I come see you in Washington?"

"Certainly. Anytime. You're with Jeff?"

"He's changed a lot," By said. "He's really changed. I can't believe it myself"—there was a muffled murmur in the background and he laughed, sounding genuinely amused—"but it's true, Willie. It's true. Maybe he'll come see you, too, and you can judge for yourself. Anyway, you can count on me. I'll stop by soon's I can after you hit D.C."

"I'll be waiting for you," Willie said with a warm assurance in his voice that he found was already beginning to come easily. "I'll do what I can. I really do appreciate your call, By, I really do."

"Well, congratulations," By said, suddenly sounding shy again. "I just wanted to let you know how great I think it is. And to ask your help."

And there, Willie thought as he turned back to the now rapidly dwindling crowd—there's my first promise. I hope I can keep it.

Two other calls, as he had rather expected, leapfrogged blithely over some years of hard work and preparation in the House that hadn't even begun yet.

"Hey, buddy!" Aram Katanian said from Fresno, where he was already a well-established lawyer. "Count me in when you run for Senator, O.K.? I'll handle your Central California campaign."

"Wait a minute," Willie protested, pleased but amused by this enthusiastic pledge from the close friend he had trounced for student-body president in the golden long-ago before the war. "I haven't even taken my oath as Representative yet. What's this Senator business?"

"You'll make it," Ari said with complete conviction. "You don't really doubt it, do you? Come on now! Who am I talking to, Willie or some cruddy, unambitious jerk?"

"Cruddy, possibly," Willie said with a laugh, "but not unambitious. As you know. However, I must point out again, I'm not even a Representative yet. So hold your horses."

Ari chuckled.

"I've got the job, though, when the time comes, right?"

"Yep. Don't call me, though, I'll call you. Timing is everything."

"I tell you what I'm going to do," Ari said. "Helen and the kids and I are coming down this weekend and you and Billy and I are going to sit down and plan how you're going to become Senator, all right?"

"Can't I even take a little vacation first?" he inquired with a half-humorous plaintiveness. "I've got to get a little rest, man. I'm *beat*."

"Nope," Ari said. "Not until we get you in the Senate."

"That'll be the day," Willie said. "Meanwhile—"

"See you Sunday in time for lunch, O.K.?"

"But—"

"Great! Sometime between eleven-thirty and noon. See you then."

And, cheerfully, he hung up. Within minutes a call from Washington, which its initiator said had been in the works for three hours, finally got through.

"Well, by God, Senator!" Tim greeted him from the National Press Club lounge where he and a couple of hundred other reporters were blearily waiting out an all-night vigil in front of the club's radios and flickering television sets. "You did it! A fresh wind is blowing from the West. A new day is dawning on the Coast. A new star is ascending over the American horizon. A new—"

"Oh, for Christ's sake, will you be quiet? Ari called a little while ago with the same 'Senator' crap. He wants to plan my campaign already. I'm not even in the House yet."

"In our minds, Great One," Tim said solemnly, "you are even now rolling down Pennsylvania Avenue on your way to the White House. House—Senate—those are mere details. All—all—will fall before you. All hail, Willie, great leader of our century!"

"Jesus, knock it off. I'm superstitious, man. You're scaring me. I've got mountains ahead of me—"

"And valleys, too, no doubt," Tim said cheerfully, "but you will rise supreme above them all. All hail, Willie, our maximum—"

"Timmy," he said sternly, "you're drunk. Now knock it off. I'm just one little dot in this whole big picture of 1952. What's the latest on Ike?"

"Not bad. Just a landslide. Ike's in his heaven, all's right with the world."

Willie chuckled.

"He called me 'Willie,' once. Do you think that will give me privileged entrée to the White House?"

"You will be allowed to polish my boots and brush my uniform, Major. I'm afraid there isn't much more I can do for you. When are you and the family going to get back here, late December?"

"I'll be coming first, to find us a place to live. Probably right after Thanksgiving."

"Dinner on me that night at Hogate's," Tim said. His voice suddenly became completely sober. "I really am glad as hell about this, Willie. It's really wonderful."

"Well, thank you," he said, equally solemn.

"In fact," Tim said, dropping his voice even lower and simulating a muffled sob, "I may cry."

"Oh, go to hell," he said with a happy laugh. "Just go to hell, Bates. See you in three weeks."

"Right, Mr. President," Tim said smartly. "I'll be on hand with a band."

And there it was, Willie thought as the last of the happy stragglers left the ranch around three-thirty and the hilltop finally became still. So much happiness—so much hope—so much trust, placed in him. Not anybody else now. Just little Willie, focus of it all.

Well, he told himself as he fell completely exhausted into the bed where Donna was already gently snoring, I will justify it. I will be good. I will be the best damned Congressman who ever hit Washington. I will do great things for my country.

Just you wait and see, he told anonymous millions off there somewhere in his fast-fading consciousness as it plunged finally into sleep.

Just you wait and see!

I'm Richard Emmett Wilson and I will serve you well.

I *will*.

3

1

The Eisenhower years, in retrospect, seemed to have passed almost as in an amiable dream. The Kennedy years were a golden nightmare in which image was all and public-relations fantasies were employed to conceal compulsive sexual weakness and dangerous gambling in the Cold War's most potentially explosive era. The Johnson years began.

Willie's own career prospered. Constituents and country perceived him to be a rising star, confident, decisive, contributive, successful.

In due course he became acquainted with the infinite sadness of the world.

Inevitably, as a maturing adult—inexorably, as a member of the Congress of the United States, upon which as upon no other institution beat all the fragile triumphs, the ever-threatening tragedies, the endless strivings and endless frustrations of humankind.

Hope, he found, does indeed spring eternal. So, too, do disappointment, desperation, anguish, despair.

"Dear Congressman [written in pencil on a ragged piece of brown grocery bag], my husband has the T.B. and can't get no work. Can you help?"

"Dear Rep. Wilson [a formal letterhead, a secretary's initials], I write to you in desperation because we are faced with the loss of the properties which have been in my family since Spanish days. *We need subsidies, and we need water.* Your assistance will be gratefully received and suitably rewarded with our support at the next election. I hope we can count on you."

"Señor Wilson [again a pencil and a dirty scrap of paper], I no speke or rite Ingles varry well. I los my arm two months ago on the —————— Farm and they won pay me no money to help. My family is hongry I am in pane. Please, please, *please*, amigo, *help me*."

"Dear Rep. Wilson [on the chaste three-word letterhead to which members of Congress write], The President was most interested to receive your kind letter relative to the plight of your constituents in the San Joaquin Valley. He has asked me to assure you that he will pass the matter along to the Department of Agriculture. He is confident your views will be most carefully considered there." And at the bottom (never missing an opportunity), the almost illegible notation, "Good to hear from you. Come see me." And the initials, hastily scrawled, prized but more often than not meaningless for any effect the professed friendship might have on the course of events.

In the broader arena, on the great stage on which leaders and led alike perform their given steps in the universal dance toward death, the unceasing clamor also rose as humanity hurtled ever faster away from the evanescent triumphs and swiftly forgotten lessons of the war that was supposedly going to restore stability to the world.

Fifty million dead, horrors beyond imagining, to achieve a victory so frightfully won—and still, as he had on V-J Day, Willie could sometimes demand unhappily, "For what?"

"At least the world is still here," Tim pointed out dryly.

"Sometimes just barely," Willie retorted.

"Maybe that's all humanity can hope for," Tim responded. "When all is said and done, *we're still here*."

"It isn't enough," Willie said glumly. "It isn't enough."

But it was his job to try to make some sense of it, both domestically and in foreign affairs. He found it to be the most challenging, and often most trying, endeavor he ever expected to undertake.

Day in, day out, week in, week out, month in, month out, year upon year upon year for him and for his 534 fellow members of the Congress, the drumbeat never stopped. The endless problems, the endless tragedies, the implacable destruction of hopes by events, the bewildered beseechings of individuals, races, nations, states—help us, somebody, help us, America, help us, Representative or Senator, help us, help us, *help us!*

He often wondered how he and his colleagues endured it, the never-changing, never-abating flood of human hope, disappointment and despair; and the endless contrivances of the clever as they attempt, often with much success, to evade the law and do evil where only good has been intended by the lawmakers.

"Does one ever feel that he is accomplishing enough?" he asked the Speaker in unhappy frustration after he had been in office six months.

The answer was a quizzical look, a dogged shake of the head, a somber reflection:

"Don't take it too heavy, son. Do what you can, don't worry about what you can't do, otherwise you'll go crazy. We're only human on this Hill. Most of us never know a full day of resting easy. You just have to keep plugging away."

Which, he realized later, was sound advice, based as it was upon the mind's ability to operate simultaneously on several levels, carrying the burden of the world's agonies side by side with necessary day-to-day concerns and the goals of ultimate ambition. But while it gave him a warm, we're-all-in-this-together feeling, it did not help greatly if one was young, conscientious and still full of idealistic, insistent dreams about "doing something for the country."

In time, though never forgotten, he found that the dreams were modified. The endless give and take of the Hill, the ponderous slowness with which most legislation moved, the inescapable necessity of compromise if one wanted to accomplish anything of any substance, gradually wore down Young-Lochinvar-Come-Out-of-the-West into Representative Richard Emmett ("Willie") Wilson, steady, dependable, practical and pragmatic member of what the leadership thought of as "the young guard."

The process took about three terms to mold him into the reliable and effective figure he presently became. He often sang ironically to himself the opening words of one of the popular songs of the day: "Put your dreams away/For another day"—They applied, he told himself. Oh, how they applied!

The only saving grace was that the dreams were still there, on the shelf but not forgotten. And someday, if one could only achieve a position of sufficient power and influence—someday—

Out of 535 members, he told himself in the same ironic mood, there were probably 400 thinking the same thing. The public, perceiving only the foibles, scandals and shortcomings of the irresponsible fringe, did not understand the reservoir of idealism that underpinned the Congress. It accounted for the occasional crusades, the sudden, unexpected challenges, the surprising campaigns launched by one, or a handful, or sometimes even a majority of one party or the other, against a presidential program or nomination, a popular shibboleth, an international figure or event. It was as though by concentrating their energies on some particular well-publicized item perceived to be noble of intent and righteous of purpose, they could divert attention from many failures of accomplishment and also justify to themselves the maze of compromise and often downright futility through which they had to struggle every day.

When he had been going about the Hill paying his respects in his first days in office, his first call had been upon California's senior Senator. The advice he received was terse and to the point:

"Know your district—answer your mail—help when you can—pick out two or three main issues you want to become an expert on and do something about—and study, study, study, concentrate, concentrate, concentrate. For the time being you're a little frog in a big puddle— not that you won't [a fatherly, deliberately flattering chuckle] soon become a bigger one—but for now, narrow it down, be selective, decide what you really want to give your heart and mind to—and work at it. It's the only way to accomplish anything here. Work at it!"

He had already decided this for himself, but with the easy deference his elders found so appealing—and which he found he was more and more using as a deliberate manipulative tool with them—he had professed to have received a revelation for which he was profoundly grateful. It did reinforce his own conclusions; and it encouraged him, as the junior Senator told him half an hour later, to "do the job and leave the glamour to others."

This last was not entirely sincere, as it was already obvious to all of them that increasingly ubiquitous television, and what was becoming generalized as "the media," would soon have a major effect upon politics and government. A beaming Eisenhower, a strained and earnest Stevenson, had already amply proved that: the Big Smile swamped the Knitted Brow. It was a lesson not lost upon the political world. Willie, if he did say so himself (which he didn't, except to his family), was an attractive young newcomer. He worked hard but he also made sure that he was available to press and particularly television. It was not long before he found himself increasingly called upon for interviews, not long before he became one of the first to be queried when comment was required on some new or developing issue.

This put him to some extent ahead of his legislative generation, "the class of '52" as it was called on the Hill. His name became increasingly familiar as it recurred more and more often in newspaper stories. Thanks to *Meet the Press* and its imitators, on which he was a popular guest, the face began to go with the name. Midway in his second term it gave him an unexpected and gratifying thrill to be hailed on Michigan

Avenue in Chicago. Someone had seen him on what were coming to be known as "talk shows," expressed admiration, asked for an autograph. Such recognition—"A long way from the San Joaquin!" he reported to Donna with satisfaction—presently became routine. He was becoming famous, in a modest but growing way.

In the House, where it really counted, his increasing prominence brought its rewards. He was considered a "comer," given committee assignments and legislative duties commensurate with what the leadership perceived to be his future. After his second reelection, at the start of his third term, he found himself assigned not only to his original committee, Agriculture and the Agriculture Subcommittee of the Appropriations Committee, but the Judiciary Committee and, biggest prize of all, Foreign Affairs. And this in spite of the fact that, as he had accurately predicted to Johnny Herbert in his first campaign, he was finding himself increasingly opposed to the accepted establishment wisdom concerning America's place and responsibilities in a world overshadowed by the aggressive, imperialistic, outward-pushing, peace-sabotaging Soviet Union.

In those days of the steadily widening Cold War, when it was not fashionable in media, publishing, academe, the arts, to vary one inch from the rigidly orthodox line that the Soviets were not a threat, that the United States was the only villain in the world and responsible for all its ills, he found it impossible to ignore what common sense and logic clearly said: that the men in Moscow were literally out to conquer the world if they could, and that in pursuit of that objective they balked at no deceit or deception, no means however monstrous or murderous. The evidence was there every minute of every hour of every day in the daily flow of the news. Only the willfully blind refused to see it. Unfortunately for the country, the willfully blind were in charge of what the country read, saw, heard and received as education in its schools. A rigidly pro-Soviet orthodoxy clamped itself upon the mind of the American intellectual community in the postwar years and only the hardiest dared defy it. Those who dared to raise their voices against the hallelujah chorus were constantly criticized, harassed, denigrated and as much as possible denied access to print, tube, airwave, theater, screen, gallery, public platform.

It was not lightly undertaken, the challenge to the establishment's drearily predictable pro-Communist orthodoxy. His independent character and quizzical, free-ranging mind impelled him, but some of those closest to him were dubious. His parents and Billy, though apprehensive, supported whatever he did. He supposed his wife and Tim Bates were the most decisive of the voices raising caveats.

"You've been doing so well up to now," Donna said when he came home on a steamy Sunday afternoon after appearing on *Meet the Press*. "I don't see why you want to jeopardize it by taking on half the most powerful people in Washington."

"More than that, probably," he said, relaxing into a chair on the shady lawn of the modest brick home he rented just over the District line in Bethesda, Maryland. He gave her the carefree grin that always annoyed her when he used it in the midst of serious discussion. "Why, what did I say that was so awful?"

"You told the Secretary that you didn't think he was preparing us adequately for a possible attack by the Soviet Union."

"No more is he. He's a jerk. The most incompetent Secretary of Defense we've had in my years here."

"I hope you don't go around saying that on the Hill."

He smiled with a complacency that annoyed her further.

"It's my opinion. And I'm not alone. A lot of people feel that way."

"And then to compound it by making that crack about 'unthinking people in government and media who play the Soviet game by constantly denying the clear evidence of Soviet aggressive intentions.' "

"Sorry nobody followed it up to ask me who they are," he said crisply. "I would have told them."

"Sometimes, Willie Wilson," she said, "you can be too independent. It isn't funny and it isn't smart—"

"But it's me. Don't you want me to be me?"

She sighed impatiently.

"Of course I do. But not to just butt your head quixotically against a stone wall. You're beginning to get a name for always being against things—"

"But I'm not always against 'things,' " he said in a reasonable tone. "I'm for a lot of 'things.' That's where they get you with the public, you see. They spread the word that you're 'against *things*,' which raises this vague fear in constituents and others that you're probably against God and motherhood, which presently successfully conceals the facts of the very real and specific things you are against. Like a weak defense—and muddle-minded attitudes toward the Soviet Union—and wishful thinking that they love us and will be nice to us if we just lie down and let them walk over us. I don't like *those* 'things.' How about another beer?"

"I'm glad it's so clear in your own mind," she remarked, rising to go in the house and get him one. "That isn't the reputation you're beginning to get."

"I hope I'm getting the reputation for having integrity and being independent," he called after, "because that's what I am."

In the pause before she returned, Washington's oppressive summer heat settled upon him full force. Cicadas hummed in the magnolias, sleepy birds twittered, he could almost hear the grass growing. Latt was supposed to have mowed it yesterday but in mid-teens he was not always so reliable.

Latt.

That was something else.

She returned with his beer and a replenished lemonade for herself. He decided to plunge right into it.

"I thought that boy was supposed to mow the lawn."

"If by 'that boy' you mean your older son," she said more in asperity than jest, "he has a name."

"To which he rarely answers. At least agreeably. Where is he this afternoon, anyway?"

"He and Senator Macon's boys have gone down to Cobb Island to go sailing on the Potomac. He won't be back until around nine tonight. You were told that."

He studied her for a moment.

"I probably was. It isn't as though I have anything else on my mind."

"Oh, Willie," she said in a tired tone. "Don't be sarcastic. It's such an easy escape."

"I'm not escaping," he protested with a tiredness of his own. "When do you stop defending him? When does he start growing up?"

"I don't always defend him. Only when you're unreasonable—"

"It's not unreasonable," he snapped with a sudden anger he knew he shouldn't indulge but seemed powerless to stop, "to expect him to keep a bargain when he's told he can go somewhere if he completes his chores and then he ducks out and goes without doing them. I have a right to expect some integrity and making him keep his promises is one way to inculcate it. Hard to do when his mother gives in and lets him go anyway."

"So blame me," she said bitterly, a long way from always bright, always upbeat, always sunny Donna of campus days. "That, too, is an easy way out."

"But it's true," he said indignantly. "It's the fact. You do let him go. How can you deny it?"

"He had this chance to go with the Macon boys, that's all. He promised me that he'll get up early tomorrow morning and do it. Will that suit you? What difference does it make if it's tomorrow morning instead of today? He'll do it."

"No, he won't," he said, tone almost triumphant.

"Why?" she demanded. "Are you going to do it yourself, Congressman? I thought you were too important to do anything as mundane as mow the lawn. Surely that's beneath you."

"It isn't beneath me," he said angrily, "as you know very well. When you grow up on a ranch—"

"We know all about that," she said dryly. "You tell us often enough."

With a great effort he did not raise his voice.

"The reason he is not going to do it," he said as calmly as he could, "is because Amos is. He's in there helping Clayne make some sandwiches. When I came home I said, 'Where's Latt? I thought he was going to do the lawn.' Clayne said, 'He's out someplace,' and without hesitating a moment, which is like him, Amos said, 'Don't worry about it, Daddy, I'll do it.' Which, I am very much afraid, is going to be the story of his life where Latt is concerned."

"He worships him," she said. "He always has."

"Well," he said, "there are objects of worship and there are objects of worship. I'm not so sure Latt is a worthy one, particularly for Amos. He's too sweet-natured. Latt definitely isn't."

"Well," she said, "Billy seems to have survived you. Maybe Amos will survive Latt."

For a second he felt an anger so deep he didn't trust himself to reply. So he didn't, simply sitting there absently dangling a leg over the arm of his chair, while nearby the cardinals flashed through the dogwood and over everything lay the pall of summer. Finally he managed to speak in a normal tone.

"The boys leave next week for the ranch, don't they?"

"Six weeks in the Valley," she said politely, "the regular schedule. Then we go out with Clayne to get them, stay another month while you button up all the loose ends in the district, and come back here in time for school."

"Dad will redress the balance," he said. "And Jose has never let Latt get away with anything, either. They both keep an eye on him. I'll call Dad and talk to him about it."

She gave him a sudden sharply hostile look.

"Then I'll have to call your mother and talk to her, too. I'm not going to have the men ganging up on Latt."

"Amos is the one who needs protection," he said with equal sharpness. "Latt can take care of himself. He always has and he always will."

"And that's what you resent. You want a Daddy's boy, and he isn't, he's too independent. He's like you. That's why you don't like him."

"I do like him," he protested. "For Christ's sake, Donn, he's my elder son, my firstborn. *I love him.*"

"Yes. But you don't like him."

"He's a handful," he said thoughtfully. "He's always been a handful. He always will be a handful. For someone named after a soul as gentle as Bill Lattimer, he sure is different. Amos is the one who should have been named after Latt. *You* give some thought to Amos."

"I do," she said. "I give thought to all of them. And to this chopped-up life they lead—you lead."

"Oh. So now we're back to my career again."

She was unmoved.

"We're never far away from it, are we? It's all our lives are—what your life permits."

"Donn," he began patiently, "we talked all this over back home when I first thought about running and you said—"

"I know what I said," she retorted with an unamused little smile. "I said what I had to say."

"Which was—"

" 'Go ahead.' What else could I say? Nothing would have stopped you."

"And you thought I might be able to do some good. Am I not doing some good?"

"Oh, of course," she said impatiently. "Nobody denies that. Brightest young man in the California delegation. Darling of the Speaker. Popular with his colleagues. Popular with the White House. Popular with his constituents, most important of all. Keep an eye on this man. He Will Go Far."

"Actually," he said with a faraway look, "I *am* thinking about the Senate."

"Actually, you always have thought about the Senate. And that isn't all."

"Nope." he said cheerfully, "that isn't all. So are you with me or against me? Want to check out? Want to take the kids and run for

cover? Not the Donna I know, Big Woman on Campus, into everything, vice-president of the student body, shrewdest politician in the
family. 'Everybody admires Congressman Wilson but everybody just
loves Donna.' Such a doll! Such a help! Such an asset! The standard
introduction at a hundred ladies' clubs in the district: 'She's really the
Congressman, girls, we all know that!' I could drop dead tomorrow
and you'd be elected my successor in a landslide. So much for the
nonpolitical, domesticated housewife who hates the public life her
ruthless, domineering, overly ambitious husband has dragged her
into!"

"Nonetheless," she said, persuaded momentarily into grudging
laughter, "it is a hectic life, it really isn't good for the kids and it is
detrimental to many marriages—"

"Right now this conversation is occurring in at least three hundred
out of five hundred thirty-five households," he agreed promptly. "As
it has in political households since the founding of the Republic. And
sometimes it winds up in divorce, affairs on the side or cold, dull
silence. I don't want a divorce, do you?"

"No"—tone becoming exasperated again—"I don't want a divorce."

"And I don't want affairs, too much trouble unless you're in the
White House protected by a loyal staff and an adoring media. And
neither of us is exactly the cold, silent type, so that probably wouldn't
work, either. Better stick with me and keep smiling, Donn. The
alternatives aren't very feasible, are they?"

She shot him an appraising look, as though considering a stranger.

"In fact, for a politician's family, there are no alternatives, right?"

He uttered his quick, charming laugh.

"Apparently. Tough, isn't it?"

"Well, don't sound so—so light about it," she said. "You aren't fair
to me or your family."

He looked thoughtful.

"Or myself, really. But that's the choice we've made. I suppose if
we didn't have this conversation every six months it wouldn't be us,
right?"

"I think I'll go in and see how the kids are doing with those sandwiches," she said, standing up abruptly. "I know I bore you—"

"No, you don't bore me," he protested vehemently, though they
both knew that for years this had been at the root of it. "Now bring
on the lunch and let's talk about something more cheerful."

But later, as on many similar occasions, he had to admit to himself
that essentially she was right. Tim told him so frequently. Tim was a

much bigger name now than he used to be, "As aren't we all," he sometimes remarked with the humorous self-deprecation that was popular with many in government and media. It did not quite conceal their satisfaction that, yes, they were pretty big—at least in Washington's eyes, which, in Washington's eyes, was all that mattered. Certainly he and Tim were "bigger" in the sense of national prominence than any of their friends from college days. They knew nobody could challenge them on that.

They met for lunch quite regularly now, no longer in the capital's cheaper restaurants as in early days, but at Duke Zeibert's and Sans Souci and the Jockey Club or, more regularly, at the Metropolitan, Cosmos and University clubs, favorite haunts of upper-level government and media. These places were what Tim called "ego-feeders," which was apt since the egos at one table were only exceeded by the egos at the next. All Washington egos, as Tim also noted, were based upon power. It didn't matter what sort of character you brought to it or how well or badly you used it, the only criterion of judgment was how much you had.

His first book, a study of it, had been entitled: *Cardboard Camelot: Shadow and Substance in the Kennedy Era.* The fact that they had now left the Kennedy era and were well into the Johnson had only supported his basic thesis. At their most recent meeting, which occurred in August 1964, just after passage of the Tonkin Gulf Resolution, he told Willie that he was now putting finishing touches on a successor volume: *Leadership and Substance: L.B.J. and the Uses of White House Power.*

"He won't like you for that," Willie remarked, looking around the dignified dining room of the Metropolitan Club wherein he saw the Secretary of State, the Undersecretary of Defense, the Attorney General, three Senators, four ambassadors, a whole gaggle of news-bureau heads and a flock of high-ranking staffers from various departments and agencies. "If there's anything Lyndon doesn't like, it's being held up as the paradigm of arm-twisting, browbeating, gotcha-by-the-balls-and-thanks-for-your-vote power. He loves it but he's a bit sensitive about being described that way."

"Oh, we get along fine," Tim said dryly. "He's not a man to argue with a column syndicated in two hundred thirty-one newspapers with more pending, plus a weekly radio commentary broadcast in thirty-

two states, plus regular appearances on *Capital Insiders*, plus magazine articles, books—"

"By God, Timmy," Willie interrupted, "you *are* busy. Little did we
think when we read all those searing pre-war anti-Hitler editorials in
the *Daily* that you'd emerge as one of America's Busiest and Most
Respected Young Pundits. Or not so young, as the case may be."

"Coming up on forty-six," Tim said with a rueful shake of the head.
"Gad, where have they gone?"

"Search me," Willie said, pretending to look around his chair.
"They were here yesterday, but *whoosh!* they aren't here anymore.
Time goes faster every day. I don't think we've done too badly with
it, though. Certainly you haven't."

"Or you. Don't try to be modest, Senator, it isn't like you. Talk
about busiest and most respected. You're everywhere. Cover of *Time*
next, I suppose."

"They're making sounds, but that doesn't mean they'll do it. Anyway, there are plenty as busy on both sides of the Hill. And also more
respected. One junior Senator doth not a summer make."

"A pretty prominent one, though," Tim observed. "After all the
drama of that squeak-in victory in '62. And your general prominence
in foreign policy, civil rights and now on the Vietnam issue, which is
apparently going to get bigger and bigger. Why did you vote for the
Tonkin Gulf Resolution, anyway?"

"Well," Willie said thoughtfully, "he called me in and sat me down
on a sofa and grabbed my lapels and talked and talked and talked and
talked and *talked*—and after a while I was too exhausted to say anything but a feeble, 'Yes, Mr. President.' Plus the fact," he added,
more seriously, "that on the whole I agree with what he's trying to do.
After all, he inherited it from Jack and at the moment there doesn't
seem to be anything better to do than just go ahead and wrap it up as
swiftly as possible. Which is what he says he intends to do."

"We could get out right now," Tim suggested. "Anybody ever
think of that one?"

"My young Latt has," Willie admitted with some unhappiness.
"We've had some furious go-rounds about it in the past couple of
months. He doesn't approve of his father's vote *ay*-tall."

"Maybe when he gets to the University he'll mellow. He's entering
next month, isn't he?"

"Yes, and if you think that's going to be any guarantee of mellowing, in this climate, I think you're a bit naive, Brother Bates. The
campuses are beginning to get a little restive, from what I hear."

"But surely Latt has enough balance from you to judge things sensibly for himself."

Willie snorted.

"That's how much you bachelors know about families. You've always seen this kid on his best behavior for Uncle Tim: you haven't seen the other side. Sometimes I don't think we know him at all. He's so different from Amos and Clayne, neither of whom would hurt a fly. Latt would, if it got in the way of what he wanted to do, or what he believes. He's a tough one. I regard him with considerable misgivings, starting college, as he is, at this particular time. What he'll be four years from now—"

"Well," Tim said bluntly, "let's wind the war down and get the hell out, then. I've got a column coming out tomorrow: can we afford to fight it? Can we afford to do to the country what it appears we may be about to do if we keep on? Are we prepared to take on the burden of everything that may happen?"

Willie gave him a quizzical smile.

"You always were ahead of your times. You always were a lot more farsighted than the rest of us—"

"You're God damned right I was," Tim snapped, unamused. "And I still am. And I say to you and your bullheaded friend in the White House, you'd better be prepared for a mighty big storm, because by God, you're going to get one."

"That's not the general attitude in this town—"

"Ha! Give it a few months and see. The liberals are all for it right now because they inherited it from dear Jack, but that'll be changing pretty damned fast. You wait and see. And I would suggest to my friend the distinguished Senator that he might listen to his son and keep an ear on that generation, because I have a hunch it's going to be heard from, loud and clear. On this issue and a lot of other things as well."

"Well," Willie said, "you may be right—"

"I know I am. And I'd suggest you trim your sails a little bit on the Soviets, too, while we're at it."

Willie looked surprised.

"What, now that they're openly helping North Vietnam against us as a deliberate means of weakening us? Where's the logic in that? And, I might add, where's your own consistency? You've been as alarmist about the Soviets since Nikita browbeat Jack in Vienna as you ever were about Hitler. What do you want me to pull my punches for?"

"That's all right," Tim said, unabashed. "We're in different categories. Anna Hastings runs me in *The Washington Inquirer* and a lot of other papers print me to achieve what they see as balance, but they're not as tolerant of you. You're becoming too effective. I make noises. You cast votes. A lot of people listen to you. You're perceived to be a threat to the liberals' pet obsessions that the Soviets are terrific but America's the shits. You can't subvert their dearly held beliefs like that, Senator! They'll get you for it. It's the crime of the century."

"Donna is always telling me the same thing."

"Donna is right. She always has had a good political brain. Listen to her. Don't be as stubborn as Latt."

"Yes," Willie said ruefully, "I suppose that's where he gets it. But I'm not going to pull my punches any more than you are. You know me better than that. Anyway, the war will be over soon and there won't be any necessity to be pro or con. Right?"

Tim shot him a troubled glance.

"I hope so for your sake. For all our sakes. But I wouldn't put any money on it. It's already dragged on too long. If we're going to win it we should have won it by now. I just have an uneasy feeling that it's going to drag on for a while longer, and that you're going to get caught in the middle of it."

Willie looked thoughtful.

"I think my position is pretty reasonable. I'm for winning and winning fast. Go in full bore and get it over with. The objectives of keeping the Communists out of Southeast Asia, keeping the dominoes in place, acting as a shield for democracy in that part of the world—all those seem to me worthwhile objectives."

"Providing it *is* fast. But I don't see too many signs of that at the moment, despite your faith in Lyndon. It all seems too slow and calculating, to me. Too Lyndon-like, as a matter of fact."

"Well," Willie said, resorting to the all-purpose comment Washington uses when discussions run smack into the impenetrable future, "we'll just have to wait and see. It will be interesting."

"That it will," Tim said dryly, "that it will. . . . Are you going to the reunion?"

"Twenty-five years," Willie mused. "That's a big one. Talk about time flying! Yes, I am. As a matter of fact, Donn and Latt and I are going out together."

Tim smiled.

"That should be an interesting journey."

"Yes," Willie agreed rather glumly. "A last chance for Good Old Dad to impart a few final words of wisdom. Which will be summarily ignored."

"Don't push it," Tim suggested. "He has to find out things for himself."

Willie snorted.

"I'm sure he has found out things you and I never knew about at eighteen. These kids nowadays are so far ahead of us— Are you going?"

"Oh, yes. The class things sound like fun, and as you know from Johnny Herbert's letter, there's going to be quite a do at the house, reception, banquet, reminiscing and the works. Plus a big party Sunday at Tony Andrade's winery up in Napa Valley. A grand chance to compare notes and bemoan our fates. I wonder how many will be back?"

"Johnny called me yesterday. Very important I should be there, apparently. He says they want to build the whole thing around me."

"Always," Tim said dryly. "After all, you're our most famous member. And anyway, how could we function without Willie? It was ever thus."

"Yes," Willie said with equal dryness. "Well. Anyway. He told me he's had about fifteen acceptances so far. People you'd never think of, like Suratt and Carriger and MacAllister and Marc Taylor and Randy Carrero—excuse me, Bishop Carrero—and God knows who-all."

"I look forward to it," Tim said. "It should be interesting."

"That it will," Willie echoed with a smile. "That it will."

When they finished lunch and had suitably greeted all those in the room to whom it was socially expedient and politically advisable to speak, Willie caught a cab to the Hill and Tim decided to walk back to his office in the National Press Building. It was toward the rear of the building, away from the temptations of the Willard, which in any event was already going into a decades-long decline and bereft of much of its former sociological interest. Tim sometimes wished idly that he still had its human circus to watch during periods of slow-moving inspiration, but perhaps it was just as well. The more earthy concerns of humankind might still be among his reasonable personal interests but they were not among the professional interests that concerned one whom *Newsweek* had recently referred to as "one of the major formulators of Washington and U.S. opinion."

This was flattering and he supposed there was some modest justification for it, though he never took himself quite as seriously as others did. Quite seriously, he had to admit—even Donna kidded him about "loosening up a bit," though Lord knew she was serious enough herself—but not that seriously. Which was just as well because he was, he had to admit, doing very well indeed in the worlds of Washington journalism and national opinion.

He was not yet one of the great pachyderms like Walter Lippmann or Scotty Reston, but he was getting there. Give him time, give him time. He told himself often that he must not become egotistically and intellectually arrogant, which seemed to be the inescapable characteristics of the major practitioners as they settled more deeply into age and honors; but he could see himself slipping sometimes. He had been a pretty cocky kid before the war when he was editor of the *Daily,* he realized that now; and he still had mighty firm convictions concerning the value of his own opinions. Fortunately a great many of his editors and readers agreed, even though they might differ on some of his conclusions.

He went up in the Press Building's creaky old elevator, walked down the musty corridor past the clicking typewriters and chattering news-tickers of adjacent offices, unlocked the door of his small, cluttered, one-room cubicle. He reflected that he was influential enough so that his views on Vietnam and other matters of urgent interest did have some impact on Washington and so, he hoped, on the country as well.

He and Willie had seen eye-to-eye on many things during their parallel times in Washington, but he realized that they were going to part company to some degree now. He regretted this because he hated to see his old friend take a wrong turning that might well disrupt a public career that Tim believed (as he knew Willie did) held much promise for the future. It might not include the White House, which Tim knew was Willie's unspoken goal ("Isn't it everybody's?" Willie had asked dryly when Tim queried him, though he always played the no-comment game with everyone else), but there was no reason Willie shouldn't give it a damned good try. Providing, that is, that he did not trip over his growing reputation as "a perpetual aginner," as one of his critics in the Senate had recently described him to Tim.

By this, Tim knew, Willie's colleague did not necessarily mean that Willie was agin worthwhile things or that his positions were unsound.

The Senator just meant that Willie was against things that "the establishment" (or, as Tim catalogued them variously in his own mind, "fashionable wisdom" . . . "herd orthodoxy" . . . "groupthink" . . . "herdthink" . . . "phony liberals" . . . "Right-Thinkers" . . . "the Great Gullibles of the West" . . . "Everybody Who Is Anybody") were for. Opposing the establishment, as everyone involved in politics and the making of public opinion knew, guaranteed animosity instant, virulent, unforgiving and unrelenting.

For the moment, as their luncheon conversation and Willie's vote for the Tonkin Gulf Resolution indicated, Willie and the establishment were on the same side regarding Vietnam. Kennedy had committed some twelve thousand American troops to South Vietnam, using the pretext of "military advisers" to bolster his desperately needed macho self-image after Khrushchev's scornful humiliations. The questionable judgment of that ominous step was still being supported by right-thinkers—for the moment. The administration-engineered overthrow of South Vietnamese President Ngo Dinh Diem just three weeks before Kennedy's own assassination had started an undertow of doubt. Now it was growing rapidly, aided by Lyndon Johnson's personal unpopularity among the faithful.

A still-muted but soon to be open washing-of-hands and shifting-of-blame was under way. Soon, Tim was convinced, the establishment would have justified to itself a 180-degree turn and its leading members would be out front leading the parade against the war. And Willie, as on so many other things, would be with them no longer—unless he changed.

This Tim knew he would not do—or if he did, too late to recapture his reputation among the opinion-makers whose power increased every day in direct ratio to the enormous expansion of the communications industry that employed them. Tim had watched Willie's shifting relations with them with considerable concern as, in his five terms in the House and two years in the Senate, he had moved further and further away from their herd-minded orthodoxy. In the House, where his popularity with his constituents had become steadily more solid as his tenure lengthened, his independence of mind and attitude had at first been a rather amusing novelty to the media.

It had brought him a sort of kindly, patronizing attention. This had soon changed.

"At the moment they think I'm one of their pet conservatives," he had told Tim in early days. "Someone like Bill Buckley who is *allowed*. But I'm not conservative, I'm independent, which is infinitely more dangerous to their peace of mind. When they find that out I won't be *allowed* anymore."

It did not take long for him to prove himself correct.

And yet, Tim reflected now as he gave his column for tomorrow a last routine check before taking it down to the syndicate office three floors below to be sent out on the wire, Willie's record, judged by any fair-minded standard, had been essentially middle-of-the-road. On such issues as national health insurance, fair application of taxes, civil rights, he had been far to the left of the accepted "conservative" position. At the same time on labor, foreign policy, the character and integrity of certain famous individuals, publications and news broadcasts, he had been outspokenly skeptical of the accepted faith and disturbingly irreverent toward many of its leading practitioners.

"He's so snide and snarky," a major lady pundit had once remarked at a fashionable Georgetown cocktail party attended by Everybody Who Was Anybody—conveniently forgetting how often she was exactly that way herself in her boringly predictable column.

"So hidebound and reactionary," agreed one of her equally famous, equally predictable male colleagues noted for his slavish devotion to group-think in his nightly television "editorials."

"And you can't ignore him," sadly remarked their fabulously wealthy hostess, staunchly right-thinking and aglitter with diamonds from brow to breastbone. "He's so—so—*obstreperous*."

"But I'm not that at all," he had protested with a cheerful grin when Tim, amused, passed on the comment. "I just say what I think."

But saying what you thought, if you did not think correctly, was not popular in Washington. And since the easiest way to fight back was to tag the offender with the universally scornful, universally employed buzzword "conservative," that was the label used increasingly to attack and denigrate Willie. So it had been ever since the day, way back in '52 in his first campaign for the House, when it had first been applied to him by a disapproving interviewer from the recondite East.

"This boy means trouble," the interviewer had reported to his editorial board in New York. "Better stop him now."

"They've been trying ever since," Willie often remarked with satisfaction. "Boy, have they been trying! But they haven't stopped me yet, and by God they aren't going to."

Nor had they.

He had gone his independent way, his independence nowhere more evident than in his approach to foreign policy, national health and civil rights, the three issues he believed to be the most important facing the country and Congress in midcentury.

In foreign policy his position soon became: the record clearly showed that Marxist-Leninist Communism and its leaders in the Kremlin were out to feather their own nests and literally conquer the world if they could, employing every means of deceit, deception, subversion and both covert and overt aggression that they could possibly devise—a vast, grim, gray Nay-Saying to all the hopes and aspirations of human beings everywhere (including the unhappy multi-ethnic peoples of the Soviet Union themselves) who just wanted to be left alone to raise their families, lead their lives, express themselves as their natures prompted and enjoy a day or two of sunshine along the way.

Not so, said Communism, not so said the stone-faced lumps atop Lenin's tomb in the May Day parades. *We* will tell you how to live, you will obey *our* orders, you will do nothing without *our* permission, your lives are nothing compared to the wishes of the state, *we will not permit you to commit the crime of just being human.*

"The universal death of the mind," Willie often described Communism's ultimate goal in his speeches, prompting scathing denunciations from many in the American intellectual community.

He could understand the youthful idealism that had drawn many of them to Communism in the first place, or at least had disposed them to be forgiving toward it. He could not understand the continuing blindness as one event after another stripped away the public face of Communism and revealed the coldly ruthless greed and the humanity-hating, self-aggrandizing, world-conquering ambitions of the little gang that ran it.

The blindness, he finally decided, was the deliberate blindness of those who had squandered minds and reputations upon an intellectual fad they knew increasingly to be a fraud, but could not abandon because if they did they would have to abandon their reputations, and themselves.

Domestically, he had always been a consistent and highly vocal advocate of a universal national health-insurance plan to meet the steadily rising medical costs that were already threatening the welfare and the peace of mind of a majority of his countrymen. Almost twenty years after the end of the war in which millions of service personnel and their families had become used to generous medical assistance from their government, costs were already soaring beyond the reach of most pocketbooks—and government was no longer there. Only now, under Lyndon Johnson's leadership, was government taking the first tentative steps toward a concept known as "Medicare"—and that wasn't enough to counterbalance the egregious greed of many doctors and health facilities seeking to profit from the medical misfortunes of their countrymen.

"The single most inexcusable major failure of the American government in my lifetime," Willie had said recently in a speech to the Commonwealth Club in San Francisco, "has been the failure to provide universally guaranteed, fully adequate and as-close-to-free medical care to all our citizens as could possibly be devised."

"Socialized medicine!" cried the American Medical Association. "Subversive of free enterprise!" echoed its supporters on the Hill. "Communist!" charged several of his more flamboyant Senate colleagues. ("Oh, Lord!" he groaned to Timmy. "Get a load of that one.")

"Your views on that subject get you good points with the media," Tim assured him with a laugh. "They had to applaud you there. But don't worry," he added dryly, "you'll soon fuck it up."

And so Willie did, making some strong speech in the Senate, or maybe in a C.I.O. convention or some equally sympathetic audience, demanding that labor unions be held to account for their excesses and be made to exercise their responsibilities to social order as vigorously as they did their rights to throw the social order into chaos with strikes.

Or, equally abrasive, noting sardonically in a speech to the annual meeting of the American Society of Newspaper Editors that "I'm officially known as a 'conservative,' ladies and gentlemen. Nine tenths of you automatically label me that without thinking twice—without, perhaps, even stopping to think once. It's gone onto your pages so automatically for so long that probably you're hardly aware that it's there.

"But why am I labeled 'conservative,' ladies and gentlemen? For three reasons only:

"First, because I believe public responsibilities go hand in hand with public rights.

"Second, because I believe that the government of the Soviet Union and Communism as an ideology are engaged upon an unceasing, unrelenting, ruthless campaign to destroy freedom and democracy everywhere in the world and take actual physical possession of the globe if they can possibly do it.

"And third, because I say that certain major publications and commentators are slanted, unfair, totally irresponsible in their deliberate twisting or outright suppressions of the truth, fawningly favorable to those who toe the line politically, ruthlessly critical and often outright suppressive of those who refuse to yield their independence of mind and judgment to the demands of the herd.

"For these things I am labeled 'conservative.'

"I submit to you that this is nonsense—vicious, unmitigated, contemptible nonsense."

"I think they heard the boos on that one all the way to the Golden Gate without a television set," Tim remarked when they had lunch next day at Duke's.

"Oh, that's all right," Willie said with a happy grin. "I'll come out tomorrow with a tax proposal they can label soak-the-rich and we'll all be pals again."

"And you wonder why you're a controversial figure!"

"I don't wonder at all," Willie said cheerfully. "I know exactly."

And the infuriating thing for his critics, Tim thought now as he began to marshal his thoughts for a piece the Sunday *New York Times Magazine* had asked him to do on "L.B.J. in the Kennedy Shadow," was that Willie meant each of the views that were often diverse and sometimes appeared, at least superficially, to be in conflict with one another.

"The only consistency is me," he had said once when Tim pressed him on it. "I'm my own consistency. I'm too much middle-of-the-road and too challenging to their pet assumptions to lend myself to easy understanding by sloganeers and categorizers. That's the reason I make them so uncomfortable."

This was certainly true, Tim had to agree, in the postwar climate.

How that climate had developed was one of the subjects that fascinated him as a student of his times and commentator upon them. He intended to analyze it in some detail in his Sunday magazine piece. He was not going to be surprised, he told himself ironically, if somehow the editors did not find his analysis suitable for publication:

"With an increasingly grim determination since the war, the establishment has refused to admit, greeted with scathing sarcasm or deliberately looked the other way when evidence has surfaced of Communist suppressions and brutalities in the Soviet Union, Communist suppressions and brutalities in Eastern Europe, naked Communist imperialist aggression in the Baltic States and elsewhere, unceasing Communist attempts to subvert peace and stability everywhere in the world.

"With similar ruthlessness the establishment has glossed over, where it has not blatantly refused to report, the facts about Communist-incited dictatorships in newly freed Africa and many Third World nations.

"Succumbing to that oozing sentimentality that is now beginning to be applied to everything from the snail darter to the spotted owl to the newest 'progressive' thug to seize power in some helpless poverty-stricken country, the Great Gullibles of the West moon alike over the Noble Fish, the Noble Fowl, the Noble Animal, the Noble Communist and the Noble Savage. In pious chorus they murmur gentle 'tut-tuts' or excuse altogether all brutalities, murders, dictatorships, bloody suppressions of civil rights and ethnic enemies, cruel plunderings of defenseless people.

"The broad, complacent forgiveness extended to the Soviets is granted to any tin-pot dictator or piece of human scum who overthrows an established order, providing he is smart enough to give himself the correct political label. All that is necessary to win favorable standing with the opinion-makers of the West, as the shrewd realize—and some of them, like Fidel Castro, are very shrewd—is to work on the guilty conscience that seems to pervade the Western intellectual community. If you are a murderous thug who can successfully con the West into considering you 'progressive,' it doesn't matter how many horrors you perpetrate. You have the establishment's official seal of approval, and are home free.

"As the years draw away from the harsh realities of the wartime struggle for survival, the integrity and courage needed for an honest view of the world have become too much for the establishment. Hardly anyone in it has the guts to face up to the facts, or to the implications of having to do something about them if one does face up. Consequently it has become the fashionable, the right, the only acceptable thing, to pretend that they are not there. Consequently, much more often than not, both perspective and reportage have become sadly skewed—sometimes unconsciously, more often deliberately, suppressive of the truth.

"The inevitable result has been that readers and viewers, having nowhere else to turn for their knowledge of events, have become as skewed in their perceptions of the world as the creators and purveyors of the news themselves. Told incessantly that the Communists are just earnest, idealistic, misunderstood nice guys, occasionally a little cruel, perhaps, but essentially salt of the earth, many innocent millions in the West have begun to believe it.

"Told incessantly in many direct and indirect ways that their own country is no damned good, many millions of innocent Americans have begun to feel uneasily that this may be so."

Tim reflected that in this climate, to which he did not belong and to which he refused to contribute, he was almost as unpopular with the establishment as Willie.

They shared many of the same enemies, except that for him, as he had told Willie, there was still the saving grace on quite a few editorial pages, including Anna's, of a lingering adherence to those principles of "fairness," "objectivity," "balance," that had once, in more innocent and less willfully self-blinkered times, been the basics of journalistic practice.

No more, he thought with an ironic smile, no more, no more. The innocent ethics of an older age of journalism had begun their long retreat some decades ago. "Advocacy journalism," the bright young journalism professors called it now. Its eager young practitioners streamed from their classrooms to inundate the media.

Fairness, objectivity, balance, the truth itself—who had seen them lately?

Not many, he thought with a sudden grimness.

Not very damned many.

That, too, he decided, was a basic part of the picture. Possibly it was itself the original sin, the fundamental error from which had come all later skewed misinterpretations:

"Somewhere along the way, probably in New Deal days when the profession, like a majority of Americans, was swept up in the desperate belief that Franklin Roosevelt was the sole salvation of the Republic, it had become absolutely necessary to denigrate, diminish, if possible destroy, everyone and everything that stood in the way of what was perceived to be his golden crusade to save democracy. The result had nothing to do with the merits of his actions, which were many, or the ultimate consequences of his presidency, which will take many decades to unfold. The immediate result was a loss of perspective by his supporters, a consequent unbalance on the part of his opponents. His supporters in the then Washington press corps far outnumbered his opponents. So began a fundamental shift in what was perceived to be the purpose, and the duty, of the journalistic profession.

"The true believers who gave the nation its news from Washington in that time honestly did not realize, so deep was their partisanship, how skewed their reporting was. Slanting the news, or twisting or even suppressing it, was not considered a reprehensible or dangerous thing because it was done in the best of all possible causes—to help F.D.R. save the nation.

"So a tradition grew and began to be handed down. A hierarchy formed. True believers did not approve of nonbelievers. True believers did not hire nonbelievers. True believers hired only those young who gave promise of becoming believers. Washington gradually became encased in a cocoon of Right-Thinking that, beginning with Roosevelt, soon came to embrace almost anything, including Communism, which in any way defied tradition or stability, or challenged old, accustomed values and old, accustomed things.

"Today the effects of this process are everywhere apparent. Few and far between are those in the media today whose mentality and approach to the news has not been formed, shaped and consciously or unconsciously dictated, by the fashionable wisdom, accepted faith and ironclad orthodoxies of 'the establishment' that began with the reportage of New Deal days."

Among the renegades being of course himself. Like Willie, he too was almost impossible to categorize. "A plague on both your houses" did not lend itself to easy labeling in a shorthand age. For him too the best they could do was the easy cop-out word "conservative." But was he? He remembered his introduction to *Cardboard Camelot: Shadow and Substance in the Kennedy Era*. What did his labelers make of its opening paragraphs about the sainted Ike:

"For all the bland haze that now in retrospect seems to hang over the Eisenhower years, there was not a great deal in them to stem the tide of increasing world disorder.

"It is true that the President's barracks-room bullying stopped the British-French-Israeli attempt to recapture control of the Suez Canal from Egypt, but the lack of grace and balance with which it was done weakened still further the influence of older civilizations and made even less effective their war-weakened but still valuable abilities to contribute experience and some stability to the world. It was an act of blatant politics by a President determined that no crisis should upset his drive for reelection to a second term. As ruthlessly as any other candidate, he made sure his own interests were protected.

"It is true that the Korean War was ended, but it was ended in a draw by a President determined to rid himself of a political liability, not in any clear-cut victory for any kind of moral value or purpose—or with any real justification for fifty thousand dead. And it ended with American troops apparently destined to be stationed into the indefinite future on the 38th parallel.

"Finally, the awkward presidential attempt to lie his way out of the U-2 incident, in which the Soviets downed a U.S. spy plane and captured its pilot, provided them with yet another opportunity to denounce the United States and spread ever more widely among the world's ignorant the myth of America's subversions of world peace."

Then the subject changed but his critical tone remained. How did his labelers handle that? By screaming bloody murder. But he felt what he had to say needed saying:

"Nor do the Kennedy years, now that the glamorous presence is gone and the public-relations apparatus has been dismantled, seem any better. They were, in fact, worse: a brief period, gravid with consequences far beyond its brevity, in which the Cold War escalated into its greatest tensions, its greatest gambles and its greatest mistakes.

"The inexperienced young President, scarcely six weeks after the Bay of Pigs had ended in a disastrous failure of presidential courage, emerged pale-faced from his vicious bullying by Nikita Khrushchev in their meeting in Vienna in June of 1961. The Soviet leader, apparently convinced he had taken Kennedy's measure, promptly moved his chessmen on the board.

"There ensued constant rumblings out of Moscow, noisy threats of aid to Castro, loud promises of help if there were any further American attempts to invade. There was a declaration that Moscow would conclude a treaty with East Germany and 'rebuff' Western attempts to maintain access to Berlin. The Berlin Wall was constructed without warning in August of 1961. In October Soviet tanks rolled up to the border to aid East German authorities attempting to stop Americans from crossing: a few hours later, having suitably rattled the West, the tanks were removed. Finally, in November, in a contemptuous what's-all-the-fuss? manner, Khrushchev announced that he was perfectly willing to postpone the Berlin issue to some more salubrious time.

"Badly shaken by Vienna, Kennedy reacted to all this in an 'I'll-show-*him*' mood not conducive to the best of judgment in Cold War matters. Then he, too, had an election to worry about, the off-year Congressional election of 1962. At first his desire to keep everything calm to aid his party at the polls prompted him to try to brush under the rug the greatest challenge of all: the installation of Soviet missiles in Cuba. It was not until then-Senator Kenneth Keating of New York released photographs of them to the press that the President was forced to acknowledge their existence and face up to the inescapable fact that he must, at last, do something.

"There followed 'the Cuban missile crisis,' closest the world has come so far to nuclear war. Aided by the fact that Khrushchev and the Kremlin were not quite prepared to take the ultimate gamble, the President and his advisers won out. Yet even then there was deliberate deception: it was officially denied that Khrushchev had been offered the quid pro quo of withdrawal of American missiles from Turkey. A few weeks later American missiles were quietly withdrawn from Turkey.

"And finally, there was—and is—Vietnam. Kennedy inherited from Eisenhower the initial investment of American 'military advisers' to the South Vietnamese government. He did not choose to reverse it: the 'I'll-show-*him*' macho mood still controlled. Instead he raised the ante to twelve thousand. Three weeks before his own assassination his administration encouraged and supported the coup that resulted in the overthrow and assassination of South Vietnamese President Ngo Dinh Diem. The Vietnam entanglement, which Kennedy inherited, increased and handed on, grows steadily more ominous now."

All of which, he thought, was a pretty good cross section of the Tim Bates approach to a plague on both your houses. Of course when *Cardboard Camelot* was published the establishment's tunnel vision saw only one thing. Its members reacted, as he remarked to Willie, like stuck pigs.

The book had been greeted with a withering critical barrage as news seeped through the ranks of the right-thinking that he had actually dared to be less than awed by the fallen idol. From major publications in the East all the way across the land in the reviews of the many lesser journals that automatically and slavishly followed their lead, the book had been denounced with a vitriol so hysterical that it struck him as almost certifiably insane.

"These guys and gals are literally crazy," Willie agreed when Tim showed him some of the most savage. "Are sane adults actually writing stuff like this? Are they really that unbalanced?"

"I'm in your category now," Tim predicted wryly. "I'm tagged for life. They'll never give up. Critics now living will savage me for the rest of their days. Critics yet unborn will imbibe the anti-Bates gospel with their mothers' milk."

"And most of it," Willie said, "will have only the remotest relation to the quality of your writing. It will all have to do with the fact that you dare to challenge the idols and ideas of the establishment."

For a little while, despite his outward jauntiness, Tim had been disturbed by the intensely personal tone of his critics' denunciations.

Then he had concluded:

So be it.

I will call the shots right down the middle of the road as I see them and if that makes permanent enemies of the establishment so be it.

Fuck them all.

This, he reflected with a grim irony—aware of its price in damaged reputation and diminished commercial success—was known as integrity.

He knew his more hysterical critics would never recognize it.

They saw so little of it in their profession, and had so little themselves.

His mood lightened, having reached that familiar point in his contemplations of the downside of his own life and the world's at which there was no way to go but up. He walked his copy down to the syndicate's office, collected the pink telephone message slips the secretary had recorded for him, returned to his cubbyhole. Three calls were from the House, four from the Senate, one from the White House press office, one from the pleasant widow he occasionally dated on a no-commitments, necessary-Washington-socializing basis.

At the bottom of the pile was a message that brought a smile because it called up a subject on which he, Willie, the President and almost Everybody Who Was Anybody were all agreed. He answered it first.

"Maryetta?—Tim. Is By there?"

And presently, with the comfortable familiarity he could never have mustered twenty years ago but that now came easily as a result of their long association and the genuine friendship they had developed in the cause:

"Hello, you black troublemaker. How the hell are you?"

This casually kidding, genuinely fond greeting, By thought with a pleased little smile, was what he got in Washington from the White House on down—leaving aside those few rabid examples of the older and still fighting South whom he found in House and Senate. Occasionally he had to deal with them. When he did, relations were unremittingly frigid and scrupulously polite. He told Tim once that he had two titles for an autobiography, he didn't know which was better: *I'm* Mister *Nigger, Now*—or, *Nobody Calls Me Nigger Any-more*.

"Not to my face, anyway," he added dryly. "I'm sure the minute I step out in the hall and close the office door, they let me have it."

On the surface, across desks and in committee hearings, it was always, "Mr. Johnson" and "sir" and, in a few more relaxed cases, even an occasional "By." But the shield was always in place, the line was always there. To this day, after passage of the Civil Rights Act of 1964 banning discrimination in public facilities, creating the Equal Employment Opportunity Commission and guaranteeing equal voting rights to his people, and the Twenty-fourth Amendment to the Constitution banning discrimination in public facilities, the barrier still hadn't diminished to any noticeable degree. What he called "silent discrimination" still persisted in a sullen and as yet unconvinced South, and not only there but all across the country. In actual fact it still knew no geographic boundaries. He sometimes confessed to Maryetta with an unhappy sigh that he doubted it ever would.

This of course was the wrong thing to say, as it flew directly in the face of her vehement and oft-expressed belief that reason, right, justice and harmony could be imposed on any troubled human condition if only the imposers were sufficiently fierce, unyielding and ruthless in their efforts.

"I swear to goodness," he told her once in exasperation after they had moved up to Washington, "I think you'd kill somebody if you thought it would make him perfect."

"Or her," she amended automatically. "You're right," she added, completely without humor, "I might not hesitate, at that. It would depend on the Cause"— giving it, as she always did no matter what it was, a strong capital *C* that hung in the air almost visibly, like a flag. "Anyway, you're so defeatist. I don't think you've ever been really convinced, in your heart of hearts, of the value and wisdom of what you've been doing."

"*What?*" he demanded, voice rising in sheer, annoyed astonishment. "Are you crazy, girl? How the hell could I have been through all this struggle if I didn't believe in it? How could I have been a part of, and supported—"

And he launched, as he had so often, into the record he knew by heart, beginning with the Supreme Court's 1954 decision in *Brown* v. *Board of Education of Topeka, Kansas* that the South's long-standing policy of "separate but equal" facilities was unconstitutional . . . Rosa Parks' refusal in 1955 to sit in the back of a bus in Montgomery, Alabama, leading in 1957 to Martin Luther King, Jr.'s organization of the successful boycott that forced the bus company to desegregate . . . the passage of the Civil Rights Act of 1957 creating a national commission to study racial conditions . . . King's formation in the same year of the Southern Christian Leadership Conference to launch nonviolent protest . . . and the response in 1960, by those impatient with the slow pace of nonviolence, of the formation of the Student Nonviolent Coordinating Committee, which belied its name by openly advocating and practicing militant direct action to secure black rights. . . .

And so on to the crisis of 1962, when Kennedy sent federal troops to the University of Mississippi to enroll black student James Meredith and protect him until his graduation a year later . . . and the 1963 march by two hundred thousand in Detroit to demand equality . . . and the televised demonstrations in Birmingham, Alabama, in April and May of 1963, put down with dogs and firehoses by Sheriff "Bull" Connor and his men . . . and the murder of Medgar Evers, field secretary of the N.A.A.C.P., in June of '63 . . . and the 250,000-strong march on Washington in August of 1963 and King's "I Have a Dream" speech.

"And all the way," By concluded with a bitter triumph, "I was right there working for the N.A.A.C.P. and the Committee for a Better Day and helping out! And you have the nerve to tell me I'm 'defeatist' and 'not convinced'! I don't know what conviction is, if that isn't it! You tell me!"

Her sharp-featured little face, bare, freckled, barren of any kind of makeup, which was an affectation she despised, stared at him from beneath its inevitable bun of drawn-back, mousy-gray hair. She looked absolutely humorless and sternly angry, the expression he seemed to remember, when he was away from her, more often than any other. Perhaps it had been a good thing that he had been so often away from her in these years of anguish and struggle, otherwise their marriage might well have collapsed a long time ago. He knew she could smile, sometimes even be quite relaxed and happy, particularly with Ti-Anna and Melrick, but not very often. The Causes were too many and too heavy.

"You tell me!" he repeated. "When I've been in the thick of it all these years!"

"Well!" she retorted, momentarily stopped. "Well! You helped the N.A.A.C.P. some in the early days, nobody can deny that. But your precious C.B.D.! What a laugh that's been, playing plantation patty-cake while other people have been out there dying! A real contribution that's been!"

"I haven't played 'plantation patty-cake'!" he exclaimed, beginning finally to get angry himself. "Just because Jeff happens to own some plantations—"

"Pal Jeff! Friend Jeff! Buddy Jeff! I remember what Jeff Barnett did to you—"

"Maryetta!" he interrupted loudly. "That was twenty-five years ago! That was *in college*! A person can't spend all his life worrying about what went on in college. You have to grow up."

"Some people," she said darkly, "never get over what happened to them in college, and I think you're one. You're still flattered to have Massa Barnett patronize you, after all he did to blackball you from the fraternity. You're so grateful to him it just oozes out of you. He's making big points just because he deigns to act decent to you."

"He is not!" he cried desperately. "He is *not*! Jeff Barnett is a real friend of mine now and I don't care a damn about what he did to me twenty-five years ago."

"Oh, yes, you do," she said with the smugly superior certainty he couldn't abide. "Oh, yes, you do."

"Maryetta—"

But just then, as often happened, the front door slammed, there was bustle in the hall, the other part of their lives together came in. Saved by the kids once more, he thought with a wry grimness as Ti-Anna, seventeen, entered with her cool style and grace and Melrick, fifteen, lumbered close behind with the amiable awkwardness of the high school football star he was.

"Are you two fighting again?" Ti-Anna asked calmly. "Mel, make them stop."

"Can't do it," Mel said with a grin. "They don't listen to me. You make 'em do it, T. You're the one who runs things around here."

"I try," she said with an elaborate sigh and the exaggerated, humorous patience that could usually calm down even her mother, "but, golly, they are *difficult*. 'Nothing prepares you,'" she added, mocking and paraphrasing, as she often did, one of her father's more profound statements, "'for raising parents. There just aren't any rules that can really tell you how to bring them up. You just have to do the best you can and hope they'll turn out O.K. when they finally become adults.' Right, Daddy?"

"That's right," he said with a somewhat sheepish grin, returning the kiss she placed lightly on his cheek. "Your mother and I appreciate the patience you both show toward us."

"It isn't easy," Mel said, dropping into a chair with a thud that seemed to shake the house. "What's for dinner, Ma?"

"I haven't even thought," she said, still stiffly, still the crusader but "mellowing a little around the edges" as By put it, in the presence of her offspring, to both of whom she was usually just simply that—Ma.

"I'll get it," Ti-Anna said. "Anything good in the freezer, Ma?"

"Some pork chops," Maryetta said, starting to get up. "I'll do it, you rest. You've had a busy day, both of you."

"Nah, take it easy," Mel said, rising and pushing her back down gently but firmly. "I'll help. In fact, I'll do it all, T., if you like. Any girl who has just been accepted by the University—"

"No!" By exclaimed as Ti-Anna suddenly flushed with pleasure and the excitement she had obviously been holding back for what she deemed the right moment—characteristic, he thought, characteristic. "That's wonderful, T. That is really wonderful."

"It's very nice," Maryetta said, also obviously pleased but never quite able to relax fully. "I hope you will have a more successful time there than your father did."

"Oh, *Ma!*" Ti-Anna said. "Don't spoil it. Can't you ever relax?"

"I think we should all have a drink," Mel suggested quickly. "Don't you agree, Daddy?"

"I do," By said firmly, getting up and heading for the kitchen liquor cabinet.

"Can I have a martini?" Mel asked innocently. "Just this once, because it's a big occasion?"

By laughed.

"I don't see why not. Just this once. Because it's a big occasion."

"By," Maryetta said sharply. "That boy is fifteen years old—"

"And you're a hundred and ten," Ti-Anna said with one of her sudden unexpected revelations of the temper she had inherited. "Mother, *please* relax."

And after a moment during which she flushed but said nothing, Maryetta to their surprise did so—at least as much as she ever could.

By mixed the drinks and, conviviality gradually restored, they celebrated Ti-Anna's entrance into the University, and whatever that might portend.

Which, By thought uneasily later after they had finished their meal and the kids had gone up to their rooms to study, would depend in large part upon Ti-Anna herself. She was a beautiful girl who had inherited rather more of his genes than her mother's, so that she was not as black as he, not as white as Maryetta, an appealing café-au-lait somewhere in between. From By, former basketball star, she had received her height of five feet eleven and the lithesome natural grace with which she carried it. From him she had received a basically good-natured attitude toward humanity, from her mother the occasional sharp impatience and scornful anger that could flare when human nature failed to measure up to impossibly high standards. Other than that, her name summed her up at seventeen in this moment of triumph.

The birth certificate said "Tiana" after By's mother. A year ago she had announced that hereafter it was to be "Ti-Anna." When Maryetta demanded why, Ti-Anna just shrugged and said, "Because it's my name and I like it that way. I like to be different."

"Isn't Tiana different enough?" her mother objected.

"Not for me," Ti-Anna answered—calmly, but in the tone even Maryetta recognized.

"Are we still allowed to call you 'T.' in the family?" By inquired with a twinkle his daughter did not respond to.

"Of course you may, if it suits you," she said grandly. "I am concerned with the wider world."

"Oh, my goodness, listen to Miss Priss!" Mel exploded with a whoop of laughter. "Just listen to that high-and-mighty girl!"

"Very well," she said in the same grand manner, scooping up her books and departing for her room. "I shall see you all later when you have gotten over this uproarious family joke."

But she made it stick, By thought admiringly. When T. made up her mind, as they had discovered at about age six months, she made it stick.

Where this would place her in the world of the University he could not at the moment predict; but it made him uneasy. Like Willie contemplating Latt's imminent departure for the same campus, By was not altogether happy that his child was entering just as major national controversies seemed to be increasing in intensity. The black cause, with which she had been surrounded in this house all the days of her life, still had a way to go, he thought with a sigh: still a way to go. There was still much to be done, still, in all probability, a lot of pain and anguish before equality became a reality. And even when it did, as he feared despite Maryetta's vehement idealism, it might be equality of opportunity but he suspected that it would not, for the majority, be equality of acceptance or respect or really genuine liking. Some would be lucky enough to receive that from genuinely good-hearted whites, but for most the wall would still be there.

He wondered if Ti-Anna would face it at the University and how she would handle it if she did. And, more broadly, how both his kids would handle it when they moved on from college into a world in which, though they knew themselves to be half-white, they would always be categorized instantaneously on the basis of their color, which was not white. He had been doubtful about his marriage for that reason; his parents, fearful too, had violently objected. Maryetta, in her not-to-be-thwarted way, had swept all that aside. "Everything will be all right," she insisted many times, "if you will *just stop being afraid.*"

Which was all very well for her to say, he sometimes thought bitterly: she had nothing to be afraid of in the white man's world. But what of her children who, caught between the races, might very well, unless very lucky, have lives difficult indeed? She wasn't a worrier about consequences—not Maryetta. She was a hell-with-'em kind of girl; and that, he thought glumly, created a lot of hell for other people.

It had always created a lot for him, he knew that. His life in the civil rights movement would have been a lot easier if, as he put it to himself, he hadn't had to lug Maryetta along like a sack of feed potatoes everywhere he went. At first he had tried to convince her to settle in some northern city where their mixed marriage wouldn't cause too much comment, and keep her head down while he went south to work in the movement.

"Keep my head down!" she echoed with a snort. "When did I ever do that, By Johnson?"

"I know," he said glumly; and with a rare retaliation of his own, "That would be asking too much consideration for other people, I suspect."

"Listen!" she said, flaring up inevitably. "If I didn't have consideration for other people, I wouldn't care what you do or what happened to your precious 'movement.' I am considerate! I do care! Nobody in this world cares more than I do about the humble and downtrodden [being the kind who was so obviously earnest that she could use words like that in ordinary conversation and get away with them] and nobody is more determined than I am to help Negroes achieve their full and rightful place in American society. You'd be crazy not to make use of my abilities in the Cause. Absolutely crazy!"

So she went along with him everywhere in those early days, and pretty soon a little doggerel attached itself to their names in civil rights circles and trailed them through the South:

> "Bayard had a little lamb,
> Her fleece was white as snow,
> And everywhere that Bayard went,
> His lamb was sure to go.
> She pushed him north, she pushed him south.
> She never closed her G.d. mouth.
> If words could tumble Jericho,
> They'd be Maryetta's, white as snow."

So when he and Jeff announced the creation of the Committee for a Better Day, whose board of directors was split evenly between the races, she had insisted that she be made secretary.

"Are you sure that's wise?" Jeff inquired with some dismay when By told him.

"No, I'm not," By said, sounding miserable, "but you know Maryetta. She just keeps after me and after me and *after* me."

"Yes," Jeff said, remembering all too vividly their college days, "I do know Maryetta. Well . . . all right, if that's what you want."

"I don't," By said gloomily, "but she won't give me any peace unless we give it to her."

"Well," Jeff said, gentleman in all circumstances, "she is very good at organizing, and that will be a big help. So maybe it will be a real plus for us to have her aboard."

Their relations were very cool, however. Maryetta obviously had never forgiven him for organizing the opposition to By in the fraternity house, and so, after offering a warmer friendship based on the hope that bygones might be bygones, Jeff had retreated into a scrupulous politeness and as little direct contact as possible.

"Give her her head," he advised his fellow board members privately, "and she'll soon be out of here."

After antagonizing a majority of them with her headstrong crusading, she was politely eased out and her duties were turned over to a placid young Negro girl equally idealistic but a whole lot calmer.

This was also a very good thing from the standpoint of her own safety, as Jeff pointed out to By, who agreed, because the South was not yet ready for abrasive white crusaders, particularly partners in mixed marriages. She received a number of serious threats to her life, which she grandly ignored until By almost hysterically insisted that she pay attention to them. His fellow civil rights workers were almost equally hostile, not life-threatening but deeply resentful of what they referred to as "her domineerin', slave-drivin' ways."

She absorbed the blow to her pride with the serene conviction, which always fortified her, that she was right and her husband wrong in what she saw as his ineffective ways and his lack of what she called "real zeal" for the Cause. She began to go north on lecture tours, carried the word to forums where audiences were respectful and receptive; and at home she never let up on By, constantly hammering him to be more active—"more strong," as she put it, "the major leader you ought to be, the tough leader you can be."

"Maryetta," he protested more than once down the increasingly tense decades of conflict and advance, "I'm not strong—at least not what you mean by 'strong.' I like people, I don't like to fight with 'em if I can avoid it. I like to conciliate, I like to reason, I like to build bridges. In the long run I think that's even more important than legislation. Legislation is the foundation but the foundation has to rest on solid ground if it's to hold. That's what I want to help create—solid ground that will support the foundation, and last. It isn't going to help much if we have the foundation in place but the ground of real conciliation crumbles away beneath it. Isn't that right?"

She was scornful, accusing him of "making speeches," but he was satisfied with his own record. He was doing his full share to bring about corrective legislation, taking many chances as a field man for the N.A.A.C.P. He too had received threats, his life at times had been in real danger. On one occasion he had been captured by a drunken group of farmers on a back road in the swamps and only their drunkenness had enabled him to escape, otherwise he would have wound up in the mangroves as one more blowtorched corpse to add to the others. He had learned early in his marriage not to tell Maryetta everything, "She makes such an all-fired fuss about things" as he commented to Jeff, so she didn't always understand the risks he took. He let her rave: after a while it went off his back like water off a duck. It was the only way he could keep sufficient peace of mind and inner certainty to keep on doing his job.

The creation of the C.B.D. had been greeted with a mixture of alarm and scorn in the South, a patronizing skepticism in the North. No one had been more sarcastic than Maryetta, who again felt that it wasn't "strong" enough.

"It's just a way for Jeff Barnett and his so-called 'progressive' fellow millionaires to avoid reality," she predicted. "It takes the heat off them to pretend they're doing something. It won't add up to anything. They won't let you and your friends have any influence. It won't be anything but a front for inaction."

This was the accepted wisdom in the North, expressed in leading establishment editorials and commentaries. In the South the C.B.D. was portrayed as a Trojan horse being inadvertently brought within the gates by "innocent and sadly mistaken do-gooders such as State Representative Jefferson Barnett of South Carolina" (Jeff having by then been propelled into politics by birth, family, tradition, influence and "an itch to get into the thick of things," as he told Willie when Willie called from Washington to congratulate him on his election).

"We are very skeptical," the general theme ran, "that Rep. Barnett and his no doubt well-meaning fellow whites will be able to withstand the pressures for radical activism that are sure to come from such hotheads as the well-known agitator Bayard Johnson. It is another example of woolly-minded innocents making themselves prisoners of shrewdly calculated ruthlessness."

"Is that me?" By inquired wryly. "Hothead, well-known agitator, shrewdly calculating, ruthless? And are you a woolly-minded innocent?"

"Ignore 'em," Jeff advised. "They think they have to say somethin'. Let's just put our heads down and keep plowin'."

Which was what they did as they approached the mid-sixties and the civil rights movement grew under the leadership of a committed and effective man in the White House. Lyndon Johnson meant it and knew how to do it: his leadership helped immeasurably. They all felt that much remained to be done, but things seemed to be moving in a smooth and constructive way.

By felt with considerable pride that the C.B.D., in addition to supporting King and other nonviolents, had contributed a lot to this with educational materials, broadcasts, press statements, frequent Congressional testimony and general national exposure, including its well-publicized public forums in the South at which Maryetta, to her angry dismay, was seldom invited to speak. By felt that the organization was becoming both the bridge and the foundation he had hoped to build. Jeff also seemed satisfied, and by a policy of hammering away at the advantages of "reasonable, fair-minded, peaceful conciliation," he was able to fend off political opponents who called him "nigger-lover" and "traitor to his race."

"Barnett dignity and Barnett money can beat those rednecked bastards," he assured By: and so they had, at least so far.

By's own reasonable approach was equally unpopular with many blacks. The nonviolent were jealous of another prominent figure in the field, the violent found him "much too wishy-washy," to quote his wife. It was with them that he had the most trouble.

He told Maryetta that he had "won some sort of objectivity award" when, shortly after he had received a particularly venomous anonymous threat, Mel came in from practice one evening to report "a funny-looking package" by the back door of the Washington house.

After the D.C. bomb squad defused it, By read the savage message that had been tossed in the bushes alongside. It called him an Uncle Tom (for the ten-thousandth time), and was signed with the symbol, in blood, of one of the radical groups that were increasingly trying to take over the movement. It promised more bombs if that one failed. For a while he accepted police protection, discarded it when nothing further happened. But it made him and the family permanently uneasy.

Stubbornly, however, he continued, along with King and other members of the Southern Christian Leadership Conference, on the nonviolent path; and even though there presently were signs that King and some others might be veering toward the more violent in an attempt to preempt their growing influence and retain control, he did not budge from his position.

"You're going to be left behind," Maryetta told him. "You and Massa Barnett are going to be out there in the cold with your black-and-white tea parties and history is just going to go right on by and forget you. You were riding the wave but you aren't anymore. Even Martin knows that. If he can see it, why can't you?"

He remained stubborn. He often asked himself if it was because he *was* flattered by Jeff's friendship and cooperation, if he was a white man's captive as his harsher critics sometimes called him—if the adult By was still impelled by the gratitude of the rejected-then-embraced, the adolescent's wound at last healed by the adult's overeager desire to grovel in a patronizing fellowship.

He could not believe it. No one could have been more committed than Jeff, once convinced of the realities that faced the South.

"Hell, man," he said, "it's our whole society's at stake down here.

We've got to adapt, we can't stand still or the wave's goin' to roll right over us. We all can live peacefully side by side, I know we can. We've got to."

At first, it was true, he did not openly espouse any advance beyond living together peacefully side by side, and it was quite a while before he and Mary Dell felt comfortable enough to invite By and Maryetta and other black leaders to their house. But the day did come, and after that there was never any question that his name, his wealth, his busy energies and his formidable personal charm were wholly dedicated to the cause. The Barnetts had always been leaders and when their most recent and most vigorous head of family (his father having died of a heart attack on the golf course) took a position, it had great influence with both races. He was, as King once remarked, "an invaluable help in the struggle for equal justice in the South." The praise was taken up and repeated many times even in those Northern circles normally most suspicious of born-again racial reformers.

He had been enormously pleased and flattered, though he told no one but By and Willie about it, when he received a letter from Dr. Chalmers at the University that said, in part, "I always knew that Jeff Barnett would someday do us proud; and now you have, in an area in which your energetic support and your great charm and abilities are absolutely essential if the South is to make the necessary, inevitable transition."

So By always wound up concluding that he was Jeff's true friend because Jeff was a sincere and genuinely good man who, whatever his traditional hurtful Southern attitudes might have been in college, was a genuine convert now. As such, By was proud and happy to be his friend and associate. If any little doubts still lingered about his own reasons for this, he successfully put them aside. He and Jeff Barnett together formed one of the strongest bridges anywhere between the races. By knew it would last their time, and that from it had come, and would continue to come, many solid and lasting benefits for his people.

And now he had just received official recognition of this, and had turned immediately, as had become his habit at points of decision, to what he referred to privately (and not to Maryetta) as "my three advisers," Jeff, Willie and Tim.

It was the first offer of a federal position he had ever received. It had come to him, the familiar voice said, "because Ah need people in there Ah can trust to do the job Ah want 'em to do, which is to guarantee every Nigrah boy and girl in this country a chance at a good job and a decent livelihood. Ah need you, By. Your President needs you! And"—a characteristic drop in tone, an earnest emphasis—"your *people* need you, which is more to the point and far more important than Ah will ever be."

"But, Mr. President—" he had begun instinctively. But if he really had any objections, which the President bluntly doubted, they were swept away in ten minutes of fervent exhortation about his great personal qualities, his magnificent record in the civil rights struggle, his invaluable contributions to race and country, his unbeatable qualifications for this position—and perhaps beyond. Who knew? If he did a good job there, which was absolutely certain given his superb abilities, he might well find himself a candidate for public office someday.

"Ah'd be for you, By, you know that! But first you have to accept this appointment and do the great job Ah know you can. Don't let your President down now, By! Don't let your people down!"

By promised to think it over and get back by 6:00 P.M.

When he called Jeff in Charleston for advice, Jeff was delighted and told him he would be a fool not to accept. Then he called Willie, with whom he had also become close again as his own activities and Willie's unflagging support of civil rights legislation had gradually restored the old trust and friendship. Willie said the same, volunteered to introduce him at the Senate confirmation hearings and promised to do everything possible to help. Now he was hearing from Tim, who told him flatly to go to it. His political analysis echoed Willie's.

"Of course he needs a moderate in there, to head off any pressure to name one of the radicals. It's the old Lyndon policy of co-opt 'em before they get strong enough to do any damage. That doesn't mean, though," Tim added hastily, "that you aren't thoroughly qualified. You are. It's a great appointment. There won't be a bit of opposition in the Senate, doesn't Willie agree?"

"That's what he says. I hope he's right."

"He's right. When will it be announced?"

"Later this afternoon, the President says."

"Good," Tim said. "I'll get to the typewriter this minute and start a column: 'The President's appointment of Bayard Johnson to be assistant chairman of the newly formed Equal Employment Opportunity Commission is one of those ideal choices that does not come often in an administration. It both recognizes "By" Johnson's many invaluable contributions to the civil rights cause and it brings his great abilities as a conciliator between the races to bear upon the most pressing of all Negro problems: gaining fair access to the nation's job markets and having the chance to establish the economic security without which civil rights legislation fades and becomes meaningless on the books.' And so on. How's that?"

"It's true," By said. "I mean, what you said about economic security in relation to rights legislation."

"Of course it is," Tim said with a chuckle. "I don't write things that aren't true. At least, I hope not. How about lunch?"

They agreed on the following Tuesday and hung up. An hour later the phone rang again. Maryetta took it, as she usually did because one never knew what crank might be on the other end and she was more effective than he at telling them to fuck off. Not that she ever put it that way, but the tone was sufficient. This time she handed him the phone with a puzzled look.

"It's Dr. Chalmers at the University," she said, hardly bothering to cover the mouthpiece. "What does that reactionary old fuddy-duddy want?"

"Shhh," he whispered sternly. Something of the old deference came back into his voice.

"Yes, sir, Dr. Chalmers," he said. "It's nice to hear your—"

"Don't grovel!" she hissed. "Don't Uncle Tom!"

"I'm not Uncle—" he began sharply, as abruptly silenced himself. "Dr. Chalmers," he said firmly, "it is good to hear from you, sir, after all these years. What can I do for you?"

"By," the president said, ignoring background noises he must have heard, "it's good to hear you. I have watched you from afar, as I do a lot of our graduates who go out of here and on to bigger things, and I must say I have admired your career and your devotion to your people's advancement. I believe I wrote you a letter a few years back—"

"You did," By said, suddenly ashamed of himself for ignoring it on Maryetta's tart advice. "One gets so busy—"

"Well I know," Dr. Chalmers said, "well I know. I assumed as much and took the will for the deed. I am calling to congratulate you on your appointment—"

"Is it out already?" By asked blankly. "I haven't even told the President I would accept yet."

Dr. Chalmers chuckled.

"A fast-moving man. I wish all presidents were able to be so decisive. He only has a Congress to contend with, I have the board of trustees. Anyway, it's a great move and I know you'll do brilliantly. I suppose much of your job will be basically public speaking, public education—public relations, if you like. I'm calling you to invite you to make your first speech as a federal official here. How about inaugurating our new Herman and Gretchen Krohl Memorial Lecture series?"

"Is that Rudy Krohl?" By demanded sharply. "I'm not sure I want to speak under his auspices."

"It is," Dr. Chalmers admitted. "He's a member of the board of trustees now, you know—"

"No, I didn't," By said in a tone of complete reserve.

"Yes, the formal announcement will be made at reunion weekend. He's given us a very handsome endowment for the series, which he's establishing in his late parents' name to bring us lecturers 'devoted to the advancement of American ideals and values.' You more than qualify, in my book."

"Does he know about this? I can't imagine someone with his racial ideas—"

"We would only accept the endowment if we retained complete freedom of choice with speakers. He didn't like it but I made it stick."

"And this is your joke on Rudy," By said, sounding bitter though he tried not to.

"Join us," Dr. Chalmers suggested comfortably, "and let's have the last laugh on him together."

By was silent for a moment.

"I hadn't thought of it that way," he said softly.

"And of course," Dr. Chalmers said, resuming dignity without a hitch, "you are very famous and you are very well qualified, and I think it would be a real triumph for the University to have you here. The emolument is five thousand dollars plus airfare and accommodations for you and your wife for two nights. It's Maryetta, isn't it?"

"Formerly Bradford."

"I believe I remember her," the president said. "Very active. Very social-minded. Very—'progressive,' is that the word?"

"Or 'liberal.' "

"But the main thing is 'active,' " Dr. Chalmers suggested with a chuckle. "Isn't that right?"

"That's right," By said. "She may not come. She doesn't approve of our alma mater these days. If she ever did."

"But you will."

"I'll have to think about it," By said. Again Dr. Chalmers chuckled.

"I can't just announce it without your permission, like the President did?"

"Better not. I might refuse."

"I was your president before he was," Dr. Chalmers pointed out. "Bear that in mind when making your decision. You'll call me, then? I'd like to make arrangements as soon as possible."

"I will."

Maryetta was scathing, scornful and opposed.

"Why would you want to go out there?" she demanded. "Why would you want to give status to that—that—insufferable Nazi? And why should you do Chalmers any favors? He just wants to give the University a free ride on your coattails. They've always been so racist."

"They're taking a lot of Negroes now," he said. "And it is, after all, a fairly prominent institution. It wouldn't do me any harm to speak there. They might benefit but so would I."

"Well, I'm not going with you."

"That's all right," he responded, unmoved. "You heard what I said to Dr. Chalmers. He doesn't expect you."

"I suppose you'll get all gooey-eyed with sentiment and let them make a big show over you. Dr. Chalmers' pet civil rights leader! Dr. Chalmers' pet monkey!"

"Oh, Maryetta," he said, tired and exasperated. "For God's sake. Knock it off, will you?"

"Well, I don't think you should go. But of course you'll suit yourself."

"Probably," he agreed in the matter-of-fact tone he used when it came to the point where she had hectored so much that he refused to take it anymore. "Probably will, Maryetta."

To which his "three advisers" all said amen when he told them. Willie pushed it a step farther, so casually it almost took By's breath away.

"You'll be there, we'll be there. There'll be a big reunion at the house and a big party at Tony Andrade's winery up in Napa Valley. Why don't you be my guest and join us?"

"But—but—"

"Not 'but,' " Willie said calmly, "just 'yes.' That's simple."

'But—but—they rejected me, Willie. They blackballed me. They didn't want me."

"Bayard Johnson," Willie said severely, "that was twenty-five years ago. That was before the war. That was when we were all kids. We're grown-ups now, for God's sake. You're buddy-buddy with your principal opponent, Jeff, anyway. What makes you think anyone else is going to give a damn at this late date?"

"I give a damn," By said softly. "*I* give a damn."

"Well, it's time for you to stop it," Willie said bluntly. "If anybody still remembers—"

"They'll remember," By predicted bitterly. "It was a really big deal in your senior year, wasn't it? They'll remember."

"Yes," Willie conceded, "but the point is, they won't care anymore. Things have changed so much since then that nobody will care. Life's moved on, By. We're all a hell of a long way from where we were then. So let it go, O.K.? I'm sure Maryetta will tell you that."

"She hasn't forgotten. She remembers. She won't want me to join you."

"Well—we—do. So how about it?"

There was silence for a long moment.

"I'll have to let you know," By said finally. "I'll just have to let you know."

"Nope," Willie said, "that's not good enough. I don't want you to fret and worry and let Maryetta work on you. I don't want you to wiggle out from under. What's your answer, yes or no?"

For another long moment there was silence while By struggled with it. He feared it and wanted it. There would be the risk of a new rejection, though he had to concede that Willie was probably right, it was unlikely. There would also be the satisfaction of "rubbing their noses in it," as he put it to himself. It was a terrific tug-of-war for a moment, ended when Willie with his usual perspicacity, went to the heart of it.

"And don't have any thoughts of 'rubbing their noses in it,'" he added, "because that isn't worthy of you. That isn't my motivation and I hope it wouldn't be yours. It's a straight up-or-down proposition, offered in friendship and sure to be accepted in that spirit by everybody, I'm confident of it. Yes or no?"

By's answer when it finally came was almost inaudible; but clear enough.

"Good," Willie said, pleased but managing not to sound as relieved as he felt. "Great. I'll send word along to Johnny Herbert, then, who's handling arrangements at the house, and to Tony in Napa Valley. And we'll all have a great time. Right?"

"If you say so," By said with a touch of rueful humor.

"Never underestimate the power of Willie Wilson," Willie said with a self-mocking flourish. "This time, it's going to work."

"This time," By said, "since it's rewriting history, it had damned well better."

"Donn and Tim and I are going to fly out together," Willie said, briskly moving on before By had time to change his mind. "Why don't you join us on the same flight? My secretary can set it up for you."

"Well—O.K. Better get me two seats. My daughter Ti-Anna's been accepted for fall quarter. We'll be sitting together."

"Good. Our son Latt will be with us. He's entering too."

"That's good," By said. "They'll be able to start off with someone they know on campus."

"Great," Willie said. "That will be nice for both of them." He started to chuckle and add something further, then stopped.

By started to respond in kind, and stopped.

For a moment they had teetered on the edge of cliché, knew it and backed away.

"I'll have my secretary call you as soon as she's got the tickets," Willie said. "See you in a couple of weeks. Tell Lyndon yes."

"I will," By said wryly, "though it isn't necessary. He's already accepted for me."

Later that evening he found Dr. Chalmers had, too.

The phone rang; Maryetta again intercepted. This time she sounded genuinely pleased because the caller by now was very well known nationally in All the Circles That Really Mattered.

"It's Dr. Suratt from the University," she said. "I imagine he wants to congratulate you on the E.E.O.C. appointment."

"Perhaps," he said—with reserve, for he too had heard much of Renny in the intervening years.

"Bayard *Johnson*!" Renny exclaimed, giving it a resounding note of fulsome awe. "It *has* been a long, *long* time! And what *miracles* you have wrought for your people since you left the University! We are all *enormously* proud of you! And of Mrs. Johnson, who is such a well-known crusader for so many noble causes! Please give her, too, my most *profound* and most respectful congratulations!"

Which, he told himself, should be a sufficient amount of bullshit to soften up even the most stubborn Negro, which he had heard from many sources By could be when he got his back up. They all loved flattery, Renny had found (not aware of the scornful little smiles that had often been exchanged behind his back when he was, as he put it, "laying it on with my interracial trowel"). He was convinced that praise from him was flattery indeed, now that he had achieved such a major position in the worlds of academe, social thought and political controversy.

"Dr. Suratt," as he had carefully planned from the moment of his war-end decision to return to the University and if possible become a teacher there, was now a major institution on the national scene, an entity almost separate from himself which was recognized and accorded instant and automatic respect by the establishment. Now as he approached his sixteenth year of teaching, publishing, commenting, lecturing upon and participating actively in, social and political issues, Dr. Suratt *was* the establishment, as much as anyone could possibly be.

Right-thinkers everywhere knew him as one of those seminal figures whose challenging and disrespectful views of the *other* establishment blended with his magnetic platform presence to make him a formidable, slavishly admired icon. He was worshiped from New York City to the Golden Gate.

"One of the major social and political theorists of our time . . . a voice of sanity and reason in a troubled age . . . a prophet of coming events whose dynamic and exciting views must be studied and absorbed by all who wish to understand the profound transformations of the twentieth century . . . one of those paradigmatic figures who illuminate the world for all of us . . . a guru for the enlightened . . . a leader for our times."

So sounded the reverent hallelujah chorus, from good gray newspaper to twinkly bright television talk show to ponderously pompous national radio network.

At forty-five, Renny was an inseparable and unassailable part of that great interlocking directorate of mutual puffery, publicity and back-patting that controls the American intellectual community. They reviewed his books—he reviewed their books. They praised his speeches—he praised their speeches. They quoted him—he quoted them. He told the world how wonderful they were—they told the world how wonderful he was. The drumbeat was incessant, implacable and irresistible.

From the winding back roads of Martha's Vineyard to the windswept dunes of old Nantucket to the lush green lawns of Georgetown, they passed the word. On campus after campus, at political fundraisers and at increasingly raucous protest rallies, wherever the four winds blow, Renny returned the favor.

It was all very jolly and completely typical of what passed for independent American thought in the second half of the twentieth century.

Inevitably this gave him a virtually impregnable status on campus, a position in which his tenure in the minds of Everyone Who Really Mattered was so solid that more conservative colleagues, the board of trustees and even those few students who dared to be openly skeptical of his views were helpless to challenge him. He was set for life and he knew it. He had found his niche in the interlocking world and nobody, but nobody, could dislodge him from it.

He was also an avid womanizer who went from one young female student to the next like a hedgehog in heat; a vanguard figure who was already noted for his long hair, his insolent manner, his dirty-looking (though, secretly, carefully laundered) clothing and his increasingly open use of drugs. He was ahead of his times (although his times were rapidly catching up with him) in his experiments with marijuana, cocaine, heroin, LSD and anything else he could get his hands on. The word on campus, increasingly, was, "If you want it, old Renny can help you get it."

Young minds in which others such as Duke Offenberg, Johnny Herbert and Moose Musavich were valiantly and against increasingly heavy odds trying to instill some modest basic standards and decencies were turning instead to the pied piper who sang his siren song from a professor's podium in a musty corner of the Quad.

Looking down from the elevated lectern on which he leaned in his customary casual Look-kids-I'm-one-of-you slouch, he would survey the upturned faces of postwar youth with the inner contempt he felt for the great majority of his fellow beings. Not only did he know that he was mentally superior to, and much more mentally agile than, all but the tiniest fraction of the minds that came into his hands every year for instruction and conditioning, but he was the Teacher; and no matter how disrespectful and independent college students might like to think themselves, that fact gave him an extra edge that, combined with a personality increasingly forceful and a confidence constantly expanding, gave him a terrific impact upon the young. These minds were there to be told, and he was telling them. Whatever crap they got elsewhere, they got realism from him.

In his way, he reflected with satisfaction, he was just as influential, and just as famous, as pompous Tim Bates and high-and-mighty Willie

Wilson. "Timorous Tim" and "Senator Squeak-In," Renny referred to them when his lectures got around to what he titled "The Fuzzy Middle."

"Then we have Timorous Tim and Senator Squeak-In," he would say to approving smiles and titters from the class. "Tim Bates, our number-one reactionary columnist in these whole United States, and famous Willie Wilson, our Senator, winner by 2,561 votes in one of history's closest contests, examples par excellence of the fuzzy middle.

"The three of us, you may not know, were fraternity brothers in the Alpha Zeta house right here on this very campus. I examined their minds then, I examine them now. They were full of amiable middle-of-the-road twaddle then, they are full of amiable middle-of-the-road twaddle now. They do not, I am afraid, give us much of a lead in a time when America seems to be drifting in a conservative stupor toward a pileup on the sharp rocks of domestic and international reality. History does not allow us time for the so-called 'balance' and 'objectivity' of a Wilson and a Bates. History demands of us that we take sides. *Whose side are you on?* That is the question you must decide for yourselves, my young, earnest, valued, *thinking* friends. I am only your helper. The basic decisions are up to you."

And having neatly skewered Willie and Tim and flattered the students, he would proceed to tell them what those decisions should be. His prescriptions were not comfortable for many of his own generation.

"The Suratt problem," as Dr. Chalmers had described it recently in a frustrated discussion with Duke, was one that had stable heads in the University upset and concerned; and this, of course, Renny knew and enjoyed and made the most of. He particularly liked to twist the knife when it came to drugs, although of course he was far too clever to speak of them openly. The message was clear enough.

"There are those on this campus," he would say with dramatic sternness, "who do not believe that you and I have a God-given right to challenge every false assumption, defy every outmoded standard, try everything that will expand and enrich our experience of life. They do not want us to think! They do not want us to experience! They do not want us to grow and liberate our minds and bodies! I tell you, my young friends, do not let them get away with it! Do not let them cripple us! Do not let them cripple *you*! You are only young— once. You will only have the courage and the fine, brave anger to defy them—once. Do it now my friends! *Now!*"

And quite a few—and their numbers were growing rapidly as the frazzled sixties roared forward—were doing just that.

The satisfaction this gave Renny was a peculiar mixture of things he did not stop to analyze too closely—perhaps could not—perhaps dared not. But his fraternity brothers did.

"He's always been jealous of all of us," Johnny said one warm spring night when Duke and Shahna had him and the Musaviches up for dinner. "He never liked anything in the house. He never respected any of us, he never believed in even the minimum decencies of getting along with people. He could never get along with anybody."

"Because he never tried," Duke said. "He would sacrifice anything for something clever. He made himself alien to everybody. Dr. Chalmers asked me about him when Renny applied here. I told him, but he couldn't be convinced. Renny can get along with people when it's to his advantage and he worked on Chalmers because he wanted a job. Once he got established, it was his show and it's been his show ever since. I don't like to think about the damage he's done to a lot of kids."

"The little Carlson girl, for instance," Johnny said, recalling the sad, aborted pregnancy and its chaotic aftermath when the girl was expelled and her parents sued the University and Renny. The University made a substantial out-of-court settlement. Renny, pleading innocence and prior occupation of the same premises by others, got away scot-free, his reputation on campus only given an extra spice.

"Or my boy Bill Gregorio," Moose said, remembering the bright-eyed, always-smiling young football star who had been mesmerized by Renny's urgings to "try drugs, you'll like them and they'll help your game." A suicide came out of that one and, for a short time, a halt to experiments among the team. Now, Moose confessed gloomily, there were signs that experimentation had resumed; and again, he said flatly, Renny was the major influence responsible for it.

"I've rarely known a truly evil person," Duke said thoughtfully, "but I'm beginning to think that Renny may be. He likes to destroy just—to destroy."

"The world thinks he's wonderful," Johnny observed ironically. "Have you read the reviews of his books? He's the greatest thing since Plato. If you want the laugh of the week, compare his reviews with mine. Or Tim's."

"He's certainly a darling of the media," Duke agreed. "That makes him a really tough problem for the University. You can't just up and fire him, it would be the scandal of the age."

"And he doesn't really give you grounds to," Moose said. "There's nothing open about the sex or drug business—he doesn't preach it in the classroom—or rather, he does, but not directly enough to pin him on it—and the kids of course won't tell on him. Those who are involved wouldn't do it, and those who aren't wouldn't think it was right to endanger the job of someone who wasn't doing them personally any harm."

"And as for his general lectures," Johnny said, "you and I are old-fashioned, Moose, we're really out-of-date. We believe in certain standards, we believe in our country, we think the kids should be given some basic decencies to live by—I mean, good God, man, how antiquated can we get? We're not smart and fashionable and—destructive—the way he is."

"That's the mood of the times," Duke said gloomily, rising to walk to the edge of the patio and stand staring down through the rolling hills and valleys to the lights of the University half a mile below. "What are they all thinking down there? What are they making of all of us, in those busy little minds?"

"About what we did in our day, I guess," Moose said with a smile. "We thought we knew it all and the faculty was just a bunch of old fuddy-duddies."

"But there were exceptions," Johnny said. "There were quite a few we respected, and in those days, I like to think, most of them were worthy of respect. Nowadays the respect seems to go to teachers like Renny who want to tear down everything—"

"And not to thee and me, who favor the status quo," Duke said humorously, returning to his deck chair as Shahna and Diana Musavich came out with dessert and coffee.

"Not altogether the status quo," Johnny objected. "I'm not against change or challenge to established ideas, but when I teach American history I want to be as fair and honest and objective as I can make it. I don't want to take sides and I don't want my students to take sides. Renny and the establishment that thinks he's so wonderful want people to take sides. And the sides are always against. Always against. It's getting so that nothing positive is being taught about America or the world anymore. It's always destructive. Always ruinous. Always disruptive. Always tear down, tear down, tear down. That's not the way I was brought up to think or teach, and I don't like it."

"Me, either," Moose said, unconsciously rubbing the long jagged scar down his right forehead as he had done ever since the war when really concerned. "I don't like it when my kids come home with that attitude and I don't like it when I come across it in other people's kids. I try to fight it on the field, which is the only pulpit I have, and not too much of that. If you're eighteen or nineteen you usually don't get into philosophical discussions with the head coach, there isn't much time for stuff like that. But there are ways of conducting yourself, ways of playing, ways of treating the other guy—things come up, I get the chance to put in a word or two now and then. I'm not working on the intellectual level you guys are, but on the level of everyday conduct and how to act like a decent human being, I suspect I have some influence. I try to act as though I do, anyway."

"You do, Mooser," Johnny said in the affectionate tone they had always used with Moose when he became earnest. "I'll bet you're a wonderful influence."

"You remember the popularity contest the *Daily* ran last year," Duke reminded. "Favorite male teacher, Coach Moose Musavich, yeay, yeay, yeay!"

"That's just because I've had a winning streak for a couple of years," Moose said, "and that's only because some damned good boys have turned out for the team. Not much to do with me."

"Oh, yes," Duke said. "Oh, yes. Your popularity goes deeper than that. The kids think you're a good man, Mooser, good in the old-fashioned sense, which a lot of them secretly admire even though it isn't very fashionable nowadays."

"It isn't with this faculty, that's for damned sure," Moose said somberly. "Renny isn't alone and it isn't just the kids who are impressed. He has a lot of influence and a lot of followers all through the faculty. We all attended the last academic senate meeting: you know how the majority thinks. All these bright young twits who are against everything and urging the kids to do every damned irresponsible, smart-assed thing they can think of to defy authority, destroy tradition and disrupt sound education. It's a microcosm of something much bigger that's spreading all through American society right now. It's a cancer. A damned cancer."

"Why is it so fashionable nowadays to be *not* good?" Johnny inquired wistfully. "Why is everything supposed to be so damned *negative*? Where did things get so off-track and topsy-turvy?"

"Now, now," Shahna said with mock severity. "You're all being reactionary, conservative, old-fashioned, right-wing, far right, antediluvian, unprogressive, insensitive, uncaring, unthinking, narrow-minded, unable to grasp the realities of our times and unfit to instruct the generation of tomorrow. Or so I am given to understand by some of the things I read and hear. Aren't you ashamed of yourselves?"

"I'm not!" Johnny said stoutly.

"Nor I," Duke echoed humorously.

"I'm too busy to be ashamed," Moose said. "Did you make this chocolate cake, Shahna? It's damned good."

And the talk turned, for the time being, to lighter subjects.

The frustrating thing about it, though, was that they knew Renny wasn't ashamed, either, and that it was Renny who was riding the popular wave of the times, and not themselves.

That same evening Renny was playing host in the lavish family home he still shared with his parents in Hillsborough—though "shared" was perhaps too intimate a word. They had deeded over to him the old gatekeeper's home, six hundred yards down the winding eucalyptus-lined drive from the main house, and he had converted it into a very comfortable and entirely private three-bedroom bachelor's domain. There he entertained frequently. Tonight's gathering was typical: three girls, three boys, all a little frightened but all anxious to try what one of them referred to, with nervous jocularity, as "old Doc Suratt's special giggle-stuff."

Renny knew, with satisfaction, that the evening would progress as it always did: increasing detachment from reality, increasing nakedness, a final free-for-all in which nobody knew exactly who was doing what to whom but everybody was happy. Renny told them it was an experiment in liberating their minds and spirits, and since he chose his subjects with considerable care, he knew none of them would talk. If they weren't too much in awe of him to tell what went on there, he made sure, as ringmaster, that they emerged so ashamed of what they had done that they would never dream of revealing it to anyone.

And suppose they did, he often told himself ironically: he would just unleash another sensational speech or savage book attacking America and the resultant coast-to-coast hosannas would silence any uncomfortable whispers that might attach to his name.

He did, as he often congratulated himself, lead a well-protected and well-rewarded life. Starting with his first book, *America: The Myth That Couldn't*, a scathing dissection of what he called "the Little Train I-Think-I-Can mentality of unimaginative middle-class America," he had consistently received front-page reviews in the book sections of every major right-thinking publication.

Number two had been *The Balding Eagle: America's Uncertain*

Role in World Affairs, in which he had argued "with the incisive insight and devastating logic that we have come already to associate automatically with Dr. Suratt's name" that the country's postwar policies were leading straight to what he described as "appalling disaster—a situation in which the twin dreams of 'world peace' and 'a stable world society' supersede and cancel out all concepts of simple right and justice on this unhappy globe."

Number three, *Janus: America's Two-Faced Foreign Policy,* featured "his usual infallible choice of the right word, the right phrase, the right thesis with which to demolish all those old-fashioned ideas that hinder a clear perception of the inevitable curtailment of the arrogant dreams and foolish imperial ambitions that besmirch America's present world record."

And in his most recent, *American Abyss: Disaster in Vietnam?,* he was "already warning, with his usual characteristic searing pen and irrefutable logic, of the tragic catastrophe that will soon engulf America if the administration does not speedily reverse its course in that unhappy sector of the world."

Four front-page reviews, four No. 1 best-seller-list positions, one lasting six weeks, one seven, one fifteen and one twenty-three—what more could "a guru for the enlightened, a leader for our times" desire?

He had been true to, and expressed unceasingly, the basic thesis of the philosophy he had first stated in a discussion in the fraternity house just prior to the war in 1939. Smith Carriger had been his opponent then. (He had noted that Johnny Herbert's preliminary bulletin had listed Smitty as among those who planned to return for the reunion. Renny wondered scornfully if that corporate fat cat still thought or felt deeply about anything now, let alone his ridiculous assertion that moral judgment had an absolute place in the world.)

In that long-gone bull session Renny had articulated his own basic belief—done it more to shock fraternity brothers whose general level of intelligence he despised, than anything else. He had applied it then more to world affairs than domestic, but over the years he had come to believe it applied across the board. It conditioned everything he wrote and the whole burden of his teaching, which he knew such conservative dunderheads as Johnny, Duke Offenberg and poor old Moose Musavich all disapproved of.

He had summed it up to Smitty:

"The blame is equal—everybody shares it—nobody can take a high moral ground because there isn't any—nobody's to blame for anything because everybody's to blame for everything—everybody's morally equal because everybody's immorally equal—nobody can judge anybody else because we're all bad. Isn't that great?"

Smitty had first looked shocked, then disgusted.

"That's the popular way to teach and argue nowadays. But I—don't—believe it."

"Me, either," Tim had chimed in. "How do you arrive at any kind of judgment on anything, if that's your theory?"

"You don't" Renny said blandly. "And the world stalls at dead center. That's the beauty of it."

"You're nuts, Suratt," Tim said.

"Not only nuts," Smitty observed. "But dangerous. *I* think."

"Me?" Renny demanded cheerfully. "Me, dangerous? Come on, now. How do you arrive at that?"

But now, he told himself with some relish, he had become dangerous: dangerous to all their silly half-baked beliefs, their half-assed "patriotic" assumptions, their complacent lives, their sick, confused country, their greedy, money-grubbing, off-balance, unequal, unfair society—dangerous to the very foundations upon which they lived— dangerous, as they saw it, to their children.

Not because he believed in Communism or any other stupid foreign-born ideology, he was too smart and too independent for that—not because he had any particular alternatives to offer except "Do it differently"—but just because, as Duke said, "He likes to destroy." He liked to challenge and turn things upside down; he took perverse pleasure in being different, the longhair, the drug advocate, the radical. He had always been, and was becoming more so, the spoiler.

And so be it. They deserved it and he was going to let them have it, as long as he could draw breath and use pen.

And now, just as he was beginning to work on book five, *Crossroads: America Waits for Racial Justice*, By Johnson had been delivered into his hands—a chance to remind his right-wing critics and the Negro world that he was on the side of the civil rights movement, and at the same time preempt By's name and position to push him in the radical direction Renny thought he should go.

When Dr. Chalmers had called a few minutes ago to ask Renny if he would like to introduce By at the first Krohl Memorial Lecture,

Renny had been astounded. Why would Chalmers, whose disapproval he knew he had and reveled in, ask him? The answer tickled Renny: Chalmers had portrayed it as a shared joke on racist old Rudy. On that basis Renny had quickly accepted. But did Chalmers have other motives in asking him, such as having a "liberal" scapegoat set up if By was too radical or otherwise fell on his face? After a moment's reflection Renny dismissed that: the opportunity outweighed the possible embarrassment. He decided with a sardonic smile that whatever the reason, he had the assignment. He would give an introduction no one would forget for a long, long time.

So for the moment he was mild as butter with By, whose immediate, instinctive reserve was quite apparent in his cautious tone.

"Renny Suratt," he said. "I remember you a little bit from the Alpha Zeta house."

"An absolute crime," Renny said promptly. "I voted for you, as you know."

"I was never entirely sure who did and who didn't," By said. "But I believe you," he added hastily.

"Please do," Renny said. "I understand you're going to kick off the Krohl lectures, which is a nice irony indeed. Dr. Chalmers just called and asked me to introduce you. May I?"

"But why—" By said, almost stammering in his surprise. "Why would you want to do it?"

"Oh, let's just say because I admire you greatly," Renny said smoothly, "and it would be a great honor for me—and I am an ardent believer in your cause—and it would be a great pleasure to welcome so distinguished an alumnus back to campus—and—many reasons. Why, do you object?"

"No," By said hastily. "I'm just thinking . . . I wonder why, with your great national reputation, you think it's worthwhile for you to do."

"What's in it for me?" Renny inquired wryly. "The reasons I state. And because I think perhaps, together, we can present an even stronger case for maintaining the momentum for civil rights. And even increasing it. Does that make sense to you?"

"Well," By said slowly—Renny reminded himself that they *were* pretty slow mentally, it sometimes took them a while for the wheels to start going around—"I'm not sure, from what I've read of your writings, that we agree entirely on the pace of things—or methods either, for that matter. My approach isn't all that radical, you know. I believe in working within the framework of mutual agreement and compromise."

"You still think that's the best way to go about it."

"Well—yes," By said, but sounding a little more uncertain, Renny thought. "I know you're inclined to be more radical—at least," he added almost apologetically, "that's your reputation, anyway—but it's been my experience that you can gain more by reasoning with people than by ramming things down their throats."

"Oh? That's how you make progress with lynchings and police dogs and bullwhips, is it? You reason with them?"

"You present them with a moral force they can't withstand," By said with a conviction that disgusted Renny. It sounded like Smitty Carriger in 1939.

"Maybe," he said. "Just maybe, if you have unlimited time. But your people don't have that much time. America doesn't have that much time. The world doesn't have that much time."

"I know you like to think globally," By said, and for just a moment Renny thought he might be being made fun of—but of course they weren't usually that intelligent or sophisticated. "I sometimes feel that one can do more working county by county and state by state than one can by trying to swing the whole country overnight."

"Your younger people don't agree with you," Renny pointed out. "They're getting impatient. Even Martin Luther King sees that. He knows he's got to accommodate them—if he can. Why don't you take the leadership away from him? This would be a great place to start, out here."

"I have some ideas of what I want to say," By remarked in a tone that closed the subject. "If Dr. Chalmers would like you to introduce me, that would be fine with me. Don't be surprised if I disagree with some of the things you say, though."

Renny laughed.

"That would make it even better. A little controversy never hurt anybody. We could both handle it."

"It will be interesting," By said uncommittally. "Are you going to the house reunion?"

"Yes, I think so," Renny said, frankly surprised. "Are you?"

"Willie's invited me."

"Willie! He would! What a guy!"

"Do you resent it?" By inquired sharply.

"No, no," Renny said hastily, "nor will anybody else. It's just Willie's capacity to still be Willie, that's all. Sometimes it's hard to realize that guy is a United States Senator. He still acts sometimes as though he were right back here telling us what to do."

"Anyway," By said coolly, not sounding mollified, "that's what's going to happen. So I'll see you there. And thanks for doing the introduction. I know it will be a good one."

Renny couldn't resist a cheerfully sardonic little laugh.

"Don't be too sure, By. I have a reputation for being outrageous, you know."

"Yes, I know," By said. "Nobody works harder."

And hung up before Renny, a bit startled, could devise a suitable rejoinder.

So much, he told himself, with an ironic little smile, for our colored brethren. Sometimes you couldn't rely on them to be properly respectful. He ran into that sometimes in his classes nowadays, when the University's black population was steadily increasing. He could count on most of the whites to be suitably impressed but sometimes the blacks seemed to be almost as disrespectful of him as he secretly was of them.

Not disrespectful of anyone, ever, was the tall, distinguished, pleasantly graying American being seen off to San Francisco at Leonardo da Vinci Airport outside Rome by an equally pleasant, equally distinguished matron and a boy and girl in early teens already promising to become as tall as their father.

That famous composer Edward Paul Haggerty was returning to the States on his annual visit, bringing with him this time the score of his new opera, *Ebon*, fourth in what he was beginning to think of as a modest cycle of musical dramas of his times. "Modest" was his word. The general public was more complimentary.

The first, *Plymouth and Salem*, had its obvious genesis. So did *Philadelphia*. And so, of course, did *Wounded Knee*.

Now, in *Ebon*, he had tackled the most difficult subject, as he saw it, that now confronted the country. As with all his major dramatic works, he had tried to be balanced and fair, an attitude that over the years had caused a certain uneasy concern among leading music critics. They were as sensitive as critics in any other field to the rigid restrictions of groupthink—had their pets and their causes—and, as with Willie and Tim, nothing offended them more than attempts to be reasonably objective, which they equated with defiance and independence. Plymouth, Salem and Philadelphia were sufficiently remote in time to be regarded as interesting experiments, but when you turned to subjects of such magnitude and sensitivity as *Wounded Knee* and *Ebon,* you began to tread on dangerous social ground. The militant cadres of herd orthodoxy charged abruptly to the fore.

Hack was a problem for them because he not only worked in a field relatively difficult to subject to politically motivated criticism—the one area in all the arts, perhaps, where, aside from national anthems and other obviously ideological themes, it was most difficult to artic-ulate a political line. He also, as even his most suspicious critics had to concede, was just too damned good to be destroyed by politically slanted criticism. The putative stockbroker of college days, having finally abandoned an essentially artificial career to do what he had really always wanted to do, had matured steadily into a master com-poser of a skill and integrity that could not easily be challenged. So far he had written two symphonies, his *Roman Suites,* a number of flow-ingly melodic atmospheric pieces such as *Walden Pond, The Tuileries* and *From the Golden Gate Bridge* and a handful of short violin and piano concerti. His three previous operas had all received respectful and successful productions in New York, San Francisco, Los Angeles and Chicago, where critics were sometimes uncertain but the public took him to its collective heart. He had already contracted for pro-ductions of *Ebon* in the same four cities. When he had received Johnny Herbert's letter a couple of months ago, he had arranged for a first reading to be held at the University early in fall quarter not long after the class and house reunions.

He was approaching the latter with more excitement and anticipa-tion than he had thought would be possible twenty-five years after graduation. What had happened to them all since he had left the house in '39?

He had not been one to maintain correspondence and old ties over long periods of time; he had not belonged to that inner circle of Willie-Unruh-Tim-Gulbransen-Moose-Franky-Lattimer that had been so tightly knit in school days. He rather expected that some of them might not have maintained all that much contact, either. He hoped a lot of them would return, and the juniors and sophomores, too, all that pre-war bunch whose developing lives had revolved around each other so importantly then. It would be good to see them all.

His own life, most of them would probably be surprised to dis-cover, had moved far from the pattern that had seemed inevitable in those days. The break with Fran had swiftly become permanent, the tentative meeting with Flavia Lampadini had turned into the greatest love, and the greatest satisfaction, of his life.

Their noontime meeting at the House of Livia on the Palantine had stretched on into a typically leisurely Roman lunch at Tre Scalini in Piazza Navona that had not ended until almost five o'clock, when she said she really must be getting home. They had parted with casual promises to meet again, knew they would do so within twenty-four hours if they could possibly manage. They did and things progressed rapidly from there. Her husband, a lawyer, was frequently away on business in Milan. Her two children, twin boy and girl aged fourteen, were at school during the day. The two elderly servants left at noon, returned at seven to prepare the evening meal—and in any event, as she confided with a laugh, "They were with my family, they only suffer Sylvio but they adore me. I am sure they would connive at any crime I asked them to commit."

"Even—?"

"Even," she said with a smile, suddenly shy, that aroused him greatly.

Divorce took longer in Italy than it did in the States, but in a year and a half they were both free, he had given up Transit Obligations and his modest teaching job in San Francisco and moved to Rome to devote himself to the full-time composing her family wealth could easily support. Life seemed to stretch out ahead serene, untroubled and happily productive. And so it had turned out to be.

The twins, Sylvio Jr. and Gioia, had at first been wary but had soon decided that this amiable, rather wry, even-tempered, considerate gentleman their mother had found on the Palatine was no threat to them and indeed was a really good addition to the family. Their relations with their father had always been rather formal and were maintained on that basis with regular, dutiful visits. Their relations with Hack, once they discovered he wouldn't bite even if they sometimes did interrupt his concentration in the music room, grew steadily warmer and closer.

"Some of us in the arts," he said with an easygoing smile, "make a big deal publicly about working ten hours solid without a break, but I suspect if truth were known we all welcome an interruption now and then. There's a limit to how much fresh stuff you can produce in a given time."

"I thought you would pull your hair and curse us," Sylvio Jr. said, returning the smile. "Isn't that what geniuses do?"

"Not this one," he said. "Anyway, I'm not a genius. I just write music."

"And terrific, too," Gioia said, and giggled. "Not my taste, but I can tell it's terrific."

"On that basis of understanding," he said, "we can all live happily ever after. Someday I'm going to write a rock-and-roll opera and then you'll really be happy with me."

"You!" she said. "You'll never write rock and roll!"

But he thought about it sometimes. It would be a surprising switch and might even turn out to be delightful. He might try it yet.

The twins grew up. They were now twenty-six, Sylvio Jr. married with a son of his own, Gioia also married though as yet childless. Along had come his own Paolo and Sophia (also, surprisingly, twins) now an all-arms-and-legs eleven and threatening to shoot up at least to his shoulder, if not taller, before they were through. And every day there was the serene, even flow of days that Flavia provided, perfect for domestic felicity, perfect for a happily constant productivity.

Once in a while there would be some sharp reminiscence of Fran, whom he supposed he would always love as long as he lived. An Italian archway somewhere would suddenly recall their long, humorous-serious banterings along the Quad, an expression on some girl's face would recall Fran's youthful earnestness. Sometimes there were more intimate memories of domesticity that could reach him even in the extremes of love. *This* was Flavia, *that* was Fran—but sometimes this and that were so alike—or so different, as the case might be—that both were suddenly in his heart—and in his arms—at the same moment.

He supposed Flavia sometimes had the same experience with him and Sylvio Sr., but they never exchanged these memories. Neither, in fact, ever talked about their previous marriages. Of course Sylvio Jr. and Gioia were constant reminders of hers, but he had long ago accepted that, aided by their quick acceptance of him; and steadily and determinedly they had all built the new home, the new life. It had worked from the first. It was impregnable, happy with a solidity he almost dared not acknowledge, in the superstitious thought that such good luck might yet be struck down by the jealous gods.

For this, at least in its early stages, he knew he owed a lot to the one fraternity brother with whom he had maintained, or rather resumed, close ties over the years. They had not been particularly close in the house—friendly, as one was with most of one's fraternity brothers, but not really intimate. It was only later, well after the war, that the friendship had really begun. He ranked it up there alongside his new family, for whose successful creation he felt much indebted to it.

He remembered distinctly that it was about three weeks after he and Flavia met. They had returned to the Forum for a visit that already had heavy sentimental overtones. They had been walking along through the golden October afternoon, not touching but in perfect harmony, when he had suddenly seen across the Sacred Way, sitting on some once-monumental pediment, a figure, lost in thought, that looked vaguely familiar. The fact that it was dressed in clerical robes at first put him off; he had never associated this particular individual with anything religious. Then in a flash, he had thought: Latt, of course—contrition—atonement—it could easily be that. It must be that.

"I know that priest," he said, voice filled with a pleased excitement. "I'm sure we went to college together. Come!"

And he had hurried her across the Sacred Way just as Randy looked up. A smile of sudden recognition lit up his face. He jumped up, held out his hand to meet Hack's and for several moments they stood there grinning foolishly, pumping hands as though they might drop off.

"Why, Hack!" Randy kept saying. "Why, Hack! Where in the world—"

"Where in the world yourself," Hack said happily. "Of all people! I can't believe it!"

"Believe it," Randy said with a grin. "Just don't tell *him*"—he gestured off toward Vatican City—"how surprised you are. He thinks I'm sincere. He thinks it's all real."

"Don't believe this man," Hack said hastily to Flavia. "He is sincere, it is real. He's just always liked to joke."

"I know," Flavia said with the easy smile he was already learning to rely upon, and treasure. "I have met just enough Americans so that I know. Many of you like to joke. So do we, though our humor is sometimes not so turned upon ourselves. Or upon the Pope, for that matter. At least not before total strangers."

"I'm sorry," Randy said with mock humility. "I'll confess my sin tonight."

"Don't you dare," Flavia said lightly. "*He* has absolutely *no* sense of humor."

"Who is this delightful lady?" Randy asked. "And what the hell, if you'll forgive my language, are you doing in Rome?"

"I think I may be getting ready to marry her," Hack said. "But come along. We're going to get some lunch pretty soon. This is Randy

Carrero, incidentally—Father Carrero—and this is Flavia Lampadini—Signora Lampadini."

"We won't be formal for very long," Randy said. "I can see that."

When they were settled in one of Flavia's favorite little trattorias, in Piazza dei Croceferi alongside the noisily splashing waters of Fontana di Trevi, they brought each other up to date. Randy told of his decision to enter the Church under the persuasions of his cousin and the still-heavy burden of Latt's death, Hack related his early years of marriage, the growing rift with Fran, his sudden decision to retreat temporarily to Rome, his meeting with Flavia on the Palatine that might well make his stay much longer.

"How long will you be in Rome?" he asked.

Randy shrugged.

"I don't quite know. I understand it's more or less up to me—in the sense, that is," he added hastily as he caught a little twinkle in Flavia's eye—"that it depends on how well I do at my studies, how well I perform the duties I am given to do—"

"How often you manage to stumble into *Il Papa*'s way as he is coming along the corridor," Flavia interrupted. "How well you make yourself known to the hierarchy. How familiar they become with bright, earnest, appealing young Father Carrero. How well you perform at what I suppose we might call 'Vatican politics.' Is that not correct?"

"I've only been here a couple of weeks," Randy protested. "I don't really know—" Then he dropped it and grinned. "Absolutely," he agreed cheerfully. "My bishop back home told me that's how it's done. But I thought he was just a cynical American. I didn't know Italians were that cynical, too."

"Italians," Flavia said, and went off into a gale of laughter. "My God, Randy! How much you have to learn about us!"

"Couldn't have a better teacher," he observed. "When are you going to marry her, Hack? What's the tie-up?"

"I'm not divorced yet."

"But you've made up your mind to be."

Hack sighed heavily and for a moment his expression darkened.

"I don't know that you ever knew Fran very well," he said, "but she's—quite a lady. It isn't easy."

"I'm sorry," Randy said quietly. "I didn't mean to make it worse."

"No," Hack said, reaching out a hand to take Flavia's. "It'll work out all right. If this girl will stand by me."

"I am married, too, you see," Flavia said with a rueful little laugh. "What a tangle you have stumbled into, Father Carrero!"

"I'm supposed to help," Randy said cheerfully, and Hack suddenly remembered from the house: he always did, anyone who was unhappy or had a problem, which was roughly 99 percent of the college population at one time or another.

"I think we can count on Randy," he said. "I'm thinking tentatively of going home next week to get things straightened out and start the divorce, and then come back here to live, at least for a while. Will you look after her while I'm gone?"

"That's very nice of you," Flavia said with a smile, "but I will be quite safe. I do have my home, you know, the children, my husband—"

"Keep her occupied and out of the house as much as possible," Hack directed with a sternness that began as a joke and ended quite seriously—too seriously, he knew, but couldn't seem to lighten it. Randy, already taking up his responsibilities, did.

"I'll keep her busy," he promised. "After all, I'm the one who needs to be entertained and gotten out of the house—*that* house. It's dark over there! I keep stumbling over cardinals and Swiss guards. I need to get out—out—*out!*"

"I shall try to provide you with the opportunity," Flavia said with a laugh. "Lunches are always possible. We give dinners from time to time. A bright young American priest would be an interesting addition. My children like to be taken out to a favorite ruin on the Via Appia for picnics, which my husband does not particularly enjoy. The young priest would be a good chaperon for that. We shall manage until this man returns. If he returns."

And she gave Hank a disconcerting look that both embraced and examined him.

"You're not sure of that," Randy said.

"I am cautious," Flavia said. "It is a big step for me, too. I am not sure of anything yet."

"You'd better hurry back, Hack," Randy said. "I'll be around as much as possible, but you're the guy who's got to get back here."

And true to his word during Hack's projected one-month absence—which lengthened into two, then three, then four, as things at home proved more difficult to settle than he had anticipated—Randy did become an outwardly casual, privately indispensable part of Flavia's life. She treated him almost as though they were meeting in the confessional, the principal confession being that she was indeed "cautious" if not downright panicked by the whole prospect of divorce and remarriage. Sylvio Sr., who turned out to be a plump, somewhat stiff and awkward but basically easygoing and decent little gentleman, accepted Randy as a frequent charming dinnertime visitor and occasional chaperon for his wife and children on "those antiquarian expeditions to ancient houses on Via Appia." He also accepted without question Flavia's announcement that she intended to lunch with Randy sometimes just to "talk about things." He remarked mildly that he had not known she was worried about "things," but made no objection. He was totally unprepared for her final announcement that she had decided to seek a divorce. After the initial shock wore off he thanked Randy solemnly for "your kind assistance to my distraught wife in this midlife crisis of hers."

At first Sylvio persisted in treating it as such, but Randy soon managed to convince him of what he himself had perceived at the start: that Flavia really was in love with Hack, really did desire a divorce and would be profoundly and permanently unhappy if Sylvio resisted. When Sylvio finally agreed, even waiving his rights as the aggrieved party so that the children might remain with their mother, Randy felt a deep gratitude and relief. Sylvio did not know the agonized, sometimes literally hysterical, conversations in which Randy had gently, step by step, persuaded Flavia to come to terms with her feelings and make the decision that he felt to be the only one that would really be best for her, and for Hack.

It was not until long after, shortly before he was assigned back to America, that he made his own confession to Hack.

"I'm afraid I wasn't at all nonpartisan while you were away," he said one day after lunch when they were sitting on the vine-covered terrace of the house on the Janiculum, Flavia and the children napping, all Rome spread out at their feet in the gentle drifting haze of early summer. "I know I was supposed to be, the Church would undoubtedly have expelled me if they'd known I was deliberately trying to push someone into divorce, but I made the decision and I did it. I hope you haven't regretted it." He gave his quick-flashing, cheerful grin. "I certainly haven't, given the picture of disgustingly maudlin uxorial comfort I see every time I come to this house."

"It has been the best thing that ever happened to me," Hack said, replenishing their glasses of red wine. "I've always wondered if you didn't give me a little extra help with it."

"Well, she wanted it desperately, you see—she told me that—but, as might be expected of a woman from a highly respectable old-line Roman family married to a man of identical background, she had herself all tied up in knots about it. She really was in a terrible state for a while—until I decided to cut the knots. I don't know which astounded her more deeply, that she finally had the courage of her own convictions or the spectacle of a Catholic priest actually saying, 'Forget your conscience, trust your feelings, *do it!*' She said she couldn't conceive of an Italian Catholic priest doing a thing like that. I said I was an American Catholic, which was a different breed."

"You want to be careful on that," Hack warned. "You could run into big trouble if you get too independent."

"You know me," Randy said, again with the grin. "I'm not a fool, Hack. I got into this for various reasons"—his eyes widened in thought as he looked far across the ancient umber city, temporarily hushed in the grip of siesta—"Latt's death—my cousin's obviously very sincere dedication, which was a challenge to me to be equally good—which I may or may not be—some feeling that maybe I really could be of some help to humanity—a desire to serve, selflessly, something bigger than myself. A long way from happy school days—or not so happy—" his eyes darkened—"as it turned out. Anyway, here I am, considered to be a very bright and promising young religious on his way up in the hierarchy, one of the very top students in the North American College, favorite of his elders, destined, they think, to go very high indeed —already assured of a major assignment when I go home, probably destined to make bishop by my early forties—your quintessential all-American super-duper, hell-bent-for-glory Superpriest. How about that!"

And the grin returned, irrepressible, as it usually was, with Randy.

"But not yet," Hack observed, "except in this small instance, not small to me, you understand, but not known to the hierarchy—not yet have you been in a position in which you might conceivably express a more relaxed and radical approach that would reflect the All-American background and be not quite so acceptable to all those black-robed elderly gentlemen who float about the Vatican on wings of steel. Then what?"

"That," Randy said, grin increasing, "is something we will have to battle out when the times comes."

"Well, good luck," Hank said seriously. "Thank you forever, on behalf of Flavia and me—and good luck forever, with your interesting life. We'll be watching, and praying for you, all the way."

"Thank you," Randy said, grin gone, also completely serious. "I appreciate that greatly, Hack. I suspect I may need your prayers. It will be interesting." The grin returned. "I think I can promise you that!"

And now in 1964 he was indeed bishop at forty-four, in his native New Mexico, and generally believed to be on his way higher; and now he was indeed beginning to express openly some of those more relaxed and radical ideas that were almost inevitably going to bring him soon into headlong conflict with the hierarchy; and no one at the moment, including a devoted, fearful and often-praying-for-him Flavia could predict the outcome.

The great plane swung out over Ostia and the Mediterranean coastline and began the familiar journey north to the other of the world's two most imperial, most inexhaustible cities, which Hack also loved. He was going to stop over there for a couple of days to see musical and theatrical contacts before going on to San Francisco. He belonged to both the Travelers' Club in Pall Mall and the East India Club in St. James's Square; had decided, this time, to stay at the East India Club.

Safely arrived, partially unpacked, temporarily settled in, he set forth with the old, familiar excitement of the lover of London to walk over to bustling Piccadilly, along noisy Regent Street, finally back to Shaftsbury Avenue and into the West End theater district. *Wounded Knee* was now well into its second year at the Theater Royal in Haymarket. He wondered if *Ebon* would be as well received. As always, he had future projects in mind. He kept a list of them in his head, constantly working:

The plight of the Jews, not only standard subjects like the Holocaust but the subtler, wider, more alarming aspects as they were still present, and again increasing, in the postwar world . . . the Soviet labor camps, finally beginning to surface in the public prints and public conscience in the wake of Nikita Khrushchev's exposure of Joseph Stalin's monstrosities, hitherto carefully ignored by the determinedly self-blinkered of the West . . . possibly (inspired by Randy) the defiant young religious rebel arrayed against the turgid bureaucracy of the old, established creed. . . .

And perhaps even, he thought wryly, an autobiographical opera about a gallant composer who might soon, if his view of the world and the compositions in which he expressed it continued their present trend, find that he, too, is engaged in battle with the intellectual conformists who dominate the culture of his native land. He might give it a Germanic title such as *Manfred and His Critics* and set it in Salzburg during the festival, perhaps, just to give it an allegorical air and confuse the herd a little. But their instincts for disrespect and mockery toward themselves were always quivering and as predictable as their responses.

Why not call it *Galahad at the Met* and be done with it?

He smiled ironically to himself and put the contentious thought aside. Kindlier thoughts succeeded. He really was looking forward to seeing the University, his classmates and his fraternity brothers again. A pleasant anticipation kept him company as he adjusted his seat and prepared to read and drowse, read and drowse, in his customary fashion, across the Atlantic.

Smith Carriger, newly elected president of Carriger Corporation—now named Carrigcorp—was also airborne at the moment, already on his way across the continent from Philadelphia. He had just signed final papers for the acquisition of a ten-state department-store chain, a rather far cry from the company's original oil interests but typical of the accelerating trend toward mergers that was beginning to appear in major American business.

Carrigcorp now owned, in addition to its still highly profitable oil-drilling concessions in Pennsylvania, Alaska and Saudi Arabia, a chain of what were coming to be known as "fast-food" restaurants scattered over twenty-three states; a major metals-manufacturing plant in Alabama; a popcorn-manufacturing company, just starting up but giving promise of real profits ahead; a candy company with 110 retail outlets across the country; and a firm that manufactured water-skiing equipment, "Riding the wave of tomorrow's sport," as its advertising proclaimed.

All in all, Smitty thought, Carrigcorp was becoming such a hodge-podge (albeit a shrewdly managed and highly profitable one) that he almost might have to stay home all the time and look after it instead of "batting off all over the world every time the C.I.A. calls you," as Annelle put it with worried disapproval.

Now he was ostensibly on his way to reunion and so, in fact, he was; but then he was going to slip quietly away. Twenty hours after saying goodbye at Tony Andrade's party in Napa Valley he would be showing up in Saigon, ready to do whatever the agency asked.

He belonged to that sizable group of former members of the old Office of Strategic Services and present Central Intelligence Agency who never quite broke free, because when all was said and done they didn't want to. The lure of the game was still too strong, the challenge too exciting, the satisfaction, when an assignment had been successfully concluded, greater even than the latest earnings report of Carrigcorp.

"I hate to be a bloodthirsty spy," he told Annelle half in jest, half in earnest, "and really I'm not. But I do like to score a point against the bastards when I can."

"I'm sure it's a lot more exciting than going to a party on the Main Line," she responded, and joined in his amusement with a wistful little smile when he said, "Well, yes, I have to confess it is."

He had been told that this time he would be gone about two weeks. There were various things that needed to be found out in North Vietnam. Here, as during the war and on several occasions thereafter, his compact little body (which he took great pains to keep in shape), slightly oval, slightly Asian cast of features, and easy facility with languages made his standing offer of help in the Orient most acceptable to headquarters.

He was contemplating his task with growing excitement and a pleased anticipation when someone stopped by his seat and offered a shy and tentative—after all these years! he thought, not knowing whether to pity or ridicule—"Hello?"

"Marc!" he said, standing and holding out his hand in one smoothly coordinated motion that revealed how well he did keep his body in shape. "Marc Taylor, isn't it?"

"That's right," Marc said with a shy little smile. "How are you—Smitty?"

"Smitty it is," he said firmly. "Are you in first class? I didn't see you get on. Sit down, I don't have a seatmate. Move on up here. I'm delighted to see you."

"Well, actually," Marc said, still shyly—You're forty-three or -four, Smitty told him silently, for God's sake, man, relax—"I'm in tourist, so maybe—"

"In *tourist*?" Smitty demanded. "The last time I checked Taylorite on the New York Stock Exchange, it was ninety-three and a quarter. What do you mean, tourist? Do you know something the public doesn't know? Should I sell?"

"No," Marc said, glancing quickly at nearby passengers who were looking amused, beginning to laugh a little in spite of himself. "Don't talk so loudly or you'll start a run on us. We're in fine shape, thank you." His voice lowered and he eased past Smitty into the window seat as the quickest available means to get him to speak more quietly. "Somehow I've always just thought I should fly tourist, that's all. I like first, but it seems sort of—flaunting, somehow."

"Nonsense," Smitty said as a stewardess approached. "My friend here will have a drink. And I will, too. Gin and tonics all right, Marc?"

"Well—" Marc hesitated as the stewardess asked politely, "Are you in first class, sir?"

"He's with me," Smitty said firmly. "If you give him any trouble, he'll buy the airline. He can afford it, too. So be a nice girl, all right?"

"Well, sir—" she said doubtfully.

"Two gin and tonics," he repeated, turning back to Marc. She hesitated, then turned away; to get the drinks, he hoped. "Now, Marc, tell me about yourself. Johnny Herbert wrote that you'd be coming out to the reunion, but I'm sorry I didn't think or I would have contacted you to make sure I'd have your company. Anyway, I do have it and I'm delighted. So how goes it?"

"I meant to call you, too," Marc said. "But you know how it is. I've been in Philly on business, too, I could have called you. Things are going pretty well, actually. I know they are with Carrigcorp."

"Yeah," Smitty said. "Are you diversifying? We're diversifying like hell. It seems to be the next big thing."

"We're thinking about it," Marc said, "although we're doing so well just sticking with office equipment of all kinds that there isn't much urge. My dad doesn't like it and he still pretty much runs things."

"Ought to look into it," Smitty suggested. "Lots of good deals coming up before long, I have a feeling. Married?"

"No," Marc said, startled by the abruptness. Still shy, Smitty noticed. One of those people who never get over it, apparently. Nothing better for that than a good solid marriage.

"So," he said briskly. "And why not, may I ask? Surely you've had plenty of opportunities."

"All arranged," Marc said with a rare gleam of humor. "Made me feel like an absolute Asiatic, so I haven't done it. But you wouldn't know about that."

"That's right," Smitty said without missing a beat. "The Mysterious East. I haven't been there enough to know. Well, I'm married, to a lovely girl. Wellesley. Three kids. Happy as a clam. Next time you come over from Pittsburgh on business, you let me know. I'd like you to meet them. O.K.?"

"O.K.," Marc said. They were both convinced he wouldn't, but you never knew.

"Thanks, sweetheart," Smitty said as the stewardess came back with the drinks and a tray of hors d'oeuvres. "When he does buy the airline, you'll be the first to be promoted. Bring him lunch when you feed me, please."

"Sir," she said, "you know that's not possible."

"O.K., bring me two portions. I'm a big eater."

"Oh, no," Marc said hastily. "I'll go back where I belong when the time comes, miss. All right?"

"Well," she said with a suddenly relaxed smile, "If Mr. Carriger will vouch for you in the meantime."

"You're a doll," Smitty said. "What a nice girl," he added more loudly, beaming at an elderly couple across the aisle. "And very efficient, too . . . So, no marriage," he said, lowering his voice to a confidential pitch again. "How's life going otherwise? Everything all right?"

And although he had asked it quite innocently, he could see at once that he had stumbled onto tender ground. Of course. That damned suicide try. Here it was twenty-five years later, as raw a wound, he could see, as the day after it happened.

"I didn't mean anything by that," he added hastily. "Really, Marc. I didn't. I just meant—things in general, that's all."

"Well," Marc said slowly, "I know you didn't, Smitty. They're O.K. I keep busy. Life goes on. Taylorite makes millions. I guess I make millions, too." He gave Smitty a shy, sidewise little smile. "Just like you do."

"Boring, isn't it?" Smitty said with a cheerful grin. "But I wouldn't want it any other way. . . . Since you raise the subject, though"—which of course they both knew Marc hadn't, but what the hell, Smitty could never resist being what he conceived of as helpful—"how *are* things? Surely you don't still worry about—that subject—do you?"

Marc looked suddenly stricken.

"How could I not?" he asked in a bleak half-whisper.

"But it was twenty-five years ago, Marc! That's silly. Everybody's completely forgotten—"

"You haven't," Marc said in the same bleak tone.

"Yes, I have! I didn't mean that at all when I said how are *things*? I just meant *things*, I didn't mean—you were the one who brought it up, I didn't. You shouldn't let it ride you like that."

"It was so weak," Marc whispered, shaking his head and looking as desolate as though it were, indeed, twenty-five years ago at that very moment.

"Well, you haven't been weak since, that's for sure," Smitty said in a no-nonsense voice. "You've had a very successful career in business that is going to go right on and be even more successful when you eventually take over—"

"I inherited it," Marc said. "It was given to me. I didn't create anything."

"Yes, you have," Smitty insisted with some desperation. "You've helped bring the firm right along. You've contributed an awful lot to it."

"I've been helped," Marc said, sounding frighteningly hopeless for a moment. "Something had to be done for Marc to give him a purpose in life, and so his parents did it. Ask anybody in Pittsburgh."

"People like that in Pittsburgh," Smitty said firmly, "aren't worth the powder to blow 'em up. Anyway, I'll bet there are a couple of million people in Pittsburgh who never even heard of Marc Taylor's little problem, or even Marc Taylor. If they've heard of him at all, it's as the highly successful vice-president and executive officer of that highly successful company Taylorite." He decided to lighten it up, grinned suddenly. "When do you want to sell it, by the way? Carrigcorp might be able to give you a damned good deal."

Marc smiled—almost laughed, Smitty was pleased to note—and shook his head.

"Thanks, but we're not selling. Not right now, anyway. But we'll be glad to keep your interest in mind." His expression became strained and unhappy again. "Now I have to go out and face everybody at the house. They'll all remember."

"O.K.," Smitty said bluntly, deciding he wouldn't pamper anymore. "What the hell are you doing on the plane then? Why didn't you stay home and hide? Nobody's making you go to the reunion. Right?"

"I thought I should," Marc said, so low Smitty almost had to lean over to hear him. "I thought it would help me. I thought it would make me face up to it and get it over with, after all these years."

"Well, it will," Smitty said in the same blunt tone. "If you'll just stop being a damned fool and let the therapy work. No wonder you aren't married. You're a case of arrested development."

"Am I?" Marc asked, and for some reason he couldn't define, something in Smitty's tone that got to him, he actually began to laugh, a shy sound that began tentatively but strengthened. Much to his amazement, he began to feel better.

"That's more like it," Smitty remarked with a tartness born of relief. "Jesus! You're a case, Marc Taylor. Young lady!" he said as the stewardess appeared. "Two more g. and t.'s, please. And my friend *will* stay for lunch."

"Sir—" she began. He favored her with his most charming smile.

"You don't know it, but *I* can buy the airline, too. So you'd better watch out. Now go get the drinks, please."

"You're incorrigible," she said, but smiling, too.

"My middle name," he said, dismissing her with a little amiable wave and turning seriously to Marc. He had just made a sudden decision he couldn't quite understand, except that he knew it would take Marc's mind off his troubles, and he knew Marc could be trusted.

"Do you know why I'm going out to the reunion?" he asked. "Do you know what I did in the war and have been doing sometimes since, unbeknownst to our distinguished fraternity brothers? Do you know what lies behind the laughing face of easygoing, lovable Smith Carriger?"

"No," Marc said, half-smiling, half-uncertain. "What have you done, rob banks?"

"Always legitimately," Smitty said with a grim. "Always legitimately. No, a little more interesting than that, I like to think." He hesitated a second, then decided to plunge on. Once in a great while he enjoyed telling somebody besides Annelle. It was kind of fun to shock and impress people with one's clandestine cloak-and-dagger life. And the very few he told always were both shocked and impressed.

"This is in absolute confidence—"

"Oh, absolutely," Marc said hurriedly, suddenly awed by Smitty's lowered voice and intensely confidential manner.

"Well," Smitty said, "it all began in the war in the Pacific, when—"

And for a couple of hours, through second drink, lunch and a bottle of wine, he regaled a suitably impressed and respectful Marc with lurid tales he could dredge up from his secret life. They were not only lurid but true, as Marc immediately recognized. The respect he had always felt for the self-contained, confident, busy little figure beside him grew greatly during the flight.

"Boy!" he exclaimed when Smitty finally fell silent. "They would never believe all that, in the house!"

"I know," Smitty said. "That's why I'm not going to tell 'em, even if the Agency would let me. That's *my* cross with the house. Here I am, this dashing figure, and they think I'm just your ordinary run of the mill, garden variety, dull-as-dishwater millionaire."

"To hell with 'em," Marc said with a laugh that sounded quite genuinely relaxed.

"That's the spirit," Smitty agreed comfortably. "It will be great to see most of 'em again, but the hell with 'em."

Fifteen minutes later Marc had drifted off to sleep, apparently completely at ease. Smitty certainly hoped so. Twenty-five years—also a millionaire—and still as uptight as a kid. He shivered slightly as he, too, drifted off. He sure hoped the weekend would take care of that.

Driving slowly down the spectacular Northern California coast with Katie, Franky Miller also was on his way; one of their typically silent rides, broken only by an occasional politely bored comment on the rugged mix of rocks, pines and crashing surf. It was a sensationally beautiful day, rare for a Pacific littoral often shrouded in fog or rain—absolutely clear, blue and sparkling, the sort that made a man feel good just to be alive.

Or should have, it he had not had so many other things to worry about.

As uneasily as Marc, Franky wondered how he would fare with his fraternity brothers. He approached them with deep misgivings. He knew he would be greeted literally with open arms, placed instantly back in the familiar easygoing slot that was labeled "Good old Franky," the specific niche that he had always occupied in what Willie used to refer to as "the balance of the house." He was sure their concept of it hadn't changed at all. He just wondered how well he could fill it now—how long before the pretense cracked and they would recognize him for what he felt himself to be, not "good old" but "poor old" Franky, who hadn't really achieved anything much in a quarter of a century.

That was how he seemed to himself, anyway, even though he knew that in Medford he had a certain position because he had been, first, "Buck Sullivan's son-in-law," and more recently, for the last eight years, "Herbie Sullivan's brother-in-law."

Contrary to Katie's confident assumption that he would inherit the auto agency when Buck went, which he did unexpectedly one Sunday morning after mass, Herbie had proved to be the one brother who genuinely wanted to take over the business. To him Buck had left ownership; and while he and Herbie got along quite amicably Franky inescapably and irrevocably had been consigned to a secondary role. Herbie assured him often, with a kindness that was quite genuine though it sometimes came across as unbearably patronizing, that his position was his as long as he wanted to remain in it.

"We'll be a team for life," Herbie told him with expansive good cheer, and before he knew it, Franky thought resentfully, twenty-five years had passed and a major part of a life was gone. And here he was, still stuck in Medford—still, in his own bitter words, "a used-car salesman."

"Is that a whale?" Katie asked quickly, pointing out across the for-once placid expanse of sea as they came around a headland.

"Where?" he responded, deciding to play along with it just to break the boredom. They had seen half a dozen already since getting onto U.S. 1, but, he thought, any whale in a storm. Not that miles and miles of silence were exactly a storm, but they sure weren't comfortable riding.

They used to be, he thought sadly; they used to be. He could remember so many times at the University, and even for a few short years thereafter, when all he and Katie had to do was jump in a car and go, and life would suddenly become an utterly carefree, happy experience. No worries, no problems, no tensions, no nothing. Just lighthearted joy and a world of their own in which life was always a ball and just being together comprised the best of all existence for them both.

He supposed it was only natural that such euphoria couldn't last. Friends told him, his own observations, his own experiences, told him. He wondered if the experience of others in the house would prove to be the same. He wondered if they would be able to reestablish old intimacies to the point where they could talk to one another frankly about it. He rather doubted it. Too many things got in the way of male confidences as one grew older. Too many things.

And anyway, how did you articulate it, how did you trace it down the years, how did you isolate the fissures as they began to develop? How could you put your finger on something and say with certainty, "This is where it began"? It all came on too subtly, too swiftly, too irreversibly. A sharper word here, an unexpected withholding of interest or attention there, a look that could be construed as disparaging, a turning away perhaps not intended to be the rejection it appeared—and the sudden desperate anguish as you realized that a parting had been reached that, for some reason you did not understand, could not be reversed—and the bewildered realization that you had hurt someone, not meaning to at all—and, after earnest attempts, the desolate comprehension that apologies were not going to be believed, amends were not going to be accepted, the dream had died.

And along with it, if you still did, in some memory of early days and in present actuality, love someone, the realization that this was how it was going to be; and that if you were in a situation you did not want to, or could not, abandon, you had no choice but to put your head down and slog along as best you could.

"There he goes again!" Katie exclaimed, and there he was, defined by a tiny plume far out on the blue-glass sea, rising briefly into the air, dissipating into spray, gone in a moment as though the silent passerby had never come that way at all.

Like us, Franky thought, like us; though all he said was, "That's seven, isn't it? We're seeing quite a few today."

"Quite a few," she agreed and turned again to her silent contemplation of the lovely coast.

And silence again, he supposed, for another hundred miles, or until some other aspect of nature called forth a communication that aspects of the heart no longer did.

He realized to his dismay that his eyes had actually filled for a moment with tears; shook his head impatiently and turned away lest Katie see; and concentrated again upon his driving. Very few cars were on the narrow road on this autumn Friday; the relatively straight stretches between headlands did not demand much attention. He did not want to think, but thoughts, unwanted, came back.

He knew he would never willingly leave Katie. He was pretty sure—hoped and prayed—that she would never leave him. It had nothing to do with financial security. Herbie had told him once, with a hearty, Buck-inherited, lord-of-the-manor air, that Franky would always have a job with him, "no matter what," and Franky believed him. So that wasn't a problem. He just wanted his laughing Katie to come back and be his great companion again, even if she had once said, as he could never forget, that he had an "innate weakness" that made him incapable of greater material achievement.

So perhaps he had not done the teaching, or the business managing, or the leading, or whatever it was they had expected of him in his early days; perhaps he hadn't lived up to the expectations of a wife brought up in an achieving household. So what? They had only achieved an auto agency, he sometimes thought scornfully, and what was that?—forgetting for a moment that it was a very successful and well-managed enterprise that had permitted them all to lead very comfortable and very respectable lives for a quarter of a century. But in a deeper context—the context in which he still placed himself for comparison when thinking about it—what had they achieved? Nothing, in terms of what he had once dreamed of being. Just nothing.

Back in college days when all life seemed there for the laughing and taking, it had been easy to be the always amicable, always joking Franky everyone expected and wanted him to be. Underneath he had wanted more for himself—although exactly what, he had never quite determined. He supposed that had been the problem. Francis Miller the philosopher, Francis Miller the teacher of youth, Francis Miller the enlightened leader toward some sort of vaguely socialistic, overwhelming good-hearted world in which nobody starved, everybody was happy and harmony presided over all their days, had somehow dwindled down into Francis Miller the good-natured car salesman. Always smiling. Always even-tempered. Always good for a joke and a jolly. Usually, good for a sale.

But at what a hell of a cost, he told himself now as he overtook a lumber truck, calculated his chances, swung smoothly out and around and back in again before the next tortuous series of hairpin turns five hundred feet above the sea-drenched rocks. What a farce, really, inside. It wasn't fair. *It wasn't fair.* He had so much more than that to give the world.

Well, it hadn't happened. Because, he supposed, he had never really been "focused," to use the jargon Franky Jr.'s teachers had used when they talked to him about his increasingly difficult son. He had just possessed an amiable goodwill toward all the world, and that hadn't been enough. He wasn't like Willie, always interested in politics, probably destined from the cradle to rise to his present eminence in the Senate, always ambitious, always determined, always keyed in and moving forward along his own particular path. Or that insufferable snot Renny Suratt, whom he had recently seen laying down the law like a modern Moses on some national television show whose goggle-eyed gabby obviously thought Renny was the greatest thing since toilet paper. Or Tim Bates, whose column was printed occasionally in the Medford paper and whose basic fairness Franky admired even when he balked at some of Timmy's less reverent views of national figures and issues Franky thought worthy of respect. Or the three doctors, Guy Unruh, Gil Gulbransen and North McAllister, with their dedicated careers—but, then, doctors always knew what they wanted to do, it seemed to go with the territory. Or even good old Mooser, automatically a national figure every autumn when he piloted the football team through a sometimes wandering and uncertain, sometimes smashingly triumphant, season.

Everybody but Franky the used-car salesman. He supposed it all probably went back to his taking the easy way out when his father-in-law offered him the job with the agency after the draft board gave him his deferment. He hadn't been particularly enthused about the war, might well have wound up in conscientious objectors' camp like Renny—what a blast, if they had been there together—but at the moment he had still been enough under the spell of his generation so that he deeply regretted not being able to share their experience with them. His visions had been of marching off with Willie and Guy and Moose and the rest into some great bright glory that would save the world and impress Katie. His rejection from service had made him really confused and uncertain. Buck's offer was ready-made, easy, and he hadn't had to exercise any particular energy or decision about it. Particularly since Katie, child of a close-knit family who wanted to stay close to it, badly wanted him to accept.

And then she had accused him of "innate weakness"! It was damned unfair.

And along had come Franky Jr. and little Rosie, and both of them were damned unfair too.

He supposed he resented Franky Jr. most. Rosie, who though she was now twenty-two was still "little Rosie" to everyone, was an innocent victim of something neither her parents, her doctors nor anyone else could ever explain. Down's syndrome had never been in either of their families, as far back as anyone knew; suddenly, with her, it was just *there*. A very sweet child, as they told everyone, doing the best they could with it. We all just love her gentle heart and smiling ways; she enriches our lives. And so she had, for she was all those things and they loved her with a tenderness and ache that couldn't go away. But—there she was, twenty-two now, and who knew how much longer? The doctors said they usually died young. The great injustice of it was something he and Katie could never bear to discuss, even with each other. Which, he supposed, had something to do with it, too.

For Franky Jr. there was no such excuse. Franky Jr. had been a supremely healthy, supremely happy baby; not your instantaneous genius-in-a-crib that some of their friends claimed to have, but a very lovable, very satisfactory child who seemed from the first to be on his guaranteed way to becoming a very satisfactory and lovable human being. Somewhere along the way something seemed to have happened. Beginning in high school and increasingly up to this very day, things had become progressively worse. At twenty-five he was, as his father had recently remarked in frustrated bitterness, "a worthless bum." And that had a lot to do with it, too.

A decade ago, Franky could remember, he had virtually worshiped Franky Jr., the sturdy little athlete who was going to recoup his father's failures. Franky Jr. had wanted to be a high school football star and then go on to play for "Uncle Moose" at the University. Uncle Moose had been his hero ever since Franky had taken him down to the Big Game in his sophomore year in high school. It had been a glamorous weekend for them both. Moose had just been named head coach and was in his glory, plowing about the stadium and the campus as though he owned the place at last. He had really laid out the red carpet for them. They were invited to last-minute practice sessions, had free run of the locker room, were seated on the benches with the team during the game, were included in all the social festivities before and after. They were also able to stay at the house and eat with the strange new, infinitely young faces that now beamed at them across the scarred old dining table, once (and still, Franky supposed) scene of so many amiable food fights. There wasn't anything, he told Katie in a delighted phone call Big Game Night, that they hadn't been able to do.

"I really think the kid is on the right track for life now," he said. "The University has worked its old magic once again."

But somehow, it hadn't. First had come high school and a football team in traditional relationship to the student body. If you were a football hero in a small-town high school's modest enrollment, you were really a hero. With that came easy access to a lot of things, including girls, liquor, fast cars (always available from Grandpa Buck, even when two were totalled in one year) and the tentative mid-fifties beginnings of the drug culture. By eighteen Franky Jr. was "a wild man," as his parents told one another with frustrated worry; and there wasn't much they could do about it. Constant tension and constant restiveness soon became open defiance and disobedience. By the time Franky Jr. left for the University, they were barely speaking to one another and even though Franky Sr. had a long, desperate talk with Moose an hour after Franky Jr. left to drive south, it hadn't done much good. Couldn't, as it turned out.

"Jeez, Franky," Moose had said in a tired tone that Franky, with foreboding, instantly recognized. "I hope I can help your kid. I'm sure not having much success with the kids down here at the moment. And my Mikey is thirteen and he's already getting to be a handful, too. God! Is there a book on how to be a parent?"

"Dozens," Franky said ruefully, "and I've read them all. They don't help."

"Not when you have to parent not only your own but forty others as well," Moose said. "It's the drugs that really make it hard. They're beginning to get in here as they are everywhere."

"We're afraid of that," Franky said. "We think he may already have experimented some."

Moose sighed.

"I'll do my best, but I can't promise you anything."

And true to his word, he had made a real effort to "cozy him along," as he put it to Diana, but of course Franky Jr. could see that coming a mile away and wasn't having any. They did have him in for dinner a couple of times, which Franky Jr. suffered with a tolerance that was painfully deliberate and painfully obvious. After that, Diana put her foot down.

"I will not be patronized by that young twerp even if he is the son of your fraternity brother," she said firmly. "I have enough on my hands at home. Maybe you can do something with him on the team. He seems to be basically a nice boy, but there are so many layers of insolence to work through that I just don't have the time, thanks very much."

Which was saying a lot, for Diana, so Moose accepted it without argument and tried instead several long private talks with his difficult young charge. That didn't work, either, and after a few months he abandoned the attempt. Then he had to tell Franky Jr. that in his judgment he didn't yet deserve to be on the first team, which, like all of them, Franky Jr. was convinced he did deserve. Franky Jr. announced grandly that he wasn't about to wait for any vague promises of "maybe next year," and quit the team. From then on, as Moose occasionally reported when a worried Franky Sr. called him, it seemed to be all downhill.

And so it had been ever since, Franky thought now as they pulled into the charming little town of Mendocino where they planned to spend the night. Franky Jr. refused to join the house when membership was offered, joined the Dekes instead and got into what in Franky Sr.'s day was called "a fast crowd." There he remained until he graduated—just barely. Four different jobs followed in quick succession, each seemingly less worthwhile than the last. At the moment he was employed by a lumber company logging redwoods near Arcata, California, doing simple manual labor. He was still heavily into drugs, which made him an unreliable worker and, Franky suspected, would soon result in his firing from that employment, too.

The last contact had been a long, rambling, harshly accusatory response a couple of nights ago when Katie had called him trying to set up a meeting. Even for her desperately hopeful mother's tolerance, that was too much.

"We won't stop," she kept saying, tears streaming down her face. "We won't stop."

Franky had tried to comfort her and for a little while they were close again; but somehow in some strange way he sensed that she blamed him—for Franky Jr., and maybe for Rosie, too, for all he knew. But God knew he had done the best he could.

So welcome Laughing Franky Miller, guys, he thought as he and Katie ate their silent dinner at the Mendocino Hotel. Here he comes, Brother Miller the Old Reliable, funny, funny, *funny*, always good for a joke a minute and a chuckle every two. What an uproarious fellow! You *would* buy a used car from this man. Many did. How could anyone resist, when he was so sure, so confident, so happy, so all-fired successful in every way?

A few miles down the coast at Heritage House, Randy Carrero, a week out from Albuquerque on a leisurely driving trip that had permitted him time to visit seminary classmates in Denver, Salt Lake and Portland, was also eating dinner—alone and, curiously, in a mood not very different from Franky's. An uneasy discontent, an uncomfortable malaise not helped by the surf that was beginning to rise a bit as sunset came on, seemed to have settled on his heart in these concluding hours of his journey. Tomorrow he would be on campus again, in his vocation as successful as any of his fraternity brothers in theirs. Why, then, was he not appropriately happy, and serene?

The Church was supposed to take care of moods like this. The Bible, the rosary, prayer, meditation, positive thoughts induced by contemplation of the dogma—those were the antidotes to the strains of living. Why were they not now coming fully to the aid of Bishop Randolph Ramirez Carrero, forty-four, that bright and rising young star of the hierarchy of whom great things were whispered in New Mexico and murmured discreetly in the Vatican?

He remembered his last conversation with Hack in the house on the Janiculum, his remark about Flavia having found his advice that she get a divorce from Sylvio hard to believe—"She said she couldn't conceive of an Italian Catholic priest doing a thing like that." And his comment, "I said I was an American Catholic, which was a different breed."

He supposed his mood now reflected what Hack had said then. He had not yet openly challenged "all those black-robed elderly gentlemen who float about the Vatican on wings of steel," but he would—he would. He knew the day was coming as surely as he knew the sea out there would be heavy in the morning. The sun was flaming down in extraordinary colors but the clouds were coming up to meet it, gray and dark and looking ominous after the gorgeous day. The coast's tomorrow might be stormy. So, in all probability, might be his.

His arguments with Rome were, he knew, the same as those of many in the American priesthood. Rising protests indicated that the number was increasing all the time. Birth control—celibacy—the attempt in latter twentieth century to keep the Church something high and dictatorial above the multitudes—the exactions of what sometimes seemed worldly greed in the guise of holiness—the constant official exhortations to the hungry peoples of an overpopulated planet to deny all restraints and breed, breed, breed—these were what upset and, for the time being, frustrated him and many others. Not too many were in a position to speak out. He wasn't yet but planned to be. When that time came, a lifetime's work would be put to test.

Once committed, he had seldom regretted his decision to become a priest. On many occasions he had found solace in the Church for a still lively and untamed heart, and he could not deny that it provided a great opportunity for service. Help was needed everywhere—how it was needed! The Church exposed you to all the terrible frustrations of humankind (including those it itself created), but at the same time it offered a cushion of belief to see you through; it enabled you to offer the same solace to others. Except that sometimes, he thought, there was no comfort, no solace, no satisfaction that could possibly soothe the unending agonies of a constantly besieged and tormented humanity.

"One can't really be at peace too much," a senior bishop had once confided moodily. "There's always someone screaming offstage."

And there were, the beaten wives, the abused children, the im-

prisoned, the tortured, the starving, the damned, the hurt, the unhappy, the endlessly striving, the cruelly rejected, the brutalized, the
unrequited, the ugly, the unloved—the endless, endless tale of un-
relieved agony. At any given moment of any given day somewhere
around the globe many thousands, perhaps millions, were being brutalized, tortured, killed, robbed of happiness, consigned to night. *At
this very moment,* he told himself with a sigh, the terrible cavalcade
went on.

Probably more intimately than any of his brethren except Willie in
the Senate, Randy was inextricably involved with the great unhappiness of the world. He would despair of it . . . and then the distrac-
tions of routine would reassert themselves . . . and the healing
balances of life would return. The sun would shine—nature would
smile—he would assist in, or hear of, some great human happiness—a
marriage would be performed—a baby would be born—hope would
revive, and go on.

But you couldn't stop to think too much or too long, or you would
be lost yourself. Close the ears to the screaming, the eyes to the
sadness, open them as much as possible to the sounds of joy and the
scenes of light—it was the only way. In the Church, as in so many
other earnest endeavors of the essentially well-meaning, there was at
least some small positive glimmer ahead to keep one going.

And yet, still remaining, were the things he objected to in the
Church, and no easy way to reform them. "Vatican II" had been a gloss;
it had not changed fundamental weaknesses. Probably they would
never change, or if they did probably not in his lifetime or in many
lifetimes ahead. The power and weight of institution were too strong.

He shook his head impatiently and blinked his eyes rapidly as if to
clear them. The waitress bringing his steak glanced at him quickly
and inquired, "Are you all right, Father?"

"Oh, yes," he said. "Quite all right, thank you. Just a touch of
headache—I'm sure the meal will take care of that."

"Let me know if you need anything."

"You might bring me another glass of red wine," he said, and when
she had, thought: there I go again. Two Scotch and waters in the
lounge before dinner, the second glass of wine now, and maybe one
more before I'm through. I'm going to turn into a typical fat old
red-faced Catholic priest if I don't watch out. I've *got* to watch out.

He thought he could honestly say that keeping in good physical
shape was his only vanity, but he felt he had to have at least one or
he might lose touch with human reality entirely and he couldn't afford

to do that. His stocky little body had always been solid, compact, powerful, as trim as Smitty Carriger's, with whom he used to compare it years ago in the house. Smitty! He wondered what he was like now, and if he still tried to watch his weight and keep himself trim. Not with two drinks before dinner and three glasses of wine with it, he'd bet. He told himself sternly that this second was the last. There would be plenty of temptation over the weekend and he might as well make up his mind to cut back right now.

Furthermore, the dietary and alcoholic indulgence he saw in so many of his fellow priests as they grew older and less hopeful and less ambitious and less willing to struggle against the comfortable cocoon of the Church could only interfere with his ultimate ambitions. If the first step was to become archbishop of New Mexico, which was what he secretly intended, he could not afford physical weakness or sloth. He had to be on his toes, as powerful in mind and heart and intellect as he was determined to be in body. There was too much competition. Like any farsighted politician in a context in which advancement for almost two thousand years had been essentially political, he knew he must be fully prepared to handle it.

He supposed his superiors would be shocked if they knew how candidly he appraised their stately flight "on wings of steel," as Hack put it, through the upper reaches. Like the proprietors of any great institution, they preferred not to be too candid about methods of maintenance and rules of preferment. They knew but they didn't say. Randy knew and he said only to his cousin Juan, now an increasingly portly, increasingly settled pastor of a modest parish near San Diego from which he probably would not go much further. He had believed from the first that Randy was destined to rise to the upper levels of the Church and took a vicarious pleasure in watching him do so. He was a good safety valve for Randy when Randy occasionally exploded in frustration at the intransigent nature of the organization. And he professed to be quite shocked when Randy said things such as, "I guess I'll just have to play politics a little harder."

"It isn't politics," Juan protested indignantly. "You wouldn't be where you are without merit."

"Conceded," Randy said, "but there are plenty of others with equal merit and they haven't got very far. I wouldn't be where I am if I hadn't sucked up to a few bishops along the way, or if I didn't know where they keep the toilet paper in the Vatican."

"You don't have to be vulgar," Juan protested mildly. "I know you have a lot of good contacts in Rome and I know a lot of people think very highly of you in America. But they do that because they think you're able. And you are able. You're very able. Why don't you drop the false modesty and admit it?"

"Well," Randy said, smile breaking through, "all right. But it still takes a hell of a lot of politicking to get ability recognized. I happen to have a knack for it, that's all. And I'm a very intelligent, very competent and, let's face it, very attractive younger man who knows how to be very flattering and complimentary to his elders. It isn't a love affair but there's a lot of that in it, let's face it. They *like* me. They're disposed to give me the breaks. And I know how to manipulate them so they'll give me the breaks. It's a relatively simple equation."

"If you're you," Juan agreed with a rueful smile, "instead of an overweight little priest like me. So be as modest as you like, put yourself down as much as you like, be as cynical as you like about the hierarchy, I still think it's destiny that the path is being smoothed for you and that you have the abilities to get where you want to go. Which is what, and what do you intend to do when you get there?"

"Archbishop of New Mexico," Randy said crisply. "Cardinal."

"And the first American Pope, no doubt," Juan said dryly. "There I stop, Cousin. It'll never happen. But it's a nice dream."

"No, it won't happen. Nor will the other two, probably. I'm a radical, Juanito. I haven't said so, much, but I think there are those who suspect. They're waiting for me. Little Randy is hardly the blink of an eye in the long history of the Church. Why should they worry what *I* think? They can squash me like a bug."

"Tell me about the radicalism," Juan suggested. "I hadn't realized." When Randy did so, he simply said, "Hmph. That doesn't sound so radical to me."

Randy smiled.

"You're American, too. These thoughts are rising here. They're not much in the open yet. One of these days I'm going to be out front for them. Then there'll be hell to pay—or, excuse me, heaven."

"You can do that," Juan agreed, "but you're probably right. They will squash you like a bug. And then what becomes of the archbishop and the cardinal?"

Randy tossed him his cheerfully impudent grin.

"I'll try to restrain myself until I become archbishop. Then watch my dust!"

But, he thought now as the sun disappeared, the sky darkened and the dining room came alight with the gentle glow of candles in the long September twilight, he really wasn't being all that discreet, or

that politically self-protective. He was, in fact, becoming a little careless in terms of what the Church would permit. Or was it simply an
egotistical desire for worldly fame and prominence, "a worldly arrogance" as they would call it if they decided to bring him to book?

It had begun with Flavia, the first time he had deliberately defied
his vows to give counsel to a troubled soul to follow her own feelings
instead of the dictates of the Church. It had continued, sporadically
but increasingly, as he had returned to America, served in several
major parishes in Denver, Seattle, San Francisco, before returning to
New Mexico. Particularly since coming home, he had more and more
counseled the poor, the battered, the too-many-times pregnant to
block conception, refuse further children, even, on several occasions,
abort when the family simply could not possibly support another, or
when there was a record of deformity or mental unbalance in prior
births. Quietly but, he knew, as subtle and far-reaching as a desert
wind, word had spread among the impoverished and overburdened:
Father Carrero is sympathetic. Father Carrero will not judge. Father
Carrero will help.

He had cautioned them all to be utterly silent, to protect him and
themselves so that he could continue to help those who needed help.
But he knew his fame was spreading along the dusty rutted roads, in
the ancient adobe villages, along the piñon-scented trails. How long
it would remain secret, how long before he could venture to indicate
some open independence, he did not know. But he knew the day
would come.

And sex and celibacy: he had seen too many priestly lives ruined,
crippled by suppressed sexuality, stale and lifeless or turning fur-
tively to outlets secret and shameful in their eyes, yet defiant because
there were times, no matter how much prayer and self-excoriation,
when the pressure simply could not be withstood. For himself, ever
the pragmatic and practical, he "took care of it," as he described it to
himself, when he absolutely had to, and didn't worry about it. But
many were not that strong. The Church forced many to feel a terrible
guilt, with often terrible consequences.

To them, and to those who came to confession with a similar problem from among the flock, his counsel was the same: ease thyself,
cleanse thyself, and try to forget. It is natural, total abstinence is not;
go, be of good conscience and good faith and live your lives so that
good works compensate, as they so often do, for whatever sins you
may think you have committed. I do not consider them so. Go and be
healed, and do not worry.

And this, too, spread among the desperate and the unhappy. And this, too, would bring down upon him in due time Hack's "black-robed elderly gentlemen who float about the Vatican on wings of steel." Add to that his intense and implacable impatience with the whole concept of the unmarried priest, which led directly to so many silent, crippling agonies, and collision with Rome seemed inevitable.

He sighed, finished his second glass of wine, stoutly refused a third and nobly, he told himself, nobly, nobly, refused dessert.

He returned to his cabin, which was out on cliff's edge directly above the restless sea, put on an extra sweater and sat for a time on the deck listening to the eternal crashing of the waves below. He felt moody and melancholy and, unusual for Bishop Carrero, uneasy and not entirely sure of the course he was setting for himself. But he knew he would not be deflected from it. He was too strong—and, he felt, too good—a man for that.

Also en route, Gil Gulbransen and Karen Ann were driving up from La Jolla because Karen Ann wanted to stop overnight with a divorced sorority sister who occupied a huge house on the cliffs at Pebble Beach ("Part of the loot," Karen Ann said dryly). Lor Davis and Angie were on the road from their own quite substantial place in Pacific Palisades. Billy Wilson and Janie were driving up from the ranch. Galen Bryce had informed Johnny Herbert that "although my psychiatric practice in Hollywood is really awfully heavy right now, I can probably arrange to have my pilot fly me up for a day or two" (which had produced a snort and a "Does he really think anybody gives a damn?" from Duke Offenberg when Johnny told him). Tony Andrade would drive down alone tomorrow from his home with its commanding view over Napa Valley: Louise thought she should stay there and make final arrangements for the daylong party ("Bring your swimsuits, the pool is great!") and barbecue on Saturday. North McAllister, flying from Salt Lake City, would also be alone because B.J. was "a little under the weather" with some complaint he and several of his fellow doctors had not yet diagnosed exactly. He and Tony had been invited to occupy their old rooms in the house and, pleased, had accepted. Guy Unruh and Maggie from Honolulu, Jeff and Mary Dell Barnett from Charleston, like Smitty, Marc and the Wilson-Johnson party, were airborne at this moment.

Only one member would be unable to make it, an unusually satisfactory turnout for a twenty-fifth: Rodge Leighton had just been appointed a deputy director of the International Atomic Energy Agency in Vienna and he and Juliette and three of the kids were busy moving. Their Ted, eighteen, was at home with his grandparents in the States, being just about to enter the University along with Latt Wilson, Ti-Anna Johnson, Mike Musavich, Alan Offenberg, Jr., Tony Andrade, Jr., Tony Davis and Grant Gulbransen. Already enrolled were Billy Wilson's oldest, Leslie, a sophomore; Guy Unruh's oldest, Wilson, a junior; and Bill Nagatani's oldest, Hiro, whose sister April was entering as a freshman. As at many a well-loved college, the house and immediate friends were well represented in the next generation.

In response to Johnny's plea that "Everybody be ready to give a brief little talk—*brief*, Willie!—about what you've been up to since the war," Rodge had written that he had "some thoughts on this situation here and I'll try to get them organized 'briefly' as you request. Maybe Willie or Moose or somebody can read them to the assembled multitude? The brothers might like to know a bit about what's going on, as all our necks are involved."

Johnny wrote back that he knew they would all be most interested and appreciative and said he'd ask Willie as soon as Willie showed up.

Which would be, as Willie estimated it, roughly three hours from now. They were over Nebraska and far ahead he could see the faint outline of the snowcapped East Front of the Rockies rising abruptly out of the flatlands in their eternal majesty. So far it had been a good flight, a little bumpy over the Midwest and, no doubt, destined to be a little bumpy over the Rockies, although the weather was clear and no storms were predicted. With good luck it might be smooth flying all the way into San Francisco. He hoped so, as Latt had always had a tendency to motion sickness and he knew Donna was always nervous about him. He could feel the tension in her arm against his as she tried to concentrate on her book while he half dozed, half listened to the music on the symphony channel. When she turned around for the fifth time to glance back down the aisle he took off his earphones and remarked mildly, "Come on, Donn. He's fine, isn't he?"

"He seems to be," she said. "But it can come on so suddenly."

"If it does, he'll just have to throw up, won't he? He has a bag. Don't worry."

"But he'll be horribly humiliated in front of Ti-Anna if he has to," she said, refusing to be calmed. "I wonder if I should suggest that he come up here with you for a while. He'd be more comfortable then, and it would give me a chance to get acquainted with her. She seems a bright little thing."

"Donna," he said with a humorous glance at her earnest face, "nothing would humiliate him more than that, believe me. In the first place, it would be Mother, hovering. In the second place, 'getting acquainted with Ti-Anna' would be about as subtle as a meat ax. He isn't going to marry her."

"I don't know," Donna said, an additional worry coming into her voice, which she abruptly lowered. Tim and By were seated together directly behind them. "I wonder."

"For heaven's sake," he protested, a little less mildly, "they've only known each other since we left Washington. You have the most vivid imagination where that boy is concerned. Anyway, what's wrong with it? She seems a lovely girl."

"Stop teasing me," she ordered in the same intense, lowered-voice way. "You know very well what's wrong with it."

"It's all the rage nowadays," he said cheerfully. "I had no idea you were so worried about it. She just happens to be the first nubile young woman he's met in his new college life. There'll be a couple of thousand more when he hits campus. Don't worry. It's just nice the kids can visit going across country, that's all. It's probably the reason he hasn't gotten sick. He's chatting away like a house afire, isn't he?"

"Well," she admitted, smiling a little in spite of herself. "They do seem to be quite engrossed in each other."

"O.K., then," he said comfortably, adjusting his seat and preparing to settle back.

"But I don't like them to be engrossed in one another!"

"Oh, Donn," he said with a mixture of annoyance and amusement. "Will you relax. Anyway, I don't enjoy having him sick around me, either. How often do you suppose it's happened in all these years? More than I want to remember."

"You'll miss him when he isn't around anymore."

"Probably," he admitted. "He's getting a little more human lately. Although we're still miles apart on Vietnam. But at least we can talk about it. We had quite a good discussion the other night, I thought. It lasted at least three minutes before he told me I was an ignorant old war-lover who hadn't had an original thought about foreign policy since the end of World War II."

"I think I should go and sit with her and let him sit with you," she said with sudden decision. "It's going to be your last chance to talk for a long time. I have to go to the rest room anyway. I'll just stop by casually on my way back."

"That will be subtle. Don't be hurt if he takes your head off."

"You're the one who has to watch out," she said with some satisfaction. "He and I always manage to get along pretty well."

"Because you always give in," he retorted as she picked up her purse, unsnapped her seat belt and prepared to move.

"I can't help it if you two are so much alike," she said, and got up and walked away down the aisle, head high, so upset she hardly acknowledged Tim and By when they smiled as she went by.

"Hey," By said, reaching between the seats to tap Willie on the shoulder. "Are you and that nice lady fighting?"

"No," Willie said in a tired voice. "I'm afraid she's going to interrupt my son and your daughter, that's all. She thinks he ought to sit with me for a while."

"They aren't doing any harm," By remarked in a thoughtful voice that sounded just a little edgy.

"That's what I told her," Willie said. "But you know Donna. Very determined."

"Does she have any reason to separate them?" By inquired in the same prepared-to-be-offended tone. Tim leaned forward with a comfortable chuckle.

"You know Donna, By," he said. "She just likes to arrange things. She always has. That's why she was such a damned good organizer in school."

"But they're just visiting—" By began, and then dropped it and sat back, with a grimace only Tim could see, to stare moodily out the window.

"Anyway," Tim said, glancing back down the aisle. "Here he comes, Daddy, so have a good time."

"Return to your seat, Mr. Bates," Willie said with more humor than he really felt, as his firstborn slid into the seat beside him. "There may be some turbulence ahead."

"Really?" Latt asked in what sounded like genuine concern. "Do you have a—yes, you do. So I'll be all right."

"Forget it," Willie said. "Just forget it, please. How's Ti-Anna?"

"Great," Latt said with obviously genuine enthusiasm. "She's a real neat girl, Dad. I'm impressed."

"I'll bet she is. Want a drink?"

"No, thanks," Latt said politely. "You know I don't believe in that stuff."

"Neither do I, really," his father said. "It just eases the wheels of civilization, sometimes."

"Meaning we can't be comfortable together without it? It doesn't bother me, Dad. . . . So," he inquired brightly, "what's up? Why did Mom want us to sit together? You have some last-minute words of wisdom to give me, is that it?"

"I don't think so," Willie said thoughtfully. "But maybe that was it. Shall we try to fool her by saying something?"

"I'm game," Latt said cheerfully. "What'll it be, Vietnam?"

"No, I think not," Willie said with a tired smile. "I think we've been over that so many times there wouldn't be much point right now. No doubt there'll be other opportunities."

"No doubt," Latt agreed.

"And, frankly, I don't want to spoil what may be our last visit together for a long time with a discussion of that subject."

"Our boys over there have to discuss it," Latt observed. "It's their lives. They can't avoid it."

"All right," Willie said firmly.

"And I hope the next time it comes up for a vote, you'll—"

"All *right*. What do you look to get out of this college experience anyway? Reaffirmation of old ideas? Or could you possibly entertain some new ones?"

"Well . . ." Latt paused and for a moment Willie looked at his son, with some wonder, for what he was: a tall, lean, dark-eyed, dark-haired kid, very handsome, very athletic, highly intelligent, shrewd, sharp, emphatic, inclined to be impatient, inclined to be somewhat dictatorial—difficult. All of which, Willie thought wryly, are direct inheritances from me. So how can I complain?

Nonetheless, he often did, wondering what he had spawned to agitate his household and, potentially, the world.

"What I'm really looking forward to," Latt said thoughtfully, "is the chance to rub elbows with other minds—if that isn't too mixed a metaphor. I have a lot of ideas about things, not just Vietnam although I know you think that's all I'm concerned about right now, but—a lot of things. There's a really good prof out there that I've heard about and I want to take some courses from him, for one thing. Of course I know there are lots of good profs out there. I want to hit 'em all before I'm through, if I can."

"What's that one's name?" Willie inquired, thinking: as if I don't know.

"Dr. Suratt," Latt said. "Did you ever hear of him?"

"Yes, I've heard of him. You won't believe it, but we're fraternity brothers. We were in the same house together. You'll meet him this weekend, no doubt."

"You've never mentioned him at home," Latt observed. "You don't like him, do you?"

"No," Willie said. "I never have."

"What's wrong with him? Everything I've heard about him has been good. What's your gripe?"

"It's too long to go into," Willie said. "He's just not a nice person, that's all. So, what else do you want to get out of it?"

"No, wait a minute," Latt said, eyes bright with combat, in them a bulldog determination Willie knew all too well. "I want to know what's wrong with Dr. Suratt."

"Tim," Willie said, turning and speaking between the seatbacks. "Tell this boy what's wrong with Dr. Suratt."

"Can't begin to," Tim said cheerfully.

"It would take a book," By agreed.

"Oh," Latt said. "I see. Some house thing, huh? Or generational— no, you're the same generation. But I gather he sure doesn't think like you all do."

"He's a special case," Tim said ironically.

"Unique," By said.

"Good," Latt said, settling back. "I like unique people. You make me more determined than ever to find out about him, Dad. Thanks."

"That's all right," Willie said dryly. "Do you have any plans to prepare yourself for a career while you're at school? Or is that too old-fashioned, these days?"

"I don't mind," Latt said. "Have to play along with the system for a while if you want to reform it. I'll probably take some history and some political science, and English, and maybe French or Spanish, probably Spanish since that will be useful in California—"

"Oh, you plan to stay in California. Your mother and I never knew that."

"Probably," Latt said. "As long as we have the ranch. It's a good foothold. After all, it helped get you where you are."

"And you're going to run for the Senate, too, someday," Willie said, trying not to sound too sarcastic.

Latt shrugged.

"Sons have. Maybe. Maybe not. Depends upon where I think I can do the most good. We're entering an era where we're all going to have to help."

"That's probably true."

"After all, if we're to change this corrupt society, everybody's going to have to pitch in and do his or her part. Isn't that right?"

"Probably right," Willie said. "I guess I just didn't realize it was quite that pressing."

"Pressing as hell," Latt said emphatically. "We're a mess. An absolute *mess*. And since your generation isn't doing anything to correct the horrible inequities—"

"We try to do our best in the Senate—" Willie began but a skeptical laugh cut him short.

"The Senate! And the House! *Those* old windbags! What have *they* ever accomplished, Dad? What have *you* ever accomplished, as a matter of fact?"

"Well," Willie said, suddenly feeling provoked beyond patience. "I'll have you know that I've—I've—"

"Yes?" his firstborn inquired, leaning toward him intently, eyes sharp, jawline unyielding. "What, Dad?"

"I can't write you a book right here," Willie said sharply, "but you know as well as I do what my record's been. After all, I'm your father, damn it! Don't you know what I've done? Do you have to be told?"

"Oh, I guess you're an adequate Senator," Latt said comfortably. "I mean, as Senators go. You vote for appropriations—you support a few good things such as national health insurance—the leadership counts on you. But I mean *really original* proposals— let's face it, Dad, you really haven't done much so far."

"Well," he said tartly, "give me time. I'm only forty-six."

"Getting along, Dad," Latt said in the same comfortable way. "Better get with it . . . I think I'll go back and talk to Ti-Anna some more now. She's a nice girl."

"Full of progressive ideas, I suppose."

Latt gave him a brilliant, tolerant, generous smile.

"Well, yes," he said pleasantly. "As a matter of fact."

And was up and gone. Tim leaned forward once more.

"Touchdown, Dad? Or did you get pushed back beyond the goal line?"

"It isn't funny," Willie said shortly, putting on his earphones again. "It isn't funny."

And when Donna came back, admitting somewhat reluctantly that Ti-Anna was indeed a nice girl—apparently no "progressive" ideas had been put forward to alarm Latt's mother—he refused to be drawn into any revelations about his talk with Latt. He knew Donn could perceive that it hadn't been a very successful one and he knew she would worry about it. So let her. It wouldn't be the first time she had worried about the two of them. Or the first, or the last, that they didn't agree.

He couldn't control Latt's courses, of course, but he wasn't going to let up on his criticism of Renny Suratt. From what he had heard from Johnny and Duke, Renny was a real youth-destroyer. He shuddered to think what might become of Latt if he got swept up in that maelstrom.

Presently he and Donna dozed off. Behind them Tim and By, after a lengthy discussion of what By planned to say in the first of the Herman and Gretchen Krohl Memorial Lectures tomorrow night, also settled back to sleep through the flight's final hours.

Back down the aisle Latt and Ti-Anna talked animatedly all the way.

Far down Palm Drive he could see the dusty summer green of the Oval, the bright mosaic front of Memorial Church, the gentle outlines of the Coast Range rising beyond. All was calm and placid in the warmth of late September afternoon.

The terrible war—the troubled peace—lives begun and already half-over—it was twenty-five years since he had last seen that peaceful sight.

It was only yesterday.

"I hope you folks aren't going to cry," Latt remarked from the backseat.

"If we want to," his mother said with a shaky little laugh, "we will. So will you, someday."

"Never," Latt said confidently. "I'll never get that attached to anything."

"Therein may lie the story of a life," his father said dryly. "Lucky you."

"I think so," Latt said in a complacent tone that annoyed them both, but what was the use? No point in an argument right now.

"Freshman dorm is off to the left," Willie said and drove the rental car expertly toward it, past the stadium, through the eucalyptus groves. Beside him he could feel Donna growing tense. The moment Latt went up those steep sandstone steps and disappeared inside that familiar old brownstone building, he would cross over irretrievably from their lives into his own. Instinctively Willie reached for Donna's hand.

Youths bounded up and down the steps, cars came and went, voices shouted, doors banged. Activity, anticipation, a rising excitement, filled the soft, embracing air.

"I'll go check in and get my room assignment," Latt said. "Back in a minute." And he was out of the car in a flash and bounding up the steps with the rest.

"There he goes," Willie said as he disappeared through the arches.

"Oh!" Donna said and began to cry. "I do hope he'll be all right."

"He will," Willie predicted firmly, though they both doubted it. "He will."

Fifteen minutes later Latt was back to get his two suitcases, tennis racket, golf clubs, six hangers bulging with jeans, shirts, one blazer, one pair of dress slacks, one necktie, a parka, a raincoat. Willie offered to help but Latt refused him hastily. Parents, Willie dimly remembered, were best not seen or heard from at this particular time.

"It looks like I've got two good guys to room with," Latt said as a youth who must be one of them appeared at the top of the steps, yelled, "Hey, Wilson, I'll help you with that stuff!" and, with a quick, amiable wave to Latt's parents, proceeded to do so.

"Mom"—Latt said, giving her a quick kiss—"Dad"—a quick handshake—"it's going to be great!"

"We hope so," Willie called after him as he and his new roommate staggered up the steps with his belongings, already so engrossed in conversation that he didn't even turn back when he reached the door.

"Hey!" Willie shouted. "Are we going to see you for dinner?"

"Probably not," Latt shouted back as he disappeared. "I told Ti-Anna I'd come over later. I'll call you tomorrow morning."

"Do that," Willie said wryly. "Be so kind."

But Latt was gone, off in a new world.

"Will we ever see him again?" Donna asked in a stricken voice. Willie gave her a hug.

"Of course. It will all be old hat by tomorrow. He'll be such a blasé, experienced college student that we won't even know him."

"Have we ever?" she inquired wistfully.

"Probably not," Willie agreed, and sighed. "Does any parent?"

2

Most who attend college reunions do so to renew old friendships and reminisce. Some others attend with a Purpose.

The three most obvious among the latter this day were the tall, bulky, humorless blond man who sat with rigid stolidity in a high-backed chair facing the president of the University in his office; the tall, thin, graying, nervous black who walked aimlessly up and down the colonnades along the Quad as they began to stir with the excited comings and goings of new and returning students; and the lean, saturnine figure with carefully sloppy clothing and carefully unkempt, lanky hair who seemed to be stalking the nervous black as he wandered, absorbed and impervious, through Friday morning's hazy sunshine.

"So!" Rudy Krohl said, relishing his moment now that he had that pompous old fart Dr. Chalmers where he wanted him. "It has been a long time since we talked in this room."

"That's right, Mr. Krohl," the president agreed, as calmly and amicably as though he weren't frightened at all by Rudy's belligerent manner, though Rudy knew he must be. "It was a rather stern moment, as I recall, but I hoped you would profit from it. Have you?"

He gave Rudy a bland, inquiring smile that momentarily—but only momentarily, Rudy told himself hastily—threw him a little off balance.

"I am here," he said bluntly. "I am a trustee now. I have profited from something, all right. But I do not think it was your kind remarks to me that day."

"Well, of course you realize," Dr. Chalmers said, in the same comfortable way as though he were still the controlling figure and Rudy the chastened subordinate, though Rudy knew that of course it was now totally the other way around, "we couldn't have the campus disrupted by violent pro-Nazi demonstrations when we were about to go to war with Germany—particularly demonstrations whose sole purpose was to intimidate and eliminate all contrary opinion."

"We had a right to protest!" Rudy exclaimed, beginning to argue, which was exactly what he had told himself he wasn't going to do because after all, he was a new trustee and this arrogant academic was his servant now. "It was our right as much as theirs!"

"Ah," Dr. Chalmers said, "but they did not attempt to stop your expression of it. You and Mr.—Hubner, was it?—and Miss Helga—Helga—"

"Berger!" Rudy snapped. "She is Mrs. Krohl now! We have four children!"

"Good for you," Dr. Chalmers said approvingly. "You probably never knew, but I had four myself, three now: my oldest boy was shot down over Germany. I believe you did not serve in the armed forces, Mr. Krohl?"

"I have asthma," Rudy said angrily. "My company contributed greatly to the war effort! I served that way!"

"And you're right," Dr. Chalmers said with an encouraging smile, "you *did* profit from it. Greatly, as I understand, for which we here at the University must be very grateful, since it has permitted you to contribute handsomely to us. And of course that was service—of a kind—and it was, I have no doubt, a real contribution to the war effort, and for that your fellow Americans must also feel gratitude. But as I was saying, when you and Miss Berger as she was then and Mr. Hubner deliberately disrupted the anti-Hitler rally organized by Mr. Wilson, Mr. Bates and Mr. Katanian, you must have perceived—in time, if not then—that I had no choice but to try to persuade you most vigorously that such was not the tolerant attitude we have always tried to maintain at the University."

"It is not so easy now, is it?" Rudy inquired with a deliberate insolence. "Not so easy now, with Vietnam."

"No," Dr. Chalmers agreed, and for a moment he, too, seemed thrown a bit off balance. "It is already taking its toll and it will take its toll increasingly as time goes on. It is going to condition our whole national discourse, I am afraid; it is going to change us into a nation uglier, more intolerant, more raucous, more harsh. And no sector will feel it more harshly than the colleges. I do not mind telling you that the prospect is very disturbing to me."

"You must put them down," Rudy said harshly. "You must put them down with an iron hand."

"Mr. Krohl," Dr. Chalmers said, "it is not that simple. The times are different."

"Put them down!" Rudy repeated. "I tell you that as a trustee! We expect it of you!"

"Some do, some don't," Dr. Chalmers said. "I am not surprised that you do."

"You did not hesitate with us before the war," Rudy pointed out with a grim persistence. "You were very forceful then, Mr. Professor President. You scolded us and humiliated us and forced us to give way. Are you afraid of this rabble now, Mr. President? Surely not!"

"I am not afraid," Dr. Chalmers said quietly, "but I am not prepared to take strong action just yet—"

"They will take it if you do not," Rudy predicted grimly. "You will see."

"I have to feel my way," the president said. "At the moment, things are not out of hand, the protests are still mild—"

"But growing," Rudy noted. "Growing everywhere."

"Growing everywhere," the president conceded, "but so far without harm to fundamental rights and decencies. So with all respects to you, Mr. Krohl, I think that for the time being I must be allowed to handle it in my own way, even though I know some of the trustees see the situation as you do and favor a tougher line. I can be tough if I have to. I don't think it's necessary yet."

"And anyway," Rudy pointed out with a return of insolence, "you will retire soon and we will have to select a new, strong president and then it will be out of your hands and we can treat it as we like."

"That's right," Dr. Chalmers agreed. "At the end of this academic year. And you can then select who you will. I would hope that he will see things as I do."

"I am determined that he will not!" Rudy said. "Anyway, I know who it will *not* be, so don't try to push him on us, because I am very much opposed."

"Who is that?" Dr. Chalmers inquired, although he knew.

"That—that—" Rudy said, twenty-five years of animosity resurfacing after the war and all that had passed between—"that *person*."

"Dr. Offenberg?" Dr. Chalmers said. "No, I shall not propose Dr. Offenberg. Yet. He needs a little more seasoning. But the time will come before long when his claim will be such that he will be very hard to ignore. I have recommended to the board, not formally but in private conversations, that they select an older man of great distinction who could logically serve perhaps three or four years until retirement, and that Dr. Offenberg be made provost with the understanding that he will succeed on the retirement of this interim head. That would be a logical and beneficial thing to do, it seems to me, given Dr. Offenberg's abilities and his devotion to the University."

"Well!" Rudy said flatly. "Your views will not weigh with this trustee, I can tell you that!"

"Then I sincerely hope there are sufficient votes to vote you down," Dr. Chalmers said crisply. "Not only on this issue but on many others as well." He stood abruptly, not offering to shake hands. Rudy perforce stood too. "Will you attend the lecture tonight? As you have been informed officially, the University is very grateful indeed for this very handsome contribution to our cultural enrichment. And also, as you know, for your other very handsome contribution recently to the endowment."

"Yes," Rudy said grimly. "I may not be popular but my money most certainly is, isn't that right, Mr. President? All colleges dance to that."

"We appreciate all contributions to the stability and future welfare of the University," Dr. Chalmers said blandly. "How could we not?"

"Yes, indeed," Rudy said savagely, "how could you not? One thing I will tell you I do *not* approve, and that is your choice of this black— *agitator*—to give the first Herman and Gretchen Krohl Memorial Lecture. I am sorry now that I ever agreed to leave selection of speakers in the hands of the University. I might have known a lot of liberal radicals would control things. *That's* where this school is going!"

"Will you attend?" Dr. Chalmers repeated in the same bland way. "If so, we would be very pleased to have you sit on the platform along with Dr. Suratt, who will introduce Mr. Johnson and also of course introduce you—"

"Renny SURATT?" Rudy cried in a tone so anguished that in spite of his best efforts Dr. Chalmers could not suppress a smile, which of course only infuriated Rudy more. "*That* perverted hare-brained phony? Sit on the platform with Renny *Suratt?* Be introduced by Renny *Suratt?* Twenty-five years ago I got my fill of Renny Suratt! No, I will not! No, no, *no!*"

"Think about it," Dr. Chalmers suggested, unperturbed. "It would be only right. It is your series, after all, in the names of your parents. Who could better pay fitting and heartfelt tribute to them than their only son?"

"Renny Suratt!" Rudy said, turning away and moving almost blindly to the door. "Renny *Suratt*! And By Johnson, too! Renny *Suratt*!"

But half an hour later, as he had expected, Dr. Chalmers received a call. Rudy would be there. "But don't expect me to say anything about Renny or By! Just my parents!"

"Very good, Mr. Krohl," Dr. Chalmers said calmly. "No one could be more appropriate or, I am sure, do a more fitting and moving job."

"Renny *Suratt*!" Rudy said again as he went off the line. "Renny *Suratt*!"

After that, Dr. Chalmers thought with a chuckle, he had better get out of the office, as he often liked to do, get a breath of fresh air and mingle with the students. The University had grown in size postwar, upward of six thousand now where it had been only three when he came on board, but he still knew many of them by name. Those returning would instantly recognize his tall, dark-suited, outwardly austere but inwardly shy figure as it passed among them with the characteristic brief nod and warm smile that lit up his craggy, dew-lapped face. The new ones would recognize him, too, for his fame after thirty years in office was synonymous with the University. He sighed. He *was* the University, in many ways, and he didn't fancy at all that he would soon have to bid his position there farewell.

One who would not grieve for that was Renny Suratt, whose reaction when he saw the president's tall figure crossing the inner Quad in front of him was: Oh, Lord. Save me from Chalmers. I don't want any homespun soliloquies today.

But when he realized that the president's objective was the same as his own, By Johnson, he increased his pace and overtook them just as Dr. Chalmers was saying cordially, "Mr. Johnson, isn't it? How good to have you back on campus!"—and then, becoming aware of Renny's rapid approach, "And Dr. Suratt. Isn't it nice to have this distinguished alumnus with us again?"

"Splendid!" Renny said. By—still shy, Renny noticed, after all these years of controversy and public appearance—mumbled something vague but respectful to Dr. Chalmers and then responded awkwardly when Renny pumped his hand with fulsome vigor and clapped him on the back. His manner clearly said *I'm grateful for your kindness* to Dr. Chalmers and *I don't believe a word you say* to Renny, which they both perceived. Dr. Chalmers actually winked at Renny, which did not make him any happier with the president's company.

"We are all looking forward very much to your talk tonight," Dr. Chalmers said. "It will be a most auspicious start for the Krohl lectures. Mr. Krohl was in my office just a few minutes ago—"

"No!" Renny exclaimed. By looked quite dismayed. "Is he here?"

"One never knows who's going to turn up on campus," Dr. Chalmers said. "Not only has he endowed the lecture series, Mr. Johnson, but he's given the general endowment a very handsome sum, too. As you both know, he's just been elected to the board of trustees, which will be announced at their meeting tomorrow morning."

"Quid pro quo," Renny observed in a dry tone that prompted Dr. Chalmers to smile and remark, "Safety in numbers."

Renny scowled.

"No safety in that gang of reactionary millionaires. He'll just reinforce all their worst instincts."

"Well, I am sure you can point the way toward their salvation in your classroom," the president said comfortably. "Dr. Suratt is quite the conscience of the campus these days, Mr. Johnson. We don't know what we would do without him."

"Is that right?" By inquired with a sudden gleam of humor that Renny wasn't expecting at all. "That isn't quite the way I've heard it."

"Oh, it's true," Dr. Chalmers said. "Absolutely true. Well, I know you probably want to talk to Mr. Johnson about your introduction tonight, Dr. Suratt, so I shall remove myself. I'll be back in my office in about half an hour, Mr. Johnson. Why don't you stop by?"

"Thank you," By said, pleased. "I'd like that."

"Good." Dr. Chalmers said. "See you tonight, Dr. Suratt."

"Of course," Renny said tartly. "I wouldn't dream of seeing you sooner."

"Of course not," the president said with a comfortable smile that embraced them both. He nodded and continued on his way, conferring upon students and faculty members alike his calm beneficence as he passed.

"Phew!" Renny exclaimed. "I do get tired of that pious soul. I expected you to kiss his ring, you sounded so deferential. You're the famous national figure, he's not."

"He's the president," By said. He smiled. "I can't help it if I revert when I see him again after all these years."

Renny snorted.

"You shouldn't. You're worth ten of him."

"I don't think so," By said. "You, maybe. Not me."

"I try to keep things in perspective for the kids," Renny said with satisfaction. "Chalmers pumps 'em full of the old conservative God-motherhood-and-the-flag crap and I shake it out of 'em and bring 'em back to reality."

By gave him a wry glance.

"So I've heard."

"Do you have a kid here now?" Renny inquired. "It ought to be about the right time, shouldn't it?"

"I do," By said, tone suddenly reserved.

"I'll keep an eye out for him—her?"

"Her," By said reluctantly, adding bluntly, "and she isn't ready for you, Renny. So keep your hands off, O.K.?"

"My goodness, yes!" Renny said, professing to be startled. "My goodness! Relax, By. I don't rob cradles."

"I hope not," By said quietly, "for I should be most distressed if you did."

"Come along to my office," Renny said with an apparent change of interest. . . . "Now," he said after a short, silent walk across the Quad, "what are you going to say tonight? Is it going to be something challenging or will it be the same old gradualism shit you always peddle?"

Fifteen minutes later, after By had made it emphatically clear that he was not going to modify his basic approach, "no matter how much you rant and rave," Renny said sharply, "Well, I always knew when you finally had your chance to make an impact here, you'd fuck it up. It's like you. You were always like that, even when you were a basketball hero. The house had you so intimidated you couldn't see straight. Now apparently the conservatives do. Are you still coming to the dinner?"

"Yes," By said sharply. "Shouldn't I?"

"Of course," Renny said calmly. "I just figured you'd probably spooked yourself out of it over the last few days, just thinking about it. I wouldn't have been surprised."

"Look," By said, suddenly feeling really angry, "if you think so little of me, why don't you just forget introducing me tonight?

I'm sure I can find somebody else. Dr. Chalmers might be willing, and I know Willie would be glad to. Why don't you just forget it?"

Renny looked smug.

"It's already been announced. We can't change it now."

"Oh, no?" By said with a sudden naked hostility that made Renny
almost visibly recoil. He reached across the desk, picked up Renny's phone, dialed operator, uttered a terse, "Dr. Chalmers,
please."

"Now, wait," Renny said, beginning to look alarmed. "Just don't
upset everything, O.K.? It's all arranged, it's been announced in the
Daily—"

"Dr. Chalmers," By said. "This is Bayard Johnson. Yes, sir, I'm still
planning to come along in a minute. First, though, I've decided not
to accept Renny's kind offer to introduce me. I know it's been announced, but—"

"It's in the program!" Renny protested in a vehement whisper.

"I thought perhaps Willie," By said, "unless you would be willing—yes, sir, I understand your position, but—oh, that would be
nice, you would introduce him and then he could introduce me.
Sure, that would be fine. He's always been my best champion anyway, from the very first day I arrived on this campus . . . He and
Donna are staying with the Offenbergs . . . Yes, this is very much
better. Very . . ."

He cradled the phone, turned back to Renny with a calmly triumphal air.

"So much, half-ass," he said, "for you."

"You can't do this!" Renny said angrily. "You'll make me look like
a laughingstock in front of the whole campus—

"I doubt it," By said, unimpressed. "You're in too solid here. But
if I did, it would be a good thing."

"Well, damn you, anyway," Renny snapped, "you black—black—
You haven't heard the last of this!"

"I'm sure not," By said, standing up and turning away. "But I'll just
have to stand it."

"I can make trouble!" Renny shouted as By stepped out the door
and set off purposefully along the Quad to the president's office. "I
can make trouble for you!"

"I believe you," By shot back over his shoulder, but said again, "I
guess I'll just have to stand it."

*   *   *

The scene was vivid in both their minds as they sat on the stage of Memorial Hall shortly before seven that night.

It was Registration Day, fall quarter 1939. Then, as now, the big room was packed, a roar of excited sound covered all. Then had come an abrupt silence. Down the aisle came the assistant dean of men, escorting a lone black youth, shy and visibly frightened, who looked neither left nor right as they made their way down the aisle to get his registration papers.

He sat down, started filling them out. Sound resumed, swiftly approached its former level. But around the lonely black figure there was a cone of silence, an obvious withdrawal, a sense of his being isolated in a shocked and startled world—not a hostile one, but one in which his presence, being so alien to everything that had been customary in that place before, set him dramatically, and inescapably, apart.

Into that void, on a sudden impulse he had never regretted, had stepped the president of the student body and his fraternity brother and close friend, "the brightest boy in school," Bill Lattimer.

"Well, well," Wilson had said softly. "What do you know."

"Yes, indeed," Latt said.

"I like his looks," Wilson said with a sudden calm decisiveness, knowing full well the impact his actions would have on his fellow students. "Let's go meet him."

Lattimer gave him a quick, affectionate smile.

"You know," he said, "you're quite a guy, Willie. Let's."

And they had walked across the open space that seemed to have grown around the boy; stood beside him for a second while he kept his head down, aware of their presence but apparently not daring to look up; and then simultaneously held out their hands.

"I'm Willie Wilson," Willie said, "and this is Bill Lattimer. Welcome to the University."

The boy gave them a great big smile they never forgot, rose to tower above them, tall as they both were, and shook hands with grateful pressure. . . .

By leaned toward Willie to make himself heard above the restless hubbub that now filled the room.

"Twenty-five years ago," he said. "In this room."

"Almost to the day," Willie agreed.

"You and dear Latt," By said. "I think that was one of the bravest—and the kindest—acts I have ever known in my whole life."

"We tried," Willie said. "We wanted to make you feel at home."

"You did," By said. "You did." A shadow crossed his face. "As much as was possible for me at that time. I'm going to start off telling them about that. They don't understand how much courage it took, back then, because they can't imagine what it was like in those days." The shadow increased. "They can't understand what it's like in these days. They think the battle is almost over."

"Tell 'em differently," Willie suggested. "It's your night."

But for a while that was not certain at all.

The first thing to break the uneasy surface of what Willie soon found himself thinking of as "the truce in the room" was the arrival of the donor of the Herman and Gretchen Krohl Memorial Lectures. He emerged suddenly onstage from behind the curtain, looking red-faced, hard-pressed, downright mad and determinedly belligerent. Some student or faculty member began to boo and hiss. Automatically it was taken up by others who had no idea what it was all about except that it seemed like a good idea. The room became filled with hostile sound.

"Damned agitators!" Rudy snapped above the uproar as he took his seat beside Willie. "Damn agitators! *You,*" he said, leaning across Willie to By, "are in for a lot of trouble. They're organized out there behind the building. They're obviously getting ready to come in. There's going to be a demonstration."

"Hello, Rudy," Willie said calmly, holding out his hand, which Rudy, after a second's hesitation, shook very briefly before shoving his hand across to do the same to By. "What's the problem?"

"I tell you they're organized," Rudy repeated. "They're coming in. You'd better be prepared to take it, Johnson. They threw a couple of rocks at me and I'm sure they're planning more than that in here. They knew who I was. They've got banners for us all."

"Just like old times," Willie remarked. "We were just talking about twenty-five years ago—"

"Very funny!" Rudy snapped. "Very funny, Wilson, you always were the big ha-ha of the campus. You'll get yours, too, before they're through. They're against By and they're against me and they're against you and against the Vietnam War. Race and business and politics and Vietnam and every other fucking thing they can think of, all mixed up together. It's a crazy, fucked-up place just like it's always been. Why I've given my money to it, I'll never know!"

"So you can honor your parents with your new lecture series and be a trustee and tell the University what to do," Willie said with a reasonable air he knew would annoy. "Isn't that right?"

"Oh, fuck it!" Rudy said angrily and turned away, greatly agitated, to fumble with a piece of paper he took out of his pocket, apparently notes for his remarks.

The hubbub in the room subsided somewhat, though the level of tension remained high. Two minutes later, though it seemed to his fellow speakers that it must be at least fifteen, Dr. Chalmers stepped through the curtains and with his usual calm dignity walked to the podium.

There was a scattering of applause, the automatic respect that the sight of him, so much a part of all their lives, could always evoke. Willie, By and Rudy had the same thought: How long, in the context of Vietnam and everything else in their hectic century, would such authority figures continue to receive even such minimal respect?

"Welcome, ladies and gentlemen," he said quietly, "to the first of the Herman and Gretchen Krohl Memorial Lectures. It is my pleasure to introduce our first speaker tonight, the generous donor who has made possible this welcome addition to our cultural programs, Rudolph Krohl, member of the class of '41."

And he turned, smiled, and with his customary air of comfortable camaraderie, said cordially, "Rudy?"

There was an abrupt renewal of the booing as Rudy came forward, but aside from an angry toss of his head, a noticeable tightening of his jaw and a momentary glare of open hostility, he paid it no attention.

Briefly but with considerable grace he paid tribute to his parents: their impoverished arrival, separately, from Germany in 1902 . . . his father's first job as a stable boy . . . his first purchase, with money patiently saved, of a horse and delivery wagon . . . their meeting at a Lutheran church picnic, their wedding, their acquisition of citizenship, his own arrival much later when they were nearing middle age . . . his father's move to mechanization, the first truck, his haulage business growing, the addition of two more trucks . . . the coming of World War I (no mention that Herman, openly pro-German, had been interned for a time as a potential subversive, his business temporarily in the hands of a trusted bank) . . . the business, greatly expanded during the war, delivering foodstuffs and other supplies on a contract basis to Army installations in New Jersey and New York . . . great expansion after the war, shrewd investments, the fleet grown to one hundred trucks by 1935 . . . the shift to much heavier moving equipment, the emphasis changing more and more to major construction projects, greatly expanded again by defense contracts in World War II (again no mention of secret loyalties), expanded even further in the postwar boom of the fifties and sixties that was still growing in mid-sixties . . . the corporate entity, nationwide and now overseas in twenty-two countries: KROHL MOVES AMERICA— KROHL BUILDS THE WORLD now emblazoned on trucks, equipment, heavy machinery, billboards everywhere . . . his parents' tragic death in a corporate-jet accident three years ago, his decision to establish the lecture series in their honor. . . .

And a brief (very brief, Dr. Chalmers noted wryly) reference to his being a graduate, no fulsome, sentimental old-grad's tribute, just at the end the simple declaration, "As a graduate and a donor I intend to do what I can to see that the University remains true to those principles of sound, constructive, *responsible* education upon which it was founded"—and the inevitable renewed boos and hisses from the politically sensitive, their antennae always quivering, always alert . . . and no mention, either, of the inaugural speaker of the lecture series. Just the final, flat statement, "I hereby declare these lectures begun."

"WHAT DID YOU DO IN THE WAR, YOU PROFITEERING NAZI CREEP?" bellowed a voice somewhere in the audience. It was greeted by a burst of approving laughter and applause.

Dr. Chalmers rose instantly, came to stand beside him, leaned to the microphone.

"I must remind you that it is one of the great traditions of the University that we receive all visitors and all shades of opinion with decency, courtesy, and respect—"

Instantly the hostile sounds increased, turned ugly. Rudy held up his hand for silence, waited stone-faced until it came. He spoke with utter contempt.

"If you discourteous swine will shut up," he said, "maybe you'll learn something. If you aren't too stupid."

At that the angry noise burst out again, roared to a crescendo of boos and hisses, lasted a full two minutes before it finally subsided into a whispering, waiting, challenge-us-again-if-you-dare-you-bastard hostility, an almost palpable presence in the room. Rudy picked up his notes and retired to his chair, angry contempt as fierce as theirs in his expression and every line of his bulky body.

"To introduce our principal speaker of the evening," Dr. Chalmers said, voice calm as he knew it had to be despite his own inner agitation in the face of yet another layer of social civility peeling away, "it is my great pleasure to welcome back to campus one of our most distinguished alumni—"

"SENATOR SQUEAK-IN!" somebody shouted. "SENATOR SQUEAK-IN!"

And the chant was immediately taken up:

"SQUEAK-IN! SQUEAK-IN! SQUEAK-IN!"

"—a member of the class of '39," Dr. Chalmers went on firmly, "a former president of the student body, the junior Senator from California, the Honorable Richard Emmett Wilson. Willie?"

And he stepped back as Willie rose and came forward. They shook hands. Dr. Chalmers murmured, "Good luck!" Willie nodded with a grimly sardonic wink and stepped to the podium.

There he simply stood for almost a full minute, quietly and without expression, hands resting lightly on the lectern, thoughts apparently completely composed and calm.

What he was actually thinking was, How shall I start? *Listen to me you crummy bastards*—? Or, *When you retarded juvenile delinquents get through with your kindergarten fun*—? Or, *Do you have any idea how much decent, civilized people despise you*—? Or, more simply, *Shut yur fucking mouths, you rude, two-bit, worthless assholes*—?

But, no, of course, none of those would do. Not all of them were bad and some of them genuinely believed that *he* was a crummy bastard, they regarded him as a retarded, reactionary adult, they despised him, they wanted him to shut his—

The only difference being, of course, that he, like most of his generation, was still conditioned to listen to opposing points of view, still believed that there was some value in rational discourse, still thought that it was possible for people to differ but still respect and be courteous to one another.

A small, generational thing, he thought wryly, but terribly, terribly important in the era they were now heading into. And destined, he was very much afraid, to wither if not completely disappear in the climate being increasingly created and controlled by the likes of Renny Suratt and all those who, mindless and gleefully irresponsible like the ones they faced tonight, were determined not only to defeat but to destroy all who dared disagree with them.

And of course he must remain civil for the sake of the audience he, Dr. Chalmers, By and even Rudy were there to speak to. He decided to concentrate on them until the noise quieted down.

Down front, close in, he could see Jeff Barnett, older, more settled, getting a little gray but still trim and very recognizable, sitting with a plump little blonde who must be Mary Dell; Moose, heavier, more stolid but unmistakably and forever Moose, sitting with pleasant, earnest Diana; Franky and Katie, whom he had not seen in twenty-five years, also older, grayer—why was everybody getting gray, all of a sudden?—smiling up encouragingly; and Guy Unruh, tanned as always from Hawaii's sun, and Maggie, her chunky little body almost alarmingly fat but sweet, rosy face as cheerful as ever; and Donna, worried and tense, sitting with them.

Further back and scattered he could spot Gil Gulbransen and Karen Ann, Gil looking noticeably older, worn and intent but still strikingly handsome, Karen Ann, perhaps aided by surgery, a little older but still basically the same blondly svelte and stylish Ice Maiden of campus days . . . Duke Offenberg, carrying his years with the dignity of the born pedagogue, Shahna dark and pleasant, a worried concern for what was going on showing through her determinedly bright and interested expression . . . Hack and Randy, pleased at being together again after too long a time . . . Tony Aldrade, heavier, quite gray, rather courtly, sitting with Lor Davis, looking ten years younger than his age, the perennial David, and an Angie who looked thinner, tinier, almost elfin now; and next to her North McAllister, a little heavier but not noticeably grayer, looking like what he was, the successful doctor and pillar of the community. Doubtless many of the others were there, too, though Willie could not separate them from the sea of faces in his quick, cursory glance.

Just as the clamor finally subsided and he gripped the lectern more firmly and prepared to speak, one last couple caught his eye. In the next-to-last row at the back, a dark, lean, handsome youth for whom he felt a sudden wave of love so overwhelming he almost cried out with it, sat with a stunningly attractive black girl who snuggled against his arm: the kids, there to see their fathers. The cliché, he thought, the cliché—here it comes again . . . and, as he caught also a glimpse of their faces happily alight with the sounds they were making, he thought bitterly: and the New Cliché, which they were apparently already embracing scarcely twenty-four hours after reaching campus.

The wave of love receded. Something harder, presaging he knew not what, began to take its place.

"Dr. Chalmers," he said calmly into the uneasy silence, "ladies and gentlemen:

"First, I think we must all pay tribute to the alumnus whose generosity to the University has made possible this lecture series and whose further generosities, I am told, will greatly enrich and strengthen the University in the future."

There was a rising murmur but he overrode it firmly.

"This is a time of memories for many of us here, and some will remember that Rudy Krohl and I did not always see eye-to-eye in our last, pre-war year here together. But nothing can diminish or derogate his generosity now, and I am happy to pay tribute to it."

The sound rose a little more, the ugly note began to intrude upon it. He ignored it and turned to smile at Rudy, who had the grace to give him a surprised and grudging, but obviously sincere, nod of thanks. He doubted that any hatchets were buried—the trustees' meeting tomorrow morning would reveal further on that—but at least for the moment the necessary civility was restored. It must be. They had to stand together in the face of this audience.

"Twenty-five years ago in this room" he went on, "your speaker and I met for the first time. Since then I, like all his countrymen, have watched his career with approval and admiration." Again the ugly murmur, something muffled that might have been, "*You* may have admired it!" He ignored it. "It has been, many times, a lonely road for him, at times a difficult and even tragic one, as it has been for so many of his gallant colleagues who have fought so long and hard to do away with the injustices to their race. Never has he flinched or compromised. He has always been a steady and constructive force for change. And he has done it with unwavering respect for the necessary tolerance and courtesy which must condition human affairs if society is not to fall into complete chaos. His decency and integrity in this respect should be an honored example to us all."

"Uncle Tom!" from somewhere halfway back. He wondered what Ti-Anna was thinking now.

"In the United States Senate where I am privileged to serve—"

"Squeak-In!" And he wondered about Latt. And, being Willie, let fly.

"Very well, you intolerant guttersnipes," he said calmly. "Vote me out next time if you have the votes and the guts. I'm ready for you."

At this the hall did explode again, shouts, yells, boos, hisses; but opposing them, he was pleased to note, a sudden surge of clapping that rose and rose until it presently drowned out the demonstration and continued until the demonstration subsided.

"Thank you, friends. And I am pleased to see that a majority of you are my friends. In the United States Senate where I am privileged to serve, we differ sharply on many things, but for the most part we manage to do it with decency and patience and a basic goodwill that eventually—" he interjected with a sudden smile, "sometimes *very* eventually, but sometimes not so long—permits constructive things to be done. In the same spirit your speaker tonight has conducted himself. He has always acted with a basic respect for the orderly process of a stable and progressive democracy. In this spirit and method he has accomplished much in the harsh struggle for civil rights; and now in his new position with the E.E.O.C., he will accomplish much more. It is my great pleasure to present to you my old friend of a quarter of a century, the Honorable Bayard Johnson, assistant director of the Equal Employment Opportunities Commission."

And he turned as By came forward, shook hands warmly and, with arm around his back, escorted him to the podium. Sound welled up again, but now, although the hostility was still present, the sounds of approval were even louder. Obviously friendly members of the audience who had been intimidated by the previous outbreaks had been encouraged by their success in applauding Willie; and obviously, as swiftly became apparent, this was noted and it was decided that sterner measures were now called for.

By acknowledged Dr. Chambers, Willie, Rudy, "ladies and gentlemen in the audience," and began:

"I, too, remember the day twenty-five years ago when I entered this room, at that time the only Negro in the University, and I remember the greeting I received. It was not welcoming, neither was it hostile. It was just—quiet. I doubt if anyone on earth ever felt lonelier than I did at that moment. Just then I became aware that two fellows were standing beside me, holding out their hands. One was a wonderful human being, a brilliant student soon to be tragically dead in an auto accident, Bill Lattimer. The other was the president of the student body, Willie Wilson. 'Welcome to the University,' they said, and I wasn't alone anymore. From that moment I was a part of this campus, and to this day Willie and I are still dear friends and always will be.

"But the significance of it was greater than friendship. Let me tell you briefly about the climate then, and what it took for me to come here, and for them to greet me so openly and warmly. Let me tell you something of the long, hard struggle of this past quarter-century, and of how it has developed in our democracy. Let me tell you how I have helped to conduct it, and what I think should be done to nail down victories that are as yet only tentative and tenuous. Let me tell you what I believe to be the best means for securing those victories and for moving ahead to secure even greater victories, which must be achieved within the framework of a mutually trusting, mutually helpful, democratic society. Let me tell you—"

But at that point the shaky truce ended. He had held them briefly with his sheer sincerity, the emotional weight of it apparent in his voice, which had trembled with it, his eyes, which had unabashedly clouded with tears as he evoked that day so long ago in another world, the impassioned rigidity of his body as he clutched the lectern and leaned forward into the microphone.

To many of them it was all so much sentimental crap and now was the time to stop it before it got out of hand and really began to convince people.

Down the aisle from the back of the hall, through the door from which he had entered the life of the University twenty-five years ago, came a stomping, shouting, pushing, shoving, banner-waving, tumbling-over-itself parade of students, locals, professors, the most famous highly visible among them—gleefully grinning, hostile youngsters—wild-eyed, desperately earnest, hair-flying oldsters—all that wild, hodgepodge conglomeration of hates, loves, passions, desires, frustrations, illusion, disillusion, blind support, blind antagonism, thoughtful concern and unthinking stupidity that, known by the generic term "protesters," would dominate the public discourse of America for the rest of the twentieth century and perhaps beyond.

A fearful riffraff, Willie thought, a blind, erratic force that knew no reason and wanted none—the Mob, created by the dreadful uncertainties of a sick, unhappy century—encouraged, coordinated and inspired by clever, anarchic minds—enshrined, most dutifully and most willingly, by television without which there would have been little impetus, whose cameras were even now panning the roiling room, the eager hate-filled faces, the shouting, vindictive demonstrators, the whole, carefree, tumultuous, happy-go-lucky scene.

GO HOME, UNCLE TOM! the placards cried . . . BACK TO THE PLANTATION, RASTUS! . . . ACTION YES, GRADUALISM NO! . . . TO HELL TO HELL WITH COMPROMISE, FIGHT FOR YOUR RIGHTS! . . . And the tie-in Renny and so many other clever minds were already working on, HEY, HEY, UNCLE TOM! GET YOUR BOYS OUT OF VIETNAM! . . . DEATH IN GEORGIA, DEATH IN VIETNAM, WHAT'S THE DIFFERENCE? . . . LYNDON'S MAN, LYNDON'S MAN, KILL AS MANY BLACKS AS YOU CAN!

"Ladies and gentlemen—" By tried to shout over the uproar.

"Ladies and gentlemen—" cried Dr. Chalmers, suddenly at his side.

"God damn it—" shouted Willie, standing with them.

"SHUT UP!" roared Rudy, red-faced and furious.

"GET THE FASCIST WARMONGERS!" bellowed an overriding voice.

And dutifully from somewhere in the ranks came a piece of brick, which, aimed with fury and the fateful skill of fanaticism, found its mark.

By staggered back, blood spurting from his forehead; swayed for a moment as Dr. Chalmers and Willie tried to catch him; collapsed into Willie's arms; and slid slowly to the floor.

Silence, instant and all-enveloping . . . not a sound anywhere save the shocked, uneasy rustling of the audience . . . everyone standing, craning, trying to see . . . everyone shocked, stunned, speechless . . . fun and games over.

Renny stopped, turned full around, held up both arms, waved furiously toward the door. Lemminglike, his ragtag army turned upon itself, its members crashing into one another as they surged back up the aisle, some in panic, some still laughing hysterically in the grip of their euphoric excitement.

"You see?" Rudy cried to Dr. Chalmers, who did not answer. "You see?"

A number of people, Jeff Barnett, Duke Offenberg and the three doctors, Guy, Gil and North most prominent among them, hurried to the stage. Willie gave each a hand as they ran up the side steps and converged upon By, unconscious and still bleeding heavily in the midst of the growing circle around him. Gil reached him first.

"Will he be all right?" Dr. Chalmers inquired in a shaken voice. Gil did not reply until he had painstakingly checked as many vital signs as he could.

"Hard to tell right now," he said. His voice sharpened. "Somebody call an ambulance. And somebody get some towels and water. Hurry!"

Three students raced backstage to comply. Gil stood aside. "Guy? North?"

Guy took the towels, applied them carefully to By's head, checked in his turn, spoke gravely. "I don't know. North?"

North did the same, spoke in the same grave tone.

"Not too good." His voice, too, became sharp. "Where the hell's that ambulance?"

A couple of minutes later, just before it arrived, a badly shaken young man and young woman pushed through. Ti-Anna dropped to her knees, crying, cradled her father's unconscious head in her arms.

Latt, white-faced, gave Willie a wide-eyed, wondering look.

"It isn't fun," Willie said harshly. "It's real."

Latt looked as though he had struck him, but rallied.

"I know," he said. "That's what I've been trying to tell you."

The ambulance came, took By, Ti-Anna, Dr. Chalmers and, by quick agreement, Gil, away. Willie started to say something further to Latt, hesitated. Latt gave him again the same wide-eyed, stranger's look, flung away, off the stage, up the aisle, out the door.

"I gather he's yours," Jeff said sympathetically. "Will you ever see him again?"

"Oh, yes, I suppose so," Willie said, and sighed deeply. "But these days, who knows?"

Five minutes later the hall was empty. By's blood still formed a big pool on the stage. Some of the friendly students tried to clean it up but it was obvious the regular maintenance crew would have to do a real job upon it tomorrow.

The media did a real job on it immediately.

RIOT DISRUPTS BLACK LEADER'S SPEECH . . . PROTEST-ERS DEMAND RIGHTS ACTION . . . STUDENTS BLAST "GRADUALISM," CONDEMN VIETNAM ROLE FOR BLACKS . . . BLACK VIETNAM DEATHS ROUSE CAMPUS . . . STRONG CIVIL RIGHTS, FEWER BLACKS IN VIETNAM, AUDIENCE DEMANDS . . .

And in subordinate headlines, smaller type, BLACK LEADER INJURED . . . MODERATE HOSPITALIZED AS VIEWS ANGER PROTESTERS . . . BAYARD JOHNSON PRO-WAR STAND ROUSES STUDENTS . . .

"We regret," the typical editorial (news broadcast, television commentary) said, "the violence which erupted at the University last night when Bayard Johnson, 'moderate' black civil rights leader, attempted to deliver the first of the new Krohl Lecture Series. But we can understand the frustration of protesters who believe his message combining 'gradualism' in civil rights with support for administration policies in Vietnam, can only result in further harm to the cause of racial justice.

"Particularly is this true of his surprising stand on Vietnam, where black soldiers form a major portion of the troops and, so far, a majority of the casualties.

"Nothing could be more unjust. . . ."

"But," Willie said, visiting the hospital early next morning with Tim and Jeff, "he didn't say anything about Vietnam. He wasn't talking about Vietnam. He didn't have a chance to talk about Vietnam. He wasn't there to discuss Vietnam. His whole argument was—"

"Oh, come," Tim said in a tired voice. "You go around this track all the time. You know how they do it. He did have a prepared text that was distributed to the press in advance and he did say, in passing, that 'In general I agree with the administration's objectives in Vietnam, even though I and many others may certainly differ on the methods and effectiveness with which those objectives are being pursued.' " He smiled. "I remember because I'm going to write a column about this whole thing. That's all it took. That's all they need."

"But the riot wasn't caused by that," Willie said patiently as they approached By's room along the busy early morning corridor. "He hadn't got to that."

"The riot was caused purely and simply," Jeff said, "because these students nowadays aren't goin' to let anybody say anythin' they disagree with. That's what's happened to our deah ole almuh mottuh since we left here. You don't listen and you don't reason, you just shout 'em down by sheer brute force. And I say it's a God damned, mind-killin', fuckin', fascistic shame, myself."

"You're not in tune with our modern age, Jeff," Willie said dryly.

"And by God I don't want to be," Jeff said flatly as they reached the room. "And you can quote me," he added in a whisper as they entered and saw By, upper half of his head swathed in bandages, motionless on the bed. Two nurses were with him. They slipped out with quick smiles and shushing motions.

"Is he conscious?" Willie whispered. By stirred.

"Hi," he said in a voice drowsy but recognizable. He spoke distinctly but very slowly. There was a great weariness, a heavy effort. "Have . . . you guys . . . come to . . . bury me?"

"Never," Willie said, giving his arm a squeeze. "That'll be a long time coming."

"You're too ornery to die," Jeff said comfortably. "How you feelin'?"

"Not . . . like . . . making . . . any . . . speeches," By said with the ghost of a chuckle. "I . . . may never . . . make any . . . speeches . . . again."

"Oh, yes, you will," Tim said firmly. "You're not going to stop fighting now. Lots and lots of people believe in you and want your message. You've got to get well fast and come right back at the mind-killers. It's the only language they understand."

"Ti-Anna . . . thinks—" By began and then seemed apparently to be overcome by some thought concealed by the bandages.

"What does Ti-Anna think?" Willie demanded, more harshly than he had intended. But he could not forget the two of them, mugging it up in the audience, not part of the organized protesters but supporting them. Against their own fathers. He found that his tolerance for "Oh, they're just kids" was almost gone.

"She . . . thinks . . . that . . . perhaps I'd . . . better retire . . . from the movement . . . if I can't be . . . more . . . positive. She says . . . people . . . like me . . . and . . . Martin . . . and other non . . . nonviolent have outlived our . . . usefulness . . . and . . . should . . . make room . . . for younger and more . . . more effective . . . leaders . . . I'm sure . . . Maryetta . . . will say . . . the same thing . . . when she . . . gets here."

"When's she coming?" Tim inquired. "Want me to meet her at the airport?"

"No . . . thanks," By said with again the ghost of a chuckle. "I'm afraid . . . she . . . regards you as . . . one . . . one of . . . the enemy."

"Oh, God damn it," Tim said in sudden frustration. "What kind of crap is that? Because I believe in nonviolence, too? Isn't she ever going to grow up?"

Again the ripple of amusement passed over the inert body.

"Probably . . . not. She'll tell . . . me . . . I . . . deserved it . . . probably."

"That's a damned shame," Jeff said. "Better not in my presence or I'll tell her off."

"Don't . . . blame . . . her." Another surge of silent humor. "She's . . . not . . . my wife, she's . . . a . . . force . . . of nature."

"She's both," Jeff said, relenting with a chuckle. "*That's* your problem."

"Anyway, friend," Willie said, "we'll go now and stop bothering you. Sorry you won't be at the house tonight. I was really looking forward to having you there—"

"We all were," Tim said, and Jeff agreed firmly, "You betcha."

"—but we'll give everybody your greetings and another time we'll do it. Meanwhile, you get well fast, O.K.?"

"The whole country's watching," Tim said. "It really is. You hit all the papers and all the networks."

"My . . . namesake . . . called a little . . . while . . . ago," By said. "He . . . wanted me to . . . know . . . that everybody in . . . the White House . . . is pulling for . . . me." Once again the fugitive amusement. "It . . . was . . . worth a . . . million . . . dollars . . . to me. . . . I . . . was . . . touched."

"Well, you should be," Willie said. "I'm sure he meant it. We'll try to get in again before we go home. Mind the doctors and get better."

"And don't chase the nurses," Jeff said. "At least not today."

"I'll try . . . not . . . to . . ." By said, voice fading in what was obviously a last effort at hospitality. "Thanks . . . so . . . much . . . it was . . . great of . . . you to . . . do . . . it."

"What do you think?" Jeff asked as they walked down the corridor. Willie frowned.

"I'm uneasy."

"So am I," Jeff said.

"And I," Tim agreed.

But they had done what they could, and there was nothing for it now but to utter a silent prayer from time to time, go on about the business of this very busy weekend, and hope for the best.

At the door of the hospital they met Ti-Anna and Maryetta coming in. Ti-Anna gave them a quick, shy smile. Maryetta was more emphatic.

"Well!" she said. "I might have known you three would be here. I hope you're satisfied, you—you—*moderates*!"

"Relax, Maryetta," Jeff said sharply. "Knock it off. Things are still very tough, he's not doing that well and he really needs you. So knock off the ideological crap for once in your life and go be a loving wife, will you?"

"I *am* a loving wife," she said, and for the first and only time ever they saw Maryetta Johnson actually break down and cry. "Don't you think I *care*?" she demanded bitterly. "Don't you think I'm terribly upset? Don't you think I wish it were me lying in that bed instead of him? *What do you take me for, anyway?*"

"I'm sorry," Jeff said, not yielding much, "but you've never shown us that side of yourself before. We didn't know it was there."

For a moment her angry, tear-filled eyes held theirs. Then she dashed a hand across them, said sharply, "Come, T.!" and they went on in.

"Now I feel like a real heel," Jeff remarked as they walked toward Willie's rental car.

"Don't," Willie advised. "It's her fault. She's always been so—so rough on him. And everybody else."

"Including, apparently," Tim said, "herself. But as you said, Jeff, how could we know?"

"Where do you guys want to go?" Willie asked. "I can drop you at the house if you like. Or the Quad. Or wherever."

"What are you going to do?" Tim inquired.

"I have to go to a meeting of the board of trustees."

Jeff looked at him.

"Don't tell me you—"

"And Rudy," Willie said with a cheerful grin. "Won't that be a great new team on the board? I can hardly wait."

"Well, congratulations," Tim said. "I guess. It's a great era to be involved with a college, I don't think."

"It couldn't happen," Jeff said solemnly, "as I have often had occasion to remark over the years, to a nicer, more noble, more worthy, more deserving—"

"I said," Willie said firmly, "where do you want to go?"

"You can drop me at the *Daily*, " Tim said. "I have a sentimental visit to make."

"Drop me at the Quad," Jeff said. "I'll just wander for a while and be sentimental, too."

"O.K.," Willie said. "Then I'll see you at the game, right? I think Moose helped Johnny get a block of tickets so we can all sit together."

"The only thing that will be missing," Jeff said with a reminiscent smile, "is one of Moose's own Fucking Asshole Touchdowns, as Franky used to call them."

"See you there," Willie said as he left them.

"Have fun," they urged.

And in a way, he thought as he parked the car near the new student union and walked along under the huge old live oaks to the room where the board would hold this special meeting to welcome its new members and discuss the selection of a new president, it would be fun.

Heated, no doubt, but back in the old familiar setting, and fun.

He had been more than a little surprised to receive a call a week ago from the president of the board, even more surprised when the caller introduced himself.

"Well, I'll be damned!" he exclaimed. "Walter! I'd lost track. I thought you were—"

"Dead?" Walter Emerson demanded with jovial relish. "Thought I was dead, did you? Not on your flaming bippy, boy! Not old Walter! Seventy-two and still kicking! You *bet*. Still alive and raising hell. Can't say I'm equally dense about you, though, Willie. I can't pick up a paper or turn on the TV without seeing Senator Wilson all over. Is there anybody else in Washington these days? Doesn't seem like it to us yokels out here in the country, I can tell you that."

"Yes, Walter," Willie said, suddenly back twenty-five years ago when he had first met Marian's ebullient father. "Calm down, now. Hold the rhetoric. It's good to hear from you. What can I do for you?"

"Marry my daughter," Walter said, and then burst again into jovial laughter. "No, no, that was long ago and far away, as the song says. Forgive my crude humor. It was just a moment's impulse."

"Sure," Willie said, recalling that he had never known Walter to have an impulse that wasn't related somehow to some objective. Maybe Marian was—what? Married and divorced? Married and not divorced? A spinster? A widow? "How is she?" he inquired cautiously. Walter of course caught his tone instantly.

"Don't run away!" he cried happily. "I can hear you retreating, old Careful Willie. She's fine. Still lives in Piedmont, near us. Divorced. Two kids—two *great* kids. Busy as a bee with all sorts of public activities. Remember she used to be quite a radical, about the comfortable life we led? She's part of it now. No more active member of society, no greater do-gooder, than Marian Sieberman. She'll be here for the game next week. You ought to look her up. It would be quite harmless."

"I'm sure," Willie said dryly, "particularly since Donna will be with me and we'll be putting our oldest, Latt, in school."

"How great!" Walter said. "Marian's oldest will be entering next year. She's quite a radical, too," he added, tone not quite so jovial. "In a somewhat different way from her mother. These kids nowadays . . . Well," he said briskly, "anyway, I know Marian would love to see you, so don't hide behind a pillar if you see her."

"I'll try not to," Willie said. "So what's up, Walter? You didn't just call after all these years to chat, knowing you. Want some money for the University?"

"Always," Walter said with a chuckle. "Always. No, we want you to be on the board. How about it?"

"Wait a minute," Willie said, "wait a minute. Do you know my reputation? I'm supposed to be a reactionary bastard, Walter. I'm not, but that's the way the establishment's tagged me. So damned conservative I put my shoes on backward so I can't take a step forward. Too much for the University, I'm sure. Not at all suited to the New Age I'm told we're entering. Just completely unsuitable. I can hear the students and faculty now."

"Fuck the—" Walter began, then laughed. "No, one mustn't use their language. Anyway, we're doing the choosing and we don't think you're all that bad. We think you're middle-of-the-road, as a matter of fact, and we want people like that on the board. God knows the members the younger alumni elect from now on are probably going to be pretty wild-eyed. That's the trend. We've got to maintain whatever balance we can."

"Senator Wilson is not the most popular man at his old alma mater," Willie observed. "I'm sure you could find a more popular choice."

"Shucks, Willie," Walter said. "Stop the reluctant virgin act. Will you or won't you?"

"As a matter of fact," Willie said, "I'm flattered and pleased and really quite excited. It will be wonderful to be back and in a position to do some good."

"It isn't going to be easy," Walter remarked soberly, "in these next few years. Things are already getting a little chaotic and I'm afraid they're going to get more so. All the campuses are getting pretty agitated over this Vietnam business. We're going to have some hot times ahead."

"I've been burned in effigy before," Willie said dryly. "Yes, I accept. And thank you and thank the board—particularly you. I know this is basically your idea."

"Marian's, really," Walter said. "So there you are."

"I'm not anywhere," Willie said, "except right where I've always been. When's the first meeting I'm supposed to attend?"

"Next week, Saturday morning before the game," Walter said. "See you then."

His tone grew warmer and genuinely pleased. "We're delighted, Willie. Really delighted."

"So am I. See you then."

And now here he was, about to take one more stand in one more place—and, he hoped, contribute something to that balance Walter was talking about. After last night's episode and today's visit with just-barely-hanging-in-there By, he approached his new duties with considerable sobriety. This was not alleviated when he recalled his talk with Duke Offenberg last night. Duke had been the Reluctant Dragon when Willie had broached the idea of his immediate appointment as president.

His first reaction had been a sharp intake of breath and a sudden wide-eyed staring down over the trees and rooftops from his commanding hill above the University's gradually diminishing lights. It had been almost ten when they had left Memorial Hall. He had suggested a drink on the patio to settle nerves after the trauma of the evening. Shahna and Donn had asked for soda and lemon, Duke had mixed himself a bourbon and ginger ale, Willie a gin and tonic. After a worried review of what they had just experienced, the girls had decided to go bed. Willie and Duke stayed on, held by the beauty of the soft September night, the peaceful quiet of the neighborhood, the flood of memories that tied them to their youth and to each other as they looked down upon the twinkling lights of their own particular, lost Eden.

" '*Into my heart an air that kills*'," Willie quoted softly from A. E. Housman:

> "*From yon far country blows:*
> *What are those blue remembered hills,*
> *What spires, what farms are those?*
>
> *That is the land of lost content,*
> *I see it shining plain,*
> *The happy highways where I went*
> *And cannot come again.*"

"And yet were they so happy?" Duke asked moodily. "I can remember a lot of times when I wasn't so happy, or so content. I didn't have such a great growing-up as you seemed to have had, Willie."

" 'Seemed' may be the operative word," Willie said with equal moodiness. "I had a lot of turmoil, too, though it may not have shown on the surface. I wasn't all that happy, all the time."

"You did seem to be," Duke said. "That last year you were really rolling, student-body president, Superman on Campus, cynosure of all eyes, everybody's hero, all women's idol, all men's model. You were riding high."

"Lots of people didn't like me," Willie said. "Lots of people don't now."

"It doesn't matter," Duke said. "You've licked everything."

"Oh, no. Oh, no. I really am Senator Squeak-In at the moment, though I hope to improve on that in '68. And the liberals and the media are after me because I don't worship with the requisite degree of blindness, as they do, at their particular altars, and they just can't forgive me for that. And I have a son who has always been a difficult and headstrong boy and now is poised, as you saw, to join the pro-test—any protest that promises excitement and opposition to what he thinks I stand for."

"Well," Duke said uncomfortably because Willie's tone had been so bleak, "at least you have a wife who—"

"Do I?" Willie interrupted, tone unchanged. "Yes, I have a wife. A wonderful, loving, helpful, supportive, decent, attractive, marvelous, boring wife. Very boring. All Donna's great qualities which were so wonderful down there—" he gestured toward the University, increas-ingly dark as its residents in increasing numbers went to bed—"have become awfully boring to me after twenty-five years. I know it's my fault, I know it's completely unfair, I haven't a thing in the world to complain about, I'm an ungrateful, unappreciative, unkind, dastardly husband, but—there it is. She bores me, Duke. No special thing, just cumulative. Completely unworthy of me, completely unworthy of her. I ought to be shot."

"Or turned free to run off with someone else," Duke said dryly. "Is that the next step in this sad tale? I've heard it before."

Willie shot him a glance, looked annoyed for a second, then re-laxed. Old friendship had its permissions.

"No, I don't think so. At least not consciously, anyway, I don't feel that way. There are lots of reasons, starting with the fact that it would be so terribly unfair to her . . . and there's the political situation."

"Others have," Duke pointed out. "Some openly, some privately. You must know of a few right now."

Willie nodded.

"Oh, sure. There are quite a few on the Hill, and in Washington generally. But . . . so far, at least . . . that doesn't seem right for me. It violates my concept of myself. It seems weak. It isn't me."

"Who's 'me'?" Duke inquired, again moodily. "I've often wondered that, about myself."

"Surely you don't feel that way about Shahna, though."

"Sometimes. Sometimes . . . but then, like you, I tell myself there's absolutely no justification, I have absolutely no right—and then I forget it."

"Always?"

"Like you," Duke said, " 'so far.' But I suppose . . . one never knows."

"It doesn't do to become too certain about things, I suppose," Willie said. "The Lord laughs . . . anyway, I'm not leaving Donna and I'm not running off the reservation and I'm not doing anything radical. I guess." He gestured again toward the University and without warning said, "You want to be president down there? I can put your name before the board tomorrow."

"Are you going to be on the board?" Duke asked, startled. "That will be great, Willie. But," he added ruefully, "the rumor's out around the faculty that the individual referred to tonight as 'you profiteering Nazi creep' is also going on. You know what that will do to my chances."

"Oh, Christ," Willie said in a tired voice. "Here we go again. You've got to be tougher than that, Duke. You can't let him buffalo you from twenty-five years ago. You won that one. And you'll win this one, too. Also, he isn't quite the creep he was. Even Rudy has matured in some ways." He chuckled wryly. "A little."

"That's it," Duke said gloomily. "Not much, I'm afraid. And now he has his millions and he'll come on the board swinging and I'll be the first objective and he'll play on every anti-Semitic instinct on the board and there are some, I've had indications, and he'll line them up against me and there will be a bitter fight and"—his voice almost broke—"I don't know whether I can stand that sort of fight at this point in my life. I'm not as young as I was."

"You're forty-five years old," Willie said crisply, "and you wanted to be a wimp then and you want to be a wimp now, and after your friends put a little backbone into you, you stood up to him and you won. So knock off the self-pity. It's your only unattractive characteristic. And it's not a good one for anyone desiring to be a college president in this day and age."

Duke looked offended for a moment, then gave him a shamefaced smile.

"I know. I know. I still let it get to me too much. But it's still there, Willie. We thought when we won the war we had that licked, too, but it's still there. And I don't like to fight it, it gets so ugly sometimes. It isn't my nature to fight. I like to be decent and reasonable with people. I don't like situations that are ugly."

"I repeat," Willie said, "if you back off in this day and age, you're done for. It's going to be a tough haul ahead, in the colleges. It's going to take a tough man to ride herd. Are you going to do that, or am I backing a weak candidate who's going to let me and the University down?"

"I hope I would never let the University down," Duke said with a first show of sharpness, "and I hope I would never let you down. But I'm not sure I should try for it right now. Perhaps Dr. Chalmers is right: I'm sure he's told you what his idea is. Get in some older man for three or four years and make me provost, and then when he retires, I would be the logical choice. That would give me a chance to consolidate my position with the faculty and perhaps be a little out of the line of fire in the Vietnam situation. And also allow the Vietnam situation to get over. Surely it isn't going to last much longer."

"Timmy thinks it will, but you know Timmy. Always the pessimist. I'm inclined to be that way myself but I agree with you, it surely can't last much longer. I think we're going to wind it up and get out of there. It's been going on since Truman and it's '64 now, for God's sake. We'll be out in a year. So what do you have to worry about? A tough go for a little while, maybe, then all-clear and away we go, Alan Frederick Offenberg, stalwart president of the University. The kids all call him Duke and everybody loves him and he totters off to pasture full of years and honor at eighty-six. It's inevitable."

"Willie," Duke said, forced to laugh in spite of himself. "You make it sound so—like a picnic. Happy-go-lucky Duke and his happy-go-lucky University. What a ball!"

"Well, it will be," Willie said firmly, "if you'll just cooperate."

"How's your drink?" Duke inquired. "Not that you need another one, you're flying high enough already."

"I will if I have you to drink to," Willie said. "Are you going to bite the bullet, sail into it, damn the torpedoes and full speed ahead, to mix a few metaphors?"

"I learned a long time ago," Duke said, "that deflecting Willie on a crusade is not so easy to do. Let's put it this way: I won't pull the rug out from under you if you want to propose me, but I won't campaign for it, either. If they ask me, I'll say I'll be honored to abide by the decision of the board, whatever it is, and will be happy, as I have been throughout my undergraduate and professional life, to serve the University in any capacity I can."

"I'm the politician," Willie said. "You're invading my territory with that kind of language. O.K., go get me that drink."

They spoke awhile longer of By down there in the hospital apparently in real danger—Gil had called just as they reached the house to report, "We think he'll make it, but he has a real fight on his hands." They spoke of Rudy and Renny and the University, and they spoke of sons, daughters, and Vietnam and the University; and finally, near midnight as the last few lights winked out and only the ghostly outlines of the Quad still lay imprinted on the velvet surface of the night, went off to bed.

So he had to face the board with an obviously reluctant candidate. He wondered now as he entered the room whether it was still worth the fight he had been prepared to put up if Duke had been just a bit more cooperative and combative. But that was Duke, and for the sake of his finer qualities, which were many, you had to work around that. He told himself that he would probably do so; but he wasn't as enthusiastic now as he had hoped to be.

"Willie!" Walter Emerson exclaimed, bounding out of his chair—or it seemed to Willie that he still bounded, though at seventy-two that might have been just a memory of the Walter he had known a quarter-century ago. He grasped Willie's hand in both his own and demanded, "How the hell are you, you old Senator, you?"

"Walter," Willie said, returning the grasp warmly and finding he meant what he was saying, "it is really good to see you again. I'm managing, how about you?"

"Hanging in there, boy," Walter said with a grin.

"How's Mary?"

Walter's bright expression dimmed, his voice became uneven.

"Not good. Not good. She's in a rest home. Doesn't know us. Doesn't know anything. It's hard for me and the girls, terribly hard. Hardest for me."

"Of course it is," Willie said. "I am so sorry." And he was: the old animosity was gone, particularly in the face of this sad news. "She was a wonderfully bright woman, who did a lot of wonderfully good things for many, many people. Please give her my love—if she would know it."

Walter shook his head.

"She wouldn't." He forced himself to brighten. "Well!" He swing Willie around to face the circle of upturned faces ringing the table, introduced him fulsomely. There was a round of warm applause conspicuously not joined by Rudy: he just scowled. Willie was both

annoyed and amused. Personal introductions and congratulations followed. The subject that was rapidly coming to dominate America
immediately surfaced.

"Many of you," Walter began, "were present in Memorial Hall last
night and those of you who weren't have of course heard about it.
What began as a protest against what some apparently perceive to be
Bayard Johnson's too-slow approach to civil rights was very quickly
transformed into one more protest against the situation in Vietnam."
He paused and added in an exasperated tone, "You can't seem to get
away from the damned thing. It seems to be everywhere."

"And so it should be," one of the board's youngest members, a
charming but now grimly determined young woman from the class of
'60, remarked tartly. "It's a terrible, disgraceful, *awful* thing. We
ought to pass a resolution condemning it right *now*. Otherwise the
University is going to be in the position of officially condoning this
inexcusable—frightful—murderous—*Lyndon Johnson* war."

"Well, now," Walter said, appearing confident he was calling a
bluff, "do you want to put that in the form of a resolution?"

"You bet I do!" she snapped, calling his, and proceeded to do so.

There was uproar for an hour or so. The generations split in the
fashion Willie knew would be inevitable. Since his and Walter's still
had a preponderance on the board, the outcome was inevitable. The
proposer and the three others of her generation who supported her
retired disgruntled; but once again what Walter had described as "the
damned thing" had divided a serious gathering of Americans. Willie
hoped and prayed that his confident prediction to Duke, "We'll be
out in a year," would speedily come true. "The damned thing" was
beginning to skew everything.

They turned then briefly to routine business, approved several
minor administrative and budgetary proposals submitted by Dr.
Chalmers; and moved on to the main subject of the meeting. Walter
introduced it in a tone that had become somewhat tense. His normal
joviality was still determinedly in place but shaken, they could all see
that.

"The final matter we have to discuss this morning," he said, "are
the recommendations submitted to us by the search committee for a
new president of the University. You have all received them and
studied them and the matter is now open for debate. We aren't under
any time pressure, incidentally, as you know; Dr. Chalmers won't be
retiring until the end of the academic year. But it is time for us to
begin making up our minds in a preliminary way. Would anyone care

to start the discussion?" He turned with an elaborate bow down the table. "Anne?"

His young opponent, whose name was Anne Greeley, B.A. 1956, L.L.D. 1960, tall, brunette, quite pretty, mother of two, "very bright girl, very bright girl," as even her critics conceded, managed a reasonable smile even though still obviously miffed about Vietnam.

"Thank you, Walter," she said. "I don't agree with this report. I have no criticism whatsoever of the qualifications of Dr. Frank Merriman of the University of Minnesota, he is apparently a fine and well-qualified man. But he is already sixty-two years old. I submit that the University needs younger, more vigorous, more—more *connected* leadership in the difficult times we are in. We need young blood, Mr. President. We don't need some old—older—man, no matter how well qualified. And," she added, "I am not at all impressed with the suggestion I have heard bruited about that Dr. Offenberg should be made provost. If this is a back-door attempt to put him in line to become president in another two or three years, then I want to give that very serious consideration, too."

"Dr. Chalmers," Walter said, "would you care to address that one?"

"Not at this point," the president said crisply. "I wouldn't want to direct your deliberations in any way, but I would suggest that selection of my successor is the paramount matter to be considered right now."

"Right," Walter said. "If that's agreeable to everybody—"

"Mr. President," Willie said. "I must confess I am impressed with Mrs. Greeley's comment—or perhaps I should say the first part of her comment. I think with all respects to Dr. Merriman that a younger man is indeed desirable at this juncture in the University's history, and the nation's history. I should like to ask Mrs. Greeley what she has against Dr. Offenberg."

"Call me Anne," she directed. "Well, I will tell you, Senator—"

"Willie," he suggested, turning on his smile full beam. She responded with an ironic glance.

"Very well—Willie. I think Dr. Offenberg, while well qualified in many ways, one of which is that he is probably young enough to meet my concerns, is in my estimation too much of a conservative in his thinking and his actions to do the job that has to be done in the shadow of this horrendous war."

"It isn't a 'war' yet," Willie remarked mildly. "The Congress hasn't declared—"

"You passed that sneaky Tonkin Gulf Resolution of Lyndon

Johnson's!" she snapped. "If I ever saw an abrogation of Congressional responsibility, that's it! You ought to be ashamed of yourselves!"

"Well, now," Walter said hastily. "Well, now—"

"Perfectly all right, Mr. President," Willie said in an amused, fatherly tone that he knew would annoy her. "Perfectly all right. It's
probably good for us to have the benefit of advice from vigorous
young minds—"

"You bet it is," she said. "It would profit you to act on it, too."

"My," he said, "you are a lively one, aren't you?"

"I try to exercise the independence of mind I learned on this
campus, Senator," she said. "Willie. I don't intend to remain silent
while the skids are greased to keep the University's academic fate in
the hands of a conservative old-boy network that hasn't had an original thought since World War II."

"World War I, probably," Walter said in an attempt to lighten
things a bit. "That's where I came in, Anne."

"That's even worse," she said. "At least you're honest enough to
admit where your biases come from. Some people like to pretend
they're more up-to-date, but they're not. Anyway," she added as
several of the older members stirred restlessly, "this is getting away
from Dr. Offenberg, which is possibly what Willie intends."

"Not at all," Willie said. "I want to discuss him because I intend to
propose him for president. Let's talk about him."

"I knew it," she said. "I *knew* it! I knew Merriman was designed to
be just a stalking-horse for Offenberg. Thank God *somebody* on the
board is living in the present! You'd probably have this railroaded
through by now if we younger members weren't here to protest."

"I don't mind protest," Willie said. "I've been protested against
many times."

"And more to come," she remarked tartly.

"And more to come," he agreed. "But if we could get away from
rhetoric and discuss the matter on its merits instead of trying to
simply batter down opposing points of view, which seems to be the
fashion nowadays—it would be a help."

"Very well," she said, looking flushed but determined, a combination he found quite charming, "let's talk merits. What are Dr. Merriman's merits, except to make way in due course for Dr. Offenberg?
What are Dr. Offenberg's merits, except to succeed Dr. Merriman?
What is so special about either that makes him so vital to the University?"

"The search committee has stated in rather exhaustive detail what it finds appealing about Dr. Merriman," Walter pointed out. "As for Dr. Offenberg, the most I have heard Dr. Chalmers or anyone else propose—until Willie, just now—is that he be made provost—"

"I'm willing to settle for that," Willie said mildly. "I don't mean to stir up a big controversy—"

"An obvious ploy," she said scornfully. "Obvious! I thought you were more devious than that, Willie. How do you manage to operate in the Senate?"

"I don't," Willie said, "didn't you know? Very ineffectual, very reactionary, very conservative. Didn't you know?"

"That's not the way I hear it from my friends in Washington," she said. "They say you're one of the shrewdest operators on the Hill. But it won't work in this instance. The machinery is too obvious."

"Well," he said, "suppose we discuss Dr. Offenberg, then. Many of you on the board know him in varying degrees; he and I are fraternity brothers and grew up together here, so I know him better than any of you, probably, except possibly Dr. Chalmers—"

"Exactly!" she said triumphantly. "Fraternity brothers! Talk about old-boy networks!"

"You did, I didn't," he pointed out. "If you mean we've known each other well for more than twenty-five years, sure, we're old boys. If you mean that would be sufficient reason to propose his name absent other qualifications, that's nonsense. I hope you'll allow somebody else to have some concern for the University, too."

"Of course you do," she agreed impatiently. "I'm not saying that and you know it, Willie. I'm saying Dr. Offenberg is simply out of sync with the world we live in now. There are very legitimate arguments against this crazy misadventure in Southeast Asia, as well as many other things that demand a more open-minded, tolerant, modern approach on the part of the president of the University—and the provost, too, I might add. Both officers are under a lot of fire and that can only increase as long as this criminal war is allowed to continue—"

"What do you want?" Rudy suddenly demanded from down the table in a loud voice that startled everyone. "Some wide-eyed, weak-kneed pinko who'll give in to every crackpot who roams around campus trying to get on TV and open the doors to drugs and uncontrolled sex and every other kind of irresponsible crap? Renny *Suratt*, maybe? Is that the kind of jellyfish you want here? I don't like Offenberg any more than you do, but that doesn't mean I'm going to vote for some lily-livered pantywaist who'll give in to every phony student demand these ill-mannered, poorly brought-up jerks can dream up. That's not how *I* intend to handle *my* responsibilities on this board, I can tell you that!"

For a moment Anne was as taken aback as the rest by his vehemence. But, Willie noted admiringly, she recovered fast.

"Mr. Krohl," she said in an icy voice, "I am not in favor of crackpots and ill-mannered jerks even when I find them present on this board. Nor am I in favor of weak-kneed, wide-eyed pinkos, lily-livered jellyfish or any other similar types. I am in favor of—Anyway," she broke off abruptly in an innocently curious tone, "what do you have against Dr. Offenberg? Don't tell me you were a fraternity brother of his, too!"

"I was," Rudy said darkly, "but not for long."

"But long enough for you to dislike him violently," she noted quickly. "Why was that, Mr. Krohl?"

"I'm not going to go into all that!" Rudy snapped, flushing with anger. "It's none of your business. I said *I don't like him*, and that's enough!"

"Not for me," she said cheerfully. "And not, I would think, for many of this board. What's the matter, Mr. Krohl? Did he steal your girl?"

"That k—" Rudy began, and stopped with an obvious effort. "My Helga wouldn't look twice at that—that *person*! She doesn't believe in mixing the races any more than I do!"

For a moment there was a shocked silence. They got it, all right, Willie could see, and obviously Anne had, too. She turned quite pale, then flushed with anger herself. Her voice became, if possible, even colder.

"Mr. Krohl!" she said. "You will be interested to know that my mother had one-half of what you obviously consider inferior blood, so I obviously have some of it too. If you are really saying, in the sixty-fourth year of the twentieth century, after the Holocaust and the war and the enormous sacrifices made to stop Hitler and—and—everything else—" she had to stop and draw a breath—"if you are saying that you are opposed to Dr. Offenberg simply because he is Jewish, then I say for shame to you, sir, I say for shame! You have just presented me with the best possible reason to vote for him for president of this University, if that means the thwarting of vicious, racist people like you! I shall certainly support him for provost, in any event. I wouldn't side with you on Dr. Offenberg for anything!"

"That's a ridiculous way to vote," Rudy said harshly. "Typical of your generation and its half-assed approach to things these days."

"Not as half-assed as yours!" she cried as Walter, finally startled out of his fascinated silence by a sharp jog on the elbow from Willie, banged his gavel furiously and said loudly, "Now that's enough, both of you! Anne, you be quiet and Rudy, you be quiet! Is there a motion on the search committee's recommendations?"

"Mr. President," Willie said calmly, "I move the report's adoption and I move the appointment of Dr. Alan Frederick Offenberg to be provost of the University effective on the accession of Dr. Merriman as president in June 1965."

"I move to separate those motions," Anne said promptly.

"I object," Willie said.

"They will be voted on en bloc," Walter said firmly and banged his gavel again. "Ayes? . . . Nays? . . . The ayes have it, twelve to four. [So much for Duke's tendency to cry before he was hurt, Willie thought.] The secretary is instructed to report these decisions to the media, the meeting is adjourned and I wish you a happy time at the game. Beat Oregon!"

"Beat Oregon!" they echoed good-naturedly and departed, a still-scowling Rudy first, a still obviously shaken Anne last, lingering to say goodbye to Willie as he stood chatting for a moment with Walter.

"Senator," she said, offering her hand. "Willie—welcome to our happy family. I think we will have some lively times together in the next few years."

"I'm sure of it," he said, pressing her hand warmly, but for the time being impersonally, in his. "You're a worthy opponent. Ever think of running for the Senate?"

She uttered a sudden lighthearted laugh that pleased him, indicating as it did that the tensions of the morning were beginning to dissipate for her, too.

"I might at that," she said. "I just might. You better watch out!"

"I'll be on guard," he said. "See you at the next meeting."

"As a matter of fact," she said, "I may be in Washington in a couple of months. My firm is arguing a case before the Supreme Court and I think I'm to be included of counsel."

"Look me up," he suggested, telling himself, Watch it, Willie, there must be twenty years' difference here. But his invitation sounded quite innocent, he was determined to keep it so, and she accepted it the same way.

"I'll do that," she said. "I want some of that fabulous Senate res-
taurant bean soup."

"It's a deal," he said. "Take care."

"Take care, yourself," she said and on a sudden impulse kissed him
lightly on the cheek. He returned it, looking a little surprised for a
moment, which made her laugh again. She flashed him a quick,
friendly smile, said goodbye pleasantly to Walter, and went briskly
out the door.

"Very nice girl," Walter remarked. "Something of a pain sometimes, but it goes with being that bright, I guess. She helps keep
things lively around here. . . . Are you having lunch with anybody
before the game?"

"I'm going to meet Donna and Duke and Shahna at the gate," he
said, "but no plans for lunch. I thought I'd just grab a sandwich at the
Union—"

"Nonsense. You come eat with us. Marian and her kids are having
a little tailgate party on Arboretum Drive near the stadium. She'll be
delighted to see you."

"And I her," he said, though for the moment he felt a surge of what
almost seemed to be panic, absurd though that was. Their brief "ro-
mance," if you could call it that—that short, uneasy, frustrating time
terminated finally by her irresolute and erratic nature and his own
decision that he couldn't take it anymore—had only lasted for about
six months. Nothing had come of it then and nothing would come of
it now. Of that he was certain, though Walter obviously had dreams
of Time, O Time, turning backward in its flight.

After the first few awkward moments their meeting moved swiftly
and smoothly into the mode they both knew it would have whenever
they met hereafter. She was still a very intelligent, very pretty woman
after twenty-five years, still able to be pleasant and good company
when she set her mind to it. It was obvious that she had done so this
day. They talked along amicably and, within minutes, like really
genuine old friends. Her daughters were bright and pretty, too, fascinated to be meeting a United States Senator and one, moreover,
who had once, mysteriously, "meant something" to their mother. The
two hours before game time passed very comfortably and pleasantly
for them all. He and Marian promised, as they walked along together
through the excited crowds to the stadium, to keep in touch; and he
thought they probably would.

Not every tension from college days revived and readjusted that easily down the years but he found he was genuinely glad that this had. And not for a moment, when he finally took his seat beside his wife and told her all about it, did he regret the decision he had made concerning Marian long ago, whatever his present problems with Donna might be.

Now over the stadium there rose the noisy clamor and stir of eighty-nine thousand people settling in. Soft-drink hawkers called, the crowd exchanged shouts, amiable greetings and mutual challenges, the cheering sections happily competed with one another, the two bands played, the roars of support welled up as the two teams trotted out onto the bright green field in the warm September sun. Overhead the small commercial biplanes trailed their banners: DICK'S CHEVRO-LET . . . EAT AT DINAH'S SHACK . . . L'OMELETTE AFTER THE GAME . . . ALBERT LOVES JEANIE XXX . . . CONGRAT-ULATIONS, MIMI AND BOBO, MARRIED TODAY . . ." And, probably inevitably now, Willie thought with a frustrated little sigh, GET OUT OF VIETNAM.

In the end zone, in the bloc of seats secured by Moose and Johnny Herbert, the returning members of the house and their wives were making themselves comfortable, those who had already seen one another around campus waving happily, those who had not greeting each other effusively.

Gil Gulbransen was talking earnestly across Karen Ann to Tim on her other side; he had just come from the hospital, he said, where By "is hanging in there, but he keeps slipping in and out of brief comas, which isn't good. Sometimes he knows us, sometimes he doesn't, quite lucid for three or four minutes as you saw this morning, then trailing off. They're going to call the house later if there's any change. Guy and North and I are going to keep checking. We feel an obliga-tion."

Tim said he thought everybody would be very glad of that, and passed the word along to Lor Davis, who was sitting on his other side with Angie between him and Tony. Hack was next to Tony, which for just a moment created a little tension that Lor, not usually the most perceptive of men but always sensitive where Tony was concerned, was aware of though he could not have known the reason—for Tony had never told him—that only Hack and Willie and gentle, long-dead

Latt had been present at that awful confrontation on the awful night when Tony's secret wanderings on the darkened Quad had finally brought their sad reward.

"Tony—" Hack had said today, holding out his hand, looking tall, gray, distinguished, every inch the successful composer.

"Hack—" Tony had responded, hesitating a split second with a wary expression in his eyes.

But Hack had gripped his hand firmly and smiled cordially and asked after Louise and the kids and Tony had relaxed and the moment had passed.

Katie Sullivan Miller was there, looking rather drawn and severe and "not quite with her usual spark," as Guy Unruh murmured to North, sitting next to him and Maggie. "But then," he added wryly, "I don't suppose any of us has it, twenty-five years later."

"That's right," North agreed, his own demons for the time being firmly under control as he thought of his friend in Salt Lake City, still miraculously loyal after twelve years, marriage and two kids of his own; and of faithful B.J., busier than ever with her civic projects, as though by being busier and busier she could somehow fend off the mysterious symptoms that were giving her face a haunted look as her doctors, including her husband, eliminated more and more possibilities and came closer and closer to the ultimate explanation, the grim answer that is finally given to many who suffer from unexplained, mysterious ailments.

In the row just in front of them Galen Bryce was sitting with Smitty Carriger, which struck everybody as a most unlikely pairing given their noticeably unimpressed attitude toward one another as undergraduates. It was, as Smitty declared cheerfully, the luck of the draw.

"Well, well!" he exclaimed. "Look at what the luck of the draw has brought me! How the hell are you, Gale? Still solving all the mental-health problems of Hollywood? That must bring you a pretty penny!"

"I have a substantial practice," Gale replied somewhat stiffly, "and I believe I am considered effective in my field."

"I'll bet you are," Smitty said, "I'll *bet* you are. Takes one to know one, eh, Johnny? We always knew Gale would end up running a nuthouse somewhere, but we didn't suspect it would be a multi-million-dollar one in Hollywood."

"It isn't a 'nuthouse'!" Gale protested angrily. "It's a perfectly respectable practice—"

"Oh, I know, I know," Smitty said. "You remember me, Gale, I'm just having a little fun. I'm sure you're very good and very highly thought of, and I congratulate you. If I had any mental problems I might come to you for them—"

"He might not have you," Johnny offered, trying to interject a little neutral humor. Gale looked as though he had been about to say that himself.

"Probably not," Smitty said with a chuckle. "Fortunately I don't have any."

"It must come from leading a thoroughly dull and normal life making money," Gale said in his primmest tone.

"That's me," Smitty agreed happily. "Dull and normal and making money. Money, money, money! Gad, sometimes I wish I had some excitement in my life!"

And he leaned over and grinned at Marc Taylor, who was seated on Gale's other side.

"That's right," Marc said, and added, "I wish *I* did," in a voice that was suddenly so honest and rather forlorn that Galen looked at him sharply and Smitty tried to cover for him with a laugh.

Randy Carrero, seated beside Marc and somehow, in some irrepressible return to the past, feeling as protective of him as he had always been, was turned toward Hack, seated behind him, resting one arm comfortably across Hack's knees with the familiarity of old friendship. He was talking a mile a minute about Rome, Flavia and the family, "really getting caught up," as he put it with satisfaction. He had decided to "dress in civvies" and was wearing a pair of gray slacks and a vivid shirt in the University's official color.

"Is this really the bishop of Albuquerque?" Jeff Barnett had demanded when he and Mary Dell had encountered him in the crowd on the way in. "I don't believe it. He looks just like any other old grad."

Mary Dell had given Randy a shrewd appraisal as she offered her hand, and smiled.

"Not quite," she said. "He's got an aura."

"It can't be sanctity," Jeff said. "Not our Randy!"

"You better believe it, boy," Randy said. "It goes with the territory."

Now, overhearing Marc's latest self-deprecating put-down, Randy turned back to him and thought, Oh, Lord. Is he still like that after all these years? I can't believe it.

"I would think your world must be pretty exciting," he said. "It's really a challenge, the way the postwar economy's grown, isn't it? The boom in the fifties, and now we're still in great shape and growing. At least that's how it seems to us outsiders."

"We're doing pretty well," Marc admitted. "And I guess it is kind of exciting to see a company like Taylorite develop as ours has. The country is certainly in good shape. I guess our American generation probably has the best of it of any generation in the history of the world. It's amazing. And how," he asked with a shy gleam of humor, "is your business?"

"Not bad," Randy said cheerfully. "We measure our profits in souls and they're doing pretty well. As far as I personally am concerned, the board of directors seems to keep on promoting me, so I guess I'm doing all right, too."

"Next step, Pope?" Marc inquired with another shy smile.

"Just between us," Randy said, "no way. I'm too independent."

"We'd all vote for you if we could," Marc said.

"You probably would," Randy said, "and I thank you for it. But not that one," he added as Renny Suratt suddenly appeared, coming up the steep flight of steps toward them.

"Oh, *him*," Marc said with distaste. There suddenly seemed to be a little silence all around them, in the midst of the steadily increasing roar in the stadium.

"Well, I'll be damned!" Guy Unruh exclaimed, leaning over to catch Gil's eye, and North's, and exchange unbelieving shakes of the head. "That nervy son of a bitch! After what he did last night!"

"I felt I had to give him a ticket," Johnny said nervously. "After all, he is a brother. But I didn't really think—"

"I did," Duke said loudly from a couple of rows above where he was seated with Shahna and the Willie Wilsons. "You should have known. You know how he acts on this campus."

"Well, I still didn't feel—" Johnny said. "What excuse could I have given?"

"I suppose none," Duke conceded. "That's how individuals like that prevail in this world. Sheer gall!"

Renny bowed and grinned and waved elaborately, and with relish, as he took his seat. With varying degrees of reserve they all gave him grudging recognition. As Duke had observed, this was how the ruthless overrode the decent: sheer gall.

Renny took his seat beside Randy, who moved away six inches or so, which, Renny made clear, amused him greatly. Billy and Janie Wilson, the last to arrive, had followed him up the steps hoping against hope that he would sit somewhere else. When he didn't they followed Randy's example. A little *cordon sanitaire* encapsulated him on both sides.

"This is great!" he exclaimed loudly. "I have a little room to be comfortable!"

And with another cheery wave all around, he turned his back, leaned forward and pretended to be concentrating intently on the field.

Down along the University benches Moose was in his element, pacing back and forth among the players, who made way for him with admiring respect. His war wound was kicking up as it always did under pressure. His forehead throbbed but he didn't really feel it: he never did when he was excited. He was fielding a good team this year and he was confident of the outcome, although he could never tell until the kids actually got out there. But he knew they were a good bunch, on the whole, well trained and well prepared; and only he and they knew what lay behind their glamorous state of public perfection.

He had confided a little of it to Franky, whom he had invited for old times' sake to sit with him on the bench. They had discussed Franky Jr., and what a disappointment he was to his parents; and Moose's Mike, just entering freshman class, who was also a handful, though Moose expressed the fervent hope to God that he would straighten up and fly right once he settled into the routine. Finally they turned to drugs and the war and what Franky referred to in frustration as "the whole damned situation."

"It isn't as though we were perfect in our day," he said, "but by God, we didn't fall apart the way this generation seems to be doing. At least we had some morals and some ethics and some common sense about things. We kept some stability going for ourselves. We used to think it was important. Silly us."

"That's how they seem to regard it," Moose agreed unhappily. "They blame us for so much, but what did we do? We just fought the war that saved them the right to be the little snot-nosed jerks and bitches so many of them are turning out to be; we didn't know we were going to save their precious future asses and make the world safe for juvenile temper tantrums, but we did . . . although I suppose," he admitted honestly, "that a lot of them genuinely think they have a gripe against the world. It really is a pretty horrible place right now in some ways, in spite of all we did. I can't see the drugs and I can't see the sinister sort of stuff Renny Suratt is preaching these days, but I can see the argument about Vietnam. It's turning into a hell of a thing; a hell of a thing. A lot of 'em are against it simply because they're cowards and want to save their own skins, but a lot are genuinely concerned. We have to respect that. . . ." His expression became somber. "It's really the drugs that have me going."

"Surely not on the team—" Franky began.

"Hell, yes, surely on the team. Do you know how hard I have to ride herd on these little bastards? There are at least twenty out of the sixty-three who've turned out for the team this year who are really into it, and of those, I think, I don't know for sure but I think, that at least five are active peddlers. They get a quick thrill out of it but they know what it eventually does to their minds, they know what it's going to do to their bodies when they're a little older, but I can talk 'til I'm blue in the face, and I do, and it doesn't do one damned bit of good. Yes, Coach. Sure, Coach. You're absolutely right, Coach. And they keep right on. It's God damned frustrating."

He broke off as an assistant coach called him; trotted over to his quarterback, instructed, urged, exhorted; trotted back. Moose, as Franky had observed years ago when he had come down to games with Franky Jr., was a damned good coach. The ugly duckling of the Fucking Asshole Touchdowns had turned into the swan of the Pacific Conference.

"You know," he said admiringly as Moose settled back beside him, eyes ranging over his charges, not missing a thing as they joked and jostled and laughed and tried nervously to build one another's morale, "they're damned lucky to have you coaching them and worrying about them and trying to help them out. You're a damned good influence."

"I try to be," Moose said moodily. "I try. It's the least one can do when you have responsibility for all these kids." He laughed without amusement. "I'm not doing too well with mine, and you aren't either, but at least I keep trying."

"So do I," Franky said, and for a moment his eyes filled with tears that he made no attempt to conceal from his old friend. "He just isn't going to get any better, I'm afraid, but there's still hope for your Mike."

"Oh, yes," Moose said. "I'm not giving up. And I'm not giving up on these kids, either. But why do we have to keep working so hard? Most of us in our generation give it our best shot, why can't we ever relax? Why don't they take what we give them and be thankful that they're damned lucky to have reasonably good parents and good sur-roundings and a great university to go to and a great country to be part of? Why are so many of them so bitter against us? What have we done?"

"We're like Mount Everest," Franky said wryly. "We're there. There has to be somebody to rebel against, and who else is there but the older generation? They think they're all perfect and we're all rotten and so, therefore, we're it. Everest."

"Of course I suppose we rebelled, too," Moose said, as the umpires began moving over the field and his assistants sent the team out to begin practice skirmishes, to the welcoming roar of the crowd.

"But we weren't so fucking *bitter*," Franky said. "We weren't so destructive. We weren't so *down* on everything."

"Nope," Moose agreed. "We were here in the approaching shadow of a great war, but we still had some hope and some self-respect. These kids are barely hanging on—and many of them going un-der. . . . Well," he said, rising and preparing to move over to the fifty-yard line, "keep my seat warm. Pray for us."

"I'll do that," Franky said with a rueful grin that Moose returned. They weren't quite sure whom they were praying for at that moment, the team or a generation.

Or two.

The University lost, 19–13, and Moose was temporarily dejected. His position with administration, alumni and students was so solid that he didn't have to worry about occasional setbacks, but still, it would have been nice to present his fraternity brothers with a victory as a reunion gift. But the kids just couldn't seem to hack it this afternoon. He sighed as he contemplated the necessity of another shower-room lecture on Monday. He hated to sound moralistic all the time, but you just had to keep hammering away for the sake of your own self-respect whether they listened or not.

His brethren and their various spouses returned to their domiciles, permanent or temporary, to prepare for the evening, which was going to be a busy one.

Ahead lay the house dinner and after that the alumni dance. Also ahead lay speeches—brief, Johnny had emphasized—the renewing of old friendships or, in the cases of Renny and Gale, acquaintance-ships—and, no doubt, some sentimentality.

They promised themselves, and each other, that there wouldn't be too much of that, but Franky predicted that "people will get sloppy," and recognized wryly that he might be among them.

Looking back, it seemed now that life had been so happy and promising then, even in the shadow of war. The ruthless events of a desperate century, combined with the inevitable erosions of ordinary living, had affected them all, in one degree or another, however successfully—or poorly—they might conceal it behind the necessary facades of social interchange.

Much to their surprise, Franky was the one who came closest to fulfilling his own prophecy. After what seemed to be a typical carefree Miller opening, his face suddenly crumpled, his eyes filled with tears, his voice choked, he was unable, for several agonizing moments, to go on.

"Are you all right?" Willie inquired in some alarm as Guy, Gil and North instinctively prepared to come to the rescue. But after a brief and obviously intense inner struggle, Franky appeared to regain control of himself and was able to finish without further difficulty. The gist of his remarks was that everything was just dandy in "the wild, wet, soggy, lovely northland" where "people are buying cars like crazy." He managed to sound so convincing that he almost convinced them—but not entirely. The episode left a disturbing little pall on their lively reunion that was not noticeably lifted when they came to the final remarks of the evening from Willie and, in an emotional reading by Moose, a letter from Rodge Leighton at the International Atomic Energy Agency in Vienna.

The evening began with great conviviality—cocktail hour, hearty handshakes, loud-voiced, back-slapping greetings; the renewal of old ties, the easy slipping back into old accustomed relationships surprisingly unchanged by the passage of twenty-five years. Wives had not been invited to this opening event of the reunion: Shahna was entertaining them at a dinner in her home above campus. "The boys are on their own," Karen Ann remarked. They were enjoying it immensely.

They agreed later that the most amazing thing about the whole evening was how very young the present house members were.

Bright, cheerful, earnest, attentive, overwhelmingly eager to please and assist their elders—who suddenly felt very elderly indeed—the present members of the house beamed all around them with a rosy-cheeked, dewy innocence they knew was deceptive but nonetheless seemed so young and immature that it was an almost physical shock.

"My God," Willie murmured to Hack, "were we that young when we were here?"

"I expect so," Hack said, surveying the willing youths who leaped to assist every time someone raised an empty glass; hung with flattering absorption upon every slightest comment to drop from ancient lips; and were apparently utterly enrapt and enthralled by these antediluvean survivors from the far-off days "before the war."

"I don't believe it," Willie protested with a smile. "Surely we weren't *that* young."

"I expect we were," Hack said. "We sure took ourselves seriously enough, didn't we? These kids apparently aren't any different."

"Well, it was serious," Willie said. At that moment Tony Andrade laughed loudly across the room at something Smitty Carriger had said, and their attention momentarily swung to him. "Some things were *very* serious."

"Yes," Hack agreed soberly. "Everything seems to be all right now."

"As far as we know," Willie said. "I gather you and Fran—"

"Yes," Hack said shortly. "It didn't work."

"I'm so sorry. She was a great gal."

"She still is. But I'm happy now."

"Good," Willie said. Something in his tone prompted a quick glance from Hack.

"And you?" he asked.

"Managing."

"Think twice," Hack said. "Divorce is a hell of a wrench if there's any basic affection at all. And the chances of coming out of it with my luck aren't always there."

"I am thinking," Willie said soberly. He sighed and repeated slowly, "I am thinking."

"Senator," suggested a bright young voice at his elbow, "may I get you another?"

He smiled.

"Oh, I think so, maybe, tonight. I usually try to keep it to one, particularly in public, but what the hell, this is special."

"I hope so, sir," the boy said fervently. "We've certainly knocked ourselves out to try to give you fellows—you men—a good time."

"You're succeeding brilliantly," Willie said. "It's a great reunion and it's great to be back in the house and see what a fine group of young men you have here now."

"Thank you, sir," the boy said with a flashing smile. "I'll be back in a minute."

"Probably thinks, 'What a dull group of old fuddy-duddies,' " Hack remarked. " 'Thank God we only have to worry about them for three hours, then we can go back to raising hell.' "

"And fornicating," Guy Unruh suggested, coming alongside.

"And rioting about Vietnam," Tim said dryly. "It's another world."

"Unfortunately," Willie said, "we're still in it." He frowned as he stared toward the door. "Is that that bastard Suratt, actually having the gall to come here tonight?"

"Why not?" Guy said. "He's a member."

And indeed he acted like one, carrying himself with the brazen manner that had always annoyed them. It was even more insufferable now, bolstered as it was by his popularity on campus and his unassailable standing in the great world of movers and shakers.

"Willie!" he exclaimed, spotting their little group and advancing upon them with outstretched hand and a deliberately exaggerated air of pleasure and enthusiasm. "How's our great United States Senator tonight?"

"Better than I was last night," Willie said coldly, ignoring his hand. "You have one hell of a nerve coming here after the trouble you caused. By Johnson is in very serious condition and may die yet. What are you grinning like an ape about?"

"That's a friendly greeting from a fraternity brother!" Renny exclaimed, retrieving his hand and managing to keep his amused expression in place, but only just. "Did you hear that?" he demanded of the youths clustered around them. "That's the kind of greeting one gets from one's old college pals, twenty-five years later. Let that be a lesson to you. Never think it isn't going to change, because it will."

"Not very much," Guy Unruh said. "A lot of us never cared for you in those days, Renny. This is nothing new for the four of us. That was a hell of a performance you put on last night."

"Insufferable," Hack remarked.

"Unforgivable," Tim agreed.

Renny's face lost its tightly held amicability, changed instantly to the arrogant anger they remembered so well.

"Well!" he snapped. "I didn't come here to be lectured by the conservative wing of American thought, or by pseudosuperior people I never liked anyway. You didn't care for me? Well, I didn't care for you! And I don't to this day. You have a *nerve* to lecture me on what I did last night, Willie Wilson! I did exactly what any sensible citizen with an ounce of concern for his country would do, in the face of this murderous, inexcusable Lyndon Johnson war. Isn't that right, fellows?"

And he turned to appeal to the house members, most of whom retreated into confused silence as they found themselves suddenly in the midst of personal hostilities whose origins obviously went back before they were born. It was apparent, however, that they agreed with Renny. The youth who had replenished Willie's drink finally spoke up, hesitantly but with growing confidence as his fellows supported him with nods and murmurs.

"I think—" he began.

"Who are you?" Willie interrupted, voice pleasant but firm.

"My name is Brad Montgomery, Senator. I'm president of the house. As I know you were."

"Yes, I was," Willie said, still smiling. "A lot of headaches, isn't it?"

"Sometimes," Brad Montgomery said, his sudden smile lighting up his face. "they *can* be a headache." He looked around the circle of his friends, who laughed and nodded.

"How many members do you have this quarter?" Willie inquired in an interested tone, but Renny saw him coming and interrupted.

"Let's don't change the subject, Willie!" he said sharply. "I'm asking these fellows if they don't agree that what I did last night was completely justified. How about it, Brad?"

"Well, sir," Brad began, "Dr. Suratt—yes, I think you have a perfect right to say what you think about Vietnam, or about anything. I think we all agree with that. Whether it is right to carry it to violent extremes—well, I don't know about that. I don't think it has quite come to that yet."

"But I do have the right," Renny said, "whatever form it takes. I do have the right?"

"Well—yes, sir," Brad said. "If that's the only way you think you can express it."

"But I *do* have the right?"

"Yes, sir," Brad said, giving way. "You do have the right."

"Thank you," Renny said. "Remind me to give you an A-plus on your term paper."

"I hope so," Brad said with an uncomfortable little laugh as new arrivals at the door reminded him and his brethren of their duties and they began thankfully to drift away.

ALLEN DRURY

"O.K., Willie," Renny said triumphantly. "Where's your support? Don't have very much of it, do you? Senator Squeak-In is on shaky ground on this one. We're going to beat you in '68, Willie. Sorry we'll have to end your wet dreams of going to the White House, but there it is. Vietnam's going to beat you. Want to bet on it?"

"Let's wait until we're a little closer to the date," Willie suggested, keeping voice and manner under control though he would have liked to give way to the visceral anger he felt.

"Let me know when you're ready," Renny suggested with an insolent grin, turned abruptly and started toward Galen Bryce and Loren Davis, who were standing near the fireplace.

"That bastard hasn't changed in twenty-five years," Guy remarked. "He is the most *un*pleasant son of a bitch."

"He's worse than that," Tim said, "now that he's a popular hero of the establishment and the media. How is By, incidentally? Does anybody know?"

"Gil's arriving," Willie said. "Maybe he can tell us."

Gil's report was not very satisfactory. By was still drifting in and out, no basic improvement discernible yet. There was still the danger that he might slip into a really deep coma and not come out of it for a while. If ever.

"Maryetta and Ti-Anna are still with him," Gil said, "and so's your boy Latt, Willie."

"Oh," Willie said, making no attempt to conceal his disappointment. "I'm sorry about that. He was supposed to join me here. I think he would have enjoyed it."

"He'll come up to Tony's in Napa Valley with you tomorrow, won't he?" Tim inquired. Willie looked bleak.

"I don't know. I have no way of telling."

"Well," Guy said briskly, "I'm going over and have a talk with North about the doctor business in Salt Lake City. Want to come along, Gil?"

"Sure," Gil said. "It's good to see old North again. . . ."

"Don't let it get you down," Tim advised. "The kid's young and impressionable. He doesn't know his own mind on a lot of things."

"That's exactly what worries me," Willie said somberly. "There are plenty of people around like Maryetta and Renny who will want to make it up for him. He's susceptible. He's already in rebellion against me, all he needs is somebody to give him direction where to go with it." He sighed. "They're waiting."

"Oh, now, don't be so gloomy," Tim said, taking his arm. "I want to find out about our millionaires. And Randy Carrero. And Jeff Barnett. *And* Moose, God knows! Come along."

And he steered him firmly across the room to where Smitty was holding forth with many humorous details about his life on the Main Line, which, to hear him tell it, seemed to consist mostly of parties and good deeds.

After a brief chat there, during which Jeff Barnett agreed that his life in Charleston was much the same, and Moose averred with an innocent envy that he wished *he* had time to go to a lot of parties, the old, familiar bell clanged through the house and it was time for dinner.

By then nearly everyone was in an expansive mood. Only Gale Bryce, wishing to verify what he had always thought his fraternity brothers would become; Randy, wishing to honor the cloth he was wearing tonight—and his own waistline; and Renny, wishing to stay alert to repel further attackers, had held their consumption down. The rest were pleasantly relaxed and ready for what Brad Montgomery predicted, as he called them to begin, would be "a damned good meal."

"Mr. President," said Willie, seated beside him, "may I offer a couple of toasts?"

"Surely, Senator," Brad said.

"Don't get gooey, Willie!" his brother Billy ordered from down the long U-shaped table. Willie smiled and stood up.

"Only moderately. First of all, to us, the classes of '39, '40, '41. We've survived. Or at least"—his voice wavered for a moment before he got it back on track—"most of us have. Dear Buff, dear Ray, dear Bob, dear Hank—and dear Latt—may God be with you, wherever you are. You live in our hearts."

There were muffled murmurs of assent, glasses raised, toasts drunk. No one else mustered the courage to speak.

"And secondly—" his voice grew lighter and more humorous though this, too, "had a lot of us on the ropes," as Moose described it later to Diana—"to three other dear ghosts without whom this house, in what *we* like to think of as its heyday though to you current occupants I know its heyday is right now, would not have been the same.

"To that large, black, always patient, always good-natured—not always *cordon bleu* but nonetheless reasonably nutritional because we all survived him—character, Dewey, our cook. I learned not long ago that he was drafted at forty-five in the war's closing days when they were after everybody who could breathe; was badly wounded in the final Italian campaign; came home to permanent residence in a V.A. hospital in Southern California; and died about five years ago.

"You kept us alive, Dewey. Don't know how you did it but you did it!

"And lastly, two characters I'm sure we'll also never forget, Josephine and Napoleon. Josephine was our cat, who dropped in as a kitten one frosty morning and lived out her days here in commanding glory, producing offspring whose offspring I'm sure can still be found somewhere on campus; and her sidekick and best buddy, Napoleon, a Harlequin Great Dane whom you, Franky, used to describe as—do you remember?"

"A God damned fucking fart machine," Franky responded. "And he was, too!"

And on that note the gooier, if not the more serious, part of the dinner came to a close in a roar of laughter as they drank the final toast and fell to on a quite impressive feast prepared by the present cook, a Filipino named Enrile who appeared midway, grinning, to take bows. The meal was served by the present members of the house who solemnly waited on their elders before seating themselves; a grandeur, as Willie confided to Brad, who laughed delightedly, they never could have imagined twenty-five years ago in their wildest dreams.

After that came, as Moose told Diana, "the heavy stuff." It didn't begin that way, so much, but by the time it reached his own reading of Rodge Leighton's letter, it was serious enough. One by one they offered brief comments on war service, wives, families, present professional occupations, outside activities if any, recreations, interests. Only Franky, fifth down the list alphabetically, disturbed the jocular flow of reminiscence and accomplishment with his brief emotional upset; after his determinedly swift recovery it flowed on, a typical accounting by the middle-aged of that generation of what they had experienced in their generation's greatest trial, and after; a relatively characteristic roster of American lives in that era, some wealthy, some more modest, some highly successful, some more moderately so; nearly all devoted in some measure to the concept of "being good citizens" and "upholding certain standards."

If these were not always the current standards, their young hosts were far too polite to indicate by so much as a lifted eyebrow or a swiftly exchanged glance that they really did have a bunch of conservative old farts on their hands. Good manners, not yet eroded by the sixties, and the reflection that, after all, these old guys *were* fraternity brothers so maybe they could be suffered on this one brief occasion, kept things mostly pleasant, and serene.

Only Renny and Tony Andrade—and, of course, Willie's brief comments and Rodge's letter—disrupted the comfortable flow of the evening after Franky's brief interlude. Renny's contribution was typical, so harsh and condemnatory that only one thing could have silenced him. It did, but not before, as he congratulated himself afterward, he had his say.

Before he spoke, Tony related his war's-end experience guarding the bridge with the Soviets in Germany.

"It was one of those things you don't forget," he said soberly. "I realized then that we were probably going to have a lot of trouble with them. In fact, I remember thinking, 'These bastards are God damned tough and they have plans we Americans don't even dream about.' I'm sorry to say I think that youthful wartime premonition was absolutely correct."

At this both Renny and some of their young hosts did stir uneasily. The accepted gospel of the age did not permit of such harsh criticisms of the Soviets even now twenty years on, after Berlin, Vienna, Cuba, Hungary, Czechoslovakia and a hundred other examples of duplicitous behavior, ruthless cruelty and imperialism both covert and overt.

"So," Tony concluded, "I guess I'm one of your typical middle-aged reactionary Americans: I don't like 'em, I don't trust 'em, I think we've got to be on guard against them every minute of every day, and I contribute time, money and effort to a lot of organizations that feel the way I do. I'm not," he added dryly, "a John Bircher, but I am an extremely skeptical and alarmed man when it comes to our friends in Moscow." He glanced down the table and added, "If this be treason, Renny, make the most of it."

"I will—" Renny began angrily but Brad Montgomery rapped sharp spoon on glass and lifted a cautionary hand.

"Dr. Suratt," he said firmly, ". . . sir. It isn't your turn yet. Dr. Bryce, Mr. Carriger, Mr. Davis, Mr. Herbert, Coach Musavich, Dr. Offenberg—then you, sir. I think it would help if we can stick to the regular order."

"Good for you," Willie whispered and received again Brad's quick-flashing smile.

"It's my responsibility, I believe in exercising it. I'm sure you did the same in your day."

"You're a worthy successor," Willie said. The boy smiled again, pleased.

For a second it seemed that Renny might rebel, so sternly did he exaggerate his expression of anger and surprise. But he had not practiced classroom and platform dramatics for so long without becoming a master. He held his expression just long enough, then gave a dismissive wave and settled back. Gale, Smitty, Lor, Johnny, Moose, Duke, offered their brief accounts. Moose's was the most dramatic.

"Rodge sent a letter and asked that I read it to you," he began abruptly (as Willie had tactfully suggested when Johnny approached him). "You guys from the old house remember that he and I were real good buddies in school. Many of you don't know that we enlisted in the Marines together and served a lot together in the South Pacific." He ran a quick hand over the ravaged right side of his face. "That's where I got these lifetime adornments. It's also where Rodge saved my life, on Iwo, along with seven other guys. I wouldn't be here talking to you tonight if it weren't for Rodge. As most of you know, he got the Congressional Medal of Honor for it." His voice threatened to break but he held it firm. "I owe a lot to Rodge. . . ." His eyes widened, he stared into far-off things. Then he shook his head impatiently and went on.

"So. He wrote this letter and I'll read it to you now, as requested.

" 'Dear Moose, Willie, Marc my old roomie, and all you guys both past and present in the house. I wish I could be with you there tonight, but you can be sure I am imagining every minute of it. I can see the dining room and the table, all those food fights, all that endless banter, all those deep discussions. Gad, we were serious then, sometimes! And despite the war coming on, those were happy days.

" 'The world isn't exactly one big ha-ha, now.

" 'Particularly am I aware of this here in Vienna, where as you know I seem to have acquired a permanent assignment in life with the International Atomic Energy Agency. I flew over Hiroshima right after the bombing and I decided then that whatever I could do to stop that awful thing, I would do. It hasn't been stopped yet, though some of us are trying.

" 'Almost my first reaction when I saw what the Bomb could do was to say: *Let's don't have any more children.* Like most of the human race, I ignored my own very sound advice and now have four, and their lovely mother, Juliette. And so I have even more reason to be dedicated to what I am doing now, which is to try to keep the monster under control so that it won't eventually blast all their hopes and dreams like it did those of the people of Hiroshima and Nagasaki.

" 'As of the reunion there tonight, the prospects don't look very good. There's the very obvious race between the Soviet Union and the United States. There's also the other factor that worries us here even more. What do we do when the Bomb and other atomic weapons fall into the hands of second-level nations, crazy dictators, terrorists, who cheat inspection, have no restraints of any kind, regard atomic weapons as just another convenient means to destroy one another—and probably us—just another weapon in their centuries-old hatreds and their crazed ambitions for power over each other?

" 'It's not a pleasant prospect, friends, and while I'd like to tell you that we are making great progress, don't you believe it. India, Pakistan, Israel—the list is growing. And it's going to keep right on growing. And when we live in a world in which the Bomb is in the hands of completely irresponsible individuals subject to no restraints whatsoever of decency or concern for humanity, it will then, I'm afraid, be only a matter of time before the world really is destroyed.

" 'And not much time.

" 'I give it maybe to the year 2000 until all the world's crazies have the Bomb.

" 'After that, God help us.' "

Moose paused and took a sip of water. They were spellbound, older and younger alike. The comfortable old dining room was a long way from food fights and banter now.

" '*Let's don't have any more children.* Well, most of us have them. So what are we going to do, as individuals, to try to stop the juggernaut before it rolls over us and obliterates this lovely planet? I don't know, to tell you the truth—except to work as hard as we can, in every way we can, to help thwart the vengeful desires of insane leaders and envious peoples, and to try to alleviate the human burdens that may prompt many of them to resort to a force of which they have absolutely no conception, and whose capacity for absolute devastation they cannot remotely imagine.

" 'I see it here all the time in discussions with some of them. If they ever did have a concept of Hiroshima and Nagasaki, except as some sort of disembodied evil off there somewhere in the dim past, they have lost it now—even if they cared. The truly terrifying thing is that some of them just don't care. They will use it anyway, because it is the most efficient means of obliterating their enemies. A bomb, or two, or three, and no more enemy. Maybe no more them, either, but I'm afraid they're not sophisticated enough—or caring enough—to see that.

ALLEN DRURY

" 'And even in the more sophisticated nations, we who were so vividly aware of the awful potentials for a while after it happened, the vividness of the memory fades. Our awareness revived for a while recently with the Cuban missile crisis, backyard shelters, schoolkids drilling to hide under desks. But it won't be long before it's all trailed away again, back into the category of things we don't want to think about because they're too awful—and what can we do about them, anyway?

" 'I sometimes feel, here in Vienna where we are lucky to progress one inch a year, if that much, toward some sort of international control, that there isn't *anything* anybody can do about it. Then I think, No, that isn't right, either. There are all those kids who, against better judgment and horrifying reality, we've brought into the world. Somehow we've got to keep trying, for them. Somehow, hope has to be kept alive.

" 'So I urge you, friends and brothers, to so live your own lives that you can contribute something no matter how small just so it's *something*, to peace and understanding and charity toward one another. Try to be helpful, try to be gentle, try to love. Maybe it will spread and, while there is still time, help to tear down the barriers and eliminate the hatreds and jealousies that separate the peoples.

" 'This is a weak and feeble proposal, I know. But what else is there? Time, in this desperate century, grows shorter every day.

" 'I've rambled enough and been much too somber. But now and then somebody has to be. Just to keep us reminded.

" 'Wish me luck here.

" 'I wish you luck there.

" 'Maybe we'll all be lucky . . . maybe.' "

Moose cleared his throat, took another sip of water, folded the letter carefully, put it in his pocket, sat down.

"Jesus!" Guy Unruh exclaimed into the silence. "There's a cheerful note!"

"Anything you want to argue with?" Willie inquired dryly. Guy shook his head. "Well, then—"

They were silent for several moments more. The abyss had opened, Rodge had forced them to look into it. Swiftly, as always, it closed. Social norms resumed. Life went on. Duke spoke, and then Brad turned to Renny, who had been waiting with barely concealed impatience while what he obviously considered a parade of minor concerns passed by.

"Now, sir," Brad said with a pleasant nod. Renny stood up.

"Thank you," he said dryly. He surveyed them carefully, face by face, up one side of the table and down the other.

"God damn it," Moose muttered, not too quietly. "Cut the posing and get on with it."

Renny shot him a savage look, quite similar to those he often used to give him at this same table years ago. Moose exchanged a grin with Tony. He didn't care any more now than he had then.

"Mr. President," Renny said, "I am not surprised to come back to this house and find its members transformed into exactly the sort of hysterical reactionary creeps I used to be convinced they would become."

There was an uneasy murmur from their hosts, not knowing quite whether to side with their guests, which they knew they ought to do as a matter of courtesy, or flatter Dr. Suratt, campus hero, with the sycophantic response he demanded and was used to. Aided by Brad's stern glance, courtesy won out. Everybody managed to look solemn and attentive.

"I am not surprised," Renny went on, "to hear Rodge Leighton's reactionary anti-Soviet opinions."

"He hardly mentioned the Soviets," Moose objected sharply. "You twist everything to suit your own purposes, don't you, Renny? You always have."

Renny ignored him.

"Rodge was never the most stable of individuals"—"What?" exclaimed Smitty Carriger in quite genuine surprise. Renny ignored him too—"and I can see where close association with an organization so filled with hysterical scientists as the International Atomic Energy Agency can induce a certain hysteria in one's self. He is too close to it, obviously. Proximity overweighs sound judgment. That must be taken into account.

"I am not surprised to hear you, Tony, confess to your reactionary anti-Soviet activities. It is what I would have expected from your Napa Valley background. Not exactly a home for worldwide vision up there, is it? Not exactly your typical hardworking, middle-class American milieu, right?"

"I work," Tony said mildly. "Raising grapes and running a winery can be hard work if you do it right. We do."

"Oh, no doubt," Renny said with an unamused laugh. "Trust you to be the all-American boy, Andrade. You always were."

"That's right," Hack spoke up sharply from across the table. "Get on with it, Renny, will you please?"

"Thank you, Hack," Tony said. Something in his surprised expression, swiftly pleased, as swiftly impassive, registered with quite a few. But only Willie knew why.

"Oh, I will," Renny said. "I will. I'm not going to take long. I just want to say on behalf of myself, and I believe of a majority of the students presently on campus, that we have moved, thank God, into a more progressive and far-seeing world in which such reactionary, war-breeding sentiments have no place. We see the Soviet Union as having some faults but more strengths. We place them beside the very obvious weaknesses of this rich, overweening, overbearing, overly reactionary country and we say, 'Give us the Soviets every time. At least they speak up for the world's poor and oppressed. At least they work for people's democracy. At least they're not conservative, war-mongering imperialists like the U.S. and its Western allies.' Isn't that right, fellows?"

Again there was an uneasy restlessness under his penetrating gaze and again Brad came to the rescue.

"That isn't exactly what we're here for, is it?" he asked. "I thought this was supposed to be a pleasant evening of reunion and reminiscence. Maybe we'd better leave that discussion for the classroom, Dr. Suratt. Sir."

"There goes your A-plus," murmured one of his brethren, and there was a burst of relieved, if still uneasy, laughter.

"Right," Renny said, changing course. "You're probably right, Brad. And it won't affect your A-plus, either. But I just wanted to put in a small disclaimer in the midst of all this hearty, self-congratulatory, red-blooded Americanism here, lest anybody think that Rodge and Tony—and no doubt Willie when we get to him—can state these reactionary views without challenge. Some of us, at least, aren't that blind to America's faults. I wanted it on record."

"I'm sure we get the message, sir," Brad said briskly. "So, proceeding apace—"

And he called on Jeff Barnett, Randy Carrero, Marc Taylor and Billy Wilson, who in quick succession reported on their lives. Marc and Billy were characteristically self-deprecating, but Billy's pride in the ranch and in his family, and Marc's in the steady upward progress of Taylorite, were clear.

Randy Carrero the students found likable and impressive as he spoke with humor of his life in the Church and then wound up with a twinkle and the observation, "I seem to have been fortunate enough to be entrusted with a certain prominence by my superiors. But I'll tell you a secret, boys. Once you learn politics on this campus, you can go anywhere."

Which amused them greatly, it was in such contrast to the habiliments he wore this night, and to his title. Jeff held them with equal skill, speaking in his broad accent of his activities in the South Carolina legislature, his glimpses of present-day plantation life "getting more highly mechanized every day," and finally his activities with By Johnson in the civil rights movement.

"I know we do not meet the high standards of Dr. Suratt," he said dryly, "because our organization is composed of both blacks and whites, and instead of being confrontational, we do try to keep things on the peaceful, nonviolent, constructive basis favored by Dr. King." He paused, obviously considering, then decided to go ahead. "As many of us witnessed last night, Dr. Suratt and his friends do not believe in peaceful, nonviolent progress. They have other agendas. Gil," he broke off abruptly, "have you checked on By in the last hour or so? Why don't you do that?"

"I was just thinking that," Gil said, rising and tossing his napkin onto his chair. "Is there still an upstairs phone, Mr. President?"

"Both second- and third-floor landings," Brad said.

"Thanks," Gil said. "I'll be back in a minute."

But he did not return for several minutes, by which time Jeff and the others had finished and Willie, final speaker by prior arrangement with Brad, was well launched into his closing remarks.

"Mr. President," he said, "members of the house past and present. I'll be brief, which professionally is hard for me to do, now"—agreeing laughter—"I just want to say, to conclude this pleasant occasion —reasonably pleasant occasion"—again laughter, a little less comfortable—"that I would not want our younger members to go away from this evening thinking that you, Renny, represent the best of a generation. You represent a segment of it, true enough, but one whose general wisdom I think a lot of us question. Particularly do we question it when it surfaces in people like yourself who have access to so many hearts and minds"—he almost said "gullible hearts and minds," but caught himself just in time—"both in your teachings and in the publications which have won you such wide national fame.

"It is my regret, as it is Jeff's, that you have not chosen to use your talents and your influence for constructive ends, but instead have devoted them to the increasingly violent purposes which many of us saw demonstrated last night. It seems to me that it ill behooves one who has ability, and such influence, to seek to destroy rather than develop peaceable and lasting solutions for our problems, particularly the problem which By Johnson has so ably represented up to now. May God grant that he can come through this tragic episode which you and your friends have provoked, and emerge with his capacities undiminished and his ability to work for peaceful solutions unharmed. It would be a real tragedy if permanent damage should prove to have been done to him personally, or to the cause of true progress which he represents. That would be an unconscionable act with inexcusable consequences. It would—"

But that was enough for Renny, who had been listening with a steadily deepening scowl that sent shivers of delicious anticipation through their younger listeners and a surge of satisfaction through the older, nearly all of whom found themselves in complete agreement with Willie. In fact, Tim and Guy and Franky were just murmuring, "Hear, hear!" when Renny, face flushed, got to his feet so violently that he toppled his chair over backward.

"Mr. *President!*" he cried in a voice that brooked no denial. "Mr. President, I demand to be heard!"

For a moment Brad hesitated. But he was, after all, a senior in college and this was the University's most famous (or notorious, depending on the point of view) faculty member and official rebel—nationally enshrined challenger of all that was accepted and stable—"Voice of the Sixties," as he was already being called by many of those right-thinking critics, editorialists, columnists and commentators who Really Mattered.

Brad surrendered.

"Very well, sir," he said, voice for the first time showing signs of strain. "But keep it brief, if you can, sir. We are almost at the end of the evening."

"Almost at the end of the evening, indeed!" Renny said savagely. "Almost at the end of the most shameful era in American history, the time when material comfort is the only standard of success, and opposition to the so-called 'Soviet threat' is the only criterion of political responsibility! End of the evening, indeed! End of America, I'd say, if it keeps on going down this futile and foredoomed path, seeking a false prosperity it cannot maintain and a destruction of Communism it cannot possibly achieve! The world of Willie Wilson! Bad cess to it, say I! It cannot possibly succeed, any more than can the pious, pompous, patronizing political accident who presumes to give us his infallible wisdom tonight! Willie Wilson! What a laugh!"

He paused, his angry glare becoming if anything more exaggerated and pronounced. He was delighted to see he had hit his target: Willie also had risen to his feet, glaring back, body tensed, preparing to hurl back the considerable vilifications of which he was capable. Only Tim's restraining hand on one arm and Brad's on the other kept him silent; and that, it was obvious, by only the slimmest of threads that might snap at any moment.

"As for By Johnson," Renny went on, modulating his voice skillfully into a dry and patronizing tone, a note of smirking triumph—"as for By Johnson, that toadying Uncle Tom who has combined with Uncle Jeffy to sabotage with mealymouthed platitudes the militant progress of his race—as for By Johnson—"

But they were not to know what he thought of By Johnson, at least on that particular occasion, for Gil, tense and terribly angry, appeared in the doorway and overrode him in a flat but implacable voice:

"Will you be quiet, you *monstrous* individual. Be *quiet.*"

"How dare—" Renny began, but Gil was not to be stopped.

"Just shut up," he said in the same flat, implacable, weary monotone. "Just *shut up*, God damn you."

"Well!" Renny spluttered. "*Well!*"

He was white-faced, all traces of triumph vanished. He appeared to be, for once, at a complete loss for words.

Gil forced his voice to a calmer, more professional level.

"Bayard Johnson went into a deep coma about an hour and a half ago and died about fifteen minutes ago." There was a general gasp, exclamations of "Oh, no!" and "Oh, my God!" Gil's voice steadied further. "His body will be removed to a funeral parlor where it will be prepared for shipment to Washington tomorrow. His wife, Maryetta, their daughter Ti-Anna and your son Latt, Willie, are with him. Maryetta seems to be hanging on, but just barely. She tells me that none of us is to come visit him, but I think I, for one, will ignore that. Willie?"

"Yes."

"Anybody else?"

"Yes," said Jeff, Tim, Hack, Guy, North, Duke, Moose.

Brad rapped spoon on glass.

"I am very sorry," he said, voice uneven but doing his job, "I am very sorry that this reunion dinner has to end on this note. But—" he sighed, sounding far beyond his years—"events overtake us, sometimes. I now declare this dinner concluded. Thank you all for coming. May your next visit to the house be a happier one."

"Thank you all for nothing!" Renny said harshly and flung away, out the door, out of the house.

Willie was pleased to note that quite a few hisses followed him. Not all were from his own generation. Some came from the students. Which, he thought with a tired wryness, might or might not signify something.

At the hospital Maryetta, eyes bloodshot and wild, graying bun of hair escaped from its usual primly careful bounds and going in all directions, almost spat at them when they entered the room.

"How dare you come here!" she demanded. "How *dare* you, you—you—*murderers!*"

"Now see heah, Maryetta," Jeff said, accent thicker than usual in the agitation of the moment, "don't you talk to us like that, girl, you heah? Don't you give us that crazy unjust crap, when we're all friends of his and admired him and hepped him and believed in him—"

"*You!*" she said, while Ti-Anna huddled at her side and Latt stood over her fiercely protective, "*you,* who blackballed him from the house—"

"And has been his friend ever since!" Jeff almost shouted. "Who has worked with him for the past fifteen years to try to bring racial justice and understanding to the South! Who has regarded him as one of my best and truest friends and hepped him in every way Ah can—can't you ever forget and forgive *anything,* Maryetta? Do you have to be this bitter still, with him on his deathbed? Now kindly stand aside, you-all, and let us pay him decent tribute!"

And he stepped forward, the others following; and the forlorn and bitter trio guarding the bed gave way.

Skull still heavily bandaged but face exposed and at last serene, the body of Bayard Johnson lay before them.

Quietly they took places around the bed.

"Willie?" Jeff asked.

"Yes," Willie said. His voice was not very steady, but he managed.

"Lord," he said, "have mercy upon this thy servant Bayard, and receive him into Thy loving peace and kindness. He was a good man who fought hard in an unhappy and difficult time for his people and our mutual country; who sought to achieve, in Thy name and Thy example, a peaceful and loving solution for all the many problems that confront his people and the nation that we share together. Receive him and comfort him, for he was one of Thy most worthy servants. We, who have known him most of his life, ask it in the name of Thy infinite mercy. Amen."

"Amen," said everyone; but even as they responded automatically the faces of Maryetta, Ti-Anna and Latt twisted again into a terrible, lonely bitterness.

"Now go!" Maryetta cried. "Just go!"

At the door Willie turned back for a moment.

"Latt—" he said. "Latt, will you be joining your mother and me to go up to Napa Valley tomorrow?"

For a moment his son looked at him with tormented, uncomprehending eyes.

"How can you?" he asked in a tortured whisper. "How can you—all of you—go and—and *celebrate*—" Willie raised a dismayed, restraining hand but his son ignored it. "Can't you see," he said in a voice so low it could hardly be heard, "that I'm in mourning?"

"Come on, Willie," Tim said quietly, taking one arm. "Come on, boy," Guy Unruh said quietly, taking the other. And after a moment, after one last agonized look at his son, whom he really thought at that moment he might never see again, he let himself be led out into the soft September night.

How terribly young Latt had sounded.

But how terribly, terribly sincere.

3

The all-University dance started in the Quad at 9:00 P.M.

The palm trees were illuminated, lanterns hung from the sand-stone arches, two bands at opposite corners alternated old, familiar tunes, banners and streamers bore class numerals and the proud insignia of the University. High above in a cloudless sky the moon rode serene. Everything conspired to produce a sentimental glow.

Unfortunately, Willie reflected, for him and for many others the present's concerns were now a little more pressing than the past's—although not, perhaps, for Hack, suddenly noticing across the center of the Quad, talking animatedly with friends, the one person he really had not wanted to see when he came to the reunion.

It must be fifteen years since he had seen her last.

Must be!

He knew damned well it was, right down to the last minute of the last day of the last week of the last month of the last year.

There you are, Mrs. Haggerty, he thought; or have you remarried? Quite likely. The tall, dark guy leaning over to laugh into your eyes, the blond guy at your elbow vying with him for your attention, the jerk coming up on the outside with a glass of something for you? They were all jerks. Fran could do better than that. How could she waste her time on such inferior human material? I feel sorry for you, he thought. It must be a hell of a life.

He was on the point of persuading himself that it was, when she turned to Mr. Tall and Dark to say something and her eyes suddenly shot past him, in that play-the-crowd glance that she had developed for the social side of her law practice, and saw Hack standing by himself perhaps fifty feet away on the edge of the happily dancing crowd.

For a split second she hesitated, obviously thought of looking hastily away and pretending she hadn't seen him. Then, characteristically, she decided to drop the pretense and sail right into it—direct, determined and strikingly beautiful, as Fran had always been. The interval was very brief but it gave him, too, time to panic, recover, think: What the hell, and abandon the childish impulse to run away.

He could see her say, "Excuse me," with a practiced, easy glance into the eyes of Mr. Tall and Dark, Mr. Blond and Mr. Jerk. Whatever any of them might be to her was not apparent in that skilled, comfortable dismissal or in their rueful but humorous acceptance of it. Apparently nobody belonged to anybody in that group. He was amazed at how relieved he felt. What was it to him, after fifteen years?

"Hi," she said, holding out her hand to take his, drawing him to her with a practiced and, apparently, quite impersonal kiss on the cheek. "Fancy meeting you here."

"Where else but the Quad?" he asked with a smile that, he congratulated himself, matched hers for friendly impersonality. "How have you been?"

"Fine," she said. "Do I look it?"

"You do indeed. Every inch the successful lawyer."

"And politician," she said. "I'll bet you haven't kept up with my career."

For a second he thought of saying pleasantly, No, I haven't, but he didn't think she would believe him.

"Yes, I have. You're in—what? Second term in the state assembly?"

"Third," she said, "and thinking about going to Washington in '66. The local Congressman is in poor health and wants to quit. He's said he'll support me if I decide to run."

"Go for it," he said. "I know you'd love it back there."

"I do," she said. "I go back a lot on the firm's business. Is Willie here?"

"Oh, yes," he said, and asked casually, "Do you ever see him when you're there?"

She looked pleased for a second. He knew it was what she wanted to hear but he hadn't thought he was going to say it. He was quite surprised at himself.

"I haven't, really, in a long time," she said. "We did testify on the foreign-aid bill two years ago on behalf of one of our overseas clients and I saw him briefly then, but that was the last time. We just chatted in the hall outside the Foreign Relations Committee for a minute or two. He was a brand-new Senator then and thrilled to death with it, though he tried to pretend he wasn't. You know Willie."

"I gather he's doing well," he said. "Want to say hello? He and Donna were over on the other side of the Quad with Moose and his wife and Suzy Waggoner a few minutes ago."

"Suzy Waggoner!" she exclaimed. " 'Welcome Waggoner!' And Moose! Does anything ever change?"

"Oh, she's changed a lot," he said with an answering laugh that he thought might wipe out the tensions that still lingered between them. It didn't quite, but it helped. "Married, respectable, about to become a grandmother for the third time—"

"Suzy a grandmother!' she exclaimed again and burst into another laugh. "Life gets curiouser and curiouser. Sure, let's go say hello to them. . . . Tell me," she said, taking his arm, ignoring its instant rigidity as they made their way through the crowd, "how is your Italian life? Are you happy?"

"Are you?"

"That's a lawyer's trick," she said lightly, "answer a question with a question. I asked you first."

He thought for a moment, really considered it, which he knew she would appreciate, then said soberly, "Yes, I am. Flavia is a wonderful wife and companion, the kids—hers and mine, she has two, we have two together—get along beautifully with us and with each other—the atmosphere at home is very comfortable and serene, she makes it easy for me to work—"

"Which I didn't."

"She's not competitive," he said, not responding directly to the challenge, making his tone nonjudgmental and matter-of-fact though he could have said a lot on the subject. "She runs the house, I do my music."

"And you're there," she said, thoughtfully but also not in a combative way. "That's nice. It's much better for you."

"Is it?" He gave her a swift sideways glance. "Do you really think so? Are we both really happy?"

She returned his glance. To his surprise—and satisfaction, he had to admit—what appeared to be a sudden glint of tears briefly touched her eyes.

"Now stop that," she said, voice determinedly light but again, he was pleased to note, not too steady. "Let's don't start down that road, O.K.?"

"Fran—" he said, but she looked away and repeated firmly. "Stop that, Hack. I don't want to get into that, please. It's pointless."

"Maybe," he said. "But not if—"

"No ifs," she said. "Look, they have a table. How convenient. My goodness, Suzy does look settled, doesn't she? I never thought I'd see the day!"

And brightly, smoothly and very firmly, she led him along to one of the many tables scattered around the perimeter of the Quad. Willie, Moose and North McAllister, who had joined them, stood up, faces alight. Everybody, Hack reflected with a wistful sadness, had always liked Fran. What a wonderful girl, and how lucky he was to have her! *Have* had her.

For the next couple of minutes everyone was involved in greeting and kissing everyone else. Fran and Donna had always liked one another on campus, still obviously liked one another now. Fran had never met Moose's wife Diana, they too obviously liked one another at once. Suzy Waggoner, gone to weight a bit but still blond, still pretty, still possessed of a wandering eye and a practiced glance, seemed somehow more sedate and less aggressive. She greeted Fran and Hack with her old knowing, sardonic smile, but it seemed kindlier and less unsettling now. The days of "Welcome Waggoner," who had once delighted in telling a naive young sorority sister that she had slept with "all" the football team, appeared to be long gone.

She appeared to have become, as Hack had remarked, "respectable"—easier to accept, not requiring the rather shocked, self-conscious tolerance they had accorded her when young. Whether that meant that she had changed—or they had changed—or the generation had changed—or the general climate had changed—they weren't quite certain; but, anyway, they all found they were genuinely pleased to see her again.

For half an hour or so they remained together, dancing a bit, chatting a lot of old times, discussing with satisfaction Willie's career, Hack's music, Moose's coaching, North's highly successful practice in Salt Lake City. Suzy inquired bluntly if Hack and Fran's appearance together "means anything" and they both replied firmly that it did not. Suzy said that was too bad and Willie hurriedly asked her to show them pictures of her grandchildren, which she did with obvious pride and the sardonic query, "I'll bet you thought you'd never live to see the day, right?"

"That's *right*," Moose said with a fervor Diana didn't understand but that secretly amused the others, remembering vividly his and Suzy's passionate involvement all through senior year. Now they seemed to be just two old, comfortable friends, although both she and Moose knew very well the instant recognition and inner tensions that stirred them pleasurably now in memory of those distant days . . . or maybe not so distant, Moose thought dreamily with a surge of reminiscent fondness he knew he should kick himself for but knew he wouldn't.

Suzy was the first to break up the group, but not before she had issued a blanket invitation to "Look me up in the East Bay. I'm in the book." She emphasized this especially to Moose and Diana, who was innocently pleased and remarked to Moose later that night when they were getting ready for bed that Suzy "seems to be such a lively, generous sort of person."

"Oh, she is," Moose agreed. "That she is."

"Maybe we can look her up sometime."

"We'll see," Moose said casually, making a mental note to check the Oakland phone book sometime just to see if she really was in it. Then he thought, I'm a married man with a great wife and three kids, what the hell am I thinking? But he knew very well what he was thinking and it didn't shock him anywhere near as much as he knew it should.

Fran and North, dancing together rather sedately to the strains of one of the slower standards, found themselves immediately back in their last conversation, on Big Game Night twenty-five years ago. On that occasion Fran had deliberately challenged what she had considered North's remoteness and lack of commitment to B.J. Now that he was long married to B.J. she wondered how things were going; and being Fran, cool and self-possessed and determined about others' lives if not always her own, she asked.

"B.J. isn't with you," she began. He frowned, voice worried.

"No, she's not. She's not feeling well and we can't quite figure out why."

"But you suspect," she suggested. The frown deepened.

"Yes. But we hope not—*I* hope not, God knows. There are two more major tests to be done and then we'll be sure. But it won't be a surprise, to me or I suspect to her, though she's being very brave about it."

"I am so sorry," she said, giving his hand a squeeze. "Such a vicious, vicious disease . . . I know you have a happy life together."

His expression was noncommittal but his voice warmer.

"We do."

"And you don't regret marrying her. I know you were quite uncertain. I remember that last Big Game Night—"

"I've never forgotten it," he said with a sudden wry little smile. "You were very inquisitive, Fran."

"I am," she acknowledged. "But I cared for you both. Still care for you both."

"I appreciate that," he said, sincerely. "I know it was all friendship."

"And worry. Worry that she would get hurt and that you"—she considered the words—"would miss out on something I felt you really needed."

"You're very perceptive," he said. "Always were. I did need it, although"—his expression darkened for some reason she had always suspected but never really articulated to herself—"I wasn't so sure I did at that time."

"And has it given you what you thought it would?" she inquired, and was aware of a slight break in tempo, a sudden brief inattention to the dance.

"Yes, it has," he said with a flash of bitterness she couldn't—or didn't want to—analyze too closely. "It's made me respectable."

She realized suddenly that she didn't really want to get in that deep, pulled back abruptly.

"But you always were respectable," she protested. "Nobody was more respectable than North McAllister!"

The bitter expression deepened.

"Respectable is as respectable does. Maybe it would have been better if I'd—"

"Now stop that," she said hurriedly. And firmly. "You've had a good life with B.J. and I know you've made her very happy. That's what matters now, and don't you forget it. I hope you never express these doubts to her."

He uttered a sad, ironic little laugh.

"How could I? That would defeat the whole purpose, wouldn't it?"

"Well, now—" she said lamely, sounding for once unusually uncertain— "I don't know about that. It depends on what the purpose was."

"Respectability, didn't we say?" The ironic tone increased. "Better drop it, Fran. You're getting in over your head." And, abruptly, "Let's talk about you. Do you ever regret leaving Hack?"

She looked hurt for a second but recovered with a determined
lightness.

"It was mutual. We left each other."

He smiled.

"And now he's the great composer and you're the successful lawyer
and politician and there aren't any kids to worry about and everybody's happy. Too bad we don't all have such well-ordered lives."

"I suppose," she said, "that I deserved that."

"No," he said. "No, not a matter of 'deserving.' Just that we all have
our reasons and probably shouldn't try to pry too deeply into those of
others."

"Just so you're really happy."

"And you are. Which is what we should all wish for each other,
after twenty-five years."

"Give my love to B.J.," she said, deliberately more impersonal as
the dance ended and they started back toward the table. "I'll call you
in a couple of weeks to find out how things are going, and then I'll
write her a letter. It probably won't be any help, but—"

"She'll be very pleased. And so will I. And, Fran—"

"Yes?"

"I do appreciate your interest," he said soberly. "I know you've
always been a good friend, always wanted the best for me." His
expression turned bleak for a second, as swiftly reverted to noncommittal pleasantry. "I'm not sure I've got it, but at least I manage."

"Just so you do," she said, giving his hand another squeeze as they
approached the table. "Just so you do."

"Did you two get everything settled?" Willie inquired lightly as
they sat down. "You looked pretty serious out there."

Fran tapped him on the arm.

"You should have been dancing, Senator, not spying on other people."

"All right," Willie said, beating Hack to his feet by a split second.
"I've got her, Hack. Come and dance with me, Fran, and tell me all
about it. So what's with old North?" he inquired casually as they
moved out into the center of the Quad and joined the hopping,
jumping, swirling, swinging—or in some cases, such as theirs, sedately and gracefully moving—dancers. "Everything O.K. with him?"

She frowned.

"As much as possible, I guess. He's always been something of an
enigma. However," she went on brightly, "let's talk about us. Do you
think I should run for the House next year?"

He guffawed and stopped dead, holding her at arm's length.

"Let's talk about *us*, should *I* run for the House next year. There's a feminine transition if I ever heard one. Yes, why not?"

"Good," she said, joining his laughter and pulling him back into the rhythm of the music. "That's exactly what I wanted you to say, of course. Will you support me?"

"Well," he said, caution learned in fourteen years on the Hill instantly shading his voice, which made her laugh again, "it's a little too early to commit to that, but depending on how things look at the time, I would certainly be favorably disposed to give the matter my most earnest consid—"

"Willie Wilson," she interrupted with mock severity, "you've become as weasel-worded as the rest. Will you or won't you?"

He had the grace to laugh outright.

"Sure. You can count on it."

"I have your word?"

"You have my word."

"That's better," she said. "It may be a tough fight but I think I can swing it."

"Why do you want to?" he asked. "It's not such an easy life."

"True. Why do you do it?"

He gave her a thoughtful stare.

"I don't know, exactly. Some combination of ambition—desire to do something for the country—belief that one can do it better than one's opponent—a concept of what America should be, can be, *must* be if this and future generations are to have a decent world to live in—a rather hazy mix of goodwill, good intentions, arrogance, ego, self-confidence, humility, desire to serve, willingness to sacrifice one's personal interests to the greater good and at the same time achieve one's personal interests and ambitions, too . . . an odd conglomeration of things. You have it, or you wouldn't be in the state legislature already. Don't stop to analyze it, just do it: so say I, seer and prophet and Senator Squeak-In, as Renny Suratt calls me."

"I forgot that character was still around," she said, "but of course he is."

"And doing very well, too, on all fronts. He's the darling of the media, the hero of the campus, and I saw him a little while ago on the other side of the Quad dancing with some little girl who looked about sixteen. I understand he's notorious for that."

"But untouchable," she said. "That's the problem with our society nowadays. The damnedest misfits become the greatest heroes. There ought to be a law."

"Join me in Congress and we'll pass one together. Are you and Hack both happy?"

She looked startled but recovered with a laugh.

"Talk about feminine transitions! That one was fast enough. Yes, we are. Or at least he seems to be, and I know I am. Why, don't we look it?"

"Not particularly," he said, giving her a glance of candid appraisal that only an old friend could have gotten away with. "I think he is, basically, but I'm not so sure about you. Any hidden romances on the premises?"

"Not on mine," she said, laughing again. "No time for them. Passing ships, of course, convenience dates, escorts when necessary—I'm sure you see the routine many times in Washington. I'll join it if I get there. But nothing I'm ready to jump off the Golden Gate Bridge about. I'm sorry."

"Don't apologize to me. Donna will just add you to her availables list for dinner parties. We'll have to think. Maybe we can set you up with someone."

"Well, thanks so much," she said dryly. "But don't strain yourselves. I'm quite content."

"One more Congressional bachelor girl," he said. "We really will have to go to work on it."

"And how about you?" she inquired tartly. "Perfect as always, I suspect, both of you. A marriage truly made in heaven, safe, snug and serene after a quarter of a century. Great marriage, great kids—"

"Listen," he said as the music began to slow toward its conclusion. "Don't get started on that. Kids—one gentle boy, one sweet little girl, one freshman just entering the University who is threatening to become hell on wheels. And as for marriage—managing."

"With Donna?" she asked, surprised.

"With Donna. But"—abruptly—"enough of that. Let me know when you want me to kick into the campaign. I'll stand by for your call."

"Thanks," she said seriously as they returned to the table. "I'll be in touch. And thanks for the dance."

"My pleasure," he said with what Donna sometimes referred to, not too happily, as his "Willie Wonderful" smile. "See you in politics."

"I'm ready," she said, as Hack, not giving her time to sit down, again swept her into the dance.

"You two must have had a lot to talk about," Donna observed, tone a little edgy. "You certainly were absorbed enough."

"She's an interesting girl, Fran. She wants to run for the House. She asked me to help and I said I would."

"Of course," she said, but he refused to be drawn.

"Come on," he said, holding out his hand and pulling her up. "Let's dance. Bayard Johnson lies dead, Renny Suratt rides triumphant, we're all twenty-five years older and God's in His heaven, all's right with the world."

"You're in a mood."

"I am. Maybe they'll play something fast and you can help me shake it."

She sighed.

"I don't know what to do when you act like this."

"Just dance," he said, giving her a sparkling Willie Wonderful. "Don't try to figure it out."

"The story of my life," she said wryly, to which he made no answer.

Hack and Fran completed their dance, this time sticking determinedly to pleasantries—the possibility of Congress, his recent compositions and his plans for more—fending off any lingering thoughts he might have had of—what? He couldn't really say. Or why he had tried to bring it up. Life had so obviously moved in different directions for both of them. It was on a bittersweet note that he relinquished her hand and prepared to move on around the Quad. Yet what was the good of feeling even that?

Elsewhere in the increasingly relaxed crowd—the stern days of "No liquor on campus" being long gone, postwar—Guy and Maggie Unruh danced placidly, Maggie's plump little body, squarer and even more solid than it used to be after three kids and a quarter-century of domesticity, snuggled contentedly in Guy's commanding arms; his thoughts, as often, far away on the latest problems of his oncology practice and the attributes of the newest nurse to join the radiation staff.

At the table to which the Unruhs presently returned, Franky and Katie Miller were listening with amusement and encouragement while Smitty Carriger vehemently urged Marc Taylor to approach a rather mousy but quite attractive woman at a nearby table; Marc, after some hesitation, was finally getting up his courage to do so. A couple of tables away Billy and Janie Wilson were sharing space with several amiable strangers and Jeff and Mary Dell Barnett, who were trying hard not to let their sadness about By cloud the evening too much for others; they were managing reasonably well but were noticeably subdued and depressed.

At another table farther along the Quad in front of Memorial Church, Tony Andrade was sitting with Lor and Angie Davis and Johnny Herbert—"the old group," as Tony remarked with satisfaction, lacking only Louise, up home in Napa Valley putting finishing touches on tomorrow's party; the old group at the moment was squeezing together to accommodate North McAllister, who had wandered by after his talk with Fran, looking lonesome.

Off by himself, subject of several wry comments from his fraternity brothers, Galen Bryce was standing near one of the clumps of palms, an unconscious expression of superiority on his face as he surveyed, with an inevitably analytic gaze, the mass of humanity that swirled in front of him with animalistic abandon to the strains of "Jailhouse Rock," "The Twist," and others of that ilk.

Tim, too, was alone for the moment, quietly smoking a cigarette as he watched the dancers; his expression appeared to be more tolerant. Actually it was absentminded and inattentive. He was mentally framing the column he would write later tonight and put on the wire tomorrow morning before leaving for Napa Valley. He could not avoid the recurring moments of depression that engulfed him as he contemplated the immediate human tragedy, and more general national import, of By's death. It weighed upon all of them but Renny, apparently; and on none more heavily than Tim.

He wondered how Renny and his establishment friends would handle it. He suspected they would make it sound like By's own fault if they possibly could. He knew he himself would pull no punches in his comments on his renegade fraternity brother, dancing so smugly tonight with what Moose referred to, with rare sarcasm, as "his youthful harem." They were all trying to ignore him, thankful that on this occasion he was apparently not quite brash enough to force himself upon them. But tomorrow?

The same thought had occurred, uneasily, to tomorrow's host. What would he do, Tony wondered moodily, if Renny appeared unexpectedly at the winery? Tony could imagine all sorts of unpleasant consequences, among them the one he had always secretly feared, some savage sally about himself and Lor, too close to the mark to be easily passed off. He was reasonably confident he could muster a sufficiently humorous and unconcerned response, but whether he could deliver it with the requisite spontaneity and blandness he wasn't entirely sure. He knew he couldn't afford not to.

He sighed. For some reason he could not define later he made no attempt to hide it. North, remaining at his side while the others went off to dance, responded. He too could not understand later why he forced the issue. Some sudden, overwhelming melancholy, perhaps— some desperate, sudden need, prompted by his talk with Fran, for reassurance and reaffirmation from someone he had always sensed would understand—it just happened.

His voice was low, intimate with a knowledge he knew Tony would have a hard time denying.

"It does get a little difficult sometimes, doesn't it?"

For a moment Tony was obviously considering bluffing it out. He gave North a startled glance.

"What's that?" he demanded sharply. But North stood his ground.

"It does, doesn't it?"

Tony stared at him for a long moment. Then the barriers at last came down.

"Yes," he agreed quietly. "How goes it for you?"

North smiled without much mirth.

"Not too bad. Married B.J., as you know. Two kids. Flourishing practice. Pillar of the community." His mouth twisted. "Occasionals, quite rarely; one long-standing. But not like you, twenty-five years going back to college days."

Again Tony for a second appeared ready to return to defenses. But there was no point; and it was a relief.

"So you knew."

"Yes. One does."

"Did anyone else?"

"Not that I ever heard of," North said. Tony made a wry sound.

"Two did," he said, acknowledging at last that awful, humiliating night; but, again, what a relief.

"Oh?"

"Yep," Tony said matter-of-factly. "Willie and Hack."

North uttered a wry little laugh.

"Welcome to the club. Willie and Billy, the Wilson brothers, short turns, vaudeville and other acts. They virtually stage-managed my marriage to B.J."

"Not mine to Louise or Lor's to Angie," Tony said with a certain unabashed satisfaction. "Those were my idea."

"So here we sit," North said with an ironic glance at Billy and Janie, dancing past their table with waves and smiles, and Willie and Hack seated at a nearby table with the Millers, the Unruhs and Randy

Carrero, "dependent on three of our fraternity brothers for the pres-
ervation of our good names and reputations."

"I've never had cause to doubt them for a second," Tony said.
"Have you?"

"Nope," North said. "I'd trust them with my life."

Tony smiled.

"We have. And B.J.'s never suspected?"

"Never. And Angie and Louise?"

"Not Angie, bless her heart. Louise is a lot sharper. I sometimes
wonder. But she never says. At least not yet. And she keeps busy
with the winery; you know, Mario's beginning to fail and she and I
work together more and more as he gradually lets go. And we have
the kids, four in our case. Lots of mutual interests to keep us going.
So—why raise the subject, why worry about it? As long as one is
discreet and pays decent regard to the obligations of marriage and the
requirements of a stable society—what of it? It's our business. Right?"

"It is," North agreed. "You sound as though you're perfectly happy
with the moral decision."

"Long ago," Tony said. "Long ago." He gave his ironic little grin.
"I figured Mother Nature was stronger than I was, so I might as well
relax."

"It took me a while longer," North confessed.

Tony studied him.

"I don't think you've really made it yet."

North's expression grew somber for a moment.

"Maybe not," he admitted. "Maybe I really haven't, even after all
these years . . . Anyway: talking to you is a help."

"Anytime," Tony said comfortably. "Anytime." He chuckled
abruptly. "We still have tonight. Three doors down the hall from each
other in the house. Want me to leave mine open?"

North looked startled, then laughed.

"I don't think that will really be necessary."

"Are you sure?" Tony inquired, and joined him in easy laughter as
the others, amused by their obvious amusement, rejoined them at
the table.

By that time Tim, having finished his preliminary mental draft of
tomorrow's column, was reviewing with satisfaction some of its more
stinging phrases. He reflected that Renny was not the only one with

a knack for the savage phrase. He himself was no slouch in that department when he really wanted to let fly.

"An unprovoked and despicable attack, designed to do grave and perhaps irreparable damage, not only to the fine American struck down but to the great cause whose fundamental decencies he had dedicated himself to preserve; an attack led and perhaps directly inspired by one of the most irresponsible figures of the irresponsible left . . . the establishment's academic darling, run amok under the heavy prod of media adoration, dabbling in the sordid depths of current American mores, using his position and the temporary hysterias of the moment to justify not only outrageous personal conduct but the most vicious and inexcusable public conduct . . . as much a murderer, perhaps, as though he had personally thrown the brick that felled Bayard Johnson, instead of simply encouraging the faceless unknown who blindly and obediently did it. . . ."

The thought crossed his mind that Renny might sue. He dismissed it. Renny wouldn't want to call attention to his possible complicity in By's death and in today's climate he couldn't win. Even for "the establishment's academic darling" the courts would not bend the First Amendment that was coming to be the media's loudest and most self-protective justification for excess.

Like most of them, Renny could dish it out but he couldn't take it. In this case, though he might scream like an eagle it would do him no good. Tim, he told himself with a cynical little smile, could be as adept as anyone else at wrapping the First Amendment around himself.

"I can see you've just told off somebody," a voice he had not heard in a quarter-century remarked with a chuckle. "I know that expression."

He came to with a start to find an old, familiar friend and his beaming little wife taking the chairs beside him: Bill and Ibu Nagatani, looking, he would swear, not a day older than when he had seen them last, standing with their beaming little parents in the crowd on graduation day.

"Tell us we look just the same," Bill suggested with a grin, reading Tim's thoughts as he often used to do. "Us slanty-eyed folks, you know, we never age. We're eternal."

"The chip on your shoulder's eternal," Tim retorted with an answering grin, rising to shake hands heartily and exchange a quick peck on the cheek with Ibu. "Where are you and what are you doing and how the hell are you?"

"Still in Fresno," Bill said, settling comfortably beside him. "Operating two farms—"

"Very successful," Ibu interjected proudly. "And three kids."

"Also very successful," Bill said. "Hiro's a senior here, going to graduate next June magna cum laude, April's entering right now as a freshman, Mary Ibu is rounding the turn in high school and is also heading this way in a couple of years. And you?" His tone became affectionately chiding when Tim shrugged. "Timmy! You're not still a bachelor! Why are you depriving the world of such good Caucasian stock?"

"And why are you still on that kick?" Tim demanded, but amicably. "Caucasian, Asian—does it matter?"

"It used to in school," Bill observed. "You really thought I was the Yellow Peril when I succeeded you as editor of the *Daily*, didn't you?" His eyes darkened for a moment. "Well, I paid for it. The farms were seized when the government took us to Manzanar and my Dad never got them back before he died of a broken heart in '49. It took me ten years after I got back, covered with medals, from service in Italy with the Nisei Battalion, the Four Hundred Forty-second Regimental Combat Team. But I got them," he said with a grim satisfaction. "The courts were finally beginning to restore a little balance. I got them back, and recovered damages, and since then I've added acreage to them and they're going great guns. Ari Katanian—you remember Ari?"

"Oh, sure. He managed Willie's Senate campaign in the Central Valley, as I'm sure you know."

Bill nodded.

"Oh, yes, I was on the committee, believe it or not. Couldn't let old Willie down, he needed every vote he could get, even us Yellow Perils. . . . Well, Ari recently overrode quite a bit of opposition and helped get me elected a director of the Fresno Chamber of Commerce. I'm quite the respectable citizen in Fresno business circles now."

"The American dream," Tim remarked with an irony Nagatani, as he used to do, caught at once.

"That's right, the American dream."

"Tell him about the newspaper," Ibu suggested.

"The newspaper!" Tim exclaimed, pleased. "You still have a hand in the business then."

"Not like you," Bill said, "our great national pundit, but in a small way. It's called *The Japanese-American*, what else, and I started it about two years ago. It's a weekly at the moment, circulation only about twenty thousand over the whole Valley, but growing. We've got a lot of support from the Japanese community, of course, and a lot of advertising building up. Of course I have dreams about a daily, with eventually San Francisco, Sacramento, L.A. and San Diego editions, too. But for the moment, doing very well, and saving our pennies, and who knows?"

Tim smiled.

"Don't want a good columnist, do you?"

"Nothing would please me more," Nagatani said with a grin, "than to have *you* working for *me*. Do you mean it?"

"I'll tell the syndicate to contact you. Do you have a card?"

"Sure," Nagatani said, genuinely pleased, reaching into his pocket and producing one. "This is our home number"—he scribbled on the back—"call us anytime. I know you make speeches once in a while. Want to come and talk to the chamber sometime soon to inaugurate your Fresno debut?"

"Anytime."

"Boy, this is going like a house afire," Bill said. "I just missed you at the *Daily* this morning, incidentally. They said you'd been in. Did they show you the editorial they're planning to run about By in Monday's paper?"

Tim nodded and frowned.

"I didn't like it."

"Much too easy on Renny," Bill agreed soberly. "Much too easy on the whole business. Stormy weather ahead on a lot of things, I think. Race, Vietnam, the economy—"

"And the general attitude *toward one another*," Tim remarked. "That's what disturbs me most, I think, this growing intolerance, this growing refusal to grant the other guy's right to expression, this growing tendency to shout down opposing views or shut them out altogether—"

Bill couldn't resist, though he grinned to take some of the sting out of it.

"Which I am sure is not the approach you're going to take toward Renny, right? You're going to give him all that nice tolerance, all that nice fairness and balance, you're going to be absolutely calm and reasonable—we're not going to get the old Bates zing-and-sting, none of the old Bates spit-and-snarl, no comparisons to Adolf Hitler—"

"He doesn't deserve tolerance!" Tim snapped. "He's scum!"

Ibu looked alarmed at his vehemence but Bill only displayed a wry amusement.

"Ah," he said, "there's my old Timmy. Kill him, boy! Kill! Kill! Kill!"

"He did," Tim remarked, cooling a bit, attempting to regain some of his normal humor but still annoyed. "I'm not going to give him much tolerance. Look at him!"

On the dance floor Renny, apparently without a care in the world, was swinging his youthful partner about with great abandon, his shirt open to the navel, his jeans unbelted but by some miracle staying up on his scrawny waist, cheeks flushed, eyes glazed, long hair flying— "the uniform" and "the attitude" correct in every respect.

"He seems to be enjoying life," Nagatani agreed. "I don't like him either, you know, and basically I agree with you. But I don't want you to get too choleric."

"There are some things in life," Tim said firmly, "that deserve being choleric about. What are you and Ibu doing tomorrow?"

"Heading home," Ibu said, relieved at the return to less controversial subjects.

"Why don't you come up to Tony Andrade's in Napa Valley?" Tim suggested. "He's giving a big blast for the house and I know he won't mind a couple more."

"And I *was* almost a member," Bill observed dryly. "Until I was blackballed."

"We wouldn't want to come without an invitation," Ibu said hastily, apparently hoping to head off that old, apparently still rankling memory. For a second Tim contemplated some sharp rejoinder, then thought better of it. He brushed aside Ibu's hesitation along with her characteristic desire to avoid unpleasantness.

"Tony won't mind," he assured her. "I don't know whether you ever knew him and his wife—Louise Gianfalco—on campus, but they'll be pleased. They're very generous and hospitable people. I'll vouch for you."

"There speaks the carefree bachelor," Ibu remarked with a smile, "never worrying about the number of people at parties. I still think—"

Bill, also deciding to relax, agreed.

"Let's go ask him," he suggested. "We'll feel better."

When they found Tony and "the group" across the Quad, Tony looked pleased and said sure, by all means come. And when Tim, on

another expansive impulse asked, "And Ari and Helen Katanian?"
Tony grinned and said, "Beat you to it, Timmy. I saw them a while
ago and they're coming, too. So you Fresno people can be a delegation . . . Say!" he exclaimed, diverted by some sort of activity toward
the center of the Quad. "What's that?"

When they got a clear glimpse through the crowd, which had
slowed almost to a stop, it proved to be one of the sensations of the
evening.

Duke and Shahna Offenberg were jitterbugging with surprising
skill, to the amused wonderment of Gil and Karen Ann Gulbransen
and a number of students, including their host at dinner, Brad Montgomery, and his cute little date.

Presently Karen Ann, with a what-the-hell gesture, pulled Gil to
his feet and joined them.

A respectful and somewhat awed circle grew steadily larger as the
four of them swung in and out together, performing with a happy
abandon until both Karen Ann and Shahna collapsed laughing with
cries of "No more! No more!"

Great applause rewarded this unexpected and impressive display of
elderly agility.

Duke, as Tim remarked with a chuckle to Tony, "probably picked
up a quite a few points in his campaign to become president of the
University."

The thought also occurred to Karen Ann and Gil when they returned to their table. They couldn't resist teasing him about it. Fortunately Shahna's always diplomatic and soothing little personality
was there to ward off the annoyance that flared briefly in Duke's eyes.

"What do you mean?" he demanded. "I *like* to dance."

"We know you do," Shahna said quickly.

"Of course," Karen Ann said calmly. "You're very good, too. You
must admit it dazzles the kids. *This* is the potential president of the
University?" she laughed her silvery peal of unconcerned laughter.
"Sensational, Dr. Offenberg! Simply sensational!"

"Well," Duke said, sounding a bit more mollified and starting to
smile a little. "I do like to dance. I just do."

"We know that." Shahna said. "And Karen Ann's right. The kids
are very impressed. And why shouldn't they be? Leaving everything
else aside, you're forty-five years old. You have one foot in the grave.
Not everybody can kick up his heels like you do."

" 'Our prexy can jitterbug,' " Gil agreed. " 'Top that, Cal!' "

"I'm a long way from being prexy," Duke said, finally relaxing. "And, I hope, a long way from the grave. Is that kid over there trying to catch your attention, Gil? He's been studying you ever since we took this table."

"Longer than that," Karen Ann remarked. "He was seated near us at the game, too. I noticed him because he was so obviously noticing you."

"Damned if I know," Gil said. "Which one is he?"

"Two tables over," Duke said. "Behind you to your right. See him? Very tan kid, good-looking. He knows we're talking about him, he's turning away now."

"He'll be back," Karen Ann said. "Turn when I tell you. . . . Now."

The boy was, as Duke said, very tan and very good-looking; tall, very thin, a somewhat Oriental cast of feature; a pleasant expression, for the moment shy, tentative, embarrassed. But it was clear he had made a decision. His gaze steadied as it met Gil's. He was obviously forcing himself but obviously determined to carry through with whatever it was he had in mind.

Gil stared for a moment very carefully. Nothing clicked. He turned back.

"Beats me. He couldn't be a med student, he's too young. And I'm certainly not famous. I don't know. It's a puzzle."

"Whatever it is," Karen Ann said calmly, "you're about to find out. He's coming over."

"O.K.," Gil said with a smile. "You're my witnesses." He swung around abruptly. "Yes, sir. Did you want to see me about something?"

The boy blushed, bronzed skin darkening. But he smiled, shyly, and stood his ground.

"Yes, sir," he said, voice pleasantly accented. "You are Dr. Gulbransen? Dr. Gilbert Gulbransen?"

"I am," Gil said. "And you are—"

"Placido Ramos," he said, and paused as if he expected recognition.

Gil's expression remained puzzled and polite. "Yes? Am I supposed to know you?"

The boy smiled as if with some secret amusement and shook his head.

"No, sir, we have never met. But I thought perhaps my mother—" He broke off, dug in a pocket of his neatly pressed jeans, held out his hand. "She told me to give you this if we ever met."

The two wings and intertwined snakes of the medical corps gleamed and twinkled in his palm.

Gil looked up. His eyes locked with the boy's. Their gazes held for what seemed a long time. Gil began to smile, broke finally into a delighted and completely unabashed laugh. The boy stood uncertain, tentatively smiling but poised for flight.

"Well, I'll be damned," Gil said. "I will be absolutely damned!" He offered his hand, which, after a moment, the boy took. "Sit down, Placido. I think you'd better meet your stepmother."

"I might have known," remarked Karen Ann, perfectly calm and as always completely unshaken and unperturbed by life's surprises, "that anyone as handsome as this might have some connection to you, Gilbert. Perhaps you'd better tell us all about it."

So Gil, as unperturbed as she, did so after ordering a round of drinks and a 7-Up, at his request, for Placido: the concluding days of the war with all their awful, nerve-racking demands upon doctors attempting to repair shattered bodies and minds . . . the pain, the strain, the loneliness, the desolation of heart and spirit . . . the new nurse in surgery, the little hut on the outskirts of Olangapo, "Sin City" near the great U.S. naval base at Subic Bay . . . the visits— "Exactly four, I believe," Gil recalled; "Enough," Karen Ann noted wryly . . . the unexpected finality of the last farewell on V-J Day . . ."and the return, I might say," Gil concluded, "to home and practice in La Jolla, and presently the arrival of your half-brother and sister, Placido, whom you will meet in due course."

"And like, I am sure," Placido ventured with a shy smile. "If Mrs.—if Mrs. Mother—" he stumbled and Karen Ann laughed, quite relaxed.

"You'll work it out as time goes by. Don't worry about it."

"Then you won't—you aren't—" the boy sounded genuinely amazed.

Again she laughed. "For heaven's sake, Placido, that was nineteen years ago, right?"

"Well, eighteen when I came along," Placido said, suddenly sounding quite relaxed and giving a big grin to which they all responded with laughter.

"Eighteen, nineteen," Karen Ann said. "Anyway, a lifetime—your lifetime. What's the point in my getting upset about it now? You're here—I'm here—your father's here—your second family is here— all's well."

"Karen Ann," Shahna said softly, "you are quite remarkable."

"She always has been," Gil said admiringly. She fixed him with the ironic gaze that had been described by her sorority sisters as "typically Karen Ann" and said dryly, "You've no idea."

Which made Gil guffaw again. Their relationship, as Duke and Shahna agreed later, had always been something of a mystery, and was now. But as Duke pointed out, "It works."

"Tell me about your mother and your other family," Karen Ann suggested. "Is she in good health?"

The boy frowned.

"Not very. She contracted tuberculosis a few years ago and her health is very fragile now." He smiled shyly at Gil. "She sends her best to you."

"And I to her," Gil said. "When you write, tell her if there is anything she needs—"

"Oh, no, sir," Placido said, sounding almost affronted. "My father"—he hesitated, again smiled shyly—"the one I think of as my father, over there—is quite rich, land, sugarcane—she did not want me to find you in order to beg. Just 'to close the chapter,' she said."

Gil frowned.

"That doesn't sound so good. I hope she is not so ill that—"

"Quite ill," Placido said gravely. "But my—father—and my sisters and brothers continue to hope."

Karen Ann looked at Gil. "Do you want to go over and see her?"

"Might," Gil said thoughtfully. "Though I am sure your—father, Placido—might not be so welcoming."

"I am sorry," the boy said. "She has not told him, only me." He smiled and spoke with the candor of his years. "Frankly, I think that is why she suggested I come over here to the University. She hoped I would find you. She said she thought knowing you and your family might add much to my life."

"We shall make sure it does," Gil said gravely. "Do you need any help financially here?"

"Oh, no, sir," Placido said quickly. "As I say, things are—quite adequate. Just friendship and support, if I might have it, from my"—he gave a sudden smile, open, trusting and completely endearing—"from my American family. That will be quite enough for me."

"You have it," Karen Ann said briskly. "Our boy Grant is entering as a freshman, too—I assume you're a freshman? Good. We'll introduce you before we leave and hopefully you'll see a lot of each other. And plan to come down to us whenever you don't go home to the

Philippines, Thanksgiving, Christmas, whenever. And write to us. Often."

"Thank you, ma'am," Placido said, sounding very pleased and a bit overwhelmed. "That will be very nice."

"In fact," Karen Ann added, "come with us tomorrow, we're going up to Napa Valley for a big party at a winery owned by one of Gil's"— she paused and smiled—"one of your father's fraternity brothers. Grant's coming. It will give you a chance to get acquainted." She snorted suddenly. "Is he going to be surprised!"

"I hope he'll like me," Placido said with some alarm.

"He'd better," Gil said with a ferocity that wasn't entirely in jest. "Now, you probably have friends over there at your table, so run along. We'll pick you up at freshman dorm at nine tomorrow morning. O.K.?"

"That will be wonderful," Placido said with a smile that embraced the whole world, and started to turn away.

"Oh," Gil said. "One thing. How did you know me?"

"I just asked," Placido said. "You told my mother the name of your fraternity, so when I saw you guys come into the stadium in a group with your little flags and blazers I just went over and asked somebody and he pointed you out. I don't know who it was but I asked him to keep it a secret and I guess he did." He grinned suddenly, quite delighted. "Is he going to be surprised, too!"

Gil chuckled.

"You bet. Now run along and we'll see you tomorrow. . . ."

After the boy left, he again exclaimed in a disbelieving voice, "I *will* be damned. I will be absolutely, positively, monumentally *damned*!"

"So will I," Karen Ann said dryly, "but let's keep it under control."

"I say again, Karen Ann," Shahna remarked with an admiring laugh, "I think you are *quite* remarkable."

Karen Ann gave her a wry look and a sudden smile that ran quite counter to the Ice Maiden reputation she had always had in school.

"Oh, well, what the hell," she said. "Life is so unhappy in so many ways that it's nice to have one or two little things go right once in a while."

After that the evening drew on to its easy, sentimental close. For a time all problems public and private were forgotten as the bands ("Off-key, as usual," Hack remarked with a wince) played the University "hymn," "The Star-Spangled Banner," "Auld Lang Syne" and, finally, "Good Night, Ladies."

They all agreed that it had been, on the whole, a satisfying and delightful affair, and departed from it with a happy glow despite the shadow of By's death and the various tensions each had brought to reunion.

"We leave with the ills that brung us," Willie remarked to Guy as the crowd moved slowly out of the Quad under the dying moon, "but soothed for a little while."

"Which is what reunions are for," offered Smitty Carriger, over-hearing. "To give us a boost for the next lap along the road."

4

Inspired by an invitation from the alumni magazine to do a piece on "The World War II Generation, 25 Years On," Johnny Herbert has been making notes all weekend.

Now as he approaches Napa Valley in the company of Willie and Donna and the Offenbergs he has decided that the article will be based principally upon his observations of the fraternity brothers he has known so long and thinks he knows so well—or at least as much, he tells himself, as one can know people with whom one has grown up in one's most formative years, when one sees them again a quarter of a century later.

He is aware that some of his impressions may be superficial. There are altered circumstances, shifts in attitude, more clearly defined traits of character—Renny is a good example—whose origins he may not altogether understand. He knows that age, inexorable, sometimes works its changes more subtly than even its most sensitive victims, let alone an outsider, can perceive. Yet conscientious Johnny, who has informally but inevitably become "the historian of the house," thinks he has at least some major clues.

He began to put them on paper last night after the dance:

"It is a generation raised in the shadow of Depression, flung into the jaws of war, matured in a materially comfortable but psychologically deeply uneasy peace. It is a generation, mostly prosperous, that still regards the future with grave misgivings despite the enormous material wealth that blesses America in the postwar period.

"White-collar salaries are rising. Blue-collar wages go up by leaps and bounds. The great housing boom, generated by the G.I. Bill, continues to generate its own momentum as more and more families acquire the civilian income to build or buy. The American auto industry has no serious competitors.

"American scientific research and know-how lead the globe. American agriculture feeds not only this country but a large part of the world. American production and American prosperity are the marvels of the earth. The American economy, virtually without challenge from any other industrial nation, dominates the world economy. The television set, symbol of American affluence, can be found in almost every American home. The newest gadgets clutter almost every American household. Well-being stalks the land.

"Fat, comfortable and sassy in the mid-sixties, America thrives.

"No generation in all history has been so materially comfortable, so materially blessed.

"None has ever faced a future more troubled and uncertain, more subject to factors that may at any moment fly wildly out of control.

"All the generation knows, a quarter-century since some of its more favored members left this beautiful campus, is that the world some of its members are now leading is a greatly troubled one. What will they do with that leadership is not yet clear. Another depression, to terminate the seemingly endless postwar boom? Another great war, perhaps, rising out of some conflict such as Korea or Vietnam? The ultimate triumph of Soviet Communist imperialism, the final decline and fall of the West? Or, devoutly to be hoped, the opposite?

"The generation does not know. Beneath its self-satisfied enjoyment of prosperity and material acquisition lie the sinister tensions of the Cold War, the increasingly embittered relationship with the Soviet Union, the ever-present, ever-growing problem of the Bomb. For all its material advances and its superficial appearances of progress, the world in mid-twentieth century is still a charnel house. It crawls with small wars, revolutions, repressions, terrible injustices, unceasing turmoil.

"Everywhere is man's inhumanity to man.

"In that fundamental sense, the world has not advanced one half-inch in all this bloody century. It has simply added modern technology to its weapons of terror. In the present era, horror is perfected in the laboratory and multiplied a thousandfold on the assembly line.

"From the point of view of day-to-day living in these fortunate United States one can—if one stops thinking—persuade oneself that the world is one big, happy picnic.

"From the broader perspective of what is actually going on out there, it is full of dark shadows and desperate uncertainties.

"The American World War II generation that to itself and to the envious foreign observer may often seem so confident and secure actually is often unsure and frequently sick at heart.

"We live with the underlying superstitious feeling that maybe our smugness defies the gods . . . that maybe we shouldn't enjoy our comfortable lives too much or too obviously, or they will become angry . . . that the picnic may any day now be overtaken by the charnel house . . . and the picnic will end."

Which, he had told himself wryly last night, is about as gloomy and pessimistic as Tim at his ultimate. It is not really characteristic of Johnny Herbert, who always manages to be reasonably optimistic even when his historian's instinct tells him that his generation and their country are adrift on treacherous seas. Yet reviewing what he has written now, he concludes that it is not, perhaps, too strong. Perhaps it is a good thing to throw, now and then, one small dash of cold water, however limited its audience, into the face of America's determined complacency.

He assures himself that at least his motivation is not that of a Renny Suratt, dedicated to destroy. It is, he hopes, to shock—to challenge and to fortify with reality—the wish to live constructively as citizens, and to preserve and strengthen the foundations of a basically good-hearted and well-meaning land.

To that, he thinks, they must all dedicate their hearts and talents if the nation, and whatever it may have to contribute to humankind, are to survive.

His reverie is so intense, and so obvious, that Willie finally offers humorous challenge.

"Johnny!" he exclaims as they leave Highway 29 and take Oak Knoll Road across Napa Valley to Silverado Trail. "Come back, come back, wherever you are. You're a million miles away. Look at the Valley! Look at the day we've got! They're beautiful!"

And so they are.

The Valley, one of earth's loveliest places, is extra lovely in the fall. The grapes are being harvested, the vines have turned autumnal, the two small mountain ranges that frame the Valley's length are soft and gentle in the misty morning light. Over all lies the golden haze of late September. It is 70 degrees Fahrenheit, predicted to rise to 82 by midafternoon.

Everything is conspiring to give them a perfect day at the Collina

Bella Winery—"Beautiful Hill" or "C.B." as it is known informally in the Valley and, increasingly, to retailers and wine drinkers across the country.

The industry is beginning to take off. Mario's instincts have been proven right. Under his and Tony's shrewd management the vineyards have grown to 595 acres, with more in prospect. The C.B. label has been in existence four years, the winery itself five. Among the old-line Italian families of upper Napa Valley who dominate the business, Gianfalco and Andrade, although relatively new names, occupy already a respected and honored place. Both Mario and Tony are actively involved in vintners' associations and activities. Tony has just succeeded Mario as president of the most powerful group. He has big plans to encourage and expand the industry. Grizzled old Italians almost twice his age, the royalty of the Valley, defer to him for leadership. It is a challenging, exciting and satisfying thing.

Now, stocky, solid, graying of hair and pleasant of expression, every inch the Valley squire, he stands on the edge of his terrace at the namesake house, Collina Bella. It is situated on a knoll high above Silverado Trail, on the east side of the Valley, along which his guests will presently come. So far none has turned off the Trail to begin the winding climb to the house six hundred feet above but soon, he expects, the influx will begin. He himself awoke at six at the University, dressed quickly and sneaked out of the sleeping house to make the two-hour drive to the Valley. He has been home for three hours now. It is almost eleven and the first visitors will soon be arriving. Louise is bustling about checking final details of food, tables, service. She has hired six young Valley college kids to help prepare and take care of things, and they will also be arriving soon.

Twenty-nine adult guests have been invited. With himself and Louise the total comes to thirty-one. If Renny—accompanied, perhaps, by God-knows-what—decides to come, it will rise to thirty-three. There is also the junior division, Gil and Karen Ann's Grant, the incoming freshman, and someone Karen refers to lightly as "our mystery guest," also, apparently, a student; and possibly Latt Wilson, although Donna confided unhappily last night, "We aren't sure, really. He knows he's invited, but—" And of course the four lively young Andrades, Tony Jr., also an entering freshman at eighteen, Mario, seventeen, Aurora, fifteen, and Theresa, thirteen.

A big houseful, one of the biggest they've entertained in quite some time. But it's a big house, with a big pool and two cabanas for changing, which Louise, in a rare fit of whimsy, has marked "Burgundies" and "Chardonnays."

"I hope to goodness they get the code," she says with a laugh and Tony, amused, predicts, "One mistake and they'll all be cued in."

Encircling the entire house is a generous terrace some fifteen feet wide from which spectacular views of the Valley can be enjoyed in all directions: south toward the city of Napa and the lower end of the Valley; north to Mount St. Helena and the narrowing jumble of hills and vineyards around Calistoga; west across the valley floor carpeted with vineyards, dotted with houses and wineries; and east, looking down into one of the small subvalleys off the Trail—the little hidden fiefdom that Mario discovered and bought thirty-five years ago and on which still flourish the original stands of sauvignon blanc, merlot and cabernet that he planted then. It is the site of the winery and of Mario's original modest "old house" that can be glimpsed at the foot of the pine-clad eastern rise of hills. He will not attend the party—he is "not feeling well," an increasing complaint that worries Louise and Tony. But so far he is clinging to his independence and won't move in with them or accept outside help.

"I'll shoot off a rifle if I need anything," he suggests with a rather impatient smile. "Then you come runnin'."

Louise says this isn't adequate but so far her father is more stubborn than she; which, as Tony reflects now, is saying quite a bit.

But, he also reflects as he does see one car on Silverado hesitate and then disappear from view in the trees below, apparently on the way up, he has nothing to complain about on that score or any other. Louise, with her swift, dark beauty, high intelligence and pragmatic shrewdness, could not be a better wife to him; nor he, he thinks he can say honestly, a better husband to her. What he thinks of as "that" has never interfered and he knows it never will. He is too careful, too cautious, and, in Lor, infrequent but complete for him as he is for Lor, he has everything he needs or wants in that respect.

Funny, he thinks, what life can do. Twenty-five years later, and here we still are; twenty-five years from now, pray God, here we still will be. I have been mightily blessed: and adds with typical wryness, In my own odd way. But blessed it is, and he is profoundly grateful for it.

He only wishes everyone in that difficult context could be so secure and so happy. Poor North obviously is not; and now, with B.J. apparently headed into cancer, as North had confided when they actually did go back to the house after the dance and drink a couple of beers together, quite innocently, in Tony's room before turning in, he knew things were getting grimmer for "one of Salt Lake's most dignified and most respected internists." That was how North described himself, with a wryness of his own. In his case, having one reliable and continuing friend had not quite seemed to resolve an inner struggle that, Tony perceived with his quick, intuitive sympathy for people, still troubled his older fraternity brother.

Well: this is party day, and he can't think too many heavy thoughts or they will interfere with his hostly duties. The car that now pulls into the parking area—it can accommodate ten; if there are more than that people will have to park down the hill and hike up—is indeed who he hoped it would be, Lor and Angie, and with them North and Randy Carrero. He exchanges hearty handshakes with Lor and North, gives Angie a warm kiss and turns to Randy with outstretched hand and welcoming grin.

"You going to bless me?" he inquires. Randy, clad again in civvies, blue jeans and Hawaiian happy shirt, grins back as they shake.

"It doesn't do any good with some people," he says with a chuckle; and for just a second his eyes meet Tony's in a glance that makes Tony think, Oh, Lord, not somebody else who knows. But then he thinks, And if so, so what? It couldn't fall in a deeper well. And quick as ever, responds, "It's your business to know, all right!"

Which makes Randy laugh; and the moment, if there is one, passes.

Tony says he hopes they brought their suits and yells for Louise, who comes out and greets them and points out "Burgundies" and "Chardonnays"; and the party is officially under way.

In rapid succession the cars come up the hill. Next to arrive are the Wilsons, the Offenbergs and Johnny Herbert. Franky and Katie, with Hack Haggerty and Smith Carriger, come next. Galen Bryce arrives, "all alone in stately grandeur," as Franky murmurs to Hack, in a rented Mercedes. Jeff and Mary Dell Barnett, Billy and Janie Wilson and Marc Taylor arrive together. Gil and Karen Ann Gulbransen, their son Grant and Placido Ramos, both boys pleased and excited, come next, Moose and Diana Musavich bring Tim Bates, Guy and Maggie Unruh. Ari and Helen Katanian and Bill and Ibu Nagatani, "the Fresno delegation," arrive in the Nagatanis' station wagon and the party is complete—Tony hopes. As the first hour passes and there is no sign of Renny, he begins to relax.

Renny, he suspects, has less innocent fish to fry; and in the secluded guest house in Hillsborough to which Renny has invited a carefully selected two boys and three girls, this is quite correct.

Within ten minutes after the last arrival, after everyone has had a chance to say hello again and after everyone has had a chance to exclaim (and secretly marvel at the calm way in which it is being handled by the Gulbransens) over a shy and appealingly handsome Placido, all the kids are in the pool. The noise level is mounting steadily as they dive and frolic and soon get into an impromptu game of water polo.

Around the deck most of the men are in trunks, most of the women in bathing suits. There are hearty but basically not really terribly amused jokes about "the waistline going south" and, "Somehow you gals seemed a little more wraithlike at the Water Carnival senior year!" They lounge gossiping in deck chairs or at one of the umbrella-shaded tables Louise had had placed at widely spaced intervals around the house.

"People can do whatever they like," she told Tony this morning. "Swim or lie in the sun or sit and talk or maybe just go to a table by themselves and look at the view, if they want to. There's no program except to eat around two and stay as late as they like."

This invitation to complete relaxation, passed on by Tony to each new group of arrivals, is accepted gratefully as soon as the six young Valley kids have filled drink orders and withdrawn to help Louise in the kitchen, and arrange place settings and condiments on the two long oaken tables that have been joined at the north end of the terrace looking toward Mount St. Helena. The volcanic mountain, source thousands of years ago of the lava flows that give the Valley its unsurpassed grape-growing soil, stands rocky and imposing, its characteristic volcanic saddleback worn and softened by the centuries, majestically and inescapably dominating the up-valley view.

Grant Gulbransen, Placido Ramos and the Andrade four continue to shout and cavort in the pool, "exhaustingly active" as Jeff Barnett remarks with a grin to Hack. He leaps up suddenly, trots onto the diving board and, to the awe of the kids and the hearty applause of his contemporaries, executes a perfect swan dive and four furious laps, so fast that they can only marvel.

"You told me you've kept yourself in shape," Guy Unruh shouts as Jeff climbs out, shaking the water out of his eyes and barely puffing, "but I didn't realize you were in *that* good of a shape!"

"I could probably give the swimming team at school a run for their money even now," Jeff yells back happily; and for a brief moment they are transported back to the days when his sleek little body led the team to victory after victory in intercollegiate competition. "Good for the ego of the older generation," as Hack remarks to North with a smile.

His sudden spontaneous demonstration typifies how they are all beginning to feel under the warm persuasions of the Andrades' hospitality and the sheer beauty of the valley at their feet and all around them. For the first time in the whole weekend, really, Willie thinks as he wanders off by himself toward the back deck overlooking Mario's lovely private domain, everybody seems to be genuinely, and completely, relaxed.

He knows that this appearance is, in a good many cases, deceptive; and yet there is something about the group—comfortable—at ease—twenty-five years along the way—everyone enjoying at least some reasonable success (some more reasonable than others, as in any group, but, over all, quite respectable)—everyone secure in old friendship, secure in their knowledge of one another—

Which prompts an ironic little smile for a moment. He finds a deck chair and sinks into it. For the moment no one has followed him here. The hum of their voices, and their occasional relaxed bursts of laughter, are muted by the bulk of the house. He hears principally the rustle of a gentle autumn breeze through the pines and live oaks that ring the deck and complement the view at carefully landscaped intervals (another of Louise's contributions). He hears too, an occasional bird . . . the grinding of a truck at late harvest somewhere in the fields below . . . the screech of a tourist car taking a curve almost too fast on Silverado Trail, as they often do. . . .

A drowsy hum lies on the world. He drifts. . . .

But he does not sleep.

Insistent, unhappy, inescapable, there comes the recurring thought of his son; and, as with all his friends here today, the other inescapable concerns of ongoing existence, diverted only briefly, no matter how pleasantly, by the Andrades' dreamworld halfway to heaven high above Napa Valley.

Latt, he feels, may really be lost to them. He and Donna had tried last night before the dance, during the dance and finally, around midnight, after the dance, to reach him at freshman dorm. Brisk young voices informed them that Latt wasn't there but the messages would be left in his room, every effort would be made to let him know, but—nothing could be promised. On the last call they had reached one of his roommates, perhaps the one who had appeared so cheerfully on the steps on that first day. Was it really only two days ago?

"I believe he had a date with somebody, Senator," the impersonally cordial young voice, indistinguishable in tone and tenor from all the rest, informed him. "If I'm awake when he comes in, I'll sure let him know. And I'll write him a note, too."

But when they tried again this morning, shortly after nine before leaving for the Valley, the word had been the same.

"No, sir, he didn't come in at all last night. I really don't know where he is. But I'll sure let him know you called, Senator."

Why this fairly characteristic behavior, not so different from the preludes to so many pitched battles in high school, should have given his parents the sudden apocalyptic feeling that it was all over, Willie couldn't really say. He had accused Donna of being too dramatic when she began to cry and voiced their mutual fear in just those words:

"I think it's all over. I think we've lost him. Oh, Willie!"

"I'm sure he's with Maryetta and Ti-Anna," he said firmly, although his own inner terrors were suddenly equally overwhelming. Why the damned kid couldn't even telephone— Didn't he know his parents would be terribly worried if he didn't?

The certainty that Latt knows exactly that and is deliberately using the knowledge to hurt does nothing to make them any happier. He is very intelligent and, when he wants to be—when it suits his own purposes, Willie thinks bitterly—very thoughtful of others. The deliberate withholding of thoughtfulness can only mean that he intends the moment to be as significant as they are beginning to think it is. It is a declaration of independence, quite clear and blatant. And about ten times more hurtful than it need have been, which Willie supposes is the exaggerated overreaction of youth. But that doesn't make it any easier to take.

They will try to reach him again this evening when they get back to campus for their last night with Duke and Shahna but it will be an effort without much anticipation of success, made tense by the grim expectation of failure. Tomorrow they have to leave campus at 5:30 A.M. to catch a 7:00 A.M. flight to Washington to attend By's funeral. Willie knows they both fear that Latt won't be there (or will be protected by his peers) when they call tonight; and probably not tomorrow morning, either, should they make an effort so nakedly abject. And once they return home, he can hide behind the telephone and the mails to keep himself isolated from appeals that Willie can see becoming more and more desperate and more and more pathetic as time goes by.

That way, he thinks, lies disaster for the family and very likely disaster for his son—an erosion inevitable unless, by the miracle sometimes not granted to parents, they can think of some way to prevent it.

The beautiful day, the drowsy dream of Napa Valley, for the moment seems a mockery. He sighs heavily and tells himself that he had better get back to the midst of the party: it isn't good to sit back here overlooking Mario's hideaway, and brood.

He rises abruptly and walks around the house to the valley side. The women, in the way characteristic of the sex, have managed to congregate happily in one large group, protected by umbrellas and suntan lotion, at one end of the pool. The men, in some cases two and three together, in others solitary like himself, are either talking quietly, dozing, or staring out contemplatively at the spectacular panorama. Donna, he observes, looks subdued; obviously she has told them all about Latt. He can only hope that, in the immemorial fashion of the United League of Women Against Men, they have been able to give her some comfort. Without, he hopes, too much damage to him.

After all, he thinks defensively, it takes two to tango. He feels he has done *his* best with Latt, even though he knows Donna thinks he has often been too impatient and too harsh with human shortcomings. If only the boy weren't so smart. If only, as Donna has often told him, he weren't so much like his father.

Again he sighs, this time impatiently, and goes to sit with Smitty Carriger and Marc Taylor, whom Smitty is apparently regaling with some adventure that has Marc wide-eyed and amused. As Willie approaches Smitty, he moves smoothly into something about Main Line parties that has them both laughing.

Inside, of course, Smitty is tensing up as he always does before he leaves for the Far East, and Marc is tensing up as he contemplates the possibility of following through on his first tentative approach to the young lady at the dance last night.

"Young lady!" She must be Marc's age if she's a day. Rather dowdy, rather dull—or, no, he thinks, coming stoutly to her defense although she's really nothing to him, really—*some* people might say she's rather dowdy and rather dull. Probably Gale and Renny would. Marc would prefer to say "somewhat conservative" and "pleasantly quiet."

After Smitty, affectionate but firm, had finally bullied him into approaching her, Marc had found the experience very nice. She is an assistant professor in the English department, teaching, among other things, "Kit Marlow and the Shakespeare Circle," which, Marc discovered, was quite fascinating if you knew something about it; is unmarried, living with her elderly mother in a modest home in the pleasant town adjoining the University; and was at first as shy and uncertain as he. But they tried a dance and it went quite well; and then Marc ordered drinks, and they went well, too; and then they really got to talking, and after a while time seemed to have passed, they heard "Good Night, Ladies," had a final go around the floor and ended with an exchange of addresses and phone numbers while Smitty beamed, not too noticeably, Marc hoped, from a distance.

Afterward, when they got back to the room they were sharing at one of the downtown hotels—"You are one penurious millionaire," Smitty remarked jovially. "I haven't shared a hotel room with anyone but Annelle for twenty years. Do you really think we can afford it?"—Smitty insisted on knowing all the details. When Marc concluded in an obvious glow, he said, "If you let this one get away, you are one damned fool, Marc Taylor. I want you to promise me you'll keep after it and *no crap*. O.K.?"

"Well," Marc said cautiously, "I did promise to call her tomorrow before I leave. And there is a meeting in San Francisco next month that I was thinking about coming to—"

"You're hooked," Smith said. "At last! We've got Marc Taylor to join the human race, everybody! It only took twenty-five years. I think I'll call Rodge in Vienna and tell him."

"Now, wait a minute," Marc protested, sounding genuinely alarmed. "I've just met the girl—woman."

"Girl to you, fella," Smitty said, "and about time! What time is it in Vienna, anyway?"

And he actually did ask the operator to put through a call and presently did reach Rodge, who promptly echoed Smitty's urgings, sounding pleased and encouraging. They told him about the dinner, about By's death, which saddened him, and about Moose reading his letter, which pleased him too.

"I didn't want to sound too gloomy," he said, "but on the other hand"—his tone became grave—"the world is in one hell of a situation with this thing, and the way we're going it's only going to get worse. I'm usually pretty closemouthed about it, you can't go around crying 'Wolf!' all the time, but I decided to level with you guys. I thought you might like to know what we face, as fathers and members of our generation."

"We're glad you did," Smitty said; and on a sudden impulse told Roger, who was also in a high-security area like himself, "what I'm up to—" very briefly, but briefly or not, it still sounded pretty heroic to Marc; and to Rodge, too, who said quietly, "Congratulations, friend. I've always known you were a great guy and now I see you're a very brave one, too."

"We all have to help in every way we can," Smitty said.

"Yes," Rodge agreed grimly. "That we do."

And now, relaxing on Tony's deck in the pleasant haze of early afternoon Smitty is finally telling Willie, also (Willie being another he can trust, and whose approval he has always liked to have; and a member of the Senate Atomic Energy Committee and himself holding top clearance). Willie, also, is impressed; and pleased they had talked to Rodge; and "particularly pleased about your girl-friend."

"But she isn't—" Marc protests again, but Willie joins Smitty in brushing that aside. Confronted by two of the strongest personalities he will ever know, Marc finally gives in.

"You do want it to happen, don't you?" Willie demands. Marc hesitates and then produces his characteristic shy smile.

"Well—yes."

"All right then. Smitty, why don't you bring back some sort of heathen idol from the Far East and we'll sacrifice to it and have it go to work for our friend here."

The shy smile broadens. Marc shakes his head in wonderment.

"Maybe I'll make it yet," he says, suddenly sounding enthused and ready for it. "I was beginning to think I never would. But maybe I will."

In something of the same spirit, seated in a deck chair at the north end of the house facing up-valley to the looming mass of Mount St. Helena, Billy Wilson is "about to take the plunge," as he puts it to himself. This is not the plunge into matrimony, which he successfully accomplished nineteen years ago, but the plunge, at last, into the career he has so willingly and lovingly deferred for his brother all these years.

Having maneuvered Hack into a private corner, Billy has been agonizing for the better part of fifteen minutes over how he is going to broach this. Hack, lounging beside him in their little enclave separated by twenty feet or so from the rest, surprises him completely by doing it for him.

"Billy," he says thoughtfully, "whatever happened to your dreams about writing plays and doing something in the theater? You were very interested in that at school, as I recall. Whatever became of it?"

Billy looks embarrassed, and shy. Hack, amused, thinks, that he has almost forgotten there actually is a shy Wilson brother.

"Well, you know," Billy says awkwardly, "Willie wanted to go into politics—and somebody had to help Dad run the ranch—and I was the younger one—and so I just sort of automatically got tagged with it. And also, you understand," he added hastily and loyally, "I wanted to do that. I *love* the ranch. I wanted to stay there and help out. It hasn't been any hardship, Hack, I assure you."

"I'm not saying that," Hack says. "I just thought maybe you'd been forced to put some good dreams on the back shelf—"

"Not 'forced,' " Billy interrupts earnestly. "I did it gladly. Because I wanted to."

"—and that they're still there," Hack concludes, undeterred. "Are they?"

Billy stares for a moment out over the lush and orderly carpet of the vineyards, mottled here and there by the red and purple leaves of autumn. And frowns. And sighs. And gives Hack a sidelong glance and a rueful, conceding smile that abandons defenses.

"They're there. They're always there. But what's the point? Willie's got his career . . . and Dad's about to retire . . . and I'm really settled into the groove . . . and I couldn't possibly break away and go to some place like Hollywood, for instance, that would be crazy, it wouldn't be fair to the family—"

"But you could write in your spare time," Hack points out. "I'm no farmer but I knew plenty around Springfield, Illinois, where I grew up, and I seem to remember there are quite a few periods during the year when you're between harvests or cattle sales or whatever, and there's slack time. Why don't you do something then? I should think the change would be a good break for you. You could do it right there on the ranch, set aside a den for yourself or build a little studio on the property. You could do it."

"I have done it," Billy says. "Quite a lot. But how would I find the contacts? I couldn't just grandly announce that I'm going to break in at my age. And without the contacts—"

"I'm a contact," Hack points out.

Billy studies him for a moment, then smiles.

"I was hoping you'd say that. But why?"

Hack smiles too.

"I don't know. You just popped into my mind a couple of months ago. Who knows why anything happens in the theatrical world, it's all so screwy anyway. You really did come out of the blue when I was struggling with a libretto for something I'm working on. I remembered that we collaborated on something for Big Game Gaieties in my senior year—"

"Yes, we did," Billy says with a pleased smile, remembering that triumphant joint contribution to the annual pre-game variety show. "We really rocked 'em, as I recall."

"We did indeed," Hack says with satisfaction. "And out of that sentimental memory of college days will now come—what? The new Rodgers and Hammerstein? The new Lerner and Lowe? The new Wilson and Haggerty?"

"Haggerty and Wilson," Billy suggests with a pleased laugh.

"We'll flip for it," Hack says. "I am thinking, quite seriously, about doing a rock-and-roll comedy." Billy looks as startled as Gioia had when Hack first broached the idea in Rome. "If you'd be interested in tackling the libretto for me, why don't you think about it? You and Janie could park the kids with the folks for a couple of weeks and come to Rome and we could sit down and get it all lined out, and then you could go home and write and I could get to work on the music, and someday—who knows?"

"We've never been to Rome," Billy says dreamily. "We've always wanted to see it."

"It's a marvelous city. Try it, you'll like it. You'll also like Flavia and our kids. I have quite a family now."

"But—" Billy says. "There are so many things to keep an eye on, on a ranch. Particularly a big one, like ours."

"Your dad can manage for a couple of weeks. Or a month, if necessary."

"Oh, I don't think I could stay away that long," Billy says in some alarm. Hack smiles.

"O.K., we'll keep it down, then. It shouldn't take more than two weeks of really concentrated work to come up with something. But *I work*, I warn you. We'll allow some time for sightseeing, and some good meals in addition to our own cook, who is sensational, but most of the time we'll *work*. O.K.?"

Billy smiles.

"That sounds great." His expression sobers. "But, really, Hack, this is harebrained. It's ridiculous. There's no guarantee at all that I could come up with anything worthy of you. I mean, you're a famous composer, man, and I'm a rancher from the San Joaquin Valley. How incongruous can you get?"

"We'll see," Hack says calmly. "This may be just the time to unleash all those caged-up demons—or clowns, in this case—inside you. It's time for a change of pace for me. And as for you, something light and clever is a great way to get started."

"I'd just be riding on your coattails," Billy says. "I don't really think so, Hack. It's a nice idea, but—"

"Willie!" Hack demands as Willie again comes wandering, rather aimlessly, around the deck, having decided, as he told Smitty and Marc, to get a little exercise before lunch. "Willie, tell this man he'd be crazy not to accept the offer I've just made him."

"What's that?" Willie inquires, perching amicably on the low stone balustrade that encircles the deck.

When Hack tells him, Billy half-balking but obviously already halfway to Rome, Willie says crisply, "I think that's a great idea. And very generous of you, Hack. I think you'd be a fool not to accept, Billy. Ask Janie. I'll bet she'll be packed within an hour after you get back to the ranch."

"Oh, I'm sure of that," Billy says with a rueful grin. "I'm sure of that. But do you really think Dad would let me go?"

"Billy Wilson," his brother says firmly, "you are forty-four years old. Yes, Dad will let you go. He told me he thinks you're working too hard and getting a bit humorless, anyway."

"No!" Billy says, sounding both dismayed and indignant. "Did he say that?"

"No," Willie says with a grin, "but he will pretty soon if you don't take a break. Go, brother, go! This kindly elderly gentleman is willing to share his glory with you. Grab it!"

"Watch that 'elderly' stuff, Willie," Hack advises with mock sternness. "You're in no position to talk. But thank you. I think you may have persuaded him."

"Doesn't he always?" Billy inquired with the rueful humor of a lifetime of younger brotherhood. But, as his tone indicates and they all know, not a younger brother persuaded when he doesn't want to be. It is obvious that this time he wants to be.

"When do we eat?" Willie asks, not too loudly, looking down the length of the deck to the tables where Louise and her helpers are beginning to bustle about. "I'm starved!"

"Go have another chip and dip," advises Tony, coming around the back corner and also, apparently, exercising a bit while he checks on the well-being of his guests.

"Making some laps?" Willie inquires. "I'll join you."

"Please do," Tony says, and they fall into easy step together.

"Everything all right with you?" Willie asks in a low voice as they head along toward where the ladies are beginning to break up and return to their spouses as the meal approaches.

"Fine, thank you," Tony says evenly. Then he flashes his sudden quick grin, a little defiant but unperturbed. "Want details?"

"Nope," Willie says. "As long as everything's O.K."

"It is, Brother Wilson. Don't worry."

Willie gives him a shrewd look.

"Not worried. Reassured."

"Thank you," Tony says with a grave little bow. "Let's walk."

Behind them Randy, circulating too, has come finally to Hack, of whom he has seen a good deal this weekend, but not since the conclusion of the dance last night. His question to Hack is very close to Willie's to Tony.

"Everything O.K.?"

"Sure," Hack says, with a slight defiance that Randy senses in his tone. "Why?"

"Oh," Randy says as he relaxes into the chair beside him, "I just wondered. After last night."

"What about last night?"

Randy studies him thoughtfully for a moment.

"I just wanted to be sure my bosom pal Flavia is doing all right, too." He grins, unabashed by Hack's expression, which has begun to be a little ominous. "I'm protecting her interests out here, O.K.?"

Hack studies him for a moment, expression still half-annoyed; then relaxes.

"She's doing just fine. Just fine."

"No regrets?"

"Always regrets," Hack says quietly. "But not operative regrets. I hope you will allow human nature that much leeway."

"I allow it a hell of a lot," Randy says cheerfully. "That's why my days are numbered. . . . Well, that's good. I just wanted to know that."

"You know it," Hack says, and holds out his hand. "O.K.?"

"O.K.," Randy says, clasping it in his for a moment. He stands up. "Well. I think I'll go in the kitchen and see if I can help Louise. I'm not bad in a kitchen. Particularly when I smell barbecue and chili and all those good things. They revive my childhood."

"Have fun and speed it up," Hack says with a smile. "We're all getting hungry."

"You guys make me ashamed of myself," Gil Gulbransen says as Tony and Willie come alongside the table where he and Karen Ann are peaceably working on their second—or is it third?—Bloody Marys. "Why does anybody want to move, on a day like this?"

"Just getting up an appetite," Willie says. "Join us if you like."

"We're too lazy," Karen Ann says, stretching and looking stylish, feline and quite stunning. "Utterly worthless people. And look at that," she adds with a gesture at the valley spread out at their feet. "I never want to leave. Just sit here forever and drink it all in. You're very lucky, Mr. Andrade."

"That I am," Tony agrees. "Have another Bloody Mary. Lunch should ready in another fifteen, twenty minutes. Lots of wine with it."

"In that case," Gil says as they move off, "this will be quite enough of the hard stuff." His gaze returns to the pool, where it has been most of time. The kids, finally exhausted, are draped around the outer rim talking drowsily and soaking up the sun. "You know," he says thoughtfully, "that boy seems to be very steady."

"Your son, I know you're talking about," Karen Ann says. "Which one, is the question." She gives him her characteristic lazy but shrewdly appraising glance.

"Yet I wonder," he says thoughtfully. "I wonder. We've certainly embraced him in a hurry. Last night an uncertain student from the Philippines, today a full-fledged all-American boy lounging by a pool in Napa Valley. Quite an experiment, we're making."

"Your experiment," Karen Ann noted. "And you made it nineteen years ago. I'm just along for the ride."

"No, you're not, either," Gil says calmly. "You're the one who made it easy last night. You're the one who invited him for Thanks giving, Christmas, up here, you name it. Mrs. Mother stepped right in. I know you're decisive but that beat all records."

"So? Do you object?"

"No, I think it was wonderful of you. I'm very grateful. And as for him, you've got a slave for life."

"I hope so," she says, "because apparently it is going to be for life."

"Oh, no. He'll go back."

She utters a skeptical sound.

"After getting a taste of the way we live here? Don't you believe it. He'll go back for a little while when his mother dies but then he'll be back. You've acquired a permanent son, Dr. Gulbransen."

"But we really don't know him at all," he objects. "He may have all sorts of traumas we don't know about. He may be a radical or a bomb-thrower or a rapist—"

"You should have thought of all that," she says tartly, then smiles. "But trust me. He's not any of those things. Just a very nice kid, with all the hang-ups nice kids have. You've occasionally thought Grant was a handful. Welcome to two adolescent boys, Doctor."

"Maybe they'll be good influences for each other."

"I hope so," she says. "Suddenly meeting a half-brother at age eighteen that you never knew you had is pretty challenging, I imagine. But so far they both seem to be rising to the occasion. And on campus they may become real pals. The first major challenge will be when they come home for a holiday under the same roof. There may be a little working out of territories then."

"Well, keep an eye on them," he says dryly. "Mrs. Mother. We'll count on your diplomacy."

"Don't you dare run out on me," she orders, half-humorous but emphatic. "You created this situation. Literally. Now you do your duty."

"Have you ever known me not to?"

Again she gives him one of her long, appraising looks through half-shut eyes.

"You're pretty good, on the whole," she concedes. "Not exactly the way I might have organized our lives, but—"

He gives her the grin that has always ensnared feminine hearts, and cocks at a quizzical angle the blond head, a little lined now but still very handsome, that has always held them, once ensnared.

"You must admit that we do have an interesting time together."

"Never dull," she agrees with a chuckle. "A little unexpected, sometimes. But never dull."

In the enormous kitchen that is Louise's domain and joy—"For a hardheaded businesswoman," Tony tells her, "you're sure one hell of a cook"—North, Lor Davis and Randy are standing around as men do in busy kitchens, nursing drinks, carrying on casual conversations with Louise, Angie and each other, "trying to stay out of the way," as North puts it; "trying to help," as Lor keeps insisting.

"Frankly," Louise says with a laugh, "you'd be more help just sitting out there waiting. But don't go, it's good to have your company."

"I'm not going," Lor says. "I might get trapped into another conversation with Galen Bryce."

"What's the matter?" Randy inquires with a smile. "Did he give you a hard time?"

Lor shakes his head in a puzzled way.

"Not really. But it was kind of spooky. Really kind of prying into my private life, I thought." A rare frown crosses the usually untroubled face of the house's other sensationally handsome blond member. Nothing will ever furrow *that* brow for long, Randy thinks with amusement, but at the moment it does appear a little disturbed.

"Such as?" Randy inquires. Lor's frown deepens.

"Oh, how often do we get up here, and how often do Tony and Louise come down to visit us, and—stuff like that. I didn't mind telling him, it's probably every couple of months or so one direction or the other, isn't it, girls?"—Louise and Angie look up from their busy projects and nod—"but what's it to him?"

"Probably running some psychological experiment on you," North remarks lightly. "Just like he used to do in school. I hope you gave him a good story."

Lor grinned.

"I just asked him to tell me about all those movie babes he's sleeping with. That seemed to stop him."

"Are there any?" North inquires dryly. Lor snorts.

"Oh, he pretends, but the way he fumbled around for a minute I decided it was mostly talk. He asked me if I knew several of their names and I said, hell, no, I'm too busy running oil wells to pay much attention to Hollywood people. He didn't seem to like that. So we were back to us again. He's an annoying son of a bitch."

"You didn't have to stay with him," North says. Lor shrugs.

"I didn't. I went over and talked to Franky and Katie Miller for a little bit and then came on in here. Gale followed me over and began zeroing in on them. I guess they're getting it now. Why did Franky cry, and what's Franky doing, and how's the auto business, and what about their kids and—*Jesus.*"

"I think it's probably just as well we don't have him around in our lives all the time," North observes.

Lor gives him a quick look that North thinks may be significant; but decides not.

"You're damned right. That would be too much. I wonder if he has anything in his life, though, really? Apparently he is damned successful, but—what else? He's always been an odd guy, *I* think. How do you figure him, Randy? You're in the same business, trying to set people straight when they have problems."

"Yeah," Randy says. "I guess so." He grins. "We belong to different religions, though. I doubt if my dogma is quite like Galen's. I'm sure my recommendations are much simpler."

"And much more tolerant, I'll bet," Lor says. "Knowing you . . . I think if I ever had a real problem," he adds in a tone suddenly thoughtful, "I might come to you. Would that be all right? I'm not Catholic, but—"

"Anytime," Randy says with a smile. "Why? Are you thinking of developing some problems?"

Lor shakes his head and grins.

"No . . . no. I just wanted to set it up, though. Just in case."

"What do you mean, 'just in case'?" Angie demands cheerfully from across the room. "You don't have any problems. You're in great shape."

"Thanks to you," he says, throwing her a kiss. "And you, Louise. And Tony, of course. You all keep me happy."

"It's disgusting," Louise says in a tone as light as his. "Angie, would you check on those chickens for me, please?"

"Why do you suppose," Randy inquires thoughtfully, "that Franky did cry? Did you get a clue, Lor?"

Lor shakes his head.

"Not really. Middle-aged angst, maybe, to use the word Gale loves to sling around. We've all got it, you know. Although I won't tell Gale."

"But I thought we just agreed," North objects, "that you don't have any problems."

"Oh, well, hell," Lor says with a laugh. "You know me, I talk a lot. You must have some."

"Yes," North says with a look suddenly stricken. "B.J."

"We know," Randy says sympathetically.

"Hell of a thing," Lor agrees soberly. "Really a hell of a thing. Do you know anything for sure yet?"

"Final results tomorrow afternoon," North says. His expression twists into bitterness. "A nice homecoming present."

"Here," Louise commands briskly, handing him a huge bowl of salad. "Put that on for me, please, and tell them we're almost ready, they can begin to find seats."

"Any particular order?" North inquires, deciding to be diverted as Louise hands Randy a companion bowl.

"No, just tell them to scramble. I figure if anybody doesn't get along with anybody after twenty-five years, that's just too bad. Lor, you take out these tacos, will you?"

"Taco kid, that's me," Lor remarks and Randy says, "My mother is a hell of a good cook, too, she'd love this," as they all emerge onto the deck.

"Chow down!" North calls, "overcoming angst," as he is sure Galen must be describing it to himself at this very moment. He decides he will deliberately seek out Billy and Janie and sit with them if he can. He and Billy have been tacitly avoiding each other all weekend but he decides suddenly that it is time for that to stop. Twenty-five years is twenty-five years; he might as well put paid to it, as much as he ever can where Billy is concerned.

As if they can read each other's minds, which they pretty well can, Billy calls from down the table, "Hey, North! Come join us!"

After a second's infinitesimal hesitation that only Billy perceives, North does so and they settle in beside one another and start making conversation. With Janie's unsuspecting but cordial help it goes quite well after the first few awkward moments.

Elsewhere down the tables everyone else settles in too. Wives more or less deliberately break away from husbands, husbands from wives. Everybody mixes, except for the kids, who cluster at the southern end despite Louise's efforts to get them to mingle with the adults. Shyness and the herd instinct are too strong at that age: there's safety in one another. Grant and Placido are hitting it off beautifully, the Andrade four are bubbling and bouncing. Respective parents exchange pleased smiles.

Conversation, general, happy and loud, resounds from under the oaks as the meal progresses. In response to loud importunings from Tony and Lor, Louise and Angie finally sit down and begin to enjoy the meal as their youthful helpers bring on the food. The barbecued beef, the tacos, the barbecued chicken, the salad, the garlic bread and all the trimmings are consumed with happy approbation. Collina Bella "Special Reserve Chardonnay" and "Special Reserve Carbernet" flow like water. Even Gale Bryce seems to relax, finally. He actually becomes a little tipsy and, as Smitty murmurs to Marc, "surprisingly human."

"The World War II Generation, Twenty-Five Years On" appears to be, as Johnny Herbert notes, well, happy and at the moment living in

Napa Valley. He reflects with a wistful regret that by five o'clock it will all be over and, with the exceptions of Lor and Angie, who will be staying over for a couple of days, everyone will be on the way home and reunion, with its old memories, new memories and all the events of the weekend commingled, will be put away until next time.

Whenever that may be, Johnny thinks with the gentle melancholy that subtly begins to touch them all as the sun sinks behind the western ridge, the long afternoon begins gently but inexorably to fade, and shadows start to lengthen across the valley floor and advance upon their happy surfeit.

Before they go Tony walks them down the hill in back for a visit to the winery. C.B.'s harvest is over, the crush has been completed, only stains and grapeskins on the concrete floor and the sour, familiar smell of wine sleeping in oaken barrels indicate that this is a place of great enterprise and caring. They can handle two hundred thousand gallons at present, Tony says, hope to expand to half a million in another couple of years. His pride is manifest. Here amid the ancient smells and the spick-and-span, latest state-of-the-art machinery, he is a man in command of his world.

Back at the house, he delivers a brief and graceful farewell, thanking them for coming, saying how happy Louise and he have been to be able to be their hostess and host, urging one and all to "Come see us again whenever you're out this way." He expresses the hope, which is greeted with laughter, applause and hearty approval, that "We can all get together again before we get too old to navigate."

For a moment the laughter is not quite so happy as everyone recalls that this condition is not really so very far away. They are a little young yet to let it weigh them down; but the thought is beginning to enter minds and hearts, a minor incubus sternly buried most of the time but annoyingly tenacious underneath. Even in mid-forties, the intimation is there. When, if ever, will they all be together again?

When Tony concludes, on a lighter note, "Hope you'll tell your local supermarket to stock C.B.!" there is a general pushing back of chairs, gathering of effects, getting ready to leave. Lines form in front of the cabanas. In half an hour everyone has changed back to traveling clothes. Handshakes and kisses are exchanged all around.

Ari and Helen Katanian and Bill and Ibu Nagatani are the first to leave. They are driving directly back to Fresno, where they will arrive near midnight, and where on Monday Ari will resume his lucrative law practice and Bill will continue to oversee his farming interests and push the expansion of *The Japanese-American*. He has already been approached by some mysterious fellow from Tokyo who says he is "interested in your paper." Bill has never considered a connection with his ancestral homeland but its increasingly impressive economic recovery is beginning to make the possibility quite intriguing. The more he considers it, the more he thinks it might be something to look into.

Ari, Willie's central San Joaquin campaign manager, shares Willie's determination to wipe out the "Senator Squeak-In" image of the last election. He will resume his preliminary organizing work, already under way, for the election of 1968.

Gil and Karen Ann collect the two boys, already, as Karen Ann notes with satisfaction "bosom buddies—as much as an adult can tell"—and start down from what Gil describes to Tony and Louise as "your magic mountain."

After them in quick succession go the others. Franky manages to say goodbye to everyone with reasonable good cheer but the memory of his brief emotional breakdown at the house dinner cannot be erased so quickly. It is with a bleak expression on his face, and on Katie's, that they turn north on Silverado and prepare to drive over the western hills to Highway 101 and on up the line to some place like Ukiah or Willits where they will stop at a motel for the night. They are engaged in a fierce, though largely silent, argument, as to whether they will make one more attempt to see Franky Jr. on the way home. Katie, though crying frequently, is grimly determined not to. Franky, though racked, insists they must. That, and the drabness of the life he faces when he gets back to Oregon, make him a sad companion. Theirs is one of the unhappier homegoings of the group.

Hack and Smitty depart with Tim and Galen Bryce, who are returning to their accommodations near campus for the night before taking off tomorrow for their respective destinations. Smitty says vaguely that he is "going to catch an early flight back to Philly," and Marc, backing him up and "providing cover" as Smitty cheerfully instructs him, echoes in the presence of the others that he will "See you on the plane." Smitty feels the rising excitement that always precedes his plunges back into the clandestine world. There is always the challenge that he may not survive it, the enormous satisfaction when he does. He may or may not kill anyone this time: he never knows. The uncertainty is something that still provides a visceral thrill for staid and steady public citizen Smith Carriger, president and C.E.O. of Carrigcorp.

Hack, thinking over his conversation with Billy, is pleased with himself for his sudden inspiration. Their collaboration on the Big Games Gaieties a quarter-century ago had been kid stuff, but clever; very clever, with the carefree gusto only college youth can bring to cleverness. He is sure Billy can produce even better material now if he sets his mind to it. Hack, a genuinely kind and decent man, is also pleased to think that he is helping Billy to "get out of the rut of the ranch." Billy really has sacrificed a lot for his brother Hack thinks; and fond as he is of Willie, he has always understood a certain basic ruthless selfishness there. Otherwise, he supposes Willie wouldn't be where he is. It takes a tough man to survive in American politics. He is sure that Willie, after a shaky start, will get wherever he wants to go. Or at least give it a damned good try.

For himself, Hack is well satisfied with his visit home. He has touched the necessary bases in London en route, will stop off in New York for a couple of days on the way back. *Ebon* is getting into shape. He has finally reached some sort of accommodation with Fran. By the time he sees Flavia and the children, things will be rising again toward one of those peaks of accomplishment that give him a happy life. And Flavia and the children, as always, will be one of the major parts of it.

Tim, enjoying Gale's rented Mercedes with a certain irony, cannot help reflecting on the earlier events of the weekend, which now come back and hit him hard after the happy, obscuring forgetfulness of the day on Tony's hill. The tragedy of By's death oppresses him anew; the column he is polishing in his head grows ever sharper and more savage. The effect on the civil rights movement, the general effect on the country of the murder whose full impact, he knows, will not really hit until Washington gets back to work tomorrow, grow ever larger in his mind. And Maryetta—and Ti-Anna—and Latt. What of the effect on them? Will Maryetta now become an even more aggressive activist, the sainted widow of a fallen hero? What will it do to the kids?

"How do you like the Mercedes?" he inquires abruptly of Gale, whose invitation to ride down with him had surprised them all. Apparently the mellowing effects of C.B. Vineyard's best had worked its magic, even on Gale.

"I love it," he says, sounding a little defensive. "It's what I have at home. German products are *so* good."

"Yes," Tim agrees with a wry amusement Gale wouldn't understand. "They are doing very well these days."

So much, he thinks, for the flaming young prophet of 1952 dismissing the prospects of German and Japanese resurgence. And score one for Rudy Krohl, predicting then what his pompous and very wealthy person had confirmed Friday night at the fateful lecture. West Germany, the Federal Republic, is humming industriously back to the economic heights; so is Japan. America is fat and dominant now, Tim thinks; but for how long, with such competition? Rudy might not deserve it as a human being, but as a hardworking and very competent businessman he had accurately assessed the future and profited from it. Tim only hopes that America will take heed, tighten up and compete. If not, he can see, with his usual prescience, a time when Bonn and Tokyo may swing more of the dog than Washington can.

Galen, preoccupied with his driving and his own thoughts, lets the conversation drop; for most of the way he is a silent chauffeur. Self-centered and egotistical though he is, he is not entirely insensitive. He can sense, indeed has always sensed, the basic attitude of most of his fraternity brothers. They don't like me, he tells himself bitterly now—they never have liked me—so, fuck them. But it is not that simple or that easy. Despite his superior approach to it, he has had to recognize a certain fundamental solidarity and support that exists in the group. There is still, after a quarter-century, an automatic acceptance, an easygoing, unpressured, automatic *being there* for each other. Not expressed, not lingered over—perhaps, in some cases, more subconscious than conscious. But there, he thinks jealously. And not for him.

Gale's life is a narrow and lonely one, though he would be the first to deny it with scathing self-protectiveness. He doesn't really "sleep with a lot of those Hollywood babes" as that dim-witted oaf Lor Davis put it; as for who it is that Lor sleeps with, Gale has *his* ideas. But, he thinks with a bitter wistfulness, he sleeps with somebody on a regular and protective basis, and who does Gale sleep with? Very few and far between.

Women don't seem to like him much. Somehow they always seem to feel that he is feeling superior, looking down on them, analyzing and observing—"making notes"; which, he has to admit to himself, does sometimes happen after the first, fine flurry has worn off. This usually occurs very rapidly. They are in and out of his luxurious little house high on Mulholland Drive so fast he can hardly remember their names from one to the next. None has struck any really responsive cord in him, and he is just honest and perceptive enough to recognize that this is probably because he hasn't taken the time—or perhaps doesn't have the requisite generosity of love—to make the effort to strike a responsive chord in them.

So he drifts through Hollywood, cold, dignified, impregnable—"A real, untouchable tower, man," as one of his famous clients put it admiringly recently. "I wish I could be like that!"

"You wouldn't want to be," Gale told him with a wry and bitter humor he didn't understand, Gale could see that. "You wouldn't want to be."

Now as he heads back from what he thinks of as "that mutually protective, mutually reinforcing love feast at Tony's," he is clinging to the thought of his own independence. At least he has that, he thinks grimly. That, nobody can take away from him.

Guy and Maggie Unruh, the Musaviches and North McAllister, who have not had too much chance to visit during the weekend, are riding down together. Moose will return to the challenging world of coaching, Guy to the challenging world of oncology. Maggie and Diana, "perfect housewifey types" (as absent, sour and at the moment still busily involved Renny described them to Johnny at the house dinner) will return to their customary domestic orbits.

Guy, as always, will be aware of pretty nurses. Moose will be thinking, as he knows he shouldn't but with an increasing excitement, about Welcome Waggoner. Good old Suzy! he tells himself with a secret little smile as he drives the five-year-old station wagon smoothly down Silverado. Grandmother, eh? He'll grandmother *her!*

He tells himself hastily that this *just isn't right.* But the secret little smile persists, all the same.

North's dread of what he is probably going to have to face when he returns to Salt Lake City is depressing him, and since they cannot ignore his glum silence, bothers the others, too. They all try to be encouraging, though Guy, fellow doctor and oncologist, can only go so far with professional optimism: they understand one another. North thanks them gravely and asks them not to worry too much. They can't help it, however. The only bright moments of the weekend have been his candid talks with Tony and the fact that he is, he thinks, reconciled at last with Billy Wilson. At least they have managed to achieve a reasonable social ease with one another, and for that he is grateful.

Billy and Janie, the Barnetts and Marc Taylor depart, as they arrived, together. Billy also has a five-year-old station wagon, a bit more battered and worn by the ranch life than Moose's, though it, too, is used principally for the transportation of kids.

Billy, although his passengers are not aware of it and might be mildly concerned if they knew, is flying down the road on Cloud 9, hardly aware he is driving but fortunately so adept at it that he is managing to negotiate quite safely Silverado's long curves and abrupt little hills and hollows. He hasn't had time to tell Janie yet but as soon as they're alone, he will. He knows she'll be as excited as he is. North is somewhere off in the back of his mind—a relieved feeling, and Billy hopes he's happy—but no longer a burden.

Billy has not realized until this moment, perhaps, how much his life has been dominated by Willie, how much he has subordinated to Willie's hopes and plans. Not that he has consciously ever resented it, he assures himself hastily; but perhaps he has, and never realized it? The thought sobers him abruptly. How could he even remotely think such a thing?

Yet looking back on it now, it seems to him that it has always been Willie this and Willie that, even though their parents have tried to be scrupulously fair and generally have succeeded. Willie has just been Willie, taller, handsomer, quicker, brighter, swifter, surer, more ambitious, more competent, more dominating—not consciously meaning to dominate, Billy knows, but he just has. Billy has always been younger brother, and that, too, without any deliberate intention on Willie's part or failure of will on his—he just has. And he has accepted it thankfully and gratefully and lovingly, first when his glamorous older brother protected him from childhood's assailants, later in college when "Willie Wilson's brother" got him into the house and assured him the welcome of many a teacher who had taught Willie first . . . and later on, when he dutifully put aside his own dreams of a career and returned to the ranch so that Willie could pursue his ambitions on the national stage . . . and when he had felt, quite sincerely, that his happy recompense had been to free Willie for his career and be the absolutely unobtrusive, absolutely loyal, absolutely indispensable supporter of all his dreams.

He has never resented this and he tells himself firmly now that he never will. Indeed, why should he? Hack has suddenly reopened the way, rescued him from the possibly terminal effects of a satisfactory but inescapably scaled-down middle age. Now he can soar again, as he puts it to himself: a perhaps maudlin but nonetheless accurate description of the way he feels at this moment. It has been a happy weekend for Billy.

For Marc, too. He has made a choice. Or at least a beginning. Not a glamorous choice, maybe, or the world's greatest Romeo-and-Juliet beginning, but one that may suit him. He has a lot of hopes, does Marc Taylor. Maybe, he thinks, the ugly duckling is finally going to have a chance to take off and fly, after all.

For Jeff and Mary Dell Barnett the trip home will be a sad one. Jeff tried to reach Maryetta this morning without success, finally called the Washington house and left word with a neighbor that he and Mary Dell will be returning via the capital and will attend the funeral. The neighbor hadn't known many details except that a familiar voice had called from the White House last night and told her to "Tell Maryetta we're plannin' services for him at National Cathedral on Tuesday." A major public farewell was apparently being organized irrespective of what Jeff suspected Maryetta's more modest wishes might be. Such is the way of the incumbent, the motivations as usual being a mingling of personal emotions and subtler political consider-ations. So, as usual with that individual, why fight it? "He's bigger than all of us," Jeff remarked to Mary Dell with a wry shrug; and so, as always, he seemed to be.

What would By's murder do to the civil rights movement, and particularly to his and By's joint project, the Committee for a Better Day? Jeff couldn't predict at the moment. It could radicalize further a movement already beginning to split into the nonviolent led by Dr. King and the violent pushing him for leadership. And it could easily destroy the Committee for a Better Day unless handled with diplo-macy and skill.

In this equation, Jeff thinks wryly, dear Maryetta can either fit in or raise hell. She has always been the more aggressive, always criti-cized By for his mildness, always attacked the C.B.D. (after its di-rectors eased her gently but firmly off the board) and probably now will repudiate it altogether and take her prestige as By's widow over to the radical side. And that will create a problem for her contempo-raries, to say nothing of what it will likely create for her daughter and son, and possibly Latt Wilson.

In the Offenbergs' new Buick sedan, an anniversary present from Shahna's father, they, the Wilsons and Randy Carrero have also dis-cussed By's tragedy and are now, as Duke drives steadily through the rolling country of lower Napa and Sonoma valleys, reminiscing more lightly about the pleasanter aspects of the weekend.

Duke and Shahna are both very pleased about his appointment as provost—"So much has happened, I've almost forgotten," he says, which makes them all laugh because it isn't true—and for a little while they kid him about that. Willie regales them with details of the argument within the board of trustees and expresses admiration for Anne Greeley, whom Duke describes as "a little difficult, but very bright—we'll have to work on her."

Willie also mentions Fran Haggerty and they agreed how nice it was to see her again, looking so well and so prosperous and so obviously on her way to more important things. Donna tells Willie that they will have to have her over next time she comes to Washington, and certainly after her election to Congress, which they all consider virtually inevitable.

"Anne Greeley, too," he suggests. "She's a pistol."

Donna laughs and says that's fine with her, Washington parties could use a pistol or two. Shahna then reduces her instantaneously and entirely unexpectedly to tears by asking in a concerned tone, "Are you going to try to reach Latt again?"

"I d-don't know," Donna says. "Ask his f-father."

Willie sighs.

"We'll try. We'll call from your house as soon as we get back."

"Maybe you should go down to the dorm and try to see him," Duke suggests. Willie looks wry.

"In that rabbit warren? You know he could hide out anywhere and I'd never find him."

"But won't you at least *try*?" Donna demands. He takes her hand.

"We'll phone and keep phoning, and we'll phone tomorrow morning before we board the plane. But I'm not going to go crawling down there and make a spectacle of myself on the off chance that my considerate offspring may be standing by to pipe the old man aboard. That wouldn't be Latt, and you know it. Right?"

"I suppose s-so," she concedes. "But, oh, Willie! We can't go back without at least talking to him!"

"We may have to," he says sadly. "He holds all the cards, at the moment."

"We could cut off his funds," she suggests with a sorrowful savagery that startles them. Willie laughs without humor.

"That wouldn't stop him for one minute. He'd manage. And I wouldn't want us to demean ourselves by using that weapon, either. Don't the rest of you agree?"

"I don't want to get into it," Duke says, "at least not right now. But we'll have him up to the house soon, and we'll get to know him and we'll see if we can't use a little gentle persuasion, and—"

"And he'll see you coming a mile away," Willie interrupts wryly, "and so much for the best-laid plots of mice and men. Randy, be thankful you don't have any kids."

"Oh, I have," Randy says. "Lots of 'em. You'd be amazed at how many parents are coming to me now and asking for help with their kids. And how many kids I talk to and try to help." He sighs. "The number grows. Drugs, pregnancies, more and more Vietnam—you name it. There are an awful lot of crazy, mixed-up kids out there. And getting crazier. And more mixed-up. Sometimes I think our whole society is getting ready to go into a tailspin. And sometimes I can't see any way out. Although that, of course, runs counter to official theology."

"To which you pay, I gather," Willie suggests, "uneasy lip service. Or is it deeper than that?"

Randy looks at him gravely.

"That could be pretty offensive to me, you know, Willie, if I chose to let you provoke me. It's a lot deeper than that. I believe in it—I want it to succeed—I'm devoting my whole life to it, after all. But I have my quarrels with it. I've thought about it a lot this weekend. I have a reputation already, you know, for being a bit of a radical. I may be heading into something more serious, soon. Hack warned me a long time ago in Rome that sooner or later I might run afoul of what he described as 'all those black-robed elderly gentlemen who float about the Vatican on wings of steel.' It may be time."

"How long have you been a bishop now?"

"Two years."

"I'd give it another couple before I challenged them, if I were you. And I'd start a definite campaign to get the media on my side before I tried anything."

Randy smiled.

"There speaks the politician. They love me already—the word's getting around. I'll cultivate it, since that's the way one has to operate in this media-dominated world."

"Just don't make the mistake of thinking they love you for yourself, though," Willie suggests dryly. "They'll love you because you're against something old—and established—and orderly. Because you stand out from the crowd. Because, in whatever context you or they may choose to put it, you're a 'radical.' Because you're news."

Randy gives him a quick, quizzical glance.

"But they don't like you very much—and you stand out from the crowd—and you're against things—and you're a 'radical'—and you're news."

"Ah-ha!" Willie says. "But what I'm often against is them and their pet ideas. That's the difference."

So, arguing mildly, debating companionably, enjoying each other's company in the afterglow of the weekend, they drive steadily on through the golden afternoon toward the University, cradler of their youth, nurturer of their minds and spirits, inspirer of their hopes, encourager of their dreams—repository, still, of their sentimental loyalties.

Twenty-five years! Willie thinks again as they pass between the two sandstone towers and start the long gradual descent down Palm Drive to the Oval.

Twenty-five years since they left this lovely womb. Toward what bright glory? Into what far harbor?

The war came, and with it the glory—sometimes, and some of it magnificent—amid the awful destructions of the worldwide convulsion.

The memory of the glory lasted—for a little while.

Out of it, though most of the generation is still here, and reasonably secure in America's current prosperity, there has come, in final balance, only increasing chaos and uncertainty for them, their children and the world.

The peaceful harbor that seemed so distant in mid-nineteen forties in mid-nineteen sixties still eludes them; and the passage toward it seems ever more difficult.

The world still faces Tim's "twentieth-century sea of shit," and its harried peoples are still desperately swimming just to stay afloat.

Will they ever reach safe harbor? Willie wonders; and although for some of his friends the quarter-century has been good, and for some of them the weekend has offered promise, the answer for the most part does not come back with a reassuring ring.